Passion's Reunion

The silence was black and engulfing. Then a silhouette appeared through the trees and disappeared again. It could be a deputy, come to get her. *Run,* Jake had said. *Go to Daniel.* She couldn't make herself move.

The rider appeared again and dismounted before her. She lifted her skirts and ran.

She flung herself into his arms. Jake, solid and alive and here...

"I left a false trail," he said. His voice was husky and broken with unsteady breaths. "They can't send a posse out until morning and by then we'll have a head start."

All she could do was tighten her arms around his lean, strong chest until he lifted her face to his and let his mouth cover hers, greedily, hungrily.

He was gone, now he was here. They were apart, now they were together. It was more than relief. It was more than joy. It was life snatched from the jaws of death; it was a second chance fiercely seized. It was being born again and not questioning why, or how, merely receiving it, cherishing it, holding on and refusing to let go.

Jessica did not know whether it was her weakness or his strength which drew them to the ground...

Also by Leigh Bristol

Scarlet Sunrise
Silver Twilight*

Published by
WARNER BOOKS

**forthcoming*

Amber Skies

Leigh Bristol

A Warner Communications Company

WARNER BOOKS EDITION

Cover illustration by Melissa Duillo Gallo

Warner Books, Inc.
666 Fifth Avenue
New York, N.Y. 10103

A Warner Communications Company

Printed in the United States of America

First Printing: June, 1987

10 9 8 7 6 5 4 3 2 1

To J.B.—for past favors

July, 1876

Chapter I

The man's boots measured angry strides on the freshly polished mahogany floor; across the portico, down the corridor, around a corner, through another short hallway. The mere sound of it was enough to send servants scurrying back to their duties and out of his path, anxiety widening the eyes of the newer employees, indulgent smiles softening the faces of the older ones.

Mister Jake was home and he was in a temper.

Jake Fielding was a strong subscriber to the theory that the best thing about going away was coming home again. He had a restless nature and was perfectly suited to life on the trail; often he was away from the ranch for months at a time with no complaint. But when the urge to roam passed the best thing in the world was knowing that home waited for him—a cloth on the table, clean sheets on the bed, neat clipped lawns and lazy afternoons under a shade tree sipping bourbon and catching up on county gossip. He had the best of two worlds, the freedom of the trail and the tranquility of trail's end, and after a long ride and a long time away the mere sight of the familiar rolling hills and meandering streams of Three Hills was enough to cause his face to break into a grin of sheer pleasure. Coming home was the best part of his life.

Except today. Today Jake had ridden in to find things in a mess the likes of which he wasn't sure even he could untangle, and he wasn't at all sure whether his ferocious temper was due more to the incredible news that had greeted him or the fact that it had spoiled his homecoming.

Daniel marked the approach of his brother's footsteps with a smile of wry amusement that grew deeper as Jake moved closer. By the time Jake appeared at the library door, Daniel had risen from his desk and was already going forward to meet him, a twinkle in his eyes, an easy bounce in his step.

"Well, well, little brother, you never were one to miss a party, were you? I should have known one whiff of Rio's chili would bring you home as fast as that old nag of yours could ride."

Jake stood on the threshold, dusty, unshaven, his dark green eyes narrowed into glowering slits. He looked like a thunderstorm about to happen. He demanded furiously, "What the hell is going on?"

Daniel feigned innocence. "Why, it's my birthday of course. It comes along about this time every year. We're having a party."

With a short angry motion, Jake tossed his hat toward an ornamental end table; it skittered off and sent a small ceramic figurine tumbling to the floor with it. He strode into the room, his lips tightening as he tried to restrain his impatience. But self-restraint had never been one of Jake Fielding's greatest talents, and when he was about three feet away from his brother he suddenly swung toward the window, then back again. "Have you lost your mind? Good God Almighty, I'm gone less than two months and you go off and do some damn fool thing like this! What in the name of hell has gotten into you?" he demanded.

Daniel's smile faltered a fraction and he winced inwardly. But his voice was quiet as he inquired, "Who told you?"

Jake made a curt dismissing gesture with his wrist. "Hell, the only person who *didn't* tell me was you. From the minute I left Fort Worth—"

There was only the slightest note of reproach in his brother's voice as he pointed out, "I *did* try to reach you."

Jake's scowl only deepened, though he looked momentarily uncomfortable. "I was on the road," he grumbled. Jake's frequent, unaccounted-for ramblings had been a point of contention between them before; he certainly wasn't up to a lecture from his older brother on that subject now.

But Daniel merely pointed out, "You had the stock in summer pasture three weeks ago. If you had come home with the rest of the hands, instead of heading into town to spend your money on cheap whiskey and cheaper women—"

Jake flashed back, "At least I didn't marry any of them!"

When he saw Daniel's muscles tense for a rebuttal, he released a long low breath through his teeth and turned away. Running a hand through his tousled black hair, he tried to get a grip on his temper—and the entire incredible situation. He should have learned by now that he never got anywhere with Daniel by raising his voice.

Jake walked over to the big leather chair by the window, pretending to relax as he sprawled his travel-worn body into it and reached for a cigar from the box at his elbow. Daniel, accepting the signal for a minor truce of sorts, settled himself on the edge of the desk, his face falling again into its customary lines of easygoing tolerance. For a time the two men did not speak.

Jake looked at his brother with a poorly disguised mixture of frustration and impatience mounting in his eyes. He was tired and filthy and a bit hung over. All he wanted was a bath, breakfast, and about twenty-four hours of uninterrupted sleep. The last thing in the world he had needed was to come home to this.

"Ah, hell, Daniel," he said with a shake of his head, "this doesn't make any sense. I'm the one who's supposed to get into trouble, not you. *You're* the one who's supposed to ride to *my* rescue, not the other way around. What the hell has gotten into you?"

Daniel laughed softly, a relaxed twinkle filling his eyes. "I'm in love," he confessed simply.

Jake stared, his teeth clamped around the cigar, his fingers poised to strike a match on the heel of his boot. After a long time he struck the match, lit the cigar and took several puffs, his eyes never leaving Daniel. "You're what?" he asked deliberately.

A tiny muscle in Daniel's jaw tightened; no one but Jake would have noticed the defensiveness, perhaps even the anger, that crept into Daniel's eyes. But his voice was mild. "I'm allowed to fall in love, Jake."

Trying to mask his incredulity but keeping his own tone quiet, Jake said, "You're out of your mind."

Daniel said nothing.

Jake couldn't believe it. He couldn't believe his brother would be such a fool. "And this woman," he measured the words carefully, "she knows what she's getting into?"

Daniel wouldn't meet his eyes. A slight stain of color

appeared at the rim of his neck. "Jessica and I . . . have an understanding."

Jake released a low breath. "Well, by God, I'll give the hussy credit for brains. She picked the one man in the county who can give her everything a husband should—except the nighttime inconvenience. I guarantee she'll be sleeping with everything in pants within a month, but if you don't mind—"

Now Daniel's voice was harsh. "There's more between a man and a woman than what happens in the bedroom, Jake. My bride—"

Jake tossed the match into a brass spitoon at his feet, jade eyes flaring. "Your bride! Gypsy tramp is more like it!"

"You haven't even met her! You—"

"I know all I need to know," Jake cut him off and got to his feet, pacing the room. "She's a goddamn itinerant, a dirty little gold digger. Nobody even knows what she's done or where she's from."

"*I* know." Daniel's voice was decisive and very cool, the way it always was when he was trying not to get angry.

For a moment Daniel felt it stir within him again, the resentment he felt for his strong, healthy young brother. Jake, who had all the answers, to whom everything was always clearly etched in black and white . . . Jake, who took what he wanted and let nothing stand in his way . . . Jake, everybody's favorite. He knew nothing about yearning, about aching for the impossible, about reaching out for something beautiful and being unable to let go. How dare he presume to tell Daniel what to do, how to feel?

Jake, who had taken their mother Elizabeth from them—

But almost before they were formed, Daniel squelched those unworthy emotions and let none of them show on his face. Jessica was exactly what Three Hills needed. A woman with his mother's spirit, his mother's beauty . . . a woman. He continued calmly, "Her father's a traveling preacher. He runs tent revivals."

"Circus sideshows is more like it! Damn it, Daniel, you know what kind of troublemakers these people are. And it's all over Texas that this man's the worst of the lot. He's been peddling his snake oil and brimstone from here to Arkansas, and he's been run out of more towns than he's stayed in. His daughter is just as big a fraud. After she's taken you for every penny she can get she's going to light out of here quicker than a hound with his tail afire!"

Daniel dropped his eyes, struggling with his temper. He merely began, in a low tone, "It's not quite that simple, Jake . . ."

Jake stopped, giving his brother a look that was as puzzled as it had been outraged a moment before. "How the hell," he inquired incredulously, "did you meet up with these shysters anyway?"

Daniel released a long sigh, spreading his hands patiently. "They were camped on our land. I had to go check it out." He shook his head slowly, a troubled look clouding his eyes as he thought back upon that first meeting with Jessica. His voice was quiet. "You should have seen her, Jake. Such a beautiful, gentle girl. And that—*father* of hers." He practically spat out the word. "You're right about that, at least. He's a charlatan of the worst sort, moving from one town to the other, fleecing the good people who flock to see his 'miracle show'—"

"With his loving daughter the star attraction." Jake's tone was sardonic. "Does she sell herself in the back of the wagon to keep him in whiskey?"

Daniel's eyes flashed. "Watch it, Jake." But he calmed

himself again. "He keeps her like a slave. She's terrified of him. She won't tell me, but I think he beats her. Damn it, don't you see that I love her? How can I let her go on living that way?"

With sudden clarity, the truth of it dawned on Jake. He paused with his smoldering cigar halfway to his lips, and the anger in his eyes changed slowly to shrewdness, then faded to understanding. Of course. Daniel, with his heart as big as Texas, never one to think twice when there was a troubled soul in need of his help, would be the first one to fall at the feet of a damsel in distress. Realizing that, Jake found it difficult to be quite as angry with his generous, gullible brother as he had been before.

Jake said, "You don't love her, Daniel, you feel sorry for her. And she's using you, just as plain as day. Hell, you're inviting her to use you!"

He began to pace again, agitatedly. "Goddamn it, Daniel, can't you see what you're getting yourself into? You feel sorry for her. Fine, give her some money and she'll be out of here in a heartbeat, I guarantee you that. Do your Christian duty, get her off your conscience, but for God's sake, there's no reason to tie yourself up with the piece of trash for life!"

Daniel's eyes darkened with warning. "I'll tell you one more time, Jake: *she is not trash.*" Then, as though regretting his near loss of temper, he spread his hands once again. "Look Jake, I'm thirty-five years old today. And, as you've so aptly pointed out, there aren't too many women who would have me as I've been since the war . . ."

The look Daniel leveled on Jake was not reproachful, but it made Jake flush anyway, despising his own clumsiness. It had never been his intention to hurt Daniel or remind him of things he couldn't control.

But Daniel ignored his brother's discomfiture, continuing easily. "A man needs a wife for a lot of things, Jake. You know I've been asked to fill Senator Laskin's unexpired term—and you know how long I've wanted the Senate. Things would go a lot better for me if I looked like a steady family man. And Three Hills needs a woman, Jake."

He cut off Jake's objection by continuing firmly, "Jessica is perfect for me. She's sweet, she's charming, she's docile . . . and voters love a pretty face," he added with a faint smile.

"She wouldn't ask for too much, Jake," Daniel continued. The meaning there was explicit, and Jake found himself suddenly lacking arguments. "I do love her, Jake; I don't care what your definition of the word is. And I'll take care of her. We'll be good for each other. You'll understand when you meet her."

He pulled his watch from the fob pocket of his vest and snapped it open, unmistakably closing the conversation. "Now, you'd better go get cleaned up before Maria has your hide for tracking up her floor. I'm meeting Jessica in an hour and bringing her back for the barbecue. We're announcing our engagement today; we'll get married when the real circuit preacher comes by in three weeks."

Not, thought Jake grimly, if he had anything to do with it.

But Jake knew when to keep his mouth shut, and anything further he said to Daniel at the moment would only fall on deaf ears. It wasn't words that were called for in this situation anyway; it was action. And there would be plenty of action when he met Miss Jessica Duncan at the barbecue.

Daniel moved forward to clap his brother affectionately on the shoulder, apparently satisfied that their differences were at an end. "I'm glad you're back, Jake. It wouldn't have been much of a wedding without you, now would it?

Or much of a birthday, for that matter.'' Then the twinkle in his eyes softened, and his fingers closed around Jake's upper arm in a gentle but explicit message. ''You're going to like her, Jake.'' It was more than a plea; it was almost a command. ''I know you will.''

But Jake, as much as he loved his brother and wanted his happiness, could not lie to him. He said steadily, ''I don't like anything about this, Daniel. And you know it.''

For a moment a dim struggle showed in Daniel's eyes, but his natural optimism won out. He squeezed Jake's arm again briefly, and said, ''You get some rest. I'll see you tonight.''

Scowling, Jake stood there for a moment longer. But Daniel's innocent, confident smile did not fade, and Jake could not argue with it any longer. He swore loudly, tossed the cigar into the empty fireplace, and turned sharply to go upstairs. This had been one hell of a homecoming.

Daniel listened to the echo of his brother's retreating footsteps and tried not to admit to himself how much the encounter had disturbed him. Had he really expected Jake to understand?

Daniel let his gaze wander to the portrait of his mother over the fireplace. Elizabeth Coleman Fielding, a legend in her own time, had been captured by the artist as a strikingly lovely girl of sixteen, with burnished black hair and mischievous eyes the color of fine emeralds. It was a face of a young woman whose feminine beauty and indomitable spirit had lingered long after she was gone, whose gentle determination had changed the lives of all she touched. The portrait had been the very first of the many niceties she had brought from her plantation home in Alabama to civilize the frontier, and her memory still dominated Three Hills, just as the portrait dominated this room.

Jed Fielding, the frontiersman she had loved and married against the better judgment of all concerned, had been among the first to bring prosperity to Texas through the cattle industry. But Elizabeth had brought something even more important: the wealth of womanhood, the vestiges of refinement. Civilization. Daniel was struck for the first time by a faint but definite likeness between Elizabeth and Jessica, the woman he intended to marry.

Daniel had adored his mother, but then everyone had adored his mother. Because of her, no one ever forgot what was important in life—dignity, grace, consideration for one's fellow beings, courage in the face of adversity. After she died, nothing was the same at Three Hills.

For ten years after Daniel's birth his parents had longed for another child, but each promise had been met with tragedy as miscarriage followed miscarriage. Finally there had been Jake, their miracle child. But in giving him life Elizabeth had sacrificed her own.

Jed Fielding, a strong, rugged man of the plains, had all but lost the will to live once his wife was gone, and when he followed her to the grave nine years later it had been almost with a sense of relief. But there had been Jake. Jake, the legacy of Elizabeth's striking good looks and indomitable spirit. Jake, all Daniel had left of his mother. For her sake, if nothing else, Daniel was devoted to the younger child.

The brothers were as different in physical appearance as they were in temperament. Daniel, tall and blond, with his strong features and subtle air of elegance, was richly handsome in a graceful, old-world way. His mildness could have been interpreted by some as weakness, but his reputation as an honest and good man brought him head and shoulders above his peers and reinforced his position of leadership within the community. No one disliked Daniel Fielding.

Jake was his mother's son, as dark as his brother was fair, as restless as Daniel was placid. Though of about the same height, Jake had a sinewy musculature that Daniel lacked; a sharp alertness, a tough spirit—perhaps even a ruthlessness—that was totally absent in the easygoing older brother. Jake was hot tempered and unsettled, too impulsive to suit Daniel's deliberate personality, but he was as quick to forgive as he was to anger. And there was great gentleness in Jake, too, if provoked by the right circumstances. Unfortunately, such circumstances were rare.

Daniel, raised in wealth and the genteel mannerisms of the gracious Southern aristocrat Elizabeth, had tried to provide the young Jake with every opportunity he had had. He had wanted to send Jake back East to school, to read the law or pursue some other calling deserving of his name and circumstances. It was abundantly apparent, however, that Jake Fielding was a man of action, not thought, and sometimes Daniel was jealous of that.

Jake was a product of the Old West, Daniel a precursor of the new. In many ways, Three Hills had always belonged more to Jake than to Daniel, for Jake loved it in a passionately involved way that reminded Daniel of his father; Daniel loved the ranch more for what it represented than what it was.

As soon as Jake had been old enough to take over the management of the ranch, Daniel had been more than pleased to turn it over to him. Daniel's talents lay in diplomacy, administration, and vision—in short, politics. Jake's natural ability with the running of the ranch freed Daniel to develop political skills that could make a real difference in the future of Texas. Jake rode the lines, handled the stock and the hands, balanced the ledgers, managed the auctions and the drives, and was in general much more proficient in overseeing the day-to-day operations of the ranch than Daniel could ever have been. Their disagreements were infrequent and never serious, for their affection for one another ran deeper than mere birthright. They genuinely liked and respected each other, and neither could have ever imagined anything seriously coming between them . . . until now.

A small frown marred Daniel's brow as he recalled the harsh words that had been spoken only moments before. Then, with a muffled sigh, he tried to put the scene behind him and look toward the future. He took out his watch, glanced at it, and snapped it closed as he strode out of the room.

By the time he reached the front steps, he was no longer thinking of Jake at all. Jessica was waiting.

Jessica spread the luscious folds of yellow polished cotton between her hands, her eyes first widening with delight and then slowly growing troubled. To Jessica, the gown was the most beautiful thing she had ever beheld, but would it be grand enough for Daniel?

There was no mirror in the dim canvas topped wagon that was the only home Jessica had ever known—Papa thought such things were sinful—but she knew every stitch of the garment by heart. She had purchased the material with money saved from her supply allotment and had spent the last two weeks painstakingly sewing by the light of a shaded candle after her father was snoring beneath the wagon. She had copied a style she had seen some of the women wearing in the southeast towns where they had stopped.

The bodice fit snugly, perhaps a little too snugly, she worried now as she ran her fingers lightly over the shape of her full breasts. And the neckline was more daring than any she had ever imagined she would wear, exposing the full width of her collarbones and even an inch or two of her shoulders. The sleeves were short and ruffled, barely covering her elbows, and the skirt fell gracefully from her tiny waist to the floor. The sunshine yellow color was magnificent, for Jessica's father had never allowed her to wear anything brighter than dark blue, and she had fallen in love with the cheerful hue on sight. Though she could have hardly known it without a mirror, the color was a stunning contrast for her cloud of black hair and made her huge blue eyes look even larger and more brilliant against her creamy complexion.

She wished she had some lace with which to trim the dress—another sinful vanity she had never even dreamed of before—and real buttons rather than the placketed hooks that fastened the front of her bodice. And, she fretted, smoothing the crisp material over her hips with an anxious gesture, the dress cried out for petticoats, stiff crinkling ones that formed a bell shape over the ankles rather than allowing the material to cling to her legs and outline her figure as it did now. She hoped Daniel wouldn't be ashamed of her. She did so want to please him and make him proud of her in front of all his friends and neighbors.

The pace of her heart caught and then increased its rhythm as she realized that in only moments she would be meeting Daniel at their special place, then going away to his grand mansion and standing by his side as his betrothed. More than once in the past month she had had to pinch herself to convince herself she was not dreaming, but after the evening to come there would no longer be any doubt . . . when they were truly and publicly engaged nothing could harm them, her father couldn't stand in their way, and she could really believe it was happening.

Quickly, Jessica picked up her comb and tried to fashion her thick mass of hair into some semblance of neatness. She had not told her father about Daniel's party or her intention to attend, and she wanted to be gone before William Duncan returned to stop her.

Jessica reached for a handful of pins at the bottom of the small cardboard box that held her few personal possessions, but found she couldn't resist. She pushed aside a pair of scissors, a skein of thread, a frayed ribbon, and at the bottom of the box found the small faded tintype. She took it out reverently, and a soft wistful smile lit her features. *Oh, Mama,* she thought, touching the photograph to her cheek. *How I wish you could be with me today, to share my happiness . . .*

Life had been so different when her mother was alive, and the memories of those early years were Jessica's most precious. They had all been happy then. They had had a real church and lived in a cozy parsonage with window boxes filled with colorful blooms. Her mother had taught Jessica to love God, to be good, and to have faith. They had been a real family then.

But when her mother died it was as though all the demons in William Duncan had been unleashed. He lost his church, began to drink, and was forced to become an itinerant preacher, dragging his wagon and his daughter from town to town, from camp to camp. From that day on Jessica's life had been built on fear, not love, and the years of her young womanhood had been a nightmare of obedience and subservience. Only those early memories of her mother had given her strength, and those same memories had been all Jessica had ever known of love, until now. Until Daniel.

Now she would recapture that wonderful time when she had had a home and a family and people to love who loved her back. She would have a husband, and children of her own, and she would build for them what had been taken from her so abruptly. Daniel would make her most cherished dreams come true. Daniel would be a father to her children. Daniel. . . .

From the first moment she had seen him he had been her knight in shining armor, so gentle, so courteous, so handsome. When he first came to their wagon she had expected him to chase them off like so many had before him, but she soon learned that Daniel was unlike anyone else who had come before. He treated her father with respect, and he smiled at her with a gentleness that made her feel hungry . . . too many years had passed since she had received kindness from another. Not only had he allowed them to stay on his land, but that afternoon he had sent over a haunch of beef to welcome them.

And the next day he had found her beside the stream. It had been the most beautiful day of Jessica's life. Together they picked wild flowers, and he spoke to her in words of poetry. He told her of his dreams and his plans for the future, and Jessica was thrilled with his vision. He was going to be a great man, and she felt humbled and honored that he would even notice her.

They began to meet more often, and thoughts of him filled her days and nights. Daniel Fielding was the only man with whom she had ever spent any time besides her father, and he was nothing like her father. He was kind and beautiful and softly spoken, and when he smiled at her he made her feel special. Those days were like a dream from which she would awaken only to find the dream continued; it was all too perfect to be true. And then he told her that he loved her and asked her to be his wife. And Jessica knew herself to be the most fortunate girl in the world.

Suddenly she was briefly blinded by the square of sunlight that flooded the room as the canvas flap of the wagon was thrown open. Jessica's father stood silhouetted in the doorway.

Jessica quickly returned the tintype of her mother to its hiding place. She took an automatic step backward as her father swung himself inside. He smelled strongly of the cherry flavored tonic he sometimes took for medicinal purposes, and was swaying more than usual. For a long time he simply stared at her, his eyes focusing slowly beneath lowering brows, and Jessica could feel his black gaze going straight through to her spine.

"What is the meaning of this, girl?" His voice was a roar that bounced off the thin walls of the wagon and crowded the small enclosure with its fury. It took all the courage Jessica possessed not to shrink from it, from him.

Lifting her chin, she said, "I'm glad you're back, Papa. I've been invited to Daniel Fielding's barbecue. I wanted to say good-bye."

For a moment William looked as though he could not believe his ears. Then he dismissed her incredible statement as though it was not worth the energy it would require to dispute. "Pin your hair up, girl. And bind yourself. You look like the devil's own whore."

Jessica's hand went nervously to her wild mass of hair, and her arm crossed self-consciously over her breasts, round and full without the tight strips of muslin her father insisted she wind around her bosom to make her womanhood less noticeable—and less offensive. A prickle of hot shame touched her cheeks, but she withstood her father's disgusted gaze and even managed to respond to it.

"No, Papa," she said steadily. "I am a woman now, and I should dress like one." A month before she would have never dared speak back to her father like that. But since Daniel had come into her life she had discovered an entire reservoir of strength she had never known she had. Since Daniel had come into her life she had discovered a lot of things.

William Duncan took a step forward, his florid face darkening further at her unexpected insolence. "A *woman* are you?" he hissed. "A shameless Jezebel is what you are! That's what that man has turned you into! I knew nothing good would come of Satan's handiwork! We should have left this place the minute I saw that man's evil face, for he's twisted your mind and corrupted your body and already sent you on the path of eternal damnation. He's a demon, that one, an angel from hell—"

"Stop it, Papa!" Jessica cried, the tenor of her voice, as well as the courage it took to speak the words, surprising her as much as her father. Her eyes blazed and her color was high. "I'm going to marry Daniel Fielding! He's not a devil, and he's going to make me his wife!"

William's eyes narrowed. "I'll see you in hell first!" he spat, and took a threatening step toward her. His smoldering gaze raked her up and down and Jessica tried not to cower. "Get out of that shameless costume, girl, and set yourself to work! We're leaving this field of perdition today, and there's not a minute to lose!"

Jessica stared at him, hardly able to believe her ears. Today, while Daniel was waiting for her . . . no, it was impossible. Life couldn't be so cruel. This couldn't happen, not when she was only inches from grasping the only true happiness she had ever known.

Her voice was very weak as she asked, "But—where? Where will we go?"

"I will go on about my work spreading the gospel to the heathen," her father replied with an imperious, unbreachable authority. "You will go to your aunt at Live Oaks where you may repent of your sins and be safe from the evil intentions of men like Daniel Fielding. Now get yourself moving, girl! And take off that trollop's garb!"

A ragged gasp escaped Jessica and her face lost some of its color. Aunt Eulalie . . . Louisiana . . . No, it couldn't happen. She wouldn't let it happen, she wouldn't be sent hundreds of miles away while Daniel waited for her, wondering what had happened to her.

"No!" she cried aloud. Though the blaze in her father's eyes frightened her, she was far more frightened of leaving Texas and what would become of her if she did. "No!" she cried again and took a step backward, trying to edge toward the door. "I won't go! I'm going to marry Daniel, I—"

William lurched forward, drawing back his hand for a blow. Jessica ducked quickly, and his closed fist landed against her ribs with enough force to knock her against the sharp edge of a trunk. She stumbled and half sprawled across it. She lay there for a moment, struggling to regain her breath.

"Is that what you want girl, to be a whore for that rutting, cloven-hooved beast?" he yelled. "To let him defile you and plant his filthy seed in you and give birth to his misshapen monsters? Is that what you want, you degenerate spawn of Satan?"

Jessica tried to crawl away as he took another step closer, but he reached down and hauled her roughly to her feet. His cherry-scented breath suffocated her, and there were flecks of spittle on his lips which mingled with the gray streaks in his beard and looked like the froth of madness. Jessica cried out as he grasped the sides of her bodice and in a single motion ripped it open to the waist, exposing the shape of her creamy breasts through her thin and worn chemise.

"Whore!" he shouted, his eyes as he followed her furtive motions to cover herself bright with contempt and rage and something very strangely like greed. "Pleasure giver!" As he spoke his hands were fumbling with his belt. Then he whipped it off and raised it above his head for a blow. "You'll pay for your lust!"

Jessica scrambled away, but not soon enough. William Duncan was not a tall man, but he was very sturdy, and the crack of the leather belt landed across Jessica's arm and back with enough force to rip the material and draw blood. Her strangled sob was lost in the sound of his heavy breathing as he stumbled toward her.

Her father was strong, but Jessica was agile, and she had not the disadvantage of the bottle of strong cherry tonic he had consumed in the hour preceding his return to the wagon. William fell over a box of foodstuffs with a cry of rage just as Jessica stumbled out through the flap opening. She landed on her hands and knees but did not look back to see how closely she was being pursued. She picked up her skirts and ran, heading toward the stand of cottonwoods where Daniel waited.

William Duncan lay where he had fallen, breathing hard and muttering curses to himself, his head spinning. He did not attempt to go after Jessica; she would return soon enough. She was his daughter, and she had no choice.

* * *

Daniel paced the ground from the edge of the small stream back to where his horse was tethered beneath the grove of cottonwoods, once, then twice. His hands clasped tightly behind his back was the only betrayal of his impatience. It was foolish to meet like two fugitives in the middle of a meadow, and he was tired of the subterfuge. But after today there would be no more reason to hide, and for Jessica's sake he would go through the motions this last time.

Briefly, a troubled frown crossed his eyes as he thought back on the encounter with Jake. He had lied to his brother, and he'd never done that before. But it was none of Jake's business, and Daniel did not have to explain his actions or motivations to him. Jessica was an innocent, a child who had to be protected from the evils of the world around her, and under his tutelage she would mature into the gracious woman his mother had been.

What he had to offer her would more than make up for the lack of a physical marriage between them, but Jake couldn't be expected to understand that. Daniel planned to tell Jessica, in time, that he could never father children. He would wait until the right time, and then it wouldn't make a bit of difference . . . but how could he explain that to Jake? Jake could never understand what Daniel felt for Jessica, nor the many reasons, practical and ethereal, that this would be a perfect marriage. He would make Jessica happy, he was certain of it, and she was exactly what he needed. Nothing else mattered.

And then he saw Jessica coming, and all other thoughts left his mind.

Jessica ran, heedless of the beautiful gown that was now torn and stained beyond repair. Daniel started toward her, but before he could reach her she had splashed across the shallow stream and hurled herself into his arms.

"Daniel! Oh, Daniel—he's going to take me away!" Her words were hoarse and ragged gasps, muffled by the crisp fabric of Daniel's coat against her face. "I had to tell you—I couldn't let him—without telling you."

"Hush, hush." Daniel's arms were tight around her, his hands soothing upon her back, but she could feel the tension mounting within him and underlying the gentle tone of his voice. "Stop, darling, get your breath. I'm here now, nothing is going to hurt you."

What wonderful, wonderful words those were. Jessica's side ached, her lungs burned, and her legs were cramping from the long and frantic run across uneven ground. Her arms and hands stung from the scratches of thorns, and the welt her father's belt had left across her back and shoulder burned dully. Her face was streaked with tears she was not even aware she had shed, and every muscle in her body was trembling. It felt so good to cling to Daniel, to let him tell her everything was going to be all right.

At length, as her shudders lessened and her breath came more evenly, Daniel eased her away. He shrugged out of his jacket and helped her into it, pulling the collar closed over her torn bodice. He looked down into her pale, ravaged face. "Now then," he commanded gently, "tell me what happened. What is this nonsense about going away?"

Jessica swallowed hard, for a renewed shudder had gripped her with the thought of her father's plans. Her small fists gripped the lapels of Daniel's jacket, holding it close. "Papa said we're leaving. He's going to send me to Live Oaks, Aunt Eulalie's plantation in New Orleans, and he's going to keep me there forever!" Her large cloudy blue eyes widened so that they seemed to dominate her face, and her grip on Daniel's coat tightened. "Oh, Daniel, I'll never see you again! It's so far away and Aunt Eulalie is so old and—"

"Hush." The word was swift and soothing as he bent to drop a reassuring kiss on her wild cascade of tangled curls. "You're not going anywhere. No one can take you away from me." He smiled and grasped her upper arms in a tender gesture of affection. He saw her wince and for the first time he understood the significance of the torn dress and terrified look in her eyes.

Daniel's face darkened, and his hands tightened, unknowingly causing her further pain. His eyes went over her swiftly, furiously, and he demanded hoarsely, "What has he done to you? By God, this I will not stand for! He's struck you, hasn't he? Tell me!"

He shook her a little, and Jessica cried out, not so much from the pain his fingers were causing as alarm at the anger in Daniel's eyes. Immediately Daniel's grip lightened, but his fury did not dissipate, and Jessica said, "No, Daniel, it's nothing, just a scratch—"

Daniel released her abruptly, turning toward his horse. "Don't lie for him, Jessica. This is long overdue, and this time he will face me like a man!"

"No!" The desperation and fear in Jessica's voice was real, and she stumbled after him, catching his arm. "Daniel, please don't! Don't go to him," she pleaded, "you don't know him when he's like this. He's like a madman and he'll kill you, I know he will! Please, Daniel!"

Daniel hesitated, and though his anger did not fade it was greatly overshadowed by concern for her terror. He looked at her, and he seemed to come to a conclusion. He said firmly, "Very well, Jessica. But you're not going back to him. You're not going back to that place ever again. You're coming home with me, now."

A rush of wonder and disbelief drew a gasp from Jessica, but she had to protest. "Daniel—I can't! I—"

But Daniel's face was set in determination, his mind working rapidly. "We'll be married today. I was foolish not to have taken you away from that man long before now. There's no point in delaying further."

Jessica's head was spinning as a mixture of joy and doubt and sheer disbelief raced through her and left her breathless. "But how can that be done?"

"It can all be arranged within the hour," he assured her, then bent to silence her remaining protests with a gentle kiss on her cheek.

His lips were cool upon her flushed skin, but Jessica tried not to notice. She was so deliriously happy that she could not ask for anything more, nor notice anything lacking in his brief, impersonal gesture of affection. She gripped his soft hands tightly, her eyes shining as she looked up at him. "Oh, I will be a good wife for you, Daniel!" she breathed. "And a loving mother to your children and—"

She stopped because something strange had come over his face with her last words, a tight, almost shuttered expression fraught with reluctance. She felt his hands go slack beneath hers, as though he wished to pull away, and he looked for a moment as though he might say something.

But before she could open her mouth to question or redeem whatever blunder she might have made, he relaxed and patted her lightly on the shoulder. "I know you will, darling. You're all I could ever ask for. Now only promise me," his eyes grew intent, searching her eyes deeply as though afraid of what he might find there, "that you will marry me now, and that you will always be as happy as you are at this moment."

How could she have refused? She could not go back to

her father. She could not let him take her away from Daniel and the happiness he offered. This was her one chance for a life filled with virtue and kindness with a man who loved her.

She laughed aloud with joy, flinging herself into Daniel's arms. "Yes," she cried, hugging him hard. "Oh, Daniel, yes, yes!"

Chapter II

For most of the year Three Hills Ranch was a repose of peaceful gentility that dominated the most beautiful corner of Texas—and therefore, the world—with an old-style regality and simple order that was unsurpassed by any of its contemporaries.

The long, low main house meandered lazily at the foot of the central of the three hills for which it was named, surrounded by stately pines, ruffled cottonwoods and meadowlike lawns. Easterly breezes billowed its lace curtains and lazy sunshine dappled its spacious rooms. An aged gardener tended the beds of brilliant zinnias and begonias which had been the late Miss Elizabeth's pride and joy, and the houseservants, under the indomitable supervision of Maria Delgades, went about preserving an orderly existence for the two Fielding men with leisurely, unobtrusive efficiency.

As far as the eye could see in any direction—encompassing an area only slightly larger than the state of Rhode Island—

Three Hills cattle fattened themselves on the rich Texas grass; ranch hands patrolled the borders with practiced ease, occasionally rescuing a calf from a tangle of briars or a stand of mud. There were few surprises at Three Hills. But three times a year, at Christmas, spring roundup, and the annual summer barbeque that marked Daniel Fielding's birthday, the quiet, predictable routine of the ranch was interrupted by a flurry of celebratory preparations.

Over two open spits in the lawn a heifer and a hog had been roasting slowly since midnight and the air was redolent with the scent of sizzling meat and slow-burning hickory. Huge cauldrons of thick hot sauce simmered over open fires, and the aroma of baking bread and spicy chili wafted from the kitchen. Long tables covered with spotless cloths had been set up on the lawn, and the morning sun created playful patterns of moving shadows through the leaves that shaded them.

Already the ranch hands were slicking down their hair, polishing their boots, and donning their brightest garb for the festivities ahead. Every corner of the great house had been scrubbed and polished within an inch of its life, the piano had been dragged outside for the dancing that would begin later in the evening, and the servants hurried back and forth in a cheerful rush to complete the last minute preparations for the arrival of the first guests. Today was July the first; Daniel Fielding was thirty-five years old, and there was more than one reason to celebrate.

Jessica had never seen the ranch house before and her first impression as Daniel and she rode in on his horse was of such wealth and splendor that she could hardly believe she was really there. That she soon would be mistress of this grand place was a concept simply too large for her to consider.

The flurry of activity for the barbecue was at its height. Servants hurried back and forth, placing armfuls of bright, polished china and silver on the outdoor tables, carrying huge bowls of punch, lugging tubs of ice brought down at great expense from the mountains. Ladders were propped up at intervals where some of the ranch hands were busy stringing paper lanterns and arguing with each other over the best way to do it. The scents, the colors, and the movement energized the lazy July day and left Jessica breathless with trying to take it all in at once. But Daniel, too excited over his own plans to give much notice to her bemusement, hurried her along.

He helped her dismount his horse and tossed the reins to a barefoot young servant who spared Jessica one delighted grin before clucking to the horse and hurrying to attend his duties. Daniel grasped Jessica's hand and she had to stretch her legs to keep up with his long strides toward the wide front steps of the mansion.

"We can't afford to wait, Jessica," he said earnestly, but his eyes were bright as he glanced at her. "Judge Waters is coming out for the party anyway, and he can marry us just as well as anyone else." Then his confidence clouded fractionally and he hesitated on the top step, looking down at her. "Do you mind, Jessica? Having a civil ceremony, I mean. I know how important it is to you to be married by a preacher, but we can still stand before the preacher when he comes at the end of the month."

Jessica was simply too bedazzled, too swept away by all that had happened in such a brief time to voice any objection, even if she had harbored one. It was a dream, she thought. Surely it must be, and she would awake any minute now. But her eyes were deep and shining brilliantly as she responded, "Oh, Daniel, what does it matter as long as you and I are truly together as man and wife?"

Daniel, looking at her bright face, so full of innocence

and joy, felt a sharp pang of guilt. She had a right to know. This was the time to tell her. Yet if he told her he might lose her.

So he only said softly, "I need you so desperately, Jessica. You have truly made me the happiest man in the world."

He reached up to gently touch the cloud of her hair, then quickly placed his hand upon the small of her back and urged her through the great door of the house, calling imperiously, "Maria! Maria, where are you?"

For a moment as Jessica stood in the cool foyer she was overwhelmed by the gracious loveliness of it all. The interior was not imposing, and there were no pretentious displays of wealth, but the house exuded an orderliness, a simple statement of endurance and quality that was as welcoming as it was daunting.

The walls were paneled in gleaming yellow pine and the dark floor was so bright Jessica could see a blurred reflection of her yellow dress in it. The scent of pine oil and beeswax floated on the summer day like sunshine. To her left was a beautifully carved fruitwood table which held a lamp of sheerest china upon which was painted a delicate lake scene; to her right a polished staircase climbed to the second floor. Two windows reached from floor to ceiling on either side of the door, and fresh air and sunshine fluttered through the white lace curtains. A woman once had loved this place, Jessica knew instinctively, and so would she.

From the foyer she caught a glimpse of another large room with a huge stone hearth and wine and dark brown leather furnishings. On the opposite side was a long low dining room with an expansive mahogany table and throne-like chairs that reminded Jessica of an etching of a banquet hall she had once seen. An enormous spray of fresh flowers dominated the center of the table, and overhead a chandelier with a multitude of crystal teardrops caught prisms of color and dispersed them in dancing patterns along the papered walls. Suddenly Jessica felt very self-conscious in her tattered dress and disheveled hair. She made a nervous gesture to adjust Daniel's coat about her shoulders and smooth back her hair just as a large, scowling Mexican woman came lumbering through the doorway from the dining room.

"Maria," Daniel said, and again Jessica felt his hand, reassuring and supportive, upon her back, "this is Jessica." There was an unmistakeable note of pride in his voice. "We're getting married this afternoon, as soon as Judge Waters arrives. I'm going to make the arrangements now. Meanwhile, see that Miss Jessica is comfortable. I leave her completely in your hands."

Then, with a quick squeeze of her waist and a warming smile, he added, "Go with Maria, darling, and she'll show you where you can rest. This is your home now; don't be afraid to ask for whatever you need."

If she felt any astonishment at this announcement it did not show in the dark woman's eyes. Her irritated scowl merely relaxed after a long and thorough perusal of first Daniel, then Jessica. With a nod of satisfaction, Maria extended her arm, beckoning toward the staircase. "And about time, too, Señor Daniel. A man your age has lived too long alone. Come along, señorita, there is much to do and little time. We must make ready."

Jessica's heart opened to the big woman who had not paused for a moment's consideration of Jessica's bedraggled appearance or the unusual circumstances, but had welcomed her without reservation as Daniel's intended bride. *I am going to be happy here,* she thought with a delirious surge of confidence. *So happy.*

Daniel patted her hand fondly as she stepped away from him. His eyes were smiling. "The next time I see you," he said, "will be at our wedding. I'll send for you the minute the judge gets here."

And then Jessica was being led toward the stairs, while Maria, with the decisive movements of a woman used to being in charge, decided, "First to wash. My Rio, he will bring up water from the kitchen, warm for the bath. And my pretty Julia will go for the flower-smelling salts the trader left, and then we must find a fine dress for the señorita . . ."

She paused, and turned back toward the foyer, bellowing, "Julia! Rio!" Then she said to Jessica, "Go along, señorita, to the top of the stairs, first door. I will follow."

With much twitching and rustling of her cotton skirts, Maria turned at the foot of the stairs, shouting commands for Julia and Rio. Jessica, with a secret smile of wonder and sheer contentment, was left to ascend the stairs on her own.

Daniel's house was as wonderful as he was, Jessica thought, and the people who worked there obviously loved him without reservation. As who would not? Daniel Fielding was undoubtedly the kindest, most generous man who had ever lived, and Jessica could never begin to repay him for the joy he had brought into her life . . . more than she had ever dreamed possible, more than she surely deserved.

At the top of the stairs Jessica paused, briefly confused, for the wide upper hallway branched into two sets of doors. Maria had told her to wait in the first room, but she had not mentioned whether it was to the right or left. With a small lift of her shoulders, Jessica opened the door on the right.

It took Jessica's eyes a moment to adjust to the dimness, but she knew immediately that the room must be a man's. The masculine scent of sandalwood soap danced upon the faint summer breeze, and a pair of worn man's boots lay haphazardly on the colorful rag rug in a pool of sunshine. Daniel's? The chifforobe was open, and a row of man's clothes hung within. There was a dusty Stetson on the bureau, and a damp towel slung carelessly over the bedpost. She was midway into the room before she noticed the form on the bed not a foot away from her.

He was sprawled on the bed facedown, and he was completely naked. His arms were stretched over his head to embrace the pillow, sinewy muscles perfectly defined even in their relaxed state. Dark hair, as smooth and silky as a raven's wing, curled gently at his neck and shadowed his face, which was half turned toward her, still and deeply relaxed in the oblivion of sleep. The skin that covered his lower arms was a rich nut brown, as though he was accustomed to rolling his shirt sleeves up, and her eyes lingered there in fascination before drifting helplessly over the taut musculature of his back, downward to his slim, smooth buttocks. His legs, shaded with silky black hair, were strong and lean and very long, and he slept as unself-consciously as a child, with one foot angled inward toward his calf, the other leg sprawled comfortably across the bed.

All of this Jessica noticed in an instant, almost before the realization that she had intruded into a man's chamber while he slept, unclothed and unaware, registered in her mind. Then embarrassed color flooded her cheeks, and she must have emitted an involuntary gasp of shame and apology, for at that moment emerald green eyes opened and looked directly at her.

It seemed an eternity that she was captured in that smoky, not-quite-focused deep green gaze, but in fact it was only a fraction of a second. He looked at her, this strong, naked man, but he did not move or speak, and Jessica was helpless to move away. And just as she opened her mouth to stammer some sort of apology, his hand reached out to grab her wrist, as quick as the strike of a snake.

Jake, having just returned from two weeks of excess in one of the most notorious cowtowns in that part of the state, was not the least surprised to open his eyes and find a woman in his room. Still half asleep as he was, it didn't occur to him that this was his own house and not some hotel room or brothel, and he acted according to instinct, not thought. With little effort at all, he tugged her off balance and onto the bed beside him, murmuring, "Well, well, what have we here?"

He registered startled blue eyes—the biggest eyes he had ever seen—and a swath of dark curly hair, flushed skin that was growing ever brighter, and he smiled drowsily to himself. *A gypsy wench, I'll be damned,* he thought and wished he weren't so tired.

Jessica gave a little cry of surprise and fear when she felt herself land beside him on the bed. She was acutely aware of his nakedness, and the aura of blatant virility he exuded was so strange she did not even recognize it for what it was, only that it made her heart leap and her skin tingle. Struggling against the sensations as much as his grip, she tried to get to her feet, gasping, "I—I—"

Jake laughed low in his throat at her maidenly behavior, sliding himself upward a bit so that his lips could taste the smooth creamy texture of her throat. He could barely keep his eyes open, but God, she tasted good, felt good, half fantasy and half reality....

"Your timing could use some work," he murmured, rubbing his cheek against the gentle curve of her half-exposed shoulder. "We might have to do this again when I'm awake."

Jessica's strength returned in a rush when she felt his lips on the bare parts of her skin, tantalizing little arrows of heat sparking through her from every place he touched. His tongue traced a hot moist pattern along her throat and the sensation made her flush all over as her pulses pounded erratically. With a strangled cry she braced both fists against his shoulders and pushed hard, every self-protective instinct she possessed propelling her to her feet.

Jake called sleepily, "Hey, it won't be that bad—don't run away!"

But Jessica did run, across the room and out of the door in an instant. Only when she was in the hallway, her hand pressed to the horrible thudding of her heart and her breath coming in gasps, did she pause to wonder why she felt less frightened than excited by the outrageous thing that had just happened in that room with a stranger. A *naked* stranger! How could she have let him touch her like that? And how, for just that most fleeting space of time, could she have thought it pleasant?

Jake, chuckling softly into the pillow, did not give the incident a second thought. He closed his eyes and was asleep almost before the door had closed behind her.

Because of the volatile encounter with his brother he had thought he would be too tense to sleep at all, but after a hearty breakfast and a welcome bath and shave Jake had stretched out on the bed for what he assured himself would be only a brief rest. Then, unexpectedly and in only a matter of a few deep breaths, the noises of the unaccustomed activity in the house faded away, his worries and his annoyance with Daniel dispersed into nothing more than drifting, disconnected thoughts, and he was deeply asleep. He did not even remember when the dream started, only that it featured a wild-haired girl with the most enormous deep blue eyes he had ever seen and skin that tasted like rich cream. . . .

It was an hour later, though it seemed to Jake no more than a minute, when the door opened again, heavy footsteps approached his bed, and a hand grasped his shoulder. Jake growled a warning and burrowed his face into the pillow, squeezing his eyes shut and searching for the fragments of the dream which had not yet grown erotic but was wonderfully close to becoming so. The hand shook his shoulder rudely as a voice demanded, "Get up, young señor, and put on your clothes. Your brother wants you downstairs this minute!"

With an oath, Jake tossed the pillow aside and sat up, scowling fiercely. The beautiful dream was completely gone.

"Damn it, Maria, you're going to get yourself shot one day barging in here when I'm asleep!"

He snatched the coverlet he had tossed aside and drew it over his lap, not out of any real sense of modesty, but more an instinctive protest against the invasion of privacy. Maria had diapered, bathed and dressed him until he was three years old, she'd nursed him when he was ill, set his broken leg, and dragged him naked out of bed on more than one occasion, and a display of shyness now would be irrelevant and misplaced. But that did *not* entitle her to wake him out of a sound sleep after the night he'd had—after the morning he'd had—and his scowl only deepened as he demanded, "What the hell's the matter with you, anyway? Coming into a man's bedroom without so much as a knock or a by-your-leave."

Maria, hands on her hips, smiled smugly. "You have nothing I have not seen before, Mr. Jake . . . and seen better of, too."

Jake searched for something to throw at her, and came up

with nothing but the pillow, which she dodged quite agilely for a woman of her bulk and years. "Get the hell out of here, you foul-mouthed old woman, before I—" But he stopped, partly because the sound of his own shout was making his head ache, partly because he had remembered something else . . . another woman entering his room while he slept. A woman with big blue eyes. A dream? Groggily, he thought he might ask Maria about that, and then he remembered what she had said and his gaze sharpened on her. "What did you say about Daniel? What time is it, anyway?"

Maria, satisfied that he was now fully awake, nodded her head pertly and informed him, "The señor wants you in the library. There will be a wedding in fifteen minutes."

The fuzzy remnants of sleep shattered in a swift burst and Jake stared at her. *"What?"*

Again Maria nodded, pleased with herself and the import of the message. "The judge, he is waiting now, and the pretty señorita is almost ready."

"Jesus Christ!" It was a vicious hiss as Jake threw aside the coverlet and got to his feet. Damn, he thought furiously. *Damn you Daniel for a gullible fool.* Another day—another hour—and Jake could have had that scheming little tramp out of his brother's life forever. But no, Daniel couldn't wait. He was bound and determined to ruin his life.

Maybe it wasn't too late. Jake stalked to the chifforobe, heedless of his nakedness, and jerked out a shirt. He whirled on Maria as he pulled it on. "Tell Daniel I'm coming. Tell him to wait for me." His face was dark and his eyes were snapping. "And by God, Maria, if that ceremony starts without me I'll have your skin. Now go! Get out of here!"

Maria left Jake muttering curses to himself and tugging

on his pants. She took her time and smiled indulgently as she went first to deliver to the groom the message from his bad-tempered brother, and then to check on the bride.

The room Jessica found after her misadventure was an airy, feminine bedroom which she learned had once belonged to Miss Elizabeth, Daniel's mother. For a moment the lovely surroundings drove away the searing embarrassment of her encounter with the sleeping man, and then the servants began to troop in, bearing a large galvanized tub and pails of hot water, and there was such a flurry of activity that Jessica hardly had time to think of anything at all.

Daniel's servants were as eager to welcome her as they were eager to please, and there was a lot of excited chatter about what Jessica should wear and how her hair should be and how good it would be to have a mistress in the house again, and children, just like when Miss Elizabeth was alive. When Julia was sent scurrying to the attic for one of Miss Elizabeth's dresses that might be altered to fit Jessica, Jessica protested, not wanting Daniel to think she was overstepping her bounds. But Maria, whose authority apparently was second only to God's, dismissed Jessica's concern as irrelevant. Of course the señor would want his bride to wear his mother's gown, and it was only a pity that Miss Elizabeth had never had a proper wedding gown to hand down to her daughter-in-law, for she, too, had eloped. Jessica was wrapped up in the whirlwind of her changing life and she hardly had a moment to catch her breath.

But at the back of her mind the memory of that man lingered, surfacing at unexpected times while she bathed and dressed in the fine lawn underthings Maria had brought from Miss Elizabeth's store. His strong fingers on her wrist, his mouth on her skin . . . and every time the memory crept upon her it brought a quick rush of color to her cheeks, a strange quivery feeling to her stomach. Who *was* he? What kind of man would behave so outrageously, and what was he doing in Daniel's house? She wanted to ask Maria, but she was too embarrassed . . . and too excited. She was marrying Daniel, not the dangerous looking, green-eyed man.

Maria tended Jessica's cuts and scratches with a soothing ointment, clucking maternally but not questioning where she had gotten them. In truth, Jessica was far too enraptured by all that had happened to her in such a short time to even hear the questions had they been directed to her. None of it was real yet. A short time before she had been in a cramped and dusty wagon, victim of her father's stern temper and about to be taken from Texas to a life she couldn't even imagine with her Aunt Eulalie. Now she was at Three Hills, surrounded by people who beamed at her and complimented her and treated her like a queen, and in only another moment she would belong to Daniel Fielding, the gentlest, most generous man who had ever lived. She could not believe it. It was all too much and happening too quickly to be absorbed. She only hoped it would last, for Jessica was certain she would never be this happy again.

And then Julia proudly brought in the dress she had hastily prepared for Jessica and laid it carefully on the bed. Jessica was so overwhelmed that tears sprang to her eyes, and she brought her fingers to her mouth to stifle a cry of sheer delight. "Oh!" she gasped. "Oh, but it's too lovely! I—"

Maria cut off further protests by pulling tight on the strings that bound Jessica's stays, causing her to momentarily lose her breath. Jessica had never worn a corset before, but its discomfort was not nearly as great as the tight muslin wrappings with which her father had made her bind her breasts, and the feel of real silk stockings and fine lawn underclothes against her skin was more than adequate compensation. She felt swathed in luxury, overcome by indulgence, and though she knew it was sinful she couldn't help it—she loved every moment of it.

"You're a tiny one," Maria grunted, tying off the corset, "but Miss Elizabeth, she was smaller. That is why she never got up from the birthbed, a fine lady such as she was never built for babies. You now, Miss Jessica, you will give the señor many little ones, strong sons and pretty daughters."

A thrill went through Jessica as she thought of children, her children and Daniel's, and the world that was opening up for her now like an unfolding blossom filled with promise. But her eyes were wide and her cheeks flushed as she was drawn, on compulsion, to the magnificent confection of pink taffeta that was spread across the bed. She touched it gently, then whirled to Maria, her eyes shining through her hesitance. "Are you sure? Are you sure it will be all right—to wear it?"

Once again Maria's face was briefly creased with an indulgent smile, but it was quickly replaced by sternness as she crossed to the bed and took up the gown. "Hold up your arms, señorita, we must hurry. The judge is waiting downstairs and we have a wedding to start."

Still unable to shake the feeling of a dream too wonderful to be true, Jessica obediently lifted her arms as the folds of magnificent taffeta were dropped over her head. *Oh, Daniel,* she thought with a surge of joy so intense it made her weak, *how will I ever be able to thank you for all you've done for me?*

Jed Fielding had died when Jake was nine years old, and since then Daniel had been everything to Jake: mother, father, brother, best friend. Daniel had taught him to ride and rope, and had bought him his first pair of spurs. Daniel taught him to shoot, and made him practice for hours on end under the hot Texas sun until he was good enough to carry his own weapon. To Jake had gone their father's treasured Patterson-Colt five-shooter, which had been a gift to Jed Fielding from Sam Houston, and which rightfully should have belonged to Daniel. But Daniel had parted with it unhesitantly to honor his younger brother.

When Jake had gotten sick off his first whiskey, it had been Daniel who held his shoulders, chuckling indulgently, while he disgraced himself in bushes on the side of the trail. Daniel was the one who bound Jake's wounds after his first fistfight and saw him through his first case of puppy love. Daniel taught Jake to defend the weak, respect the strong, and take care of himself. Daniel had given Jake all he had ever known about his mother, and about the man his father had been before his wife died. He had made him proud of his heritage, and never made him feel too bad when he didn't always live up to it.

Daniel had gone off to fight in the War Between the States and Jake thought he had lost the last thread of continuity in his life. When Daniel had returned, a hero but a cripple in a way that would have destroyed other men, Jake would have gladly given his own life to spare his brother that suffering.

Jake's affection for Daniel went beyond fraternal loyalty; it was fierce and protective and unquestioningly devoted, as Daniel's was for him. In all the world, they had only each other to depend upon, and Jake would not allow his brother to ruin his life anymore than Daniel would have stood by and let the same thing happen to Jake.

He could not keep silent.

"Are you out of your mind?" Jake hissed, ever mindful of the alert ears of Judge Waters, who, for all his many virtues, was one of the biggest gossips in East Texas. He saw no need to air family linen in front of a stranger—although if Daniel was foolhardy enough to go through with this preposterous marriage more than dirty laundry would be held up for the whole county to mock.

Daniel started to turn away, but Jake grasped his arm. "Damn it, Daniel, don't you see what a fool that woman is making out of you?"

Daniel said tiredly, "Jake, I'm not going through this again. You don't know anything about her."

With another impatient hiss, Jake ran his hand through his recently trimmed and neatly combed hair, ruffling it slightly. His eyes fell upon the portrait over the mantel. "Good God almighty, Daniel, Mother would be spinning in her grave if she knew you'd brought a woman like that into the house! For God's sake, will you think about what you're doing? Will you just take a minute and *think?*"

Daniel's smile was tolerant if a bit strained. "Mother," he told Jake gently, "would like Jessica very much."

Jake held his brother's gaze. "Give me five minutes with her, Daniel. I'll pay her off, get her out of your life."

"Stop it, Jake." Daniel's voice was clipped, and loud enough to make Judge Waters, who was pretending to peruse a fine leather-bound copy of Plato's *Republic*, glance up curiously. Daniel continued in a lower, though just as determined tone. "Just listen to *me* for a minute. This is my wedding day; I'm marrying the only girl I will ever love and you can't stop it. But you can do a lot to cast a shadow over what should be the happiest day of my life."

A brief flicker of guilt made Jake avert his gaze, but Daniel pursued quietly, "How much do I really demand of you, Jake? Is it too much to ask you now not to spoil my wedding day?"

Jake would have replied in anger and stubbornness but for two things. The first was the genuine hint of pain beneath the simple plea in Daniel's eyes. Jake had never willingly hurt his brother, and he did not know whether he could make himself do so now, even if it was for Daniel's own good. But the second thing was a soft rustle of movement at the door. Jake turned to look at Jessica Duncan and it was too late.

Jessica sensed the tension in the room immediately, and it was so jarring to the fairy-tale atmosphere which had pervaded her senses from the time she had walked into the house that for a moment she faltered. Then she looked into the icy green eyes of the dark-haired man who stood next to Daniel and her heart stopped.

He was dressed in a crisp white shirt, string tie, and tailored dark gray pants and vest. His shiny dark hair was slightly disheveled—only enough to give him a rakish, devil-may-care appearance—and it shadowed his forehead in a natural sweep that defied whatever effort he might have made to brush it back. There was absolutely no mistake about it: he was the same man Jessica had last seen lying nude upon his bed, the man who had grasped her wrist and begun to kiss her.

But it was not that memory that caused Jessica to shrink within herself in a protective gesture or sent the color into her cheeks. There was not the slightest flicker of recognition in the man's eyes, and there was no reason to be embarrassed. What *was* in his eyes was a dislike so strong it almost could have been called hatred. The emotion confused Jessica as much as it disturbed her.

His sun-darkened face was hard, his lips compressed, and

the hostility that radiated from him toward Jessica was almost tangible. Jessica did not understand. She did not even know this man: why should he be angry with her? What had she done? Who was he?

Jake stared at her, this gypsy girl of his dreams, the woman with the incredible blue eyes whose skin had tasted like honey and whose softness had filled his arms . . . Jessica. Daniel's bride. And what he felt was a mixture of shock of recognition, embarrassment at his behavior, however unwitting, with his brother's intended, and most of all pure anger. He had been right. She *was* a tramp, and looking at her now, all dressed up in his mother's clothes. . . .

Daniel walked toward her, his hands extended, his face so full of pleasure that for a moment Jessica let all thoughts of the dark-haired man fly completely from her mind.

"Darling," Daniel said softly, grasping her hands. "You are an angel."

The color that tingled in Jessica's face now was from pleasure as his eyes swept her up and down. The satiny pink gown was a bit tight, but, Maria had assured her, it only accented her full figure and would please Daniel enormously. The heart-shaped neckline was low, revealing, to Jessica's chagrin, a definite hint of cleavage which was so blatantly seductive she had begged for a shawl to cover it. But Daniel didn't seem to mind. If there was anything immodest in her dress at all, Daniel didn't seem to notice. The full skirt with its stiff petticoats was over twenty years out of fashion, but Jessica did not know the difference, and if she had it would not have mattered. She had never felt so elegant, so pampered, so beautiful in her life.

She was a vision in pink and white, her dark hair a startling contrast, her enormous eyes shining, her skin glowing with the curious expectation of unadulterated happiness. Daniel said huskily, tightening his fingers on hers briefly, "Surely there has never been a more radiant bride."

"Oh, Daniel," Jessica whispered, absorbing and returning the wonderful light in his eyes. "You are so good to me. I promise you will never have cause for regret. I will be the best of wives to you." And she meant it with all her heart.

Daniel brought her fingers to his lips, and then paused, a momentary regret shadowing his eyes. "I'm sorry there wasn't time for me to get you a ring." He smiled. "My mother didn't have one either—except a woven ring my father made for her out of willow bark. She wore it until the day she died." His eyes met hers, tender and smiling. "Perhaps it's a trait of the Fielding men—to be so impulsive in their marriages they forget to buy the wedding ring. But we'll go to Fort Worth next week and pick out one together. The most beautiful ring in Texas."

Jessica said softly, "Oh, Daniel, you've already given me all I want. I don't need a ring."

Her eyes were brilliant, earnest and adoring. Daniel felt his heart swell looking at her. How could anyone say what he was doing was wrong?

Daniel could feel his brother's grim, accusing eyes on him. With all the strength at his command, he ignored him. It didn't matter what Jake thought. Daniel had to do what was best for himself. And it would be best for Jessica, too. He was certain of it.

Quickly, Daniel turned, drawing Jessica forward. "Jessica, this is my good friend Judge Harold Waters, who will be performing the ceremony." Jessica smiled shyly at the portly, gray-haired man who stepped forward to bow over her hand. "And," Daniel turned to the dark-haired man who had stood silently all this time, "my brother, Jake."

His brother! Daniel had never mentioned that he had a

brother, or if he had Jessica had forgotten it. Astonishment mixed with growing embarrassment as memories of their encounter came tumbling back, for it somehow seemed much worse knowing he was Daniel's brother. But Jake gave no sign of acknowledgment, or welcome, or anything at all. He simply looked at her with cold, hating eyes for a long moment, then turned away.

"Well," said Judge Waters boisterously, ushering them forward. "You've got a yardful of thirsty guests, Daniel, and I confess I'm anxious to be one of them. What do you say we get this happy occasion under way?"

Through the reeling confusion of the encounter with Daniel's brother Jessica found herself positioned before the desk, where the Judge stood with an open book in his hand. Witnesses were called in, and the library door was closed on the private ceremony. Her arm was tucked possessively through Daniel's, her hand held tightly, and she could feel Jake's inexplicable anger burning into her back. But then there was no time for confusion, nor worry, nor fear, for Judge Waters had begun to speak:

"Dearly beloved, we are gathered. . ."

The sun had just slipped beyond the grove of cottonwoods, casting a dusky pink twilight over the frenzied gaiety of the celebration on the Three Hills' lawns. The lanterns had been lit, their bobbing lights flickering like pale ghosts against the subtle blue sky. The musicians played one lilting reel after another and dancing couples flew up and down the hard-packed soil dance floor, laughter ringing, skirts twirling. The guns were locked away in the library, as per the standing rule at Three Hills parties, for Daniel Fielding had learned at his father's knee that guns and whiskey did not mix. And there was an abundance of whiskey.

Jake did not drink much. He tried to make it a rule never to drink when he was angry. His temper alone was enough to get him into trouble; combined with whiskey it could be deadly. And nothing would have given him more satisfaction at that moment than to turn that murderous combination on the shameless little seductress who was flaunting herself in his mother's clothes and turning his brother into an apish fool in front of half the county.

Jake became aware that George Casey had sidled up next to him and was standing there, sipping whiskey, his eyes as intent on the graceful whisk of pink taffeta skirts as Jake's own had been. Casey had been Daniel's sergeant in the army, and never tired of telling the story of how Daniel had saved his life at Bull Run. He had brought Daniel home after Daniel's injury, and, as a measure of respect and loyalty, had kept the exact nature of that injury secret all these years. He was ranch foreman now, a good worker and unerringly devoted to Daniel, and for that Jake had to like him, even though now he found the man's presence inexplicably annoying.

"I never would've believed it," Casey muttered with a doleful shake of his head. "A sensible man like the cap'n to be taken in by a hip-swinging little heifer like that. What the hell can he be thinking of?"

Jake found his own thoughts, when voiced aloud like that, distinctly unappealing, and he tightened his hand on his glass, wishing it held something more substantial than the lightly spiked fruit punch. Jessica's laughter, as light as a sleigh bell on a winter morning, reached him over the music. The fact that she had managed to charm her way into the hearts of everyone present—or almost everyone—only irritated Jake further. And the look of satisfaction on his brother's face when he gazed into that devious little tramp's eyes made Jake want to step behind the bushes and empty his stomach.

"Never figured the cap'n for going and doing something like this," continued Casey sadly. "I mean, the man's got a reputation to keep up, I can see that, so's he'd think to get married. But why pick a ripe little article like that? Why, anybody can see she's good for just one thing."

"Watch your mouth, Casey," Jake snapped. His hand itched to curl into a fist. "You're talking about my brother's wife."

Jake took a swift, short gulp of the watery punch, his eyes narrowed on the laughing approach of Daniel and his glowing bride. Casey, shaking his head in sorrowful confusion, wandered away.

Daniel, a little out of breath from dancing almost every tune, drew up before him. "Where have you been hiding all day, Jake?" he demanded. "You've broken the heart of every pretty young thing here."

Jake tried to smile. His eyes flickered over Jessica, her face flushed and damp with exertion, a few curls loosened wantonly around her face, her nearly exposed breasts rising and falling shamelessly. Oh yes, she was beautiful, dangerously so. Jake knew the twinge of desire he felt was echoed by every man at the party, and she was enjoying it, anybody could tell that. Daniel was a fool.

"I'm still a little tired, I guess." Jake turned to place his cup on the table behind him. "As a matter of fact, I was just about to go in."

"Not before you dance with the bride," Daniel insisted.

Before either Jessica or Jake could do anything to prevent it, he had placed his bride's hand firmly in Jake's and held it there. He looked at them for a moment, his hand covering both of theirs, and his face was alive with happiness, his eyes deep with hope. "You are the two people I love most in the world," he said gently. "I want you to get to know each other." And then, with a swift clap on Jake's back, he grinned. "Go on, dance. Give me a chance to catch my breath and Jessica's toes a chance to recover."

A waltz was starting, and Jake had no choice but to slip his arm around Jessica's waist and lead her into the dance.

Jessica's heart was racing from more than the recent physical exercise. Jake's hand was strong and warm against the small of her back, his thighs brushed her skirts, his other hand held hers lightly but firmly. His entire body was rigid with anger.

He was light on his feet and guided Jessica easily in the steps of the dance she had never performed before, his instinctive grace finding a natural rhythm in her and matching it. Jessica looked up at him with a smile of gratitude and pleasure for the dance, but his eyes were dark and insolent, not the least bit friendly.

"So, Miss Jessica," he drawled. "We're supposed to get to know each other. I would say you already know a lot more of me than I do of you—or maybe I should say you've *seen* more of me."

Jessica's face flamed, not only for the rudeness of his remark when she had truly wanted to use this time to make a friend of Daniel's brother, but for the sudden memories that flooded her. She knew the shape and texture of his arms that now held her so impersonally, the strength of his thighs which brushed her skirts, the flow of his slender waist to taut hips in vivid detail. In a rush she imagined that his shoulder against which her hand now rested was not covered by the barrier of vest and shirt, and that her fingers touched only smooth bronze skin. It was all she could do to keep from jerking her hand away.

But too much was at stake for Jessica to allow herself to be intimidated. It was very important to Daniel that she and Jake get along, and it was important to Jessica. She could not understand his hostility, and was certain she had done nothing to provoke it. It had been Jake, after all, who had grabbed her in his room, not the other way around. And he surely realized she hadn't been spying on him on purpose.

She faced him steadily and said, "You don't like me, do you?"

"You're right." Jake's reply was curt and impersonal as he swung her around in time to the music. "I don't like anyone who takes advantage of my brother."

Jessica's mouth opened in astonishment. "But I'm not! I love Daniel!"

Disdain filled Jake's eyes as he glanced down at her. "You love Daniel's money," he corrected in a cool, distant drawl. "And that's about the extent of what girls like you know about loving."

Jessica stiffened. She did not know what she had done to deserve this treatment, but the hurt went deep. If it had not been for Daniel, who loved his brother so much, she would have left the dance and walked away from Jake at that moment. But Daniel was depending upon her.

With as much gentleness as she could manage, she said, "That's not true. But I see you've already made up your mind about me. I don't understand why. Daniel wants us to be friends, and I think we should at least try. We have to live together, after all," she reasoned.

"Not necessarily." Jake looked down at her without any emotion at all, save the low disgust that lingered far back in his eyes. "For a thousand dollars you could disappear tonight; the marriage would be anulled and Daniel would have his life back. I have the money, lady, and it's all yours. What do you say?''

At some point during his speech they had stopped dancing, and now stood, still in the pose of the waltz. Jessica stared at him, speechless with shock and hurt and outrage, and Jake returned her gaze coolly. Then there was a murmur in the crowd, the music wound down slowly to the angry sound of hoofbeats, and Jessica turned to see her lovely fairy-tale wedding day turn into a nightmare. It was a nightmare that had only begun.

William Duncan parted the crowd with his horse, his face like a thundercloud. ''Daughter!'' he bellowed. ''I knew I would find you here, cavorting in iniquity! Come here, you shameless spawn of the devil! Come here to me!''

Jessica's hand slipped from Jake's. Of their own volition, her feet carried her through the parting crowd to her father's side. No, she thought, desperately. No, please don't let it be, don't let it end, don't let this happen now.

She laid her hand on her father's leg and looked up into his glowering face, fear and distress darkening her eyes. ''Please, Papa,'' she pleaded. ''Don't make a scene. Don't cause any trouble.''

''Get on the horse, daughter,'' he commanded fiercely. ''You're coming with me.''

Desperately, Jessica began to shake her head, her fingers tightening on the rough material that covered her father's leg.

Daniel made his way through the crowd, strong and calm and in ultimate control. Jessica's heart reached for him, and she turned to go to him, but her father's hand clamped down hard on her shoulder and she stood still.

"Stay your ground, man. This woman is mine, and no one takes what's mine," William Duncan growled.

Jake saw Duncan rest his hand on the shotgun strapped to his saddle, and his own hand went automatically for his revolver. After weeks on the trail a sidearm had become second nature to him, and he cursed softly when he found it was not there. Every instinct in Jake's soul bristled in awareness, and without giving it another thought he turned sharply toward the house, heading for the room where the guns were locked away.

Daniel met Duncan's furious gaze levelly. "You're welcome here, Mr. Duncan, as I hope you'll always be. But Jessica is my wife now, and you're frightening her."

Daniel started to walk toward her.

Duncan withdrew his rifle in a single smooth movement, startling a gasp from the crowd. Astonishment flickered over Daniel's eyes as he stopped and looked at him.

Terror gripped Jessica's heart. "Daniel!" she cried.

William Duncan pulled the trigger.

The scene exploded before Jessica's eyes in a slow motion collage of sound and color. The startled pain on Daniel's face, the carnations of brilliant red that bloomed against his shirt and began to spread as he crumpled slowly to the ground. The roar of movement and horror that emanated from the crowd, and Jessica's own voice, high and shrill, screaming a single word over and over again. "No . . . no!"

And then there was the rough grip beneath her shoulders, dragging her upward, flinging her facedown across the saddle; feeble struggles and the high-pitched ringing in her ears that was her own scream. Daniel was still and lifeless on the ground, and she began to struggle harder, sobbing his name, reaching for him. A sharp pain knifed across the back of her neck and grayness began to envelop her, and no matter how hard she reached she could not touch Daniel. . . . Her last thought before the lurch of the horse pushed her over the edge of consciousness was that she would never see Daniel again.

Jake heard the gunshot when his foot was on the bottom step. He not only heard it; he felt it as though the bullet had gone straight through him. His heart stopped and went cold; he turned and ran, pushing his way frantically through the crowd until he was kneeling beside the limp form of his brother on the ground.

The ragged hole in Daniel's shoulder was seeping huge amounts of blood, soaking his shirt front and dripping onto the ground. Jake pressed the heel of his hand against the wound and exerted pressure, trying to stem the flow. His chest felt swollen and he could hardly breathe. All he could hear was the frantic pounding in his ears that could have been hoofbeats or the sound of his own heart. He shouted hoarsely over his shoulder, "Where's Doc Peters? Somebody ride for him. Hurry, goddamn it, *hurry!*"

More than one volunteer began to run, somebody shouted, "Bring the sheriff!" and then the crowd began to close in on Jake.

Perspiration was dripping down his forehead, his arms were shaking in the effort to hold the pressure, and his breath came raggedly through parted lips. Someone folded a jacket under Daniel's head, someone else, who was sobbing softly, spread a shawl over his legs. Someone said, "We should get him into the house." But another said, "No, run for bandages—try to stop the bleeding here." And it all began to blur together in Jake's ears. He could hear nothing but the sound of his own hoarse breathing, feel nothing but the sticky warmth beneath his hand and the unsteady rise and fall of Daniel's chest, the only proof that he still lived.

Daniel's face was already pasty and damp with loss of blood, and his eyes, when they flickered open, were glazed with incipient shock. He looked at Jake for a long time as though he did not recognize him, and then such an expression of pain crossed his face that Jake had to press his own lips tightly together to withstand it.

"Jake . . ." Daniel's voice was weak; his hand lifted limply to touch Jake's arm and then fell again. Urgency bore through the pain on his face. "Promise me—"

"What?" Jake demanded hoarsely. "Whatever you say."

"Bring her back," Daniel whispered. "Swear to me, whatever happens, you'll bring her back. . . ."

The scene blurred hotly, Jake's lips compressed tightly and for a moment he couldn't speak. And then, quickly, before Daniel's eyes drifted closed again, he whispered, "Yes. Of course I will. Don't worry."

Daniel's hand plucked lightly at Jake's sleeve. He gritted his teeth with the effort to speak, insisting, "Promise."

Jake's eyes drifted down the curving drive that led away from Three Hills. "Yes," he answered. His face was grim and his voice was husky as he looked back to his brother. "I promise."

Chapter III

Jessica pressed her face against the iron bars that guarded the broken windowpane, lifting her face as she searched for some hint of moon or stars in the night sky—anything that would give her a clue as to the time. But the sky was overcast again tonight and a fine mist of rain congealed against her cheek. There was nothing outside but darkness, and darker shadows against a landscape of black that were the twisted shapes of trees and ragged hanging moss. *How long?* she thought in desperation. *How long have I been here?*

Her father was dead and Jessica was alone.

William had taken her from Three Hills to Louisiana, but the days of the journey were an agonized blur of which Jessica remembered little. She could hear nothing but the echo of a gunshot, see nothing but the startled look in Daniel's eyes and the red stain on his shirt, and knew nothing but that Daniel, the only good thing that had ever been in her life, was gone, and her father had taken him from her.

Jessica knew what awaited her. Eulalie had once been the envy of all the family. The youngest daughter of a simple storekeeper, she had married a wealthy planter and gone to live at the luxurious Live Oaks Plantation in splendor and contentment. But the war had taken everything from her. Her husband was dead, her bayou land confiscated, her house burned, and Eulalie herself was left quite demented. Throughout Jessica's life her father's most fearsome threat had been to send her to Eulalie. And now it was happening.

They had arrived at the burned-out shell of Live Oaks Plantation at dusk, her father, smelling heavily of cherry tonic, ranting about committing Jessica to the keeping of Aunt Eulalie for the salvation of her soul. He had dragged her out of the rented livery and up the broken steps of the decrepit plantation house. Even then everything had been embued with a sense of numbed unreality and distance in which nothing made sense and nothing mattered. The front door, warped from exposure to the elements, hung askew on its hinges and screamed like a dying woman when William shoved it open, shouting like a trumpeteer for his sister Eulalie. Still Jessica did not believe it.

And then, materializing from the dusky shadows of the ransacked room stepped the gaunt, spectral form of Eulalie. Jessica had a glimpse of unkempt, straggling gray hair, a pale and wrinkled face, and eyes that burned like coals from hell before her father gave her a rough shove that sent Jessica sprawling on her hands and knees to the dusty floor at the woman's feet.

"My daughter," he spat, the hatred in his tone chilling Jessica's blood. "She carries the devil's seed. Worms are eating at her heart! The sinful world has corrupted her mind and caused blasphemy to issue from her mouth! She must be locked away from the evil influences that would claim her soul and seek redemption through prayer and vigilance.'' He paused, wiping his sweaty brow, and announced, ''I myself am called to the great frontier to bring the gospel to the savages beyond the mountains. I charge you, my sister, with the salvation of this godless child's soul. And I would take a cup of refreshment, if it's no bother, before I'm on my way to do the Lord's work.''

Eulalie's dulcet tones drifted down to Jessica as though from a great distance. ''Of course, brother William, the colonel and I will be delighted to offer our hospitality to blood kin. Do come into the parlor while I have Cook prepare a light meal to restore you after your long journey.''

There was no parlor, and Jessica was to learn later that the colonel had been dead for over ten years. That was when she first began to awaken to the nightmare.

They dined from cracked saucers and gourds on stale cornbread and dandelion tea, with William procuring a jug of scuppernong wine for himself. Eulalie presided over it all in her threadbare dress and tattered shoes as though she were the grande dame of society she once had been.

Jessica remembered looking around the gutted room, its cobwebbed corners dimly lit by a foul smelling tallow candle. The few remaining furnishings were missing legs and arms and vomiting stuffing onto the floor, the teacart was an old hogshead barrel and the night sky was visible through a gaping hole in the ceiling. She hadn't been able to believe her father would really leave her in such a place.

The conversation had been as brief and incomprehensible as the meal. William gave terse, scowling orders to Eulalie about keeping his daughter and the welfare of her soul; Eulalie answered in sweet, refined tones about the state of her pansies or the number of guests expected for her next ball. A madhouse, Jessica had thought, with the first flicker of real emotion or conscious thought she had had since the night of her wedding. It was a madhouse and he surely did not mean to leave her there.

But when her father got impatiently to his feet he spared only a brief contemptuous glance for his daughter and her surroundings. There might, in that fleeting moment, have been a flicker of regret, but more likely it had been a trick of the sputtering candle, for immediately his eyes were stony, his face filled with hatred. "It's no better than you deserve, whore of Satan," he spat. "I'll pray for the salvation of your soul."

William Duncan left with a jug of Eulalie's scuppernong wine under his arm, riding hell-for-leather toward the Lord's calling—and out of Jessica's life.

She had screamed and run after him as the truth of it descended upon her like a bolt from the sky. Strong black arms had seized her from behind, lifting her bodily off her feet; she clawed and screamed and kicked and fought until she had been shoved into the barred storeroom which was to be her prison cell.

The next morning she had watched through the iron bars as Rafe, Eulalie's huge black manservant, carried the sodden body of William Duncan across the knee-deep weeds which once had been the lawn of Live Oaks. He had been found floating facedown in the bayou, his fingers still wrapped around the handle of the empty wine jug.

Jessica had been intimidated by her father, terrified of his temper, and eager to escape his domination, but she had never hated him. He was her father, and the code under which she had been raised taught that children respected their parents. She knew she should mourn him, but tears would not come. His death sent a numbing chill into her soul, a horrifying mixture of relief because he was gone and dread because now she was truly alone. And because the emotions that accompanied his loss were so contradictory and confusing, it was easier at last to feel nothing at all. Perhaps, someday, she would cry for him, but now it took all her energy just to stay alive.

At first she had tried to keep track of the time. She thought that surely some stranger would pass by, surely some peddler or vagrant or townsperson would stop to knock on the sagging front door and Jessica could make them aware of her predicament. What had she done to deserve such punishment? She had only married a fine and gentle man. She had brought no disgrace to anyone, had disobeyed no laws. Surely the Lord would be merciful. Surely she could be forgiven for whatever sins she might have committed and would be delivered.

But gradually, as time passed and the days began to blur into one another, Jessica realized she would not be delivered. No stranger ever passed by, and if one should, he would notice nothing but a hollow remnant of an old plantation, like so many others along the Mississippi and through the bayous. There would be no reason to stop, no reason to imagine there was any life inside. No one knew where she was. And if she could by chance send a message, to whom would she write for help? Daniel, dear, beloved Daniel, was surely dead by her father's hand. And though it was possible that in time her father might have come back for her, he too was dead now, and Eulalie was only carrying out the last wishes of a man who would never return to amend his instructions. She was alone. She had been completely abandoned in this place and there was no hope for her except that somehow she might regain her freedom through the use of her own wits.

But as the days muddled into nights without change or

hope for change, despair replaced terror, apathy dulled desperation, and Jessica could feel her will to survive seeping away as surely as the daylight was swallowed by the dusk. *I shall soon be as mad as my captor,* she thought now, turning away from the window. *And I will die in this place . . .*

The room was almost in complete darkness now, and Jessica was hungry. Hunger had become an almost constant state, for Eulalie brought her meager meals of grits or hominy irregularly at best, but Jessica did not mind the hunger as much as the darkness. Already the rats were scuttling busily in the corner, and soon the beetles would be out; huge, noisy insects as big as a man's finger, their talons making sharp clicking sounds as they scurried across the floor, sometimes over Jessica's bare feet. . . .

She shuddered and wrapped her arms around herself, chilled more from the dampness and the dread of night than the late summer air. She wore nothing but a stained and ragged nightdress, for Eulalie had taken the rest of her clothing and shredded it into rags, for reasons yet unknown to Jessica. Jessica's hair hung in limp, dirty clumps around her shoulders and down her back, for she had not had a bath or a change of clothes since she had arrived. Sometimes she used her drinking water to wash, but such measures were woefully inadequate, and she had long since ceased to sicken from her own uncleanliness.

Her heart began to speed with relief as she heard footsteps outside her door, the grating of the rusty key in the lock, and then the door creaking open.

Eulalie never came alone, so any thought Jessica might have had of escaping when her meals were brought was immediately dismissed. Two had remained with Eulalie after the war: Rafe, an ex-slave who had no place left to go, and

Will, the wiry, mean-eyed overseer who considered Live Oaks the last refuge against the carpetbaggers and scum who had invaded the South, a man who looked upon the vast unworked acres as his one chance to someday make his fortune. The two of them foraged for food, stealing when they had to, using the hounds to track down game in the woods. They protected fragile Eulalie, who was still the lady she had always been to them, cut firewood and made endless minor repairs on the house. They spent a lot of time cleaning their guns and spitting rabbit tobacco into the cracks of the sagging front porch. And they kept Jessica from escaping.

Today it was Rafe who stood guard outside the door while Eulalie delivered the evening meal and prayers, and Jessica was glad. Whenever Will came he brought with him a sense of unease, of dread, and the way his dark eyes roamed over Jessica's scantily clad body made her skin crawl.

Eulalie walked inside, carrying a tray in one hand and a sputtering pine-knot candle in the other. "Well, good evening, my dear. Are you feeling much better this evening?"

Eulalie had convinced herself that the reason for Jessica's confinement was ill health, a justification with which Jessica had long since found it futile to argue. "Yes, thank you ma'am, much better. I think I am almost fully recovered. Perhaps tomorrow a walk in the garden—"

"Oh, dear, I think you must be too optimistic. Your color seems a bit off and you will get a chill standing by the window like that. If you're not much stronger by next week I think we must send for Dr. Fortinier. I do worry about you so, my dear."

The conversation was always the same and the fantasy never varied. At first Jessica had tried to reason with her, to protest her confinement and convince Eulalie of the truth; it had availed her nothing but wasted breath and crushed spirits, and, when Jessica objected most vociferously, sometimes Eulalie did not return with her meal or her candle for a day or longer. It was much better to remain calm and pretend with her aunt.

Eulalie passed Jessica to set the tray on the floor, bringing with her the odor of unwashed clothes and decaying flesh. The swaying candle illuminated the small square room with a grayish light, revealing its mildewed walls, uneven floor, and the two furnishings: a seldom emptied chamber pot and a feather tick, unadorned by sheeting or pillow, on the floor. One scrawny rat, blinking in the light, turned and crawled for cover beneath the baseboard as she approached.

"Now, dear, we mustn't dawdle. I must get your tray back to the kitchen and oversee the laying of supper. The colonel is bringing guests tonight." As she spoke, Eulalie lifted one grime encrusted finger to her straggling, wiry gray hair, primping unconsciously as she would before a mirror.

"How lovely." Jessica moved across the room, closer to the light. She watched her aunt carefully. "Perhaps I could come down and join you."

Eulalie looked at her speculatively for a long time. "You really should stop hiding yourself away, my dear. It's long past time you had a beau. Soon you'll be past the marrying age, you know."

"Yes," Jessica said a trifle breathlessly, hardly daring to hope. "I think you're right. If—if the colonel would be kind enough to introduce me to some of the families hereabouts . . . ."

"You could wear your blue tulle." Eulalie's eyes took on a dreamy, faraway look. "And the pearls that the colonel gave me for a wedding gift. You've seen my pearls, haven't you dear? With the diamond clasp?"

"And my silk petticoats and new kid slippers," Jessica said softly, moving a step closer. She dared not breathe for disturbing the spell. Just a chance. If only she had a chance to escape from this room. "And you could help me put my hair up . . ."

Eulalie sighed. "What fun it would be to prepare a young girl for her first ball. And when you swept down that staircase all eyes would turn on you, just like they used to turn on me . . ." She let her voice drift off, reminiscing.

There was no grand staircase at Live Oaks. The once-gracious plantation had been in the path of the Union Army during the intense fighting that took place over the salt mines at Avery Island during the war, for salt was as precious as gold to both sides. Live Oaks had been devastated. The top story of the mansion had been blown off, the outbuildings burned, and the furnishings ransacked. The slaves and livestock had been driven off, the fields burned and trampled. And all of this only days after Eulalie had received news of her husband's death while fighting for the Cause. She had never recovered from the blow, and she chose to live with the truth by pretending it did not exist.

There were times when Jessica felt sorry for her aunt, and certainly wished her no harm. But day after day as her guards came and went, as the probability of escape became more and more remote and Eulalie slipped deeper and deeper into her crazed fantasy world, Jessica found it hard to understand or sympathize with the woman who kept her prisoner. What little energy and few remaining wits she had were all concentrated on finding a way to keep from going mad herself, on trying to hold on to hope. . . .

Now, unable to bear the suspended silence any longer, she prompted, "Shouldn't we be getting ready? I think I hear the colonel's horse now."

Eulalie spiraled back down to her slowly, her eyes losing focus and then, as they so often unexpectedly did, sharpening alertly. "Vile girl!" she hissed. "You tried to trick me! You want my husband! Don't think I don't know what goes on in that evil little mind of yours, you lie here night after night lusting for him. Wretched, wretched creature! William was right, you should be locked away for your own good and that of all other decent folk in the county! I'll not break my promise, William." She tilted her head to the ceiling. "I'll keep her safe!" Then, to Jessica she said, "On your knees girl, before I have Rafe take the strap to you! We'll pray for the salvation of your soul."

Wearily Jessica sank to her knees on the bare and dusty floor. She prayed for a miracle, but she didn't think it would do any good.

The man stood in the shadows of the building, his hat pulled low, his hands stuffed into the pockets of his slicker, the collar turned up against the drizzle. His face was in profile to the dim veil of light that emanated from the window, his expression a study of impatience and absent concentration.

The sheriff's posse had trailed William Duncan after little more than an hour, but had lost him less than ten miles away from Three Hills. Jake, unwilling to leave his brother until the doctor had pronounced him out of danger, had bent over Daniel's bed while Daniel gasped out the name of Live Oaks Plantation in New Orleans, and then Jake had not even waited for sunrise. He had left Three Hills with nothing but his horse, his guns, and what provisions Rio could hastily stuff into his saddlebags. There was fire in his eyes and a grim determination in the white lines about his mouth; he did not intend to return empty-handed. But it wasn't Jessica he was after; it was William Duncan.

The trail had not been an easy one, and the bastard had been more wily in covering his tracks than Jake had counted on. Jake traced him to Galveston, by then more than a week behind, where he discovered Duncan had abandoned overland travel for a steamboat. By the time Jake arrived in New Orleans whatever trail Duncan might have left was stone cold. He could only hope that his brother's guess was right: that the man had taken his daughter to the relative's plantation in New Orleans.

But Jake had been told there was no Live Oaks Plantation in New Orleans, or anywhere on this part of the Mississippi River. For almost a week Jake had cooled his heels in the city, making inquiries in every quarter, growing more furious and frustrated by the minute. Could Daniel have been wrong? Could the girl have lied about her aunt? Could that son of a bitch possibly, at this very moment, be getting away scot-free?

But Jake couldn't return to Daniel empty-handed. He had no intention of ever returning to Three Hills with his brother's shooting unavenged. And he would not leave Louisiana until he had checked out every possibility. A month after leaving Three Hills, he at last found what he'd been looking for. Yes, there was a Live Oaks Plantation, Colonel Fisher's place. It used to be the biggest shipper of indigo and rice in these parts before the war. But it was nowhere near New Orleans, not even on the Mississippi. It was way the hell out near Avery Island, on Bayou LaFourche.

Jake rode for the bayou. It was impossible to get a decent map, and of the people he talked to some admitted to having heard of Live Oaks, others just scratched their heads and looked at him as though he had lost his mind. Live

Oaks had been destroyed during the war, they told him. Nobody lived there anymore. But it was his only lead.

Jake's first sight of the gutted plantation house had proven them right, and his spirits had sunk into a cold hard knot of anger and frustration in the pit of his stomach. All this way, all this wasted time, for nothing but a dead end. The place was little more than a shell. No one could possibly live there.

But, incredibly, someone did.

There was livestock in the lean-to shelter that served as a barn. There were footprints in the mud. There was stacked firewood and the faint smell of cookstove smoke. A couple of old hound dogs were tied to a tree out back, looking mean and hungry. Jake had watched the place all afternoon; he had seen the two men, neither of whom was Duncan, and the old woman. As darkness fell, he left his horse tied at a safe distance in the woods and crept closer to the house. That was when he had seen someone's face pressed against the barred window toward the back of the house. Later, when the candle backlit the room, he had been able to recognize the person to whom the face belonged. Jessica.

He hadn't planned it like this. He had never, in fact, planned much of anything beyond finding Jessica—and, if there was any justice, Duncan. Vaguely he had imagined himself approaching the aunt, informing her he was taking Jessica back to her lawful husband, and then riding off with her to put her on the next train west. Clearly such an approach was unfeasible in this situation. It wasn't just Duncan, he realized. The entire family had to be crazed to live like rats in a place like Live Oaks. And the girl was being kept in a barred room. Jake didn't think they were the kind of people who could be reasoned with, and he had neither the time nor the patience to try.

A week before Jake had sent an anxious telegram to Three Hills, inquiring about Daniel's state of recovery. The reply had been simply, "I am well. Find her. Please."

Jake did not have a plan. He was furious and frustrated that Duncan was not with his daughter, and every moment he wasted the bastard was moving farther away. Jake didn't even have a horse for her, but the nearest town was almost a day's ride away and he would be damned if he was going back just to get another horse. He had lost enough time already, and he had no more patience for this game.

He would keep his promise to Daniel. He would get Jessica out of this place and send her back to his brother. Then Jake was going after her father.

Midnight hung like a heavy cloak over the small, airless room. The heavy, rhythmic drip of rain onto the fat leaves of a hydrangea bush outside Jessica's window was the only sound. A misty fog curled its fingers about the bars at her window, and the house was shrouded in sleep. Jessica dozed lightly on the bare mattress on the floor, the thin nightgown hiked up around her knees, one arm flung restlessly over her head, her chest rising and falling in a faint, shallow rhythm.

At first Jake did not see her, and he thought he had the wrong room. The sagging front door had been easy enough to pass. When he found the heavy padlock on Jessica's door he was momentarily thwarted, but he used his pen knife to unscrew the bolt. The door opened with a terrible screech, but apparently the occupants were used to the creakings and groanings of the old house and no one stirred.

The unpleasant odor of damp decay and human confinement assailed his nostrils as he crept into the room, searching the darkness for some sign of life. He heard her soft breathing before he saw her, and he was upon her as quickly and as silently as a panther.

Jessica's eyes flew open on a smothered gasp as a hand clamped down on her mouth. At first all she could think was that Will, that horrible, snake-eyed man, had come just as she had always dreaded he would. She struggled instinctively and with raw terror, but the man held her down easily with nothing more than the weight of his hand digging into her mouth.

"You try to kick me or bite me," he growled, "and I swear I'll knock you out. I don't have time to fool with a screaming woman and I'd just as soon carry you out of here unconscious over my shoulder as not. Now get up before you wake the whole damn house."

He jerked her roughly to her feet with one arm around her rib cage, the other around her neck, his hand still clamping her mouth. Heart thundering, she stumbled to keep from falling to her knees as he dragged her across the floor, and then, incredibly, out of the room. Her eyes were wide and terrified and her hands clawed futilely at his crushing arms, but she struggled to keep up with his long strides because . . . because he was taking her out of her cell!

The wet night air assaulted her reeling senses, the muffled sounds of a world that had gone on so long without her rushing to meet her like a song of welcome. Terror was quickly wiped away by wonder, and she twisted her head to look up into the face of the man who had made it possible. His face was dark and shadowed beneath the low-brimmed hat, but she saw his grim mouth, narrowed eyes, and rain glistening on a strand of black hair that curled against his collar. It wasn't Will at all, she realized, but a stranger. No, not a stranger. . . .

Jake! It came to her in an exploding sweep of joy and

wonder that felt too incredible to be true. Jake's strong arms were half pulling, half dragging her across the overgrown lawn, and his damp warmth pressed into her shoulders and crushed her waist. Jake . . . Daniel . . . Texas.

Suddenly from behind them came the warning growl, then the sharp ferocious bark of a dog. Jake froze, every sense alert, and Jessica imagined she could hear his heartbeat in cadence to the fear-jolted rhythm of her own. Another dog joined the first, splitting the night with their furious barks, and then there was a human shout and the sound of running footsteps on the slick boards of the porch.

Jake swore viciously, and in the same moment he released her mouth and grabbed her by the upper arm, breaking into a run. There were more footsteps, more barking, and then the explosion of a shotgun rent the air. Jessica's feet went out from under her on the slippery grass, but before she even hit the ground Jake hauled her back beside him with a painful wrench on her arm.

"Goddamn you, I'll leave you here!" His eyes were glittering and his breath scattered the fog in front of her face before he turned and began running again.

She bit back a sob of pain and terror as his fingers dug sharply into her arm, for the barking dogs were closing in and she was almost certain human footsteps followed them. This time, running for her life, Jessica kept up with him.

Chapter IV

"Jake!" she gasped as they ran through underbrush in the woods, wet branches slapping against her thighs and blinding her. Jessica turned her head and tried to shield her face with her arm. "How—Daniel—"

Her next words were choked off by a shrill scream as something caught her hair hard and sent a jolt of pain through her scalp that made a flare of brilliant red and yellow burst before her eyes.

Jake paused as he felt her arm jerked out of his grasp, more than a little inclined to keep going and leave her behind. He hadn't counted on the dogs or guns. The men he wasn't so worried about—they couldn't shoot until they had caught up with them, and the time it took them to get on those old nags they called horses would allow a gracious head start. But the dogs were killers, closing in with every breath, their deep growls painting a vivid picture of their thirst for blood. Furthermore, the animals were trackers, and could follow the trail of human prey just as easily as they could that of a possum or raccoon.

But he had promised Daniel. He whirled to grab her again, but when he pulled she screamed, and he saw immediately what was the problem.

That long, wild hair of hers had become entangled in the low-hanging branch of a tree. Her eyes were brilliant with tears, her breath contorted with pain as she tried futilely to pull it free. Jake quickly moved around her, muttering curses that Jessica had never heard before, and grabbed the tangle of curls where it was snarled in the branch. He pulled viciously. It was no use.

Sucking in his breath, Jake spared a single glance back the way they had come. The crashing sounds of growling beasts pushing through the undergrowth was closer now, almost upon them, and there was no more time to waste. He snatched his buck knife from the holster at his belt and in a single cut sliced off the offending lock of hair at the scalp. As Jessica stumbled free, he grabbed her around the waist and half carried her to the spot where the horse was waiting, stamping and pawing the ground nervously.

His fingers dug into her ribs and Jessica gave a little yelp as he lifted her off her feet and practically flung her onto the saddle. She almost slipped off and grabbed frantically at the horse's mane. The horse started to rear and she slipped further. But Jake, mounting, caught the reins, calming the beast just as his heavy weight came down behind her, his stomach pressed hard against her buttocks. She flailed for support as she lost her precarious balance again, and he flung an arm around her waist, pulling her against him with a force that almost cut off her breath as he swore, "Hold on, damn you! You fall off now and there's not a goddamn thing I can do for you!"

For the dogs were upon them, snapping and growling. The terrified horse lurched forward as Jake slapped the reins, plunging through the undergrowth at a frantic pace which threatened to dislodge them both.

Jake had seated her sidesaddle; he had never seen a woman mount any other way and it did not occur to him that that position might be difficult, even dangerous, for her to try to maintain on a range saddle. His arm ached from trying to hold her in place and her fingernails dug into his wrist with a force that threatened to draw blood. She was going to fall, he thought grimly as the horse took a small leap over a broken log and she slipped further down on the saddle. *What a hell of a mess...* But he couldn't stop now; the dogs sounded like a pack of coyotes behind him and he was certain he heard other hoofbeats trampling the path behind them. Worse yet, he didn't have the first idea where he was going.

Sobbing for breath, pushed down low over the horse's neck by Jake's weight, Jessica thought that if she didn't fall to the ground to be trampled to death her back would surely snap in two and she would die just as surely. Jake's leg was thrown over one of hers, cutting off the circulation, and the pommel dug painfully into her other hip. What had begun as a mere mist was now a definite rain; it stung Jessica's eyes and clogged her nostrils. But it was none of these discomforts which prompted Jessica to twist in the saddle, to try to turn and get a look at his face. The path he was taking was leading directly into the swamp.

"What are you doing?" she cried, terrified. "Where are you—"

"Hold still!" Jake drew reflexively on the reins as he felt her slip again.

"We can't go this way! We—"

"Which way would you rather go?" He jerked his head

curtly, indicating the sounds of pursuit that blocked off the path behind them. His face was shiny with rain and perspiration, his eyes hard and desperate as he hauled her up against him again. Her ribs felt like twigs beneath his arm, and the soft flesh of her abdomen seemed to have no substance at all. He didn't remember her being so thin on that long ago night when he had held her in his arms for the waltz . . . an insane thing to think with a pack of dogs and two men with shotguns closing in on them.

Impatiently, he drew more sharply on the reins, and in the same motion tore his arm from her grip. She cried out when she thought he was going to let her fall, but without breaking the motion he used his other arm to steady her and grabbed her knee, pulling it upward in a most undignified way to curve around the pommel. "There!" he declared on a breath. "Grab onto the pommel, not me. I don't know how much farther we have to ride and my arm sure as hell can't take any more."

Jessica, though more securely seated, was greatly aware of the absent weight of his hand on her naked knee, the warm pressure of his groin against her cold buttocks, the crushing weight of his leg over hers. And strangely, mixed with the terrors of the night, was an absurd and sweeping embarrassment for the fact that she was half-naked before the man and his body was touching hers at almost every point. She felt a hot shame and alarm course through her even as she desperately cried, "But we can't go this way! We're headed toward the swamp!" The same direction from which Rafe had carried her father's lifeless body, she thought, shivering again.

"You want to go back, be my guest," Jake replied shortly, his eyes scanning the surrounding landscape for some alternate route. "My guess is you'd make a tasty little supper for those two hounds, and what's left over your high-and-mighty relatives can carve up and use for fish bait."

Suddenly he saw a slight glimmer of light through the trees. Without another thought he slapped the reins and urged the horse toward it.

Her hair tickled his face as he bent low over her, ducking branches and limbs that snatched at his hat and scratched his face. Her heart pulsed like that of a terrified rabbit beneath his hand and her breath came in little gasps of terror. Again he remembered her in his mother's satin gown, her full breasts, soft curves, flushed cheeks, and the surge of anger that filled him was both irrational and inexplicable. She was shivering beneath him with cold and fear. Damn, he thought tightly, urging the horse on.

The sounds of pursuit were a bit more distant now, but the gleam of light was closer. A house? A coach light? The path was rough and overgrown, but it was a path—perhaps even a road at some time—and it had to lead somewhere. Jessica was right about one thing: the smell of brackish water was growing stronger by the minute, swamp sounds noisier. The direction they were taking was nowhere close to the way in which Jake had originally come.

He pushed aside a curtain of Spanish moss, drawing his horse up sharply as its hooves sank into the marshy ground. The thin curtain of rain glistened in the spill of yellow light from a lantern set on the bank before them, and a scrawny black man straightened curiously.

He held a long sharp stick in his hand and at his feet was a rusty bucket filled with gigged frogs. The dark swamp sounds were almost deafening, the throbbing hums of insects and toads, rhythmic, full, and alive, almost completely drowning out the baying of dogs and the crash of hooves.

"Evenin'," the black man said cautiously.

"Where does this path lead?" Jake demanded curtly, holding his dancing horse still. The animal could sense the approach of the dogs, and the sucking mud beneath its hooves made it nervous, not to mention the anxiety of its two riders, which was as thick and as palpable as the very fog in the air.

The man's shiny face broke into a gap-toothed grin. "Lawdy, Massa, you at it." He gestured with the stick. "It don't lead nowhere 'ceptin' right here."

Jake drew in a short breath and cast a quick glance over his shoulder. The dogs had picked up their trail again. This swamp was a playground to them.

The water that snaked between clumps of marsh grass and partially sunken trees was as black as the river Styx and about as inviting, and it seemed to go on forever. But pulled close to the bank, anchored in a patch of cattails, was a small, flat-bottomed pirogue.

Jake was off the horse in an instant, dragging Jessica with him. Her numbed legs collapsed the moment her feet touched the ground, and she went down on her knees in the mud. Jake ignored her, turning to unstrap the saddle. "How much do you want for your boat?"

The grin faded from the other man's face, to be replaced by an anxious scowl. "Nassah, I cain' sell my pee-roke. How's I'm supposed to feed my fambly? I cain'—"

Jake lifted saddle, blanket and bags off the horse, and with a slap on the terrified animal's rump, sent it crashing through the woods. He carried the saddle to the boat, his boots squishing in the marsh.

Jessica struggled on trembling legs to an upright position, her hair whipping about her shoulders as she turned her head toward the approaching sound of baying dogs. "Jake—" she said frantically.

"Massa, please don' take my pee-roke. I *needs* it! I—"

Jake dumped the saddle into the boat; Jessica scrambled toward him, cold mud oozing between her toes and dragging at the hem of her gown. Jake dug into his pocket and pulled out a coin, snapping it through the air toward the black man. "And you haven't seen anybody tonight," he commanded, stepping into the boat and dragging the pole in after him. "Do you understand that?"

The man caught the five-dollar gold piece in both hands, his eyes growing round as he turned it over and over in the light. "Yassuh," he breathed. "Ain' seen nobody. Never had no pee-roke. Thank ye, suh, I sho *does* understand, yassuh, I does."

Jessica reached for Jake's arm as he stepped into the boat, terrified he was going to make good on his threat and leave her behind. But he grabbed her roughly under the arms and swung her in, pushing her facedown on the bottom of the boat. "Don't make a sound," he growled, "and don't move."

He used the long pole to push away from the bank, and then, just as the baying dogs crashed through the bushes, he dragged it back inside and dropped his full weight on top of Jessica.

"Not a sound," he breathed against her ear.

Jessica, biting her lip as her breasts and hipbones were ground painfully into the rough flooring, nodded and tried desperately to find some way to breathe.

The little boat drifted sluggishly along the currents of the swamp, blending into the night. The dogs, catching the scent of the runaway horse, turned to follow, just as Jake had known they would. Will and Rafe, their eyes alight with the greed of the hunt, broke into the clearing, questioned the ignorant fisherman briefly, and turned to follow the dogs.

Jessica felt Jake's tense, waiting muscles relax gradually as the howling and barking grew distant and finally disappeared altogether.

But still he did not move. Jessica's breasts ached, one arm was pinned painfully beneath her, and she could feel two enormous bruises rising on her kneecaps. Something, Jake's gun belt, she thought, was digging sharply into her thigh, and she thought if she was not allowed to take a deep breath soon she would suffocate. His warm weight pinned her to the floor, his breath was slow and regular in her ear. Surely he did not intend to stay that way all night?

"Please," she gasped when she couldn't stand it any longer. "Could you get off me?"

"Why?" His tone was totally unlike any he had used earlier, low and lazy and distantly amused, bringing back sharp, poignant memories of a gracious mansion, the smell of hickory smoke and festivity in the air, a sleepy smile and brilliant green eyes . . . "You make a fine cushion."

"You're crushing me!" Jessica began to wriggle, but it was a futile gesture. He was simply too heavy.

Now that the danger had passed, the thrill of the narrow escape was heady for Jake, and he became aware of the tantalizing cradle her soft, rounded buttocks made for his pelvis and the dimly erotic sensations her motions beneath him were beginning to evoke. Having faced danger and outsmarted it was one of life's two most satisfying experiences—the second being directly connected to the impulses generated by the squirming motions of the woman beneath him—and for a moment Jake felt like grinning.

But then he remembered who and what she was, and that it was because of her that he was in this godforsaken swamp in the first place, being chased like a rabid cur by two madmen with guns and a pack of dogs while his brother lay badly shot half a state away. The surge of victory abruptly turned sour. He braced his arms against the floor and levered himself away from her, sitting back against the saddle and glaring at her in disgust.

Jessica pulled herself to a semi-sitting position, drawing in gulps of wet air and coughing as it hit her lungs. The rain was steady, plastering the thin nightgown to her body and dripping off the coiled clumps of her hair in cold spatters down her neck and between her breasts. "We'll catch the fever here!" she exclaimed, trying to control her breathing.

Jake picked up the pole, more for the sense of control it gave him than from any real idea of using it to guide the boat, and pushed angrily at a grassy mudhill they drifted past. It was too dark to do anything tonight but try to find a place to camp and wait for sunlight to show him the way back to dry land. Damn, he thought in mounting irritation. This was not the way he had intended to pass his last night in Louisiana.

The night creatures shrieked and howled while they floated by twisted black skeletons of deformed trees trailing their fingers of Spanish moss into the water. Something entered the swamp with a huge splash, and Jessica shivered, her eyes peering anxiously through the dark. What a horrid, horrid place. People died here. Her father had died here.

"We've got to get out of here!" she insisted, her voice growing a little shrill. "I told you not to come this way! This isn't the way back to the road! We've got to—"

"If you want to swim," Jake interrupted shortly, "I'm damn well not going to stop you. Otherwise, shut up."

Jessica stared at him. Of course it was insane to turn on her rescuer after such a harrowing escape, absurd to be frightened by the swamp after the nightmare she had lived through as a prisoner of Eulalie's madness. But Jessica was weak with hunger and unused muscles; her head was reeling with the aftermath of danger and a hundred unanswered questions; her nerves screaming with shock and the incredulity of the events of the past hour. Nothing about Jessica was rational any longer, and she simply couldn't take anymore. Her fists clenched. "Don't talk to me like that! Don't tell me to shut up when I'm trying to tell you—"

Abruptly the temper that had festered inside Jake for the past weeks of searching and frustration snapped. The waiting and worrying, tracking and losing, the fear for Daniel, the anger and resentment about the promise that had brought him to Louisiana only to lose the man he really wanted and be charged with this noisy, bedraggled female all culminated in a single moment. He swung the pole out of the water and centered it against her chest. His eyes were glittering and his voice was very quiet.

"All right, lady," he said lowly. "You want to talk? Talk. Where is that murdering bastard you call a father?"

Jessica's breath left her in a single gasp which had nothing to do with the uncomfortable pressure he was levering against her with the pole. The hatred in his eyes was strong enough to pierce the blackness that surrounded them. She realized abruptly that her rescue had not been a rescue at all—she had been snatched from the pit of hell only to find herself in the hands of the devil, and Jake Fielding did not care whether she lived or died.

As if to confirm her thoughts, Jake prodded her lightly with the pole. "Answer me." His voice was a low rumble, all the more deadly for the quiet constraint that backed it in contrast to the throbbing activity of the swamp life around them. "Because if you think I'd hesitate for one minute to push you overboard and leave you to the alligators you're dead wrong. In fact, I can't think of anything that would give me more satisfaction right now."

Jessica's hands clutched the side of the boat until her knuckles were white. She hardly dared breathe. Her eyes were enormous in her pale, strained face. Had Jake been less consumed by his own anger, less tired and wet and miserable, he might have been moved to pity for her, but as it was he barely noticed her.

"W-why? Why do you want to know?" she whispered.

"Because," Jake answered coldly and matter-of-factly, "I'm going to kill him."

All the fight drained out of Jessica with that, and with it, all her fear. There hardly seemed any point anymore. Her father . . . Daniel . . . and now Jake. His brief reappearance in her life had been like the answer to a prayer, a bright flare of hope—but he had not meant to help her at all. He only wanted her as the quickest means to her father, and there was no point, none at all . . .

She released her grip on the side of the boat and lowered her eyes. She said faintly, "You're too late."

The pressure on her chest lightened a fraction. "What?" Jake snapped.

She looked at him, her eyes bright and her face torn with pain. "I said you're too late!" she cried. "He's already dead! He left me in that place . . . and he *died!*"

For a moment Jake was utterly still. Then he swore, a short ugly sound that tore through the night, and he brought the pole down on the water with a force that rocked the boat and splattered their already soaked bodies with foul smelling swamp water. Jessica wrapped her arms around herself against the damp and her own inner pain, turning away from his hard, tight profile, curling into a corner of the boat as far away from him as possible. He was going to leave her here, she knew. She had been unable to deliver what he wanted, and he had no further use for her. He would abandon her in this hideous swamp and never think twice about what he had done.

Jake's eyes fastened upon the shadow of a hummock in the distance and he poled toward it automatically, his arms straining with repressed fury, his emotions in turmoil. He felt cheated, thwarted, useless. He had come all this way propelled by a promise but sustained by vengeance, and now fate had snatched justice from his hands. He was stuck in the middle of a Louisiana swamp with a girl he didn't want and a promise that bound him and all of it seemed empty. The futility of it chafed on his nerves. After a long time he spoke tightly into the darkness. "How?"

Jessica's voice was very small. "He drowned."

Jake's eyes swept the surrounding expanse of dark, sluggish water and he released a long breath through his teeth. That was just what he needed to hear.

He guided the boat until it brushed up against the grassy hill, then steadied it with the pole. The little island did not look very promising, but they could hardly drift aimlessly all night. He grabbed hold of a clump of swamp grass and pulled forward until the bottom of the boat scraped land. He stepped out into ankle-deep sludge, swearing again under his breath.

He tossed the pole onto the bank and grabbed the bow. "Get out," he commanded Jessica.

Jessica got to her feet uncertainly, hesitantly, but in Jake's present mood she had no intention of arguing with him. Gingerly she stepped out, slipped immediately in the mud, and fell onto her hands and knees. Jake, grunting as he pulled the heavy boat ashore, ignored her.

When the boat was secured Jake paused to survey the

situation, wiping drops of perspiration and rain from his face. He was accustomed to sleeping along the trail, but he wasn't very well provisioned for it this trip—and this was not exactly a trail. It would be pointless to make a fire tonight, and he was too damn tired and wet and miserable to even try. He wasn't about to guess what kind of creatures shared the soggy hummock with them, but at least the boat was broad and flat, if a little hard. They could sleep inside.

Jessica, he thought with a prickle of irritation, fell down more than anyone he had ever known, but she was on her feet again, small and waiflike, behind him.

In a voice that trembled slightly despite the forced courage that lifted her chin a fraction, she asked, "Are you going to leave me here?"

"Don't think I'm not tempted." Jake was turned away from her, searching through his saddlebags for something, and his voice, muffled by distance, did not sound as harsh as it once had. Then he said, "No. I'm taking you back to Three Hills and your husband."

"Daniel!" Jessica rushed up to him, the impact of the word sailing through her. "Daniel? He—he's alive?"

Jake had found the small leather flask he had been looking for and he sat down heavily in the boat, leaning back against the saddle, his raised knees sprawled, his head bent forward against the drip of rain. He brought the flask to his lips and drank deeply before replacing the cap. He scowled at her. "Yes, no thanks to you and that murdering scum that sired you."

Jessica fell back on her heels, her fingers pressed tightly to her lips to smother cries of joy and wonder, her eyes brilliant with unshed tears. Daniel! Daniel who cared for her and protected her . . . Daniel, the one good thing that had come into her life since her mother died, was alive! He was alive and waiting for her! All this time she had lain in that dark cell hopeless and despairing he had been waiting for her, planning to bring her back to him. Her face was alight with joy so deep she was afraid to release it, and she whispered through barely parted lips, "And he wants me? He wants me back?"

Jake spared her one curious look as he turned to replace the flask in his saddlebag. What a peculiar girl she was. To look at her one would think she was glad to hear she was not a wealthy widow, glad to be going back to Daniel. The way she looked, all starry eyed and flushed, one could almost think she was in love with Daniel, which Jake knew could not be the case.

He responded harshly, "Yes. God knows why." And she sank back into the far corner of the boat, her hands still clasped tightly before her, her face wearing a dreamy look that Jake couldn't decipher.

He scowled deeply as he dragged out the saddle blanket and wrapped it around himself, using his hat to cushion his hips as he lay back against the saddle. None of it made any sense: that madhouse he had taken her from; the crazy father who'd tried to kill Daniel; and now the daughter who couldn't wait to rush back to her husband's arms. And he was too tired and dispirited to try to figure it out tonight. The main thing he had to worry about now was how to make this journey as short as possible, but even that would have to wait until morning. He pulled the blanket up around his ears and closed his eyes.

Jessica hugged herself tightly, hardly feeling the dampness anymore for the warmth that surged through her when she thought of the miracle that had just occurred.

"Jake." She leaned toward him to ask him how long it would take to reach Three Hills, wanting to ask him a dozen questions about Daniel and the ranch and every detail that had been thought and said and enacted since she had been away. But Jake, wrapped securely in the only blanket, was snoring lightly, fast asleep. Jake was used to looking after no one but himself.

She fell back, slightly disconcerted, shivering a little in the dampness. But then she smiled, tucked the edges of her nightgown around her feet, and curled up in her own corner of the boat. Nothing could disturb her happiness tonight. It didn't matter. Daniel wanted her, Three Hills was waiting for her, and all was right with the world.

Chapter V

The morning dawned clear and beautiful. A soupy breath of white fog lay low over the water, dispersing slowly into a fine transparent mist in patches where the warmth from the brilliant cerulean sky filtered down. Small insects skittered over the clear brownish green surface, breaking the glassy smoothness with small concentric ripples of motion. A largemouth bass jumped and arced, its silvery fins a brief glitter of color in the sunlight before it reentered the water with a splash.

On the opposite shore a white egret, stark against the shadows of the bank, stood motionless and watching, while on the hummock near the beached boat a fat lazy turtle sunned himself in a patch of light. The air was thick with the almost overwhelming sweet scent of magnolias, their fallen blossoms dotting the still water with splotches of white. A riot of color and scent bloomed on either bank in the form of hyacinths, wild iris, orange and black striped lilies, while overhead the intertwined branches of oaks, cypress and tupelo, thick with hanging moss, formed a living, breathing canopy. In stark contrast to the activity the night before, the swamp in the morning was still, lazy, almost beneficent.

Jessica awoke cramped, aching, and disoriented. She tried to sit up and banged her head on the side of the boat, sending a shaft of pain all the way to her ankles. The morning sun had dried her nightgown to her in sticky patches against her skin; her face felt swollen and her hands and feet stung from the bites of a half dozen insects. She was queasy with hunger.

She remembered where she was. The frantic flight through the night, the dogs, the rain, the swamp . . . Daniel . . . Jake.

She sat up abruptly—too abruptly, since the action sent bolts of pain through her stiff muscles—and looked around frantically. Jake was not in the boat. His saddle, blanket, crinkled poncho and hat were there, but Jessica was alone. He had left her after all. He was going to abandon her on this tiny island in the middle of the swamp with no way to escape. . . .

And then she saw him. He was standing where the sloppy marsh of the bank gave way to the firmer growth of blooming plants and twisting trees, and his back was to her. Jessica sat back, weak with relief, and for a moment simply looked at him. His strong, solid shoulders were outlined by the shape of his dark cotton shirt, the loose vest covered his back, his long lean legs were encased in light twill pants, and the sun glinted off his thick jet hair, with a slice of goldenly tanned neck just visible above the dip of his collarless shirt. He seemed strong, solid, safe. Looking at him, she was filled with a sense of security simply because he was there.

He must have heard her move, because he said, without turning, "So. You're finally awake."

He turned and walked toward her, casually and without any trace of modesty at all as he rebuttoned his pants. Jessica stared, feeling a rising embarrassment which was faintly akin to horror when she realized that while she had been watching him—admiring him, even—he had been . . . had been. . . .

When Jake saw the expression on her face he grinned, a slow and nasty expression that made Jessica quickly avert her burning face. He gestured politely toward the bushes he had just left. "Feel free," he invited, a wicked sparkle in his bright green eyes. "*I* won't watch *you.*"

Jessica turned her head another fraction so she couldn't see him at all, fighting back the ridiculous embarrassment. She was accustomed to traveling with her father under conditions not much better than these, and privacy was one thing she had long since learned not to cherish. But being with her father and being with this man—Jake Fielding, with his long legs and sauntering gait and roguish grin—were two quite different things. Worse yet, she did need to make use of the bushes, but she did not know how she could get up and walk past his dancing, mocking emerald eyes.

Jake wished Daniel could see Jessica now. He had wondered what his brother had seen in the woman before, but now . . . Her hair, tangled with mud and twigs, was coiled in heavy clumps over her head and shoulders, her eyes were puffy and her face was distorted by two prominent mosquito bites, one near her mouth and another just above her cheekbone. Her lips were colorless and drawn, her fingernails black with grime. The tattered nightgown she wore had been gray with filth long before the mud and green algae from the swamp had been added. Jake felt none too fresh himself after sleeping in damp clothes on the ground, but she looked more than disheveled. She looked as though she might well be the carrier of some disease.

He shook his head in mild disgust. "Lady," he said frankly, "you are the sorriest sight I have ever seen. Why don't you at least take a bath?"

Jessica's head jerked around toward him, her face tightening in instinctive defense. She felt awful; aching and filthy and sharp with hunger and fatigue. After the night she had had she was in no mood to meekly accept Jake's barbs; she was in no mood for anything at all except to get out of this godless place as soon as possible. Furious, she started to open her mouth to tell him so.

But then she stopped. There was no point in denying the obvious. She *did* need a bath, and in fact, her last thought before she had drifted off into an uneasy sleep had been a hope that Jake would not be so anxious to leave that he would deny her a few moments to sponge off the worst of the mud and perhaps rinse out her hair. She had not had much in all those years with her father, but she had always managed to stay clean. A bath was of the utmost priority. And she also needed to make use of the bushes, very badly.

With as much dignity as possible, she climbed out of the boat, every muscle screaming in protest. She did not look at him once as she stepped over the squishy ground and then as far into the undergrowth as her tender, briar-torn feet would take her. But she could feel his laughing eyes on her back.

Jake took advantage of the time she was gone to scoop up some water into a pan and scrape off his whiskers, and even though he hated using cold water, he felt greatly restored when it was done. In fact, all things considered, he felt pretty good all the way around this morning. The rain had left the water clear and the temperature somewhat cooler, and the worst part was behind him. Before the day was out he would be back in New Orleans, and if he could get a telegram to Daniel and if everything was well at the ranch, he might just put the woman on a train and stay over a few days, enjoying a few of the finer things of life for himself. He hadn't been in much of a temper to enjoy anything when he had arrived there a week before.

He tossed the soapy water back into the swamp and rinsed off the razor as Jessica's footsteps crashed through the undergrowth again, sending birds fluttering, their screeches shattering the beatific stillness of the swamp. He acknowledged with a dry twist of his lips that at least she had managed the trip there and back without falling down. That must be a good sign for the day ahead.

Stopping a few feet away from him, Jessica said, "I'd like to take a bath, now."

Jake wiped both edges of the razor on the material that covered his thigh. "So who's stopping you?"

She stared at him. "You—you don't intend to stay here and watch?"

Jake looked at her, that slow, lopsided grin insinuating itself across his face again. "Why not? Turnabout is fair play, isn't it?"

She knew immediately that he was referring to the time she had stumbled into his room while he slept, and the memory of his long, unclothed limbs as well as what had happened afterwards made her cheeks redden horribly. Oh, this was impossible, traveling with him, depending on him. He was rude and boorish and nasty and he didn't like her at all. He was determined to make every moment of their time together as miserable for Jessica as possible, and she had little choice but to allow him to do it. Would he never let her forget that one moment's indiscretion which, in all fairness, hadn't been her fault?

Jake couldn't help but notice that the rag she wore was almost transparent. He felt a momentary twinge of conscience, which immediately turned to irritation, when he realized that she had slept in the rain last night with nothing more than that frail garment for protection. But, hell, it wasn't his fault he had had to kidnap her from that place, wasn't his responsibility that her relatives were a bunch of rat-eating white trash, wasn't even his idea to get her in the first place.

The way the material clung to the shape of her full breasts and outlined the pink shading of her nipples was suggestive if not downright obscene. And she was worried about modesty! He folded his razor with a snap and strode toward the boat, tossing over his shoulder, "I won't be seeing anything a dozen men haven't already had before, so I don't know why you should get so prissy about it."

Jessica gaped at him. She wasn't sure what he meant by that—though she had a fairly good idea—but if he thought she was going to take off her clothes and wade into the water while he looked on lazily he was very much mistaken. The man had no decency at all, and she opened her mouth to tell him so, but he straightened up from the boat, his eyes raking over her contemptuously.

"Oh, hell," he said, forcing patience he did not feel, "if it means I don't have to get into that boat with something that smells like it's been dead for three days, go ahead. I'll turn my back, for God's sake. Just wash, will you?"

Jessica tightened her lips against humiliation and indignation and the very strong urge to fling back a retort. Instead she simply asked, "Do you have any soap?"

Jake reached into the saddlebag and took out the bar he had used for shaving. He tossed it to her, then turned deliberately and walked away.

He didn't go far. For one thing, he wasn't sure how safe the water was, and he was not about to have gone through all this just to return to Daniel empty-handed. For another, he'd be damned if he'd let a cheap little tramp like her tell him what he could and could not see, where he could and could not go. He settled on a moss covered rock just beyond a slight bend in the shape of the island, out of her range of vision, but keeping her fully within his. He leaned back on his elbows, comfortable in a spangle of shade and sun, and pulled up a stalk of grass for chewing.

Obviously she didn't trust him any more than he deserved, for she waded into the water fully clothed. That made him chuckle softly, enjoying the view as the wet material molded itself to her ankles, then her calves, then her thighs and then, when the water covered her waist, floating about her in billowy puffs. When she came out of the water she might as well be stark naked, for all the good that froth of wet material would do her.

Which brought up an interesting problem. Jake's eyes drifted to the flutter of a yellow butterfly as it danced above a shadowed log a few feet away from him. He could hardly take Jessica into town dressed as she was, much less put her on a train. He was going to have to find her some clothes. Damn, what a nuisance this was turning out to be. Why the hell had Daniel brought this troublemaker into their lives?

Thinking about Daniel as he had last seen him, lying weak and white in their mother's four-poster bed, his face contorted with pain as he gripped Jake's arm and begged him to find Jessica . . . thinking about Daniel, felled by a bullet from her father's rifle, started that black anger gnawing at his insides again. Jake's eyes began to narrow, focusing on nothing at all.

He had been too exhausted to think much about it the

night before, too driven by vengeance to consider anything before then. But now the truth was unavoidable, and it bore a great deal of thinking about. The old bastard was dead—Jake's hand curled into a fist as he reviewed that infuriating piece of information—and there was not a thing he could do to avenge his treachery. The son of a bitch had tried to murder Daniel, and Jake would find it difficult to forgive anything that had anything to do with the Duncans. Just looking at Jessica he could tell she was nothing but trouble.

Jake would have died for Daniel, but where did one draw the line between blind loyalty and good judgment? How could he take this woman back to his brother knowing she was going to do nothing but destroy him?

But, damn it, he had given his word.

The heaviness of his thoughts was threatening to destroy the confident spirits with which he had started the day, and he turned his eyes back to Jessica, scowling darkly. She bent to dip her hair into the water, arching her smooth neck backwards, and when she did the tips of her scantily covered breasts pushed through the surface, her nipples puckered and prominent. Jake took a breath and jerked his eyes away, focusing on the log across from him. Trash, he thought. Pure trash.

But Daniel was depending on him. He had no choice. He would keep his promise, but he would do it on his own terms, and he'd be damned if she would set one foot on Three Hills property until he knew exactly what her game was.

Resolved, though far from resigned, he tossed away the blade of grass and got to his feet. A big catfish broke the surface not half a dozen feet away, and Jake's stomach rumbled. His last meal seemed a century ago, and he could almost smell that fresh fish frying up in the pan. But he had looked in vain for dry firewood earlier and had found nothing but rotting logs and green branches, not even enough tinder to boil a cup of coffee. Not that it mattered. They would be in town by noon, New Orleans by breakfast the next day. And what a breakfast it would be. Hotcakes and sausages, grits floating in butter, a plate of ham and six eggs and a whole damn pot of coffee. His mouth watered just thinking about it.

But in the meantime he had a few hard biscuits and a couple of slabs of bacon he had cooked up on the trail to Live Oaks two days before, and that would have to do. From one saddlebag he took out a biscuit and stuffed it with bacon, from the other he dragged out a pair of pants and a shirt.

"Hey lady!"

Jessica whirled, her lathered hair whipping around her, her eyes huge and startled as she instinctively crossed her arms over her breasts. Jake couldn't help grinning. She looked ridiculous.

He held up the pair of pants and the shirt, not knowing what prompted him to such chivalry. They were his only change of clothes, and the smart thing to do would have been to put on the clean outfit himself and let her have what he was wearing. But maybe he was still feeling guilty about the blanket or maybe he had decided it was easier to catch flies with honey than vinegar; maybe some of the manners Daniel was always trying to drum into him had finally seeped through. He said, "You can put these on when you get out."

She responded, still watching him warily. "Th-thank you."

He tossed the clothes over a nearby bush. "And hurry up, will you? I don't want to spend all day in this place."

He took his breakfast to the mossy rock and leaned back with his legs stretched toward the log. In all truth, had he not been so hungry and in need of a hot bath and a real bed himself, he wouldn't have been all that anxious to leave this place. Jake had an appreciation for the lush beauty of the swamp born of too many days on the dusty trail with nothing but the lowing of cattle and the dull wit of cow-hands for company, and for awhile it was pleasant to just sit and absorb it.

He finished off his breakfast in two bites and spent a time listening to the drone of insects and the gentle splash of water, absently picking up pebbles and tossing them toward the fallen log. From the lay of the land, he figured the marsh would thin out just around this bend, where there was bound to be a road. From there it could only be a short trek back to civilization. He abhorred the thought of going on foot—walking was something a rancher never did if it could possibly be avoided—but more than likely they would come upon a farm house before long where he might purchase horses, for Jake always traveled with plenty of cash.

He let his eyes drift lazily back to Jessica, wondering what was taking her so long. He started to shout to her to get out and get moving, for he really wanted to make town before noon, but then he thought better of it.

She was just rising from rinsing her hair, cascades of water flowing down her face and the shiny ringlets that covered her back, the nightgown molding to her breasts and waist like a second skin. Jake had no intention of looking away.

She had a damn fine figure, despite the recently acquired scrawniness that was most noticeable in the convexity of her stomach, the leanness of her ribs and the prominence of her collarbone and shoulder blades. Her breasts were high and round and full, just right to fit beneath a man's hand, her hips gentle flares that invited caresses. Watching her, Jake felt a stir in his own blood, and if Daniel had been any other man, he would have known precisely what it was his brother saw in Jessica. If Jessica had been any other woman, Jake would have been more than a little tempted to find out for himself.

But Jessica was not any other woman; she was a two-bit tramp who planned to ruin his brother, and Jake was irritated with himself for letting his thoughts drift. He focused instead on a particular house in New Orleans, where the women wore satin garters and smelled like camellia blossoms, and decided that would be his first stop—tonight, with any luck at all.

He caught his breath as Jessica, still innocently unaware that she was being observed, lifted her arm and slipped her hand beneath the open neck of her nightdress, rubbing the bar of soap along the underside of her arm and her shoulder, around her neck. He could see the path her hand took beneath the material as it moved across her breasts to the other arm, and there was no point in trying; Jake could not have looked away had his life depended on it.

His eyes followed her innocent yet powerfully suggestive movements beneath the clinging material as her soapy fingers slid over her own flesh surely, matter-of-factly; beneath her arm, down her ribcage, across the upper part of her stomach until the material inhibited her movements and she removed her hand. She bent over, rubbing the soap against first one foot and then the other. And then Jake could see through the distortion of the water that she slipped her hand beneath her skirt, stroking her calves, her thighs, moving upwards. . . .

His throat convulsed sharply and he jerked his eyes away.

"Christ!" he muttered thickly, and got to his feet, his back fully turned to her. He could hear Jessica splashing in the water behind him, rinsing off, and he took a slow deep breath, trying to concentrate on New Orleans and the scent of camellia blossoms. That didn't help matters one bit.

He fumbled in his vest pocket for tobacco and papers, intending to give her plenty of time to get out of the water and into some clothes before he went back to the boat. Damn, this was crazy, he thought. He couldn't wait to get back to New Orleans.

He rolled the cigarette, spilling a great deal of the precious tobacco onto the ground, and struck a match against the heel of his boot. The taste of the smoke only made his tight throat drier. Jessica had to be out of the water by now, probably peeling out of the wet nightgown behind the meager shelter of some bush. He tried not to think about it.

He took a few steps as though to forcefully direct his feet away from the boat, and lifted the cigarette again to his lips. His heart slammed powerfully against his chest as the shaded log on which he had been about to prop his foot opened dark reptilian eyes and, with a swish of its powerful tail, slithered down the bank and into the water.

Jake stared as the alligator—the log at which he had been gazing off and on all morning—cut a path through the swamp toward the spot where, only moments before, Jessica had been bathing. He whipped his head around, starting to call to her and point out the narrow escape they both had had, then thought better of it.

He drew another breath, and finished his smoke in determined deliberation, keeping a wary watch on his surroundings. He couldn't wait to get out of this place.

* * *

When he returned to the boat, Jessica was sitting on a stump, completely swathed in his clothes, attempting to comb out her curly mass of hair with her fingers. She turned around when he approached, smiling a little shyly and gesturing with the floppy sleeve of his oversized checked shirt. "They're a little big," she explained, almost as though apologizing.

Jake looked at her. She wore the shirt untucked and it reached to her knees. But the material clung to damp patches on her body and even its voluminous size did nothing to disguise the curves he remembered so well. His pants bagged around her bare feet, despite the fact that she had rolled them up several times. She'd be tripping on them all day.

Without another thought, he took out his knife and knelt beside her. She gasped when he caught hold of the material at her ankle. "Don't cut them," she protested. "You'll never be able to wear them again!"

He spared her a derisive look and sawed away the material. Did she think he couldn't afford another pair of pants? "You have enough trouble standing up as it is," he told her ungraciously. "All I need is for you to trip over your own feet and fall out of the boat."

He ripped away the material and her bare ankle fell free in his hand. For a moment he held it, a small delicate artwork of tendon and bone, and she did not try to pull away. Then he let her foot drop and turned quickly to the other leg, this time touching nothing but the material. "Are they going to fall off when you stand up?" he asked. "Do you need a belt?"

Jessica colored. "No." She cleared her throat a little. "They fit fine otherwise. Thank you."

Jake remembered the full flow of her hips and imagined

that the pants would, indeed, fit just fine there. Then, realizing that she couldn't possibly be wearing any underclothes beneath the fine twill of the pants, his throat tightened again and he stood abruptly. "Here." He tossed the scraps of material to her, not meeting her eyes. His voice was gruff. "Wrap these around your feet somehow. We might have to do some walking before this is over."

Jessica quickly went to work fashioning stirrup-like boots out of the leftover material, both surprised and grateful for his sudden generosity. Jake went back to the boat to put on his hat and strap on his gun belt, preparing for the day's journey.

Unable to contain the question any longer, she said anxiously, "Jake . . . how long do you think it will take us to get back to Three Hills?"

Jake looked at her sharply. She had finished wrapping her feet, a fairly neat little job, too, given what she'd had to work with, and was nervously trying to plait her wet hair. The lock of hair she had lost to the branch the previous night was quite noticeable, butchered close to the scalp near her left temple. Jake felt a small and absurd twinge of regret for that. Her hair, when it was clean, was rather pretty.

But then he was irritated with himself for the sentiment, and with her for everything, and he returned harshly, "You just can't wait, can you?"

Jessica stared at him, confused. "What? To get home, you mean?"

"Home!" Jake snorted, his dark brows lowering. "Three Hills will never be home to the likes of you, lady, and you'd do yourself a favor to get that straight right now!"

Jessica's hands fell still, and she felt as baffled as she was hurt by his vacillating attitude. One moment he was thoughtful enough to provide dry clothes for her and even to alter them so they would fit, the next he was spitting at her like she was less than the dirt beneath his feet. What had she done to make him dislike her so? And what did she have to do to prove to him that she was worthy of his respect?

She said cautiously, "Daniel is my husband."

His eyes glittered with anger and contempt. "Husband! That's a fine line. And next you'll be telling me what a perfect wife you're going to be for him!"

Jessica's fists clenched instinctively in defense while her stomach knotted with anxiety. She hated it when anyone yelled at her, and long experience had taught her the best way to deal with a man's temper was through meekness and submission, no matter how hard it was to bite back her own anger. She didn't like the way his eyes glittered, and though there were a thousand protests and denials she would have liked to have shouted back, she spoke none of them. She merely clenched her fists and sat silently, waiting for him to do what he would.

Jake took an angry step forward, lifting his arm to emphasize his next accusation, and she flinched, automatically lifting a hand to shield her face. Jake stopped, staring at her, and the fear in her enormous blue eyes was like a bucket of cold water thrown on the flame of his temper. Then he noticed his raised arm and realized she was waiting for his blow.

"Good God almighty," he said, insulted and outraged, "I've never hit a woman in my life and I'm not about to start now! What the hell's the matter with you?"

But she did not look very reassured, and when he took another step toward her, meaning only to jerk her hand away from her face, she flinched again and tightened her shoulders against him. Jake turned away with a short hiss of self-disgust and stalked back to the boat.

He lifted his hat and ran his fingers through his hair, taut with half a dozen emotions he couldn't even begin to define. *Damn*. What an irritating woman she was! He couldn't even remember now what he had started to yell at her, and the last thing he felt like doing was resuming the argument. Then he remembered that Daniel had said her father used to beat her, and Jake felt slightly sickened. What was he supposed to do with a woman like her?

"Ah, hell," he said at last, passing his hand one more time over the taut muscles at the back of his neck. "Let's get out of here."

He started to step into the boat, then paused, glancing over his shoulder. "You hungry?" he demanded gruffly.

She had risen from the stump, but was still watching him cautiously. At the mention of food she relaxed. "Yes," she said gratefully.

He dug into his saddlebag and brought out the last two biscuits. He handed one to her, bacon on top, and kept the other for himself. "May as well eat them now." He shrugged. "This'll probably be all we get until dinnertime."

A rush of saliva filled Jessica's mouth as the sight and scent of real food greeted her, and she practically grabbed the biscuit from Jake's hand, biting into it ravenously.

Jake's amusement was mixed with amazement as he watched her. "Lord, lady, didn't they feed you back in that hellhole?"

Jessica shook her head, ashamed of her manners and her greed, but unable to pause long enough to answer him. She had taken three gulping swallows before she realized her mistake.

The greasy salt pork hit her empty stomach like a fist, and prepared to return with the same speed with which it had gone down. She clamped her hand over her mouth, but it didn't help. She took a few stumbling steps away and collapsed on the ground, retching violently.

Jake, watching her, threw his own biscuit on the ground with a muttered oath of disgust. "By God, you sure know how to ruin a man's morning, I'll give you that."

He watched as she leaned over the stump, her small shoulders heaving, the choking sounds she made pulling at his own gorge. Then he whipped off his hat and slapped it against his thigh, swearing again in irritation. "Damn little fool," he exclaimed, striding over to her. "How long has it been since you had anything solid in your stomach? Why the hell didn't you tell me you were sick?"

He caught hold of her shoulder, not knowing exactly what to do for her except to let it pass, but she slapped his hand away, crying, "Don't touch me—don't look at me—please!" She broke off as another spasm seized her, and Jake stepped back, helpless.

When at last it was over Jessica collapsed with her cheek against the cool wood grain of the stump, shivering uncontrollably, more wretched and humiliated than she thought she had ever been in her entire life.

Jake said tautly above her, "God damn it all, lady, you're going to make this one hell of a trip. Now, if you think you could drag your pretty little butt off the ground—"

"Don't call me lady!" She whirled on him, her small fists clenched, her face red and wild. Jake was startled into silence. "My name is Jessica! You say lady like you mean something else, something ugly!"

"I'll call you whatever I damn well please—"

"And don't swear at me!" Her eyes glittered and her voice was shrill. "Papa says—said—it's sinful t-to swear."

And then, without any warning at all, she burst into tears. Great shuddering sobs came from deep within, sounds she did not seem able to control no matter how she tried. She flung herself away from him and buried her face in the rough texture of the stump as all the pain and terror and misery of the past month came rushing through in ceaseless, battering waves, and she was simply too tired to fight the tears.

"Great balls of fire," Jake muttered tensely. "That's all I need, a bawling woman!" He took a step toward her, but if he had felt helpless before, he was utterly at a loss now.

Jessica knew he was angry; he had a right to be angry. He didn't like or approve of her, he had obviously been forced to come on this mission, and she had been nothing but trouble to him. But Jessica was angry too. She was angry and hurt and the roiling fear inside her had to find some outlet; the tears came and she let them.

Jake felt a small tug of pity as he watched her. He listened to the sounds of her desolation and couldn't believe that one small person could suffer so much and not die from it. Dwarfed in his clothes, her tangled curls tumbling down her back, with that absurd spike near her temple where he had shorn off her hair . . . He dropped to his heels beside her, moved by an unaccountable need to take her into his arms and hold her and soothe her as he might a small child. His hand hovered above her head uncertainly for a moment, brushing against the butchered lock of her hair, and then fell awkwardly onto her shoulder. But helplessness made him impatient, and his voice came out much more gruffly than he had intended.

"Listen, laying here on the ground crying your eyes out isn't going to solve anything. And if you think for one minute that I'm going to put up with a hysterical female for the next five hundred miles you're dead wrong. Come on, get up. Let's get out of here before it gets too hot to travel."

Jessica choked back a final sob, her shoulders stiffening beneath his hand. She had not expected tenderness from Jake, or kindness, or even understanding. But his anger hurt her, just as his callousness and contempt on top of everything else she had suffered had hurt her from the very first moment they had met. She was tired of being hurt. She was tired of bowing her head meekly and accepting life's blows, tired of stepping out of the path of arrogant, finely dressed people like Jake Fielding because she wasn't good enough to walk in their shadows, tired of being pushed by the wayside and waiting for the worst to happen. He was right: feeling sorry for herself was not going to solve anything. She vowed she was not going to do it any more.

She was Daniel Fielding's wife; it was time she started living up to the name. She had a right to hold her head up high. She had survived her father's abuse and the scorn of almost everyone she had ever known; she had lived through an attempt on her husband's life, a kidnapping, and Eulalie's madness, and nothing—not this horrible swamp, not her own weakness and hunger, not even Jake Fielding himself—was going to beat her down now. She had a lifetime of security and happiness waiting for her at Three Hills Ranch, but it was clear she was going to have to fight for it.

Jessica straightened up, tightening her lips and wiping her tears away with the heels of her hands. Her voice was thick, but her eyes, swollen and bleached a very pale blue by the onslaught of tears, held a measure of determination Jake was not entirely sure he liked as she turned to look at him. "You don't have to worry about me," she said, and her chin jutted out with a gesture of what Jake very easily recognized as stubbornness—something else he had never seen in her before. "That's the last time you'll ever see me cry."

She got to her feet, head held high, and walked over to the boat.

Chapter VI

The Atchafalaya was one of the largest swamps in the country, covering almost twenty-eight hundred square miles of interlocking waterways which led, for the most part, nowhere. Its sluggish, twisting streams meandered endlessly in no particular direction before dissolving into marshy landfills or turning back upon themselves so subtly that the inexperienced pilot could negotiate their courses for days before discovering that he had been doing nothing but traveling in circles. Experienced trappers and fishermen went into the swamp never to be heard from again. Local lore was filled with tales of mappers and traders who boasted of their intention to conquer the unknown only to disappear without a trace into the black heart of the Atchafalaya. Few who went into the swamp alone ever returned.

But Jake and Jessica had no way of knowing this.

Six hours after Jake had set off so confidently for the bend in the stream which would lead him to the road he was still poling. Noontime came and went, and with it the hope of a bed and a meal by dusk. The interlocking branches of tupelo and cypress overhead grew thicker, darker, and closer. The draping curtains of willows took on a blackish hue, and the Spanish moss was so long and heavy in places that Jake had to lift the pole out of the water to knock it aside and clear a path for the pirogue.

Jessica sat tense and silent at the end of the boat. Few words had passed between her and Jake since they had begun their journey that morning, and at times she thought he had almost forgotten her presence. She had watched his face go from casual to grim as hour after hour he levered the pole into the dark water, pushing forward with a lunge and leaving behind a churning hole of mud and slimy duckweed, lifting and pushing again, over and over until the rhythm of his body seemed to blend in with the pulsing stillness of the swamp and become part of it.

Every nerve in Jessica's body was coiled into itself. She thought if she didn't scream from the silence she would surely do so from fear. So she kept her lips tightly clamped, her arms wound around herself, her knees pressed stiffly together. She had long since resigned herself to the fact that they would never see civilization again. Now she was concentrating only on surviving each successive minute.

The pirogue glided slowly under a low-hanging branch and Jake had to duck his head to miss it. His hat brushed against the fat body of a huge brown and black snake that had wound itself around the branch and the reptile hissed at him ominously. Jessica bit the underside of her lip and hugged herself more tightly. "We're going to die in this place."

She had not realized her thought was whispered aloud until Jake glanced at her. His eyes held no humor at all. "Now that's a cheerful thought." He lifted the pole again, and his tone was dark as he scanned their surroundings. "At least we won't have far to go to get to hell."

"Don't blaspheme."

He pushed savagely on the pole. His shoulders had been aching so long now that the pain was part of him. "Don't swear, don't blaspheme," he mimicked bitterly. "Tell me ma'am, is there anything I *can* do besides saving your scrawny hide?"

Jessica glared at him, surprised by her sudden surge of temper as much as she was by the relief that swept her at having someone upon which to vent her anger and fear. "If you'll pardon me for saying so, you don't seem to be doing such a great job at *that*, either. You'll be lucky if you can save your own hide!"

Churning green eyes glared at her with the threat of violence, but she met them evenly, her own eyes sparking. Anything, even fighting, was better than the brittle silence that had been hanging between them all day accompanied by an awful sense of doom that seemed to flow from the dark banks of the swamp like a fetid breath.

"You think you can do a better job?" he demanded. "I'd be more than glad to give you a chance!"

"I told you not to come into the swamp! I—"

"By God, lady, I'm not going to go through that again."

"I told you not to call me that!"

Silence rang in the flash of murderous eyes, and with a lunge that almost sent Jessica toppling forward, Jake dug the pole into the mud and pushed. "I should have left you while I had the chance," he muttered. "I've half a mind to leave you now and save myself the aggravation of a nagging woman on top of everything else. By God, I'd like to see how you do without me, you're so goddamn eager to complain."

"Your threats don't scare me anymore, Jake Fielding," she lied bravely, keeping her voice steady. "You can leave me here if you want. I've lived through worse."

His eyes returned to her, and beneath the anger of his unspoken imprecations there was something else, something very peculiar that she couldn't begin to define. Then he turned away and silently poled toward the nearest shore.

The boat scraped against the muddy shallows, and Jake leaped into the shallow water. "Get out," he commanded. "Make yourself useful."

Jessica climbed into the murky water, tugging at the bow while Jake pushed at the stern. When the pirogue was securely beached amidst a clump of bushes Jessica crawled out of the sludge and looked around at their accommodations for the night.

The ground here was somewhat drier than the hummock they had stayed on the night before, but it did not appear any more friendly. The long marsh grass looked like a dead woman's hair, spiky leaves of flowering bushes snaked along the ground like boney fingers and blackberry brambles and thorny bushes pushed through the close covering of trees with lush greed. There wasn't a clear space of ground anywhere.

Jake was climbing out of the water, brushing his hands along his forearms. He commanded curtly, "Check your legs."

Jessica stared at him, but when he gave no further instructions, she looked down at her legs. Gingerly, she caught the pants material at the knee and pulled the damp cloth up a little, exposing a few inches of her ankle above her wrapped feet. She stifled a little cry at what she saw there.

Leeches, dozens of the slimy, greedy creatures, were

fastened to the white skin of her lower legs, their bodies quickly bloating with her blood. Her stomach, already weak from the morning's trauma and her long fast, lurched horribly. She tried not to scream.

Jake, catching her expression, felt the first twinge of mirth he had experienced all day. He got down on his haunches and took out his knife. Then, with a devilish sense of satisfaction for her distress, he matter-of-factly plucked the parasites off. "Just think," he commented mildly while Jessica squeezed her eyes shut and tried not to think about what he was doing, "you were swimming in this same water this morning. It's a wonder you didn't come out with these things clinging to you . . ." He couldn't resist. "All over."

The very thought made Jessica weak. She gripped his shoulder to keep her balance.

"Yes sir, a body's got to be careful where he goes swimming buck nekkid—Ouch. Lady, take your claws out of my shoulder, will you?"

Jessica forced herself to release his shoulder while his hand impersonally pushed up the material over one leg, exposing a portion of her slender white calf, and he applied the blunt edge of his knife to her skin again. "You're not going to swoon are you?" he asked without much interest.

Jessica steeled herself against the dizziness that was sweeping through her with every breath. She tried to think of something pleasant, but couldn't remember a single thing. "No." Her voice was hoarse but determined. She would die before ever revealing to him another sign of weakness. "I n-never sw-swoon."

"Good." Jake stood and resheathed his knife. "Because if you did you'd like as not fall into a snake pit." His eyes swept the surrounding landscape with blatant disgust. "If this place isn't hell it's sure got to be one of the first outposts."

He took the pole from the boat and took a few steps into the high grass, swinging the pole in a circle around him, occasionally beating it on the ground. Something slithered out of the grass and something else scurried into the bushes. Jessica reached weakly for the support of a tree behind her, remembered the things that might be clinging to that tree, and quickly straightened up again.

Jake flattened a circle of grass around him, shoving back the cloying tendrils of a particularly persistent bush, and took out his gun. He stepped back and fired a single shot into the ground. Jessica jumped, and the sound echoed on. The trees came to life overhead as the birds took flight, and several unknown inhabitants of their campsite rippled through the grass for cover. Jake reholstered his weapon with satisfaction.

He carried the pole back to the boat, glancing at Jessica in ill-disguised contempt as he passed. "I don't suppose you know how to make a fire?"

Jessica lifted her chin. There was nothing to be done about it, she told herself. This was a horrible place but it was where they were. There was nothing to do but make the best of it. They would probably die there, but they didn't have to die that night . . . Matching her tone to his, she said, "Of course I can."

Jake nodded curtly. "Matches are in my saddlebags."

And then, without another word or even a glance over his shoulder, he walked off, pushing through the bushes and trampling down the grass until his footsteps were only a faint echo that finally disappeared altogether.

Jessica stood there for a long time, shivering in the humid heat of late afternoon, overwhelmed by an intense isolation and the oppressive stillness that accompanied his absence. A thousand eyes were watching her from the bushes, the trees, the banks of the opposite shore. She tried to conjure up a vision of Three Hills, graceful, refined, peaceful and secure, but she couldn't really make herself believe such a place existed, much less that she would ever see it again. She wished Jake would return.

But when Jake did get back he would expect a campfire, and Jessica had no intention of giving him further cause to berate her. With every scrap of courage she possessed, she put one foot cautiously in front of the other and began her search for dry wood. " 'The Lord is my shepherd,' " she murmured, and determinedly strengthened her voice. " 'I shall not want.' " It seemed to help.

Jessica was on her fiftieth recitation of the Twenty-Third Psalm when crashing steps through the undergrowth announced Jake's return. Her first instinct was to leap to her feet and cry out a joyous welcome, but she made herself sit still, calmly and methodically feeding the fire, and she didn't even turn her head. She had found a good supply of flour and sourdough starter in Jake's saddlebags; mixed with water from his canteen and seasoned with blackberries it made a rich batter to spread into the skillet and bake over the embers.

Jake, returning with a plucked and cleaned fowl for their supper, was surprised by the domestic picture she made sitting beside the fire and efficiently roasting bread in a skillet.

He had assumed that the moment he disappeared she would have collapsed into an attack of feminine vapors, unable to do anything but huddle in the boat, terrified until he returned. In fact, she had built a neat little fire and had even had sense enough to clear away the brush and grass before she started. She had somehow managed to drag his heavy saddle from the boat and was using it as a chair, and had spread his poncho on the ground to keep the cooking utensils clean. She had even rigged up a couple of torches out of pine knots and broken branches and set them by the shore, presumably to discourage alligators. Jake didn't know how much good that would do, but it was a nice touch. He wasn't sure even he would have thought of it.

It was a relief not to have her nagging him as he built a spit and arranged the duck over the low-burning flames. He was too tired to fight with her, and had too much to worry about to waste energy trying to keep her in line. If nothing else, he was grateful for her silence.

He had been trying to convince himself otherwise all day, but there was no point in denying the obvious any longer. This swamp was not going to give way into clear land around the next bend. The road was not just on the other side of the next copse. They were unmistakably lost.

Being lost did not bother him as much as having to admit the fact. He had grown up in some of the most stubborn and unforgiving land in the country. The meandering hills and tangled pastures of East Texas were his backyard, and the deserts west of the Missouri and the endless rolling plains of Kansas were as familiar to him as the back of his own hand. He could track with unfailing accuracy any trail left by man or beast, and until this very moment the word lost had not been in his vocabulary.

He glanced at Jessica suspiciously, waiting for her to make some comment or ask some stupid question that would set his temper off. What really grated at him was that she had been right about the swamp in the first place, and there was nothing in the world worse than a woman who was right. He wondered how long it would be before she felt compelled to point out to him once again just how right she had been.

Jessica turned out the bread just as it formed a delicate white crust on the top, cleared the sides of the pan by knocking it against the ground, and filled it with water to boil for coffee. She was used to taking care of her father on the trail and knew how to do it properly. The roasting duck began to sizzle as its fragrant juices fell into the fire and she turned the spit. She was light-headed with hunger, but she had learned her lesson about impatience. Tonight she would eat slowly and carefully, for she knew she would need her strength for the days to come.

Jake brought a small cloth sack of coffee beans from his saddlebag and she took it from him wordlessly, crushing the beans with a rock before adding them to the water. She had made up her mind during Jake's long absence not to provoke him to any further displays of wrath that night. And it seemed as though every time she opened her mouth she made him angry.

That was strange, she mused, giving the skillet a shake to mix the coffee with the water. Before Jake she had never raised her voice in anger to any man and would have been appalled to even envision herself doing so. But in a mere twenty-four hours he had changed her temperament, not to mention her life, drastically. She did not think that could be a good sign, for if they were ever to get out of this dismal place—and the possibility dimmed by the moment—their only chance was to work together. She decided that the best thing for both of them would be if they dealt together as much as possible without speaking.

There was only one plate, and Jessica pushed the bread to one side to serve the duck, burning her fingers a little as she pushed the heavy bird off the stick. She poured coffee into the single tin cup, and Jake did not need an invitation. He tore off a drumstick and a chunk of bread and sank to the poncho behind her, leaning his shoulders against the saddle on which she sat.

He was so hungry he wolfed the drumstick without tasting the rich, fatty meat, but the bread was a surprise. She had put something sweet in it—blackberries, he noted upon closer examination—and he appreciated it with an epicurean palate not usually wasted on the trail. "This is good," he said, licking his fingers before reaching for another helping.

Jessica replied politely, "Thank you." It *was* good. In fact, the entire meal came close to being the best thing she had ever tasted in her life, and it was with great self-restraint that she kept herself from attacking the bird with the same hungry greed Jake displayed. She carefully paced herself with small slivers of the moist, steaming meat and ladylike bites of the warm bread. This time, to her great relief, her stomach welcomed every morsel.

Jake wasted no time on drawing room manners. He devoured the fowl between gulps of thick coffee and mouthfuls of the sweet, crusty bread. He would be damned if he could figure how she had gotten the bread to brown just right like that; his always burned on the bottom and remained doughy on top. He supposed she might be of some use to have along after all.

He had filled the coffee cup for the second time before he thought to offer it to her. Jessica accepted it with both hands and sipped from it delicately. She had very small hands, he noticed when she returned the cup. Feminine.

Previously he had found her silence a blessing. But now, replete with a warm meal, settling back against the saddle with a cigarette and the last of the coffee, Jake found her subdued mood worrisome, even oppressive. He wondered if she was still mad at him for making her cry that morning. Or that afternoon, when he had lost his temper with her again. Or . . . hell, she had a lot to be mad about.

He glanced at her as she got to her feet. "You should finish that off," he said, nodding at the plate. The bread was gone, but there was still a bit of meat left. "I don't want any more."

"I'm afraid I can't eat more, either," she said. "I'll wrap it and save it for the morning."

She busied herself with storing the leftovers in his saddlebag and rinsing off the dishes at the edge of the swamp. In silence. After a time Jake said, "All we have to do, you know, is find the main tributary and let it lead us to the source. This place has got to empty into something, maybe the Gulf or the Mississippi. Nobody can stay lost forever."

She said, without turning, "Yes, I suppose that's right."

Jake followed the slope of her small shoulders, the curve of her buttocks as she bent over the water. He concentrated on the tip of his cigarette. "There's plenty of game and fish. We won't starve."

Actually, Jake wasn't a very good hunter; there had simply been no call for it in his life. On the trail he subsisted on beans and bacon, at home he feasted on Rio's plain but abundant fare. Hunting and fishing were two things a cattleman never had to learn to do, which was just as well, because he had to learn almost everything else. But here in the swamp the wild things were fat and unwary, and Jake didn't think he would have much trouble bringing in something to put over the fire at night. He was a good shot.

Jessica smiled at him weakly and unconvincingly as she returned to the fire. "I'm sure we'll be fine."

Jake wished he were sure. And he wished he knew what was making her so cautious and withdrawn.

Jessica sat on the edge of the saddle, close to the fire where the mosquitoes weren't so vicious. He seemed so confident that their situation was less dire than it looked and she wished she could believe him. But life had obviously treated Jake Fielding much better than it had Jessica, and optimism was hard for her to come by. It would be cruel beyond belief to imagine that God would give her a fine man like Daniel and deliver her from Eulalie's madness and her father's domination only to bring her to the swamp to die without ever being reunited with her husband or his gracious home. But it was not impossible. Jessica had learned not to expect too much from a stern and unforgiving heavenly Father.

Jake slapped at his neck as a mosquito found its target and swore softly. Jessica shot him a reproachful look and he scowled. He felt absurdly like apologizing, and to this uneducated, underbred little scrap of a man pleaser . . . The very notion irritated him, and her great blue eyes didn't waver from his. She did have the most incredible eyes.

Darkness came quickly in the swamp, and with its shadows and night noises a new and not entirely disagreeable intimacy formed the backdrop for their campsite. The orange and yellow flicker of the fire planed her features and softened her curves, and Jake remembered again how she had looked that night in his mother's pink dress; how she had felt moving against him in the light steps of the dance, every inch a woman. Daniel was crazy to bring her into their house.

She turned so that her profile was to him, lifting her arms to try to rebraid the heavy mass of her hair. The motion thrust the curve of her breasts against her shirt, and he wondered if she could possibly be aware of what an alluring pose she had struck. Common sense told him she was, but there was such innocence in her mannerisms that he found it hard to believe she ever premeditated anything. She had nice breasts, not too large, but firmly shaped. Jake deliberately moved his eyes away and took another draw on his cigarette. He wished she would talk to him. Even her nagging would be better than the silence.

She was scared of course. He couldn't fault her for that; he was more than a little uneasy himself. But he didn't have any serious doubts they would eventually make it out of the swamp. What bothered him was the thought of the difficulties that lay in store for them. Jake did not like hardships and preferred not to deal with them; that was one reason he had chosen to ride herd over being the gentleman rancher that Daniel thought he should be. Life was simple on the range, uncomplicated and undemanding. A man could be his own boss there, taking what he wanted and leaving the rest. He never had to worry about anybody but himself.

But now, and for the duration of the journey, he had this woman to worry about. Not only how to keep her safe until he figured out what to do with her, but what she was thinking, how she was feeling, what she was plotting. He hoped to hell she wasn't getting ready to cry again.

When he couldn't stand the silence a moment longer, he glanced at her. "Look, lady—"

"Jessica," she said firmly. "My name is Jessica."

"*Miss* Jessica." He ground out the words in irritation, and then wasn't sure he wanted to go on. What a provoking woman. He stared at the ember of his cigarette. "Listen, I know you're not too happy with the way things turned out, but pouting at me is not going to change it. If we're going to get out of this mess, it looks like we're going to have to try to get along."

"You're not an easy man to get along with," she pointed out calmly.

He chuckled, more in surprise than anything else. "No, I reckon I'm not. Daniel's always telling me I've got the manners of a wild coyote."

"He's right."

He glanced at her suspiciously, but there was no malice in her expression. It had been a simple statement of fact.

He grumbled, drawing on the cigarette again, "You're no goddamn missionary yourself."

She let her hair fall, fanning in a wild cascade of ringlets from her neck to her shoulder blades, and turned to him. Jake thought she was going to jump on him for swearing again, and he opened his mouth to put her in her place, but to his surprise she merely inquired, "Why do you hate me so? Will you tell me what I've done?"

He stared at her. "Lady, if you don't know . . ." And then, with a terse breath, he finished shortly, "Between you and your father you almost killed my brother. And if you think for one minute I'm going to let you just sashay up to Three Hills and take over, you've got another think coming."

Jessica stared at him, her face alabaster and her eyes dark in the firelight. She said unexpectedly, and so softly that Jake had to strain to hear, "I'm not sorry he's dead."

The truth came upon her slowly, something that had been gestating for weeks and whose birth had come with the surety of nature which nothing could restrain. But when she realized she had spoken it aloud, she met Jake's startled glance with a burning in her cheeks and distress in her eyes. Though she meant to retract the statement she found herself confessing instead, "My father. I know it's sinful but . . ."

She faltered and dropped her hands to her lap. "He was a cruel man, and he wasn't always honest, and . . . he tried to kill Daniel. I'm not sorry he's dead." The last was almost a whisper, and she couldn't meet Jake's eyes anymore.

What an awful, awful thing to say, she thought. If Jake had despised her before he would surely find her beneath contempt now. She tried to form a quick prayer for forgiveness but it sounded hollow. Perhaps because she knew that, as despicable as it was, what she had just uttered was the honest truth.

Jake was silent for a moment, trying to resolve this new information with what he already knew about her. It didn't quite make sense. He tilted his head on the saddle to get a better look at her and said curiously, "Daniel said the old man used to beat you."

Jessica stiffened. Perhaps to atone for her previous blasphemy, perhaps because she did not want Jake to think any less of her father, or herself, than he already did, she replied with dignity, "It's a parent's right to discipline. It's his duty."

Jake sat up slowly, looking at her. He had been raised with a respect for womankind that was almost reverence, and though through the years he had learned that certain women deserved less respect than others, striking any woman was not something any decent man would do. In the desolate towns of the Southwest where the males outnumbered females roughly twenty to one, even the whores were treated with dignity. It hadn't been so long past that a man could be justifiably shot for making a spurious comment about a woman within public hearing. Jake found the very image of any man raising a hand to this small fragile creature abhorrent—no matter how much he personally might dislike or distrust her. And she had accepted it as a way of life.

He said soberly, "No, Jessica. No man has a right to hit you, no matter who he is or what the cause. It's not decent, it's not natural. And you're a fool if you think it is."

Jessica glanced at him, not knowing whether the little thrill that went through her was due to his words, or the fact that he had, for the first time without prompting, addressed her by her name. The smile that softened her lips felt strange when it was addressed to him, and she said, "You sounded like Daniel just then. I guess you're more like him than I thought."

Jake had to look away, because that little smile of hers made her look young and sweet and incredibly innocent, and because she had no cause to direct it at him. And because things were getting more complicated by the minute and nothing was quite the way it had started out to be. He said rather curtly, "I'm nothing like Daniel. Daniel is too nice and I'm too smart."

He started to toss away the last of the coffee, and then remembered to offer it to her. She shook her head and he stood abruptly, throwing out the coffee on his way to the boat.

He returned with the blanket and a curt, "We'll sleep on the ground tonight. That boat's hard enough to crack even a cowpoke's spine."

She stood uncertainly and he immediately took her place, resting his head against the seat of the saddle and snapping the blanket over his legs. "If you need to go to the woods," he said matter-of-factly, without glancing up, "be quick about it. I've got to get some shut-eye and I can't be up all night with you tramping around."

"N-no," Jessica said a little nervously, watching him. Where did he expect her to sleep?

"Then throw some more wood on the fire and come on." He took off his hat and settled back against the saddle with a sigh, closing his eyes.

Jessica took her time about feeding the fire, and when she turned he was watching her with a frown. "What are you waiting for?" And then added impatiently, "There's only one blanket. You either share it with me or do without." He held up a corner of the blanket for her.

Jessica was quite sure that there was something indecent about sleeping with him under the same blanket. Wasn't that exactly what her father had preached about all those years? A woman who behaved shamelessly got nothing less than what she deserved, and to lie down next to Jake Fielding with his long legs and strong hands and beard-roughened chin . . . Her throat went a little dry just thinking about it.

She said, as calmly as possible, "I did all right without a blanket last night. I'll sleep in the boat."

"Don't be an idiot. It gets damp at night and you'll catch the fever. That's all the hell I need! What do you think I'm going to do, bite you? Get in."

Jessica hesitated only a moment longer. It was going to be a long trip and there was no point in making herself any more uncomfortable than necessary. She had no desire to have gotten through everything only to catch the fever before they even had a chance to get out of the swamp. And she didn't really want to sleep in the boat alone, away from Jake's alert senses and quick gun.

She tried not to think about his strong legs as she stepped onto the poncho and lay down stiffly beneath the blanket, as far away from him as possible.

Though she was very careful that their bodies didn't

touch, Jake could feel her beside him as rigid as a corpse and he was irritated. He hardly expected gratitude from her for his considerate gesture, but she was huddled at the far end of the blanket like she thought he had bugs, and there was no call for that. Besides, there wasn't enough of the blanket to cover both of them if she insisted on sleeping on the other side of the island.

"Hell and be damned," Jake grumbled. In a single movement he slipped an arm beneath her shoulders and hauled her over to him so her head was on the saddle beside his. "I'm not going to wrestle with you all night for cover."

He leaned over her and began to efficiently tuck the edges of the blanket beneath her to guard against the intrusion of unwanted creatures during the night, and almost immediately he wished he had left her where she was. Her eyes were wide with surprise and her unruly hair was already beginning to come loose from its rough braid. She gasped when his chest brushed across her breasts, which left her lips parted in an incredibly unwary invitation. Quickly he looked away and concentrated on arranging the blanket under her, but her shoulders were small and alluring beneath his hands, her hips firm, evocative swells, her thighs tense and defined to his touch. His hip was pressed against hers as he bent over her, and she was soft beneath him. Jake could feel the faint stir of her breath on his cheek. He would have been less than human not to experience some reaction.

The image of her body so thinly clad in his pants and shirt as he had seen her all day was suddenly alluring, the shape of her legs, the curve of her bottom, the thrust of her breasts. Unbidden, the thought entered his mind that it would be so easy to lower his body on top of her, to cover her parted lips with his, to feel her small arms encircle his neck. And for a moment, poised above her and captured by her wide, uncertain eyes, he actually considered yielding to the impulse. Then, because he couldn't believe he was seriously thinking such a thing, he swore.

Jessica's heart was beating rapidly, and she was certain it was from no more than the intensity of his gaze and the way his body was touching hers at almost every point. His hand had paused beneath the curve of her knee and the gentle heat from his chest brushed her breasts. She tried to keep as still as possible, hardly daring to breathe. Two buttons of his shirt and undergarment were open at the throat, and she could see a tuft of dark hair there, just below the dip of his collarbone. Staring at it, she felt her own throat grow dry.

But her voice was very steady as she said, "Don't you know any words that aren't four-lettered?"

"No," he said gruffly. He quickly finished arranging the blanket beneath her legs and then rolled away from her, making the same arrangements on his side of the blanket.

When he lay beside her again, his hands linked on his chest and his head very close to hers on the saddle, Jessica tried without success to relax. They were so close that his body heat branded her upper arm, her hip, and her thigh, everywhere his hard muscles touched. She had never been so near a man in this way before, and the strangeness of it was as uncomfortable as it was tantalizing. She didn't see how she would ever sleep.

Clearing her throat a little, she asked, "Aren't you going to take off your boots?"

He glanced at her. "What for?"

When he turned his head like that his face was very close, so close that his eyelashes could have brushed her cheek without moving much at all. She immediately felt flushed and moved her own head, pretending to seek a more comfortable position on the saddle. "It just seems like the thing to do when you're sleeping."

"Never take off your boots on the trail. You could be in trouble if you have to move in a hurry or something crawled inside." He shrugged. "I've known cowhands who take a bath with their boots on or even—" He had started to say make love to a woman, but stopped himself for no particular reason.

Jessica said, "Is that what you are—a cowhand?"

Jake laughed quietly. "Hell no, I'm a gentleman scholar, can't you tell?" Then, because she seemed really interested, and because he suspected she was about to reprimand him for his language again, he added casually, "I don't like being cooped up. Some people hate trail work, but I don't mind it so much. Daniel's a politician. He takes care of Texas. I'm a rancher. I take care of cattle. We both like it that way."

"Yes," Jessica said slowly, softly, "I can understand that. It must be . . . the best thing in the world, to ride free with no one to account to and no one locking you in. To just go and do whatever you want."

Jake glanced at her curiously, struck by the yearning in her voice, but then she asked almost eagerly, "What's it like on the trail? What do you do?"

Jake's lips turned down wryly as he settled his head securely against the saddle. "Sit around the fire with a bunch of dusty old cowpokes making up swear words, mostly."

She laughed, a sweet and gentle sound low in her throat that made Jake turn his head to her in surprise. He had never heard her laugh before. It was a pleasant sound.

But when he looked at her, her laughter faded into

shyness, and she turned her head away, looking up at the sky. In a moment he did the same.

He tried not to think about how soft her hip was where it pressed against his, nor how close his elbow was to the curve of her breast. It would be so simple to relax his arm, let it flow downward until his hand spread across her small belly, or even lower . . . He felt a heaviness tingling in his loins and it was almost more than he could do to subdue it. Jake was not used to denying himself anything, and the only thing he could do was assure himself that the last thing he wanted was this woman who was not only a nuisance and a danger, but his brother's wife.

But the heat from her small body was beginning to make him sweat, and when she stirred a little the nerve endings in his arm prickled. He tried not to notice the feel of her hair where a wisp of it nestled against his neck, silky and imbued with her scent. He tried very hard to concentrate on something else.

The interlocking network of trees and vines provided a scant glimpse of the heavens, but even if he had been able to see it was too hazy to make out any stars. During the day the sun was so often obscured by the thick foliage of the swamp that it was impossible to keep an accurate course, presupposing that the waterways would allow it. At the moment he wasn't certain whether they were traveling north or south, east or west. His own helplessness was immeasurably frustrating.

He released a heavy sigh. "God almighty, what kind of crazy relatives do you have to live on the edge of a place like this?"

Jessica hesitated. "Live Oaks used to be a great plantation."

"Well, its best days are behind it, let me tell you that." And then, because it was something he really wanted to know, he demanded, "How could you let yourself stay in a place like that?"

"Do you think I had any choice?" Her voice was tight and harsher than she had intended. How she hated to think about that place, the nightmare from which she had so narrowly escaped. But now that he had brought it up, she couldn't seem to stop thinking about it. Her voice came almost without her wishing it, low and choked. "I thought I'd go mad. When I was little, sometimes when I was bad Papa would . . . tie the flap of the wagon closed and lock me inside, and it would get so hot and I would get so thirsty I thought I would die. I thought that was the worst thing that could ever happen to anybody. But Aunt Eulalie's was worse.

"There was no light and sometimes she would forget to bring the candle and I was so hungry. There was no glass in the windows, only bars, and the rain would come through. I tried and tried to find a way to get out but the bars were strong and Rafe or Will were always there. Will . . . he really scared me sometimes, the way he looked at me. And sometimes—oh, it was awful, but sometimes I'd pray to die quickly and not grow old and mad in that place like Aunt Eulalie. And I couldn't have a bath or any clothes. And the bugs . . ." She caught her breath, refusing to go on, refusing to let her mind take her any further into that abyss of horror. "There's nothing worse in the world than being locked up," she said softly, her fists unconsciously curling at her sides with the intensity of her words. "I don't think I could have stood it another day."

Jake was appalled, and he had no words to express his feelings or thoughts. The girl had been a prisoner all of her life, first of a cruel and abusive father, then of a madwoman's asylum under conditions that would bring the strongest man to his knees. He, who had no love for confinement under the best conditions, could barely imagine what it must have been like for her. No wonder she had run to Daniel. No wonder Daniel had wanted to take care of her. He didn't know what to say to her. And he was more uncertain than ever what to do about her.

They lay together in silence for a time, listening to the throbbing chirping swamp life that surrounded them, each lost in their own reflections. Jessica was surprised when she realized that the apprehension she had felt upon first lying down with him had completely fled. She felt, in fact, as comfortable with him as she could with any man under the circumstances. She did not think they could ever be enemies again. She even began to think, for no exact reason at all, that they might even be on the threshold of becoming friends.

"But then you came," she finished simply, turning her head to look at him, and then away. "And even as much as I hate this place, as scared as I get sometimes, it's still better, because at least—at least I'm not locked up."

Jake made a gruff sound low in his throat, and did not look at her. He said, "Better get some sleep. We're leaving at sunrise."

Jessica turned her head and closed her eyes, and in a surprisingly short time the hum of the insects and frogs, in combination with her own exhaustion, lulled her into a deep sleep. But Jake lay restless and wakeful for a long time, staring at the sky and thinking.

Chapter VII

Jessica awoke the next morning groggy and sticky with the rising temperature and humidity of the swamp. She pulled aside the blanket with slow stiff movements and tried to roll away from the body that was pressed so close to hers. Something heavy trapped her leg, and she became aware of Jake's soft regular breathing at the same moment she realized it was his large hand that was curved so possessively around the upper portion of her thigh.

Immediately she was fully awake and her heart began to thump as she turned her head to look at him. How gentle he looked sleeping beside her, his thick dark hair falling over one eyebrow, his closed lashes shadowing his cheek. The rough stubble of a beard darkened the lower portion of his face, defining his strong jawline and chin, yet somehow even this rugged evidence of his masculinity was endearing. He had half turned in his sleep so that his face was a mere fraction from hers, and a strand of her hair was trapped between his cheek and the saddle.

Jessica followed the shape of his jaw downward. Perspiration glinted in a crease of his throat, which was strong yet somehow vulnerable as it swept downward to his fluted collarbone and the hollow there with its nest of dark masculine hair. Looking at him, Jessica felt the irrational urge to touch him, to smooth back the fallen lock of hair, to trace the shape of his cheekbone, to let her fingertips play over his rough morning beard. The thought made Jessica's heart speed uncomfortably and her breath to come a bit more rapidly. She was intensely aware of his strong hand curved around her leg, and there was a tightening in her stomach muscles, a quivery feeling that was directly related to the strange intimacy of waking up like this with him.

Carefully, trying very hard not to wake him, Jessica moved her hand down to his wrist, thinking to remove his hand.

Immediately Jake was alert. His green eyes opened, clear and aware, and looked directly into hers. Jessica couldn't move.

The waking reality for Jake was not so different from his dreams. Her face, flushed and soft, was a mere breath from his, her lips parted with a question or an exclamation, her eyes as big and blue as the Texas sky. Dark hair tumbled about her shoulders and breasts, touching him. Her fingers were small and heated on his wrist, her muscles distinct yet pliable beneath his fingers, and for a moment it seemed so natural to find himself so that he almost moved his hand upward, instead of away.

A mere thought would close the distance between their mouths. Already he could taste her, as sweet as wild honey, as delicate as an unfurled blossom. The thickness between his legs was definite and insistent. Her huge expectant eyes seemed to swallow him. He could feel his heart beating and it seemed so right, so easy. . . .

The moment between them was thick and rich with possibilities, and it seemed to be suspended forever. He did not move; Jessica did not breathe. Her heart was thudding painfully and more rapidly than it ever had in her life. The strange knot of anticipation, or nervousness, that had begun low in her chest began to spread to her stomach, making her feel weak and uncertain. The place where his hand touched felt heated and swollen. Jessica waited for him to move. Jake tried not to.

A blue jay screeched noisily overhead and the heavy spell that had wrapped itself around them was shattered. Jake rolled abruptly away from her and got to his feet. "No time for breakfast this morning." His voice sounded hoarse. "Let's get going."

There was a sense of timelessness to the swamp, a dreamlike quality that was a mixture of surrealistic images and unnatural sounds, of endless motion and suspended thought. It was difficult for Jessica to remember whether they had been there two days or five, a week or a month. At times it seemed as though they had never been anywhere else and never would be again. The world began and ended with the moss infested tupelos and sluggish dark water that had no course, and at the center of that world was Jake.

Things did not seem so strained between them anymore, and Jessica's dim hope that they might one day be friends seemed to be gaining substance, slowly but surely. There still was a restraint between them, a distance that he created, but matters were improving on levels both slow and subtle and infinitely welcome to Jessica. Occasionally he remembered to offer her the coffee cup before he had even drunk from it, and he did not seem to forget her presence so often anymore. Once when they camped Jake had been gone a particularly long time. He returned with a hatful of blackberries in addition to the squirrel he had shot for their dinner and requested simply, "Could you make some more of that bread like you did the other night?"

Jessica was more than happy to comply, and nothing had ever pleased her more than Jake's grunt of satisfaction when he tasted it.

It would have been against nature for Jake not to snap at her occasionally, but he didn't lose his temper nearly as often as before. The only times he ever really grew short with her was when she asked about Daniel; then his face would cloud and his eyes grow stormy and he would answer in monosyllables if at all. That hurt Jessica, but not so much as it had previously done, when he had used every opportunity to tell her just how unsuitable she was for Daniel and Three Hills.

She discovered, to her surprise, that he was easy to talk to, and he didn't seem to mind when she asked him questions about the places he had been or the things he had seen. He didn't make fun of her when she talked somewhat dreamily about all the things she had previously reserved for private fantasies—the gracious ballrooms of New Orleans, the cities in the north where the buildings were sometimes over five stories high, a place called Paris, France where she had heard even the carriage wheels were painted gold.

Occasionally, to make the time pass more quickly, he would tell her stories, and those were the best times. Her favorite was the tale of a man trapped on a desert island, which he said came from a book called *Robinson Crusoe*. There was another about a shipwrecked family who built their house in a tree and another by a man called Mr. William Shakespeare in which everyone died in the end.

Jessica did not like that one, and when she told him so he laughed. She liked to hear him laugh, but he rarely did.

There were still uncertain moments. He would lapse into long silences, and occasionally she would turn and catch him gazing at her with such an intense look it made her heart skip a beat. He would turn away quickly and, as like as not, find an excuse to growl at her soon after. And one night, as she was braiding her hair before the campfire, she felt his shadow fall over her and the very light touch of his hand on her hair. He said, with a softness that sounded utterly alien in Jake's voice, "I'm sorry I had to cut your hair."

Jessica's hand went in surprise to the stubbly lock he touched, for in truth she had all but forgotten about the incident, and her fingers brushed his. There was the most peculiar look on his face, and for just that moment, as her fingers touched the rough warm texture of his, something in her quickened, then questioned. But then his face grew shuttered and he abruptly walked away. Jessica spent a long time sitting there, touching the place he had touched, thinking about him.

That night, as all others, he lay stiff and wakeful beside her, nothing but the heat of his body brushing hers. He never touched her again, even in his sleep.

Time moved on, days and nights blending into one another, and sometimes it was hard for both Jake and Jessica to remember that they were not the only two people in the world. For Jessica's part, she could no longer remember a time when Jake had not been an inextricable part of her life. It did not even occur to her to imagine the time when he would no longer be so.

They always stopped before sundown to make camp. Jake sat on a fallen log at the edge of the clearing, whittling a stick of cypress into a toothpick, watching Jessica prepare a stew for supper. If his thoughts were restless, his mood brooding, his bland expression hid the fact. Jake knew exactly how long they had been in the swamp: seven days and seven nights of Jessica.

In less time than he cared to think about she had gotten under his skin just as surely and uncomfortably as a cocklebur under a saddle. And he wasn't the only healthy, red-blooded male on the ranch. They would be sniffing around her like hounds with the scent of a bitch and it would be only a matter of time before she turned to one of them, for chastity was an unnatural state for a woman like her; anybody with half an eye to see could tell that.

The sun had rouged her skin and seemed to bleach her eyes to a clear, startlingly bright blue. The huge tangle of dark curls which sprang over her shoulders and across her back was incredible to look at. It made a man want to catch his hands in it, bury his face in it, to see it spread out on a pillow beneath him. In his old clothes, with her hair loose and her sunburned skin she looked like a gypsy, wild and unfettered, and it heated his blood just to think about taming her . . . until she turned with one of her shy smiles and he realized she was completely unaware of her own allure. That somehow made her even more provocative.

The worst of it was that it was not only her physical allure that worked on his senses—though she did have that in abundance. She had a way about her, quiet but determined, feminine yet capable, that worked itself into his head and wouldn't let go. She was absurdly grateful for the smallest kindness, but her eyes could flash a warning that would stop him dead in his tracks over a stupid thing like a cuss word.

He found himself spending too much time thinking of ways to please her, and when he caught himself at it he was irritated. Yet that didn't stop his pleasure when she smiled at him. She was a strange mixture of innocence and courage, of childlike wonder and too much of the bad side of life that made a man want to wrap his arms around her and protect her, to hold her and soothe her and love her the way a woman was meant to be loved....

Damn Daniel anyway. If he had to have a wife—a companion, a political asset or whatever it was he wanted—why couldn't he have picked some horse-faced old maid who wouldn't know what she was missing and wouldn't care anyway? Why did he have to pick a lush young beauty like Jessica who would be a constant temptation to every man who stepped in her path? Daniel was not stupid. Didn't he realize that a woman like Jessica could spell nothing but trouble?

Still, Daniel was a politician first; Jake had lived with him long enough to know that. Daniel would think in terms of assets and debits, and Jessica's loveliness would win many votes. To Daniel, that would be important.

But it was out of the question. He couldn't possibly take her back. Daniel would be miserable, as she would be. And Jake simply couldn't imagine living in the same house with her, watching her graceful movements, catching her fleeting smiles, watching her climb the stairs at night alone to her bed....

Jake stopped whittling. The solution to all their problems came to him with simple clarity. The amazing thing was that it had been there all along. It was the very first thing he had thought of, and it made more sense than ever now.

Jessica added a handful of peppers to the stew and smiled at him over her shoulder. His eyes followed the way her hand flicked back a strand of her hair as it fell over her breast. "It should probably simmer awhile," she said. "Are you very hungry?"

"I can wait." Jake concentrated on his whittling again.

Jessica straightened up, pressing both hands to the small of her back for a moment to stretch away the soreness. She was struck, as she had been quite often the past few days, by how different Jake was from his brother. Daniel was as open as sunshine and as gentle as a summer breeze, but there was something about Jake's brooding silences and thundercloud temper that made simply being around him interesting—exciting even, the way it felt just before the storm broke. Of course Jake lacked his brother's refinement and grace, but there was that rugged strength about him that made her feel safe. And she never felt awkward with him the way she sometimes had with Daniel, as though she would never be good enough for him, as though she would forever be too awestruck by him to ever really know him. With Jake she felt like an equal. She had told him her most intimate secrets and he had accepted them. It bothered her that she had never felt that free with Daniel.

Daniel was wonderful, of course. He was gentle and generous and breathtakingly handsome, but she could never remember noticing how strong his legs were, or the way the muscles of his arms moved against the fabric of his shirt . . . with a prickle of alarm, she realized it was difficult to remember what Daniel looked like at all.

And because that knowledge felt unsettlingly like a betrayal of some sort, she turned quickly back to stir the stew. Jake was different from Daniel, that was all. She liked Jake, but she loved Daniel. She truly did. And she would be more fortunate than she had ever thought possible to have both men beside her when she returned to Three Hills, Daniel as her adored husband and his brother as her friend.

With a wistful little smile she said, "Do you know the first thing I'm going to do when we get home? Take a bath. A real bath with hot water. And do you know, I've heard that in the fancy cities they have a kind of soap powder that makes bubbles when you put it in the water, and it smells like flowers. I can't imagine anything more heavenly. And they make something called toilet water that smells like roses when you put in on your skin. My, wouldn't it be wonderful to just stroll through some of those fancy shops smelling all those things, looking at the pretty bottles and ribbons and paper flowers?" She laughed self-consciously. "I used to think about that whenever Papa would stop in a town, but of course he'd never let me go outside."

Jake said carefully, "You can do more than just look, Jessica. You can have all those things."

Jessica cast a quick glance over her shoulder, coloring. "Oh, no, I didn't mean . . . Daniel has been far too generous with me already. I would never ask him for silly frills. No . . ." She smiled contentedly as she turned back to the stew. "All I ever want in my life is just to stay at Three Hills and be Daniel's wife."

Jake was watching her, his voice thoughtful when he said, "No, you want more. You may not realize it yet, but you do. And you deserve more."

Jessica paused, casting a questioning glance at him.

"I've been doing a lot of thinking," he said, "about the things you've told me, the kind of life you've had." His expression was very serious. "It's not right, Jessica, a pretty young girl like you . . . there's a whole world out there you've never seen, a dozen things you've never had or done. You could have them all now."

Jessica felt a renewed blush warm her cheeks and she bent over the fire again to hide it. She was touched by his concern, and more than a little flustered by the fact that he had called her pretty. He had never done that before. In a rather stifled voice she said, "I have everything I want."

"You don't want to go back to Daniel, you don't want to be tied down to some East Texas cattle ranch before you've even seen what's waiting for you out there." Jake struggled to keep the impatience out of his voice. "You could live in any city in the world—New York, New Orleans, even Paris, France. You could have pretty dresses and your own coach and a fine little house. You could go to one of those fancy schools and learn how to talk and dance and play with your fan the way females like to do. Damn it, Jessica, think about it."

There was no point in trying to restrain himself any longer, and he got to his feet, his voice intense. "I've got money, more than you'll ever need. I can put you on a train to any place you want to go, you can set yourself up in style, go to parties, find some nice young man who'll be a real husband to you."

Something inside Jessica froze and twisted painfully. She could not believe what she was hearing. With an explosive flash her mind went back to that night at Three Hills—oh, a lifetime ago—when she had been dancing in Jake's arms, his eyes as dark as hate above hers, and he had offered her money to leave and have the marriage annulled. After all they had been through together, all she had shared with him, he hadn't changed. She had trusted him with her fears, her daydreams, her shames—her *life*—but all he had been thinking, all this time, was how to renew his offer. *Nothing had changed.*

She couldn't move as an awful heaviness in her chest

made it hard to breathe. "I have a husband," she said very softly.

Impatiently, Jake whipped off his hat and ran his fingers through his hair. "Damn it, Daniel's not a husband and you know it. You're throwing your whole life away and it's better you know it now than later. Listen." He tried to make his tone more reasonable. "All you have to do is write Daniel a letter, explaining how you've changed your mind. He'll understand. The marriage will be annulled and I'll make sure you're provided for. It would be better for everyone, don't you understand that?"

All Jessica understood was that an enormous sense of betrayal and hurt seemed to be swallowing her from the inside out. She wanted to scream at him, *You're supposed to be my friend! I thought you understood, I trusted you*... Her fingers tightened on the wooden spoon and the effort ached all the way up into her shoulder. She said stiffly, "I love Daniel. I'm not going to leave him."

"Love! What the hell do you know about love? You're *grateful* to him, that's all. And there's got to be a hell of a lot more between a man and a woman than gratitude to make a marriage. You're not doing Daniel any service by going back to him, can't you see that? What do you think it's going to do to him, being with you, watching you day after day, knowing he can never give you what you need? And what about you? You're a woman, and you can't pretend it doesn't matter forever. With Daniel the way he is it won't be six months before you're sleeping with everything but the stud stallions and—"

Something inside Jessica snapped. She whirled, blind with rage and hurt. With an impetus of its own her arm swung around and she struck Jake hard on the side of the neck with the spoon.

Jake staggered back with a startled yelp of pain as hot stew splattered over his lower face and neck. With an instinct born of rage and self-defense his arm shot up to shove her away, contacting firmly with the center of her chest.

Jessica's eyes opened wide and she cried out as she struggled to keep her balance. Jake's heart lurched to his throat and then stopped beating entirely as he saw her stumble backward into the fire.

Chapter VIII

It all happened in less than a second. Jake launched himself at her, dragging her out of the fire and tumbling with her on the ground, his hands frantically slapping the little tongues of flame that licked at her legs and the edge of her shirt. She was sobbing beneath him, little helpless sounds that would have been screams had she had the breath. The odor of burned fabric filled his nostrils and horror roared through his head as he rolled over and over with her on the ground, trying to smother the flames.

"Jessica—my God—I'm sorry. I didn't mean—God, Jessica are you burned? Are you all right?"

At first Jessica had been too shocked to do anything but fight off what she assumed was his attack, pummeling him with her fists and crying out as he hit her. Then she had realized her clothes were on fire and she was incapable of anything but terrified, whimpering sobs as he rolled her over on the ground, killing the flames with the damp grass and his hands. Now he lay on top of her, his face white and wet with perspiration, his eyes dark with fear as she gasped and shuddered with the aftermath of the narrow escape. She couldn't form an answer for a long time.

"No-no," she finally managed in a hoarse whisper. "I'm n-not burned . . . I'm all right."

His eyes closed slowly as his muscles relaxed. He lowered his face to rest against her breasts and he breathed, "God, I'm sorry. I didn't mean to push you."

It was such an intense moment that Jessica didn't even think about the intimacy of their position. Her head was still pulsing and whirling with shock, her chest was aching with short, choppy breaths, and her limbs were shaking. It seemed the most natural thing in the world to lift her arms to his neck and hold onto him as he was holding her.

She could feel his breath, hot and heavy on her breasts, and the weight of his torso pressing her down. Her fingers slipped into the thick fall of silky hair at the back of his neck and dimly she was aware of the sensations: prickly hair on the backs of her knuckles, warm skin beneath her fingertips, Jake's heartbeat against her ribs and his head cradled against her breasts. It felt so right to be embraced by him, to be embracing him, that the horror of the moment that had just passed was all but forgotten. Wrapped together in relief and the weak aftermath of terror, there was safety, there was strength. There was wonder.

Slowly she became aware of other sensations, more acute and rather disturbing; confusing but strangely compelling. One of his legs was between hers as she lay sprawled on the ground, his hipbones were sharp against hers and his cheek was warm and abrasive through the thin material that covered her breast, making her nipples prickle and tingle strangely. Her heart began to beat faster when she thought how unseemly their position was, and when she realized that she wanted it to go on forever the surprise within her doubled the rate of her pulse.

Jake must have come to the same awareness in the same moment, for she felt his muscles tense and he pushed himself away without looking at her. He rolled over onto his back and lay on the ground beside her, still breathing unsteadily, and Jessica felt strangely bereft when he was gone. His hand was open loosely over his chest and she could see the slight movement of his fingers which registered the jerk of his heartbeat.

Jessica made herself sit up, though her muscles felt like water and her heart was as unsteady as his. She told herself it was from no more than the scare.

"What about you?" she managed, in a moment. "Are you all right?"

Then she noticed several small red blotches on his neck where the stew had splattered and her heart constricted. She hadn't meant to hurt him. She couldn't believe she had hit him. Her fingers went without volition to lightly touch the injuries, and when they did his eyes met hers. There was something there, a swift awareness, a gentle need, something that reminded her of the way she had felt a moment before, lying with her arms around him and wanting to hold him forever; it took her breath away.

Then he sat up, lowering his lashes as he said hoarsely, "Yes. I'm all right."

He got up and walked to the fire, kicking the few scattered logs back into the circle with a shower of sparks, bending to feed it a bit more tinder. Amazingly, the pot of stew had not tipped over.

Jessica sat where he had left her, drawing her knees to her chin as she had done when she was a girl, and there was silence for a long while. Then, not even trying to keep the pain from her voice, she asked quietly, "Why did you say that, Jake? Why do you always have to say such—ugly things to me to hurt me?"

He turned to her, the pull of helpless and conflicting emotions clear in his eyes. After what had just happened he couldn't bring himself to be short with her. She looked so small and childlike in that huddled position that he was not capable of yelling at her. But neither could he ignore her plaintive demand for an explanation, as much as he would have liked to.

"Damn it, Jessica, I didn't mean to hurt your feelings." There was unaccustomed gentleness behind the impatience in his voice. "I don't sit here all day trying to figure out ways to make you feel bad. I'm trying to *help* you, don't you see that?" And it was true, he argued with himself, for his opinion on that matter had not changed. It would be better for everyone—not just for Daniel and himself—if Jessica went somewhere else, anywhere but Three Hills.

Jessica's expression was calm, her eyes unflinching. "No, I don't see that. Why do you say Daniel isn't my real husband when you know he is? You were there when we were married, and even though it wasn't a preacher—"

Exasperation was beginning to play in Jake's face and tone, and he had to turn away, pretending to mind the fire. "You know that's not what I mean."

"Then what?" Her voice was also growing frustrated and defensive. "I *will* be a wife to him—a good wife. I may not be a fine lady like he's used to, but I'll learn. I'll mind his house and care for his needs and mother his children."

Jake turned slowly. "You'll *what?*"

The blatant astonishment in Jake's expression caught Jessica off guard. What had she said wrong? "I—I said I'll be a mother to his children. . . ."

Jake couldn't believe what he was hearing. He stared at her. Her enormous blue eyes that he had come to know so well were filled with nothing but what she considered the truth, her chin was lifted in a defiant assertion of her own abilities and rights, and if there was a little quaver in her voice it was only due to confusion at his reaction. He didn't understand. How could this be possible?

Very carefully, watching her with growing uncertainty, he asked, "Jessica . . . you can't mean . . . Didn't Daniel tell you?"

There was nothing in her face but increasing confusion. "Tell me what?"

It couldn't be. Daniel had assured him that she knew—or had he? Had he actually said he had explained matters to Jessica or had he merely evaded the question? All this time Jake had been wondering why a woman like Jessica could give up her youth and beauty for a man who could never offer her a real marriage and she hadn't even known!

He couldn't believe it. Daniel would never be so deceptive. He had told her, of course he had. Daniel wouldn't lie.

Jake's voice was tight though carefully even as he demanded, "Come on, Jessica, you know what I'm talking about. Didn't you and Daniel ever discuss—" He felt stupid, but he didn't know how else to put it. "Children?"

Her face clouded. She did not know what Jake was trying to say, but she knew it was important and unpleasant. And suddenly, for no clear reason, she was remembering the look on Daniel's face the one time she had broached the subject of children with him, an innocent comment much like the one she had just made to Jake. The shutter that had come over his eyes then was only a darker reflection of the dread she saw in Jake's eyes now.

She said, wondering why it was suddenly so difficult to

speak in a normal tone, "No, not exactly. It never seemed . . . we never had much chance."

Jake ran his fingers through his hair with a low oath that was unintelligible to Jessica, but its meaning was perfectly clear. He stared at her as though he were seeing her for the first time, as though she were a strange swamp creature that had crawled aground and bore both fascination and amazement for him.

He took a step toward her and then turned away. He couldn't believe this of Daniel. Why would he have lied? Why would he have deliberately pulled this desperate girl into a trap of a marriage without telling her the full price for his protection? It didn't make any sense. He couldn't believe his brother would do such a thing.

Perhaps Daniel had been so dazzled by her beauty, so filled with pity for her circumstances, that he had acted on impulse, thinking to explain the whole to her later. Perhaps he had even been so enchanted by her and so overwhelmed by her gratitude that he thought it didn't matter. But it *did* matter. Anyone could see that. This was not something that one could just ignore and hope it would go away. Surely Daniel must have realized that.

Jake didn't know what Daniel had been thinking and didn't understand it at all. But even through his confused and cautious disillusionment over his brother's behavior he did see one thing very clearly: It was imperative that Jessica know the truth, now more than ever.

He said, simply and cleanly, "Daniel can't have any children, Jessica. Ever."

She stared at him. The words pounded in her head, echoing hollowly in the pit of her stomach. The world seemed to go cold. It couldn't be true, she thought. Daniel would have told her if it were true. Of course they would have children. It was part of being married. It was an integral part of the glorious future she had planned. Jake was teasing her, cruelly. It was all some obscene joke. It couldn't be true.

Her voice sounded hoarse as she accused, "You're lying."

"Damn it, why would I lie?" His face was grim. "I'm only saying what I thought you knew—what Daniel should have told you."

Looking at him, she knew he wasn't lying. Why, indeed, would he? Absorbing it, she felt stunned, betrayed, deeply hurt—but numb. "But he didn't," she said dully.

She saw a flash of impatience in Jake's eyes and the lines around his mouth tighten. "He told me you knew. I never thought I'd see the day when I'd be ashamed of my own brother, but there's no excuse for this. He *lied*—to me and you. He had no right to do that."

Quickly, instinctively, Jessica rose to Daniel's defense. She just couldn't believe he had meant to hurt her or deceive her. Bravely denying her own pain, deliberately turning her back on her shattered illusions, she asserted, "Many people are never blessed with children. It's tragic, but it doesn't mean that their lives cannot be just as full in other ways—"

"Damn it, Jessica, that's just the point! Your life *won't* be full in other ways!" Jessica could not fathom the frustration that churned in his eyes, and she stared at him blankly. "It's not just children," Jake said deliberately, taking a short step toward her. "It's *everything*."

Jessica only looked at him, plainly uncomprehending.

Jake did not know how much clearer he could make it. He couldn't believe that anyone could be so obtuse. And he couldn't stand looking into her wide, mildly questioning eyes another moment. He turned and began to search the ground for his hat.

His back was to her, and his voice was as calm as he could possibly make it when he said, "Daniel was injured in the war. He was lucky he didn't die . . . hell, I guess for the first year or so he must have thought it would've been better if he had." He found his hat and bent to retrieve it, smoothing back his hair with a tense motion before arranging it on his head. Then he had to turn and face her. "It's not just children," he told her painfully. "Daniel can't make love to a woman. At all."

Jessica did not take the time to try to analyze the meaning of Jake's words; she was far too anxious and confused by the expression on his face, the look in his eyes. There was pain mixed with reluctance in them, something that looked like anger but wasn't quite . . . and her voice was very small as she asserted, "That's not true. Daniel is very affectionate . . ." Dimly she remembered Daniel's brotherly kisses upon her cheek, his affectionate squeeze of her hand or pat upon the head, and irrationally, almost treacherously, recalled how cool his lips had been, how dry his hand. But he cared for her, he was affectionate.

Jake burst out in a single impatient rush, "Damn it, I'm not talking about hugging and kissing! I'm talking about what goes on between a man and a woman in bed, in the dark."

She said nothing, just continued to look at him with a steady gaze, only a hint of denial beginning to lace through the question in her eyes. And something incredible began to occur to Jake.

He said lowly, staring at her, "For God's sake, Jessica, haven't you ever mated with a man?"

As though a valve inside her had suddenly burst, understanding rushed through her. Heat scorched her cheeks and shock tingled her fingertips. Of course she knew what happened between men and women; her father had lectured her on the evils of carnal pleasure in extensive, mortifying detail. But to hear Jake refer to it now. . . .

She burned beneath Jake's sharp, disbelieving gaze, writhing with the import of his words. She couldn't look at him, and it was all she could do to stammer, "No—no, of course not. I-I wouldn't . . ."

Jake did not know why he was surprised; perhaps on the deepest level he was not surprised at all. She was an innocent in every sense. He must have known that from the first moment he had met her but had been too set in his ways to admit it to himself. God only knew how she had remained that way this long with the kind of life she had led, but it was unmistakably true. And what could he say to her now?

She tried to prevent him from saying anything. Miserable with confusion and shame that a man like Jake should ever speak to her of such an intimate matter, she straightened her legs, clasped her hands in her lap and stared at them fixedly. Her voice was barely a murmur through the thickness of her embarrassment. "It—doesn't matter. Daniel—"

"It *does* matter." He spoke swiftly, harshly, and without thinking at all. "To Daniel as well as to you." He took an agitated stride toward her, his hands unconsciously clenched inside his vest pockets. "It's the most important part of men and women; it's the only reason we're made differently. How can you say it doesn't matter when you don't even know what you're talking about?"

Jake knew he should drop the subject; he knew he was on dangerous ground. Later he would look back and would never believe he had said these things to a woman, would never understand what propelled him forward. But he was in too deep to back out now, so he got down on his haunches beside her and clasped her scorched face in his fingers to make her look at him. The misery he saw there softened his voice, gentled his touch, and he took a breath.

"Jessica," he said, "it's not right. It's not natural." He searched for words and cursed himself for his own inadequacy, fighting a sudden surge of resentment against the brother he had always idolized. Why wasn't it Daniel saying these things to her, Daniel who had the education and the smooth tongue and the pretty phrases? All Jake knew was blunt speech and ungilded truths. He had never felt so clumsy or awkward in his life. And she kept looking at him, waiting.

"There's a part of you," he began, struggling, "that's made to fit with a man. It's what makes you a woman . . . The stirrings will come on you in the long dark hours of the night and there'll be no one to fill them for you, no one for you to turn to, and you'll be left feeling empty, and bad . . . Because when a woman joins with a man, it's more than just a way to make babies, or at least it should be—it's being what you were fashioned to be, and there's pleasure in it, and I can't even explain it to you because I don't know the half of it, but it's something you'll never know."

God, he was making a mess of it. Why was he doing this? She should have had a mother, some female to tell her these things. But clearly she had not. The scarlet embarrassment that burned his fingers was fading to blotches and her eyes were no longer as reluctant as they were earnest, curious but confused, trying to understand. And what could Jake tell her about love, about loving? He knew whores and eager widows and the girls on the border towns who knew no shame, and he understood a woman's pleasure. He knew nothing about how to make an innocent like Jessica understand that with love there should be more.

She saw the frustration in his eyes and she started to drop her own, but his fingers tightened slightly. "And what about Daniel?" he demanded, for this he did know. "Have you thought what it will be like for him, knowing you, being with you, seeing you every day, and never being able to . . . He can still *want* you Jessica. And when a man wants a woman it's like—like a fever in the blood, a fire that burns day and night, and all he can think about is the way your skin feels, and the way you taste and smell, and he wants to make love to you because giving pleasure gives pleasure. . . ."

His voice had thickened, and without being aware of it his grip had loosened on her chin and his fingers spread lightly over the warm and silky texture of her cheek, stroking it. There was no more fear in her eyes, just an expectancy and a gentle anticipation that worked its way into his own chest and tightened there.

"Making love is the most beautiful thing a man and a woman can do together, Jessica," he said hoarsely. Unable to stop the action, his eyes moved toward her lips. Soft and rosy, he knew they would taste like sunshine. "A man was meant to be inside a woman, and a woman was meant to take a part of him. It's God's way. To want a woman and know you can never have her . . . there can be no worse torture for a man."

One fingertip wandered to the corner of her lips and he felt the slight tremor there. Abruptly he realized that he had not been talking about Daniel's feelings at all. He had been talking about his own.

His throat convulsed and he lowered his eyes. He got to his feet stiffly and awkwardly, and neither one of them spoke for a long time.

Then Jake mumbled thickly, "I'll serve up supper."

He turned away and busied himself with the movements of what had become their daily life, but Jessica did not follow him. She sat there for a long time, staring at her hands, not knowing what to say. Not even knowing what to think.

Little was said between them the next day. The afternoon was thick with humidity, still and heavy. It was as though the mood between the swamp's two lone occupants had communicated itself to the very environment around them; life itself was poised in expectancy, like a held breath or a half-formed question. Jessica felt as though she were waiting for something to happen—anything—that would break the stifled tension which radiated between them as thickly as the lazy waves of heat or the dense clouds of insects.

Though she tried to push it out of her mind, fragments of Jake's conversation with her the previous night kept returning to haunt her, and she worried them as a dog might a bone, anxiously, deliberately, unable to let go. There was so much she didn't understand, so much she could never ask.

Jake had said that what she felt for Daniel was not love, only gratitude. Though her instinct was to push that idea away, to deny it immediately with all her heart, she found that she could not quite make herself do it. How was she to know? How was she to know what she felt for Daniel? Their courtship—if it could be called such—had been so hasty, so determined on Daniel's part and so breathless on hers. Of course she was grateful to him. She had every reason to be grateful to him. But was that the same thing as love?

She cast a covert glance at Jake, his strong body towering above her, muscles straining as he dug the pole into the muddy water, pushing toward shore and an early camp. His face was taut, his profile distinct, and when she thought he might look at her she quickly avoided his eyes, her pulse speeding a little. Daniel had never made her nervous like this for no reason. Daniel had never been able to pierce her heart with one brooding glance, and as hard as she tried, she could not remember what color Daniel's eyes were.

A vague sort of despair seized her as confusion ebbed and flowed. Jake could not be right. She had not made a mistake. She *did* love Daniel, and she would be a good wife to him. Daniel was all she had; it had to be right between them. She wondered what Jake had meant about the stirrings that would come upon her. Could it possibly have anything to do with the way she felt sometimes lying beside him under the blanket, listening to his breathing, feeling his heat, when her palms went clammy and her heart beat faster just because he was close? Merely thinking about it made her feel embarrassed, and quivery inside, and she deliberately did not look at Jake again because she knew if she did he would read what she was thinking and she did not want him to do that. None of it made any sense anyway.

She wished Jake would talk to her, though. Easily and freely, like he used to do. She wished she could think of something to say to him. She felt that if something didn't happen soon to relieve this awful tension between them she would surely scream.

Then something did happen.

Jake was pushing close to the bank where the intertwining branches of willows and gum made a low-hanging green canopy. When he lifted the pole out of the water it knocked against one of the branches and something thin and ropey and squirming dislodged itself and fell with a plop into Jessica's lap.

She screamed, jumping to her feet and sending the snake tumbling to the floor of the boat, where it lay writhing furiously in confusion. Outraged squirrels and birds chattered and chirped overhead as she screamed, "Get it out! Get it away from me!"

Jake gave a startled hoot of laughter, not in the least concerned. "It's just a green water snake. It won't bite you! Stop acting like a fool."

But to Jessica this was her worst nightmare come true and she could not stop gasping, could not stop the screams that kept building in her throat, could not forget the way that hideous thing had felt when it landed on her... "Get it *away!*"

Then, with a swishing sideways motion, the reptile started to propel itself toward her, and she let out another cry, backing as far away as possible until even that wasn't far enough and she put one foot on the edge of the boat, prepared to jump out if necessary.

"Stop that infernal racket! I told you it's harmless." Jake bent and grabbed the writhing creature behind the head, and when he lifted it he took a step toward her. "Get down from there, you brainless female, before you—"

Jessica did not notice that his amusement had changed to alarm, nor that there was command, not teasing in his voice. She only saw him coming toward her with that hideous squirming snake in his hand and she scrambled backwards with a panicked wail.

She balanced precariously on the edge for a split second; Jake flung the snake away just as he lunged to catch her. She flailed and grabbed at his arm, but it was too late. All she succeeded in doing was unbalancing him as well and both of them pitched forward into four feet of slimy, fetid water.

Jessica came up gasping and sputtering, green strands of duckweed clinging to her hair and dripping down her face, the taste of filth in her mouth. Jake was swearing vociferously behind her. "You harebrained little idiot! Look what you've done! Goddamn it all, I'm soaked to the skin. Why the hell didn't you tip over the boat while you were at it? Then we'd be in a *fine* mess!"

"It wasn't my fault! You scared me—"

"Even my goddamn gun is wet! How're we supposed to get anything for supper now, just answer me that!"

Their voices were raging at full bore amidst the thrashing and sucking sounds of water and mud, their eyes flashing as at last they had excuse to give vent to the strain that had been building between them like a thunderstorm. Jessica floundered to the shore, wringing out the hem of her shirt in disgust as she accused heatedly, "You were laughing! I *told* you to get that thing away but you—"

"I should have let it bite you!" Furiously, Jake waded the few feet to catch the boat which, due to its heavy-bottomed shape, had mercifully not tipped over during the foray. With a hissing, grunting tug, he began to drag it toward shore. "Of all the stupid, female things to do."

Jessica clambered onto the bank, gooey mud sucking at every step. "It serves you right, getting wet! If you hadn't—"

Her words locked in her throat and her heart stopped as the air was split by a sudden, horrible sound behind her. It was the mind-rending, blood-chilling sound of Jake's scream.

Chapter IX

It echoed forever, that horrendous, hoarse, terrifying wail of a man in agony. Jessica felt the blood drain from her face, felt her fingers grow numb. Everything seemed to be in slow motion as she made herself turn and stumbled toward him.

"Jake—what—oh, dear God!"

Even her voice did not seem to be her own and every step she took into the greedy mud and tangled weeds seemed to push him farther away. He had collapsed at the edge of the shore, half in and half out of the water. His face was a ghastly white and torn with pain, his arm stretched forward toward the leg that was still underwater.

"*Son of a bitch,*" he gasped, and it was a twisted, involuntary sound that barely formed words. "Jesus Christ, something—"

"Jake, what?" She finally reached him, falling beside him on her hands and knees. Panic and horror clamored inside her chest in place of prayer and she grabbed hold of his arm, wanting to shake him, wanting to demand something from him, wanting to save him from whatever it was that was threatening him. *"What?"*

"My leg! Something—Jesus Christ, it's a trap!" Each word was a grunt, a struggle for breath, and his face went a shade paler as he bent down, reaching with both hands for the mechanism that had fastened around his ankle. The muscles of his shoulders strained and shook as he tried to free himself and Jessica noticed that the water was beginning to stain a murky red. He was bleeding.

Jake sat back, his head falling against the bank, breathing hard. "God, it hurts . . ." His lips tightened and his eyes squeezed shut.

The pain that twisted itself around Jessica's chest was like a huge fist, squeezing at her heart. She reached beneath the surface of the water until she contacted Jake's leg, following the shape down until she encountered the vicious steel jaws around Jake's ankle. Her movements stirred up the bloody water but nothing else. Helpless panic rose as she tried to open the sides of the trap and succeeded in doing nothing but dragging a weak, choked sound from Jake.

And then, from the distant shore, she heard the heavy plopping sound of something entering the water. And another.

She stared at the swirling pattern of blood that was beginning to float on the current. Her terror-stricken eyes scanned the water for the rippling motions of approaching carnivores. There was slithering in the underbrush, another splash in the swamp, and everything within her was galvanized into strength, certainty and determination.

"Jake, you've got to try to stand up." Her voice was hoarse and raw and as she spoke she scrambled up the bank behind him. "Get out of the water." She slipped her arms beneath his, locking her elbows beneath his armpits as she dragged him backwards. "Hurry. *Try.*"

If Jake had noticed the sounds he was too dazed by pain to understand their significance. But something in her voice must have communicated itself to him because he stiffened his free leg and tried to stand, and with more physical strength than Jessica ever dreamed she possessed she managed to drag him clear of the water. They both realized at that moment that safety was short-lived. The dark eyes and weathered snouts that approached at such a sluggish, inexorable rate would follow the scent of blood onto the bank in a matter of moments.

With a little cry of desperation, Jessica fastened her hands on either side of the slimy jaws that held Jake's ankle, pushing hard to separate them. It was a wicked, deadly looking thing, with razor sharp teeth that had penetrated Jake's boot and fastened themselves into his muscles. Its hold was unforgiving. Jessica strained and gasped, sweat of panic and exertion rolled down her face, but the trap would not give.

Jake heaved himself forward and added his strength to hers, but even with their combined effort they only succeeded in budging the jaw enough to make Jake cry out and release his hold. No, Jessica thought, terror whirling through her mind. It couldn't be. There had to be a way out. How did the trappers gather their prey if the combined strength of two people could not release the trap? The swishing, gliding motions of the powerful predators drew ever closer and dread rose like a scream in Jessica's throat.

Then she saw it.

Jake had gathered himself to try again, his pain ravaged eyes racing across the water, but Jessica brushed his hands away. "No!" Beneath his foot was a flat, round lever attached to a spring lock mechanism. She worked her hands inside the trap, bracing the heels of both palms against the lever, and pushed down hard. The trap sprang open with a snap.

Jake drew a ragged breath and grasped his leg with both hands, lifting his foot carefully, pain etched in every breath. As soon as he was clear, Jessica released the spring, and the sound the jaws made as they slammed shut twisted in her stomach.

But there was no time to waste on relief or congratulations. Jessica scrambled to her feet as Jake sank back, ashen-faced and gasping, trying to gather his strength. The boat had drifted a few feet away and without hesitation Jessica slid down the bank toward it.

"Jessica, don't!" Jake cried hoarsely, sitting up. "Don't go in the water!"

But she was already hip deep and she didn't dare look around, didn't dare listen, didn't dare think what might even now be charging toward her. She caught hold of the pirogue with both hands and dragged it backwards, where Jake was waiting at the shore. He fell inside, grabbing Jessica beneath the arms and pulling her over the side just as something huge and hard bumped the boat, almost sending them both overboard again.

Jake's face was gaunt with effort, the pain darkening his eyes as he used the pole to pull himself to a standing position. Bracing himself, he swung the pole hard at the water. It cracked viciously against something and the water thrashed. He took advantage of the turmoil to push the pole against the bank and shove into the slow current.

Jake leaned heavily on the pole, his breath ragged and strained, gathering his strength. Jessica remained where she had fallen at his feet, still shaking with sweeping currents of shock that made her teeth chatter and her vision blur. Over, she thought, and held on to the word. Over. They were alive. Alive. It was over.

"Jake, sit down." Her voice was hoarse and not quite steady. "Take off your boot. Let me look at your foot."

"No." She saw him grit his teeth and his color terrified her as he swung the pole into the water once again and pushed forward. "It's all right."

It was not all right. The leather was neatly torn and even now beginning to stain with blood. Her voice was harsh as she commanded, "Don't be a fool. You have to take off your boot so we can tend to your cuts. Sit down, Jake, for pity's sake!"

"If I take off my boot," he returned shortly, "my leg will swell and I'll never get it on again." He took a breath, and with the motion she could see him forcefully infusing his muscles with strength, pushing the pain away as fiercely and determinedly as he pushed at the muddy bottom of the swamp. But his voice was a bit more controlled as he added, "It's not broken. Just bruised and bleeding like hell. The best thing I can do is try to use it if I can. It'll be all right. We've got to keep moving."

Jessica cast an uneasy glance at the shapes converging behind them and could not argue with that logic. She looked at Jake and wanted to believe he was all right, but conviction fell short when she saw his face. There was agony in his every movement, though he staunchly tried to subdue it. His skin was ashen and as wet as though the dunking had occurred only moments before. He could barely put any weight at all on his injured leg, and every time he pushed against the pole he almost fell.

Jessica opened her mouth to plead with him again but knew it would do no good. He was beyond hearing her and his stubbornness would only intensify with her protests. A few more yards, Jessica thought. A few more yards just to satisfy him and she would make him stop and make camp. She would make him take off his boot, too.

Jake lifted the pole a dozen times, perhaps two. Jessica kept her eyes behind them, watching for encroaching danger, but there was nothing but the sounds of his harsh breathing with each push. She released a cautious breath. It was all right. When she glanced at Jake, he did not seem as unsteady as before, and if his face was grim, it was with concentration. He was going to be all right. They were going to be all right.

And then Jake said, very steadily, "Jessica, I need you to do me a favor."

Her eyes flew to him, and his expression was intent, as though focusing on some distant object beyond her view. His lips were the color of ashes and his knuckles, as they gripped the wooden pole, were bone white. He said, "Take the pole. Keep us moving as long as you can. I don't think I can—"

She was on her feet, grabbing the pole in one hand and trying to support him with the other arm as he sagged heavily to the floor. She knelt beside him, a dry sob of fear and concern rising to her throat, but he protested dizzily, "All right." He tried to wave her away. His breath made an unnaturally harsh sound as it struggled through his lungs. "Just—hurts like hell. Need to rest a minute."

Oh, God, oh Jake, please . . . But her cries were stifled deep inside as she cradled his head and his eyes drifted closed. Biting fiercely into the underside of her lip to force herself to remain calm, she moved Jake's head to rest more comfortably on the saddle.

He grabbed her arm and his eyes opened. "Keep moving." His voice was very hoarse. "I've got the smell of blood all over me and we can't—stop. It's easy. Just push the pole into the mud and lean forward. You can do it."

"I know I can." How strong and confident her voice sounded! She was breaking apart inside. It was getting dark and she did not know what to do for him. The alligators and snakes were everywhere, there were bears and cougars in the woods along the banks and what would happen to him if he didn't get treatment for his wounds? "Don't worry."

He nodded, swallowed hard, and closed his eyes.

Jessica got to her feet. She could do it. She knew she could. Jake was depending on her. She dropped the pole into the water, found a hold, and pushed. The boat moved crookedly. She tried again, putting all her strength behind it. She made a bit more progress that time, but the boat veered sharply toward the shore. Quickly she swung around to the other side to correct the movement.

Perspiration beaded on her neck and rolled sluggishly down her body beneath her already wet clothes. But it was fear, not exertion, that pounded in her chest and dampened her brow. How long could she keep this up? What would happen if she stopped? Jake—how bad was his injury? She knew about gangrene, about pustulating fevers that could overtake a person and kill in a matter of days . . . Oh dear God, she couldn't let that happen to Jake. He had to have help. She had to do *something*.

And then it occurred to her. A trap. Someone had to have set that trap. It had not mystically appeared from nowhere. *Someone had put it there*. They were not alone in this place. If there were traps there was a trapper nearby, and if there was a trapper there was the possibility of help. The first and faintest flicker of hope dawned and she turned to Jake, her lips parted for a promise, but his eyes were closed. She said nothing.

She would keep moving, but she would not move far. There was shelter near, another human, help. She knew it. All she had to do was find it.

She drew the pole out of the water and thrust it down again. Perspiration dripped into her eyes and stung like tears. She whispered, " 'Yea, though I walk through the valley of the shadow of death, I shall fear no evil: for thou art with me; thy rod and thy staff they comfort me . . .' "

Jake fought his way in and out of reason through lapping tongues of fiery pain that seemed to consume not just his leg, but his whole body. His muscles strained to fight it and he gritted his teeth against it, but it was useless. He could hear Jessica's voice, but not her words. He tried to focus on her shape through a hazy cloud, but that too began to slip from him. Desperation was a thin wire inside him that only fueled the pain, and his last conscious thought before the fog overtook him was, *Don't let me die now. I can't die now. If I die she'll be all alone. . . .*

At dusk she saw it. Jessica did not know how long she had been propelling the boat, back and forth, back and forth, never going more than three hundred yards in any direction away from the site of the original trap. On each pass her eyes scanned the shoreline, peering through the trees, and on each pass she was convinced she had missed something. She was certain there had to be a sign somewhere, so she would turn and begin again. She could no longer feel the magnificent ache of her shoulders, the strain in her leg muscles. Breathing was a harsh, grating effort that scraped at her lungs and tore at her sides, and every time she lifted the pole she thought she could not possibly do so again.

The world had taken on an unreal quality of grainy

twilight, fatigue-blurred vision, and movement for its own sake. She must have passed the small hut several times without seeing it, and when she did she could not believe it.

The hut looked like part of the tangled forest that surrounded it. Cypress pilings were driven into the bank perhaps fifty feet from shore, looking like nothing more than tree trunks. But upon them, rising into the foliage and almost invisible in the midst of the leaves, was built a haphazard structure of cedar shingles covered with a palmetto leaf roof. Immediately there flashed into her mind a recollection of Jake's story about the shipwrecked family who had built their house in the trees, and with a choked cry of triumph, Jessica began to pole toward it. Shelter. Habitation. Safety.

She stumbled into the water, heedless now of whatever might be lurking to attack. Grunting and straining, slipping more than once, she managed to pull the pirogue forward until the bow rested securely on shore.

"Jake." She shook his arm gently, and then more firmly. "Jake, please, you've got to try to get up."

She cast an anxious glance over her shoulder, a wet rope of her hair slapping against her face as she did so. The little shack was dark and for all appearances deserted, and she did not know how she was going to get Jake up the steep, ladderlike steps that led inside. "Jake." She tightened her hand on his arm. "Please."

His eyes opened, but they seemed very dull. She wasn't at all certain he even heard her. "We've got to go now." She kept her voice forceful and calm, and she grasped both his arms to pull him to a sitting position. After a moment he seemed to gather himself and began to help her. He was breathing heavily.

"Why did we stop?" he demanded hoarsely. "I told you—"

"It's all right. I've found shelter. But you're going to have to try to walk."

He looked at her as though she had lost her mind, but Jessica did not have the energy to argue with him. "Come on," she said, and pushed the pole into his hand. "Use this to steady yourself. You can do it, I know you can."

It took many tries before Jake, with her help, pulled himself out of the boat, and then he stood there, leaning heavily on the pole, sweating profusely and trying to regain his strength. Jessica had the foresight to gather his saddlebags, flinging them around her neck like a harness, and she slipped her arm tightly around Jake's waist, urging gently, "It's not far. You can make it."

The short distance between the shoreline and the cabin seemed to stretch forever. Several times Jake sagged and almost fell, and Jessica felt every muscle in her back strain as she struggled to support him. Even in the rapidly failing light she could see his white skin, the grimness in his eyes. He wasn't going to make it, she thought in despair. And if he fainted before she could get him inside there wouldn't be anything she could do; she would never get him up those steps alone.

But she had underestimated Jake's strength of will, which fought off pain and dizziness with the same fierce determination with which he had fought off snakes and alligators since the beginning of their journey. He managed the torturous climb up the stairs on his hands and knees, each movement sending glassy shards of pain and whirling dizziness through him. Jessica, supporting and encouraging him from behind, was certain that in the very next moment he would topple backwards, and fear and anxiety grew within her until she thought she would scream. "Only a little further," she whispered. "Almost there. . . ."

The little shack was prefaced by a sagging covered porch. The door swung open easily when Jessica pushed against it. Jake was leaning on her heavily now, so that she was dragging more than guiding him inside. Her eyes adjusted rapidly to the dark interior and she made out its sparse furnishings: a table, a straight-backed chair, a stove and a rope bed in the far corner. With the very last of her strength she guided Jake to the bed, where he collapsed heavily. His eyes closed and his breathing was labored.

Jessica bent over him for a moment, bracing her arms against the cypress frame and trying to catch her breath. When she straightened every muscle in her body screamed protest, but she barely noticed. She had to do something for Jake.

She found a lantern on the table and matches in Jake's saddlebag. She turned the flame up and looked around for what assistance she could find in the hut.

It was a spartan little place, and smelled damp and gamey. There was a tin stove, a low shelf containing a few dried foodstuffs and some pots for cooking, and little else. Traps of all sizes and descriptions hung from nails on the walls, and Jessica couldn't prevent a shudder when she saw them. There was a dusty bearskin rug on the floor before the stove, and on the table was a clutter of sharp, evil looking knives. Jessica picked up the largest of these, and with it, and the lantern, she went over to Jake.

She set the lantern on the floor and knelt beside him, looking at him for a moment. His face was twisted in pain even on the border of unconsciousness, his wet hair sticking to his forehead beneath his hat. When she lifted her hand to remove his hat he did not move, and when she smoothed away his hair his skin felt too warm. She whispered, "I'm sorry, Jake." Then she gritted her teeth and dug the knife into the soft leather of his boot, sawing downward.

The swelling of his leg had constricted against the tight fit of his boot enough to inhibit circulation and stop the bleeding, and there was truly no other way Jessica could have gotten the boot off except by cutting it. He groaned when she peeled off the leather that encased his leg and pried his blood encrusted foot from the heel. She lifted the lantern to examine the damage.

The lower part of his leg, from mid-calf to the foot, was at least double its normal size, darkened an ugly blue. A neat series of deep gashes were beginning to ooze fresh blood, and it was impossible to tell from the dried blood that smeared his leg and foot whether poisoning might have already set in. Swiftly she left him and returned in a moment with his canteen and his flask of whiskey.

Jake made no sound or movement as she cleaned the wound as gently as she could with water, but when she poured the stinging whiskey into the wounds he gasped loudly, pain bringing him back to consciousness. "What the hell!"

"Whiskey will drive out the poison," she replied, and he bit back a cry as she poured more on the wound.

"Give me that." His voice was tight and weak as he stretched his arm toward her.

Jessica hesitated, and then delivered the flask into his hand. Jake levered himself onto one elbow, took a long swallow, and collapsed again, gasping. "Goddamn, woman, what're you trying to do, kill me?"

Jessica's spirits soared with relief because it was the first full sentence he had uttered in hours. Retrieving the flask from him she said, "This is the only Christian thing your whiskey has ever been used for."

"What did you do with my boot?"

"Cut it," she replied calmly, and the stream of profanity that followed filled her with a brief and satisfying certainty that he was regaining his strength.

But the burst of energy was short-lived and possibly induced by nothing more than the whiskey, for he collapsed in the middle of an imprecation, exhausted and short of breath. Jessica left him in search of something to use for bandages.

"What is this place?" he asked weakly after a moment.

"A trapper's hut, I think."

"Any sign of life?"

Jessica shook her head. "No, but I'm sure the man who lives here will be back eventually. We can rest here until he comes."

Jake was silent, gathering his strength. "How did you find it?"

Jessica discovered some scraps of cloth that weren't too filthy and returned to him. "I knew it had to be here somewhere. There couldn't have been a trap unless there was a trapper."

As she knelt beside him again she thought she saw a flicker of admiration in his pain hazed eyes. His lips twitched with what might have been an effort to smile. But immediately his lips tightened and his eyes squeezed closed as she took his foot gently in her hand. "More . . . whiskey," he grated after a moment, and her own face was torn with his pain as she shook her head.

"I can't, Jake. I need it to soak the bandages."

"Christ! My leg's on fire!"

She wrapped one whiskey-soaked cloth around his ankle and with his stifled cry she had to bite down hard on her lip, forcing her hands to do the things that were causing him such agony. His fingers dug into the mattress and she could feel him straining against her, but he did not utter another sound.

"There's a little left," she whispered, and her hand shook as she brought the flask to his lips. He was too weak to sit up, so she edged her knees beneath his shoulders, supporting his head with one arm while helping him hold the flask with the other. There was only a swallow or two, but Jake was grateful even for that. He was glad he had forgotten about the flask for most of their journey, for there would have been nothing left when he needed it most.

He let his head fall back heavily and she cradled it in her lap, her fingers making soothing motions through his damp tangled hair. His senses were spinning and the throbbing pain that gripped his entire body was as steady as his heartbeat. He felt as though the whiskey had gone straight to his head, although he knew the few drops he had taken could not be responsible for the way he was feeling.

There was a cluster of spiderwebs on the roughly hewn wall next to him; that he could see very clearly. But the glow of the lantern diffused the rest of the room—even Jessica's face—to a yellow-white blur. He could feel the gentle stroking motions of her fingers in his hair and the softness of her legs beneath his head, but not her warmth. He fought against the pain and struggled to maintain consciousness, and fighting made him weak until at last his body, as well as his mind, seemed to be drifting in a hazy vortex of pain that was so familiar he hardly hated it anymore; he accepted it like a reluctant friend.

"Ah, Jessica," he mumbled thickly after a long time, "how the hell did we end up in a place like this?"

Jessica started to answer him, and then she realized that the question was rhetorical. He was fading into delirium, and that, at the moment, was probably the best thing for him.

Jake closed his eyes, tired of fending off the inevitable, but rest was not so easy to find. The words kept coming and he did not know from where; he was merely possessed by the need to speak and it didn't matter why. "I was always bent for hell," he murmured matter-of-factly, "even as a boy. Daniel was the good one, like our mother. I took after Pa. He was just a crusty old rancher she could never civilize, try as she might . . . I never knew my mother. She died when I was born. But I felt like I did. She was everywhere. No one ever forgot her. She brought culture to Texas. She made Pa build her a fine house and planted flowers and put shoes on the servants and brought a piano. She was a legend. I wish I had known her. Who knows? I might have turned out different if I had."

She thought he smiled, but it was too weak a sign to be encouraging. She bent low over him, placing her hand quietly against his hot cheek. The fever was building swiftly under swamp conditions, as she had feared it would. "Hush," she said softly. "You should try to rest."

He looked at her intently. "Do you wish I was different, Jessica?"

Her heart speeded just a fraction, for his eyes looked so earnest, so anxious, it was hard to remember it was just the fever talking. "I like you fine the way you are," she soothed. "Please try to rest."

He frowned a little, as though against pain, or slipping memory. He knew he should be quiet; he didn't know what was pounding at his brain this way, making him want to talk to her, telling her things he had never told anyone, things no one had a right to know. But the words kept coming, like restless energy.

"Sometimes I wish I was different. More like Daniel. Most of my life I've wished I was like Daniel . . . but the harder I tried, seems like, the worse I got at it." His speech was interrupted by a long shuddering breath, and he shivered a little. Jessica felt the wetness of his clothes against her knees and knew she should build a fire to keep him warm. She tried to slip away, but he groped for her hand, holding it to his face. "Don't leave," he murmured. "It feels good when you touch me."

Jessica's heart twisted a little for his helplessness, and she stayed where she was, stroking his face, letting him talk.

"He always took care of me. After my mother died, Pa went into a decline, I guess, and there never was any light in his eyes as long as I knew him . . . They say I was raised wild, but I wasn't. Daniel always took care of me, tried to show me the right things to do, tried to make me into the kind of man my mother would have wanted . . . But it wasn't any good. I just never fit. And when Daniel went to war, I was so mad because I was too young and they wouldn't let me go instead. But it should have been me . . . I was the fighter, not Daniel, and it should've been me that was shot, not him . . ." His eyes suddenly lifted to hers, bright with fever and a ferocity that superseded physical pain. He demanded intensely, "You see that, don't you Jessica? Everybody saw that. It should have been me because Daniel had so much to give . . ." Again he shivered. "And I—I was good for nothing but trouble. I wish it had been me."

Her voice was soft but her eyes wide with alarm as she bent near him. "Don't say that! You don't mean it. It's wrong to question the ways of God."

His eyes drifted closed as he mumbled, "Then you would have been happy, Daniel would have been happy. God was wrong." A shudder shook the length of his body and his face tightened with pain. "I'm so cold..."

Jessica got up then, moving his head to rest against the mattress, and though his hand tightened on hers briefly it soon fell away with another onslaught of shivers. There was a stack of cooking wood by the stove and she built a fire rapidly, but the stove was not made to radiate much heat, nor was the hut built to hold it. She moved back to Jake and knew she must remove his wet clothing.

First she tugged at his other boot, but removing it would have been no easy task under normal conditions; to try to do so without hurting him was almost impossible. When at last the boot fell to the floor, she was panting and Jake had lapsed into restless semi-consciousness, muttering half-formed words she could not understand and was sure she did not want to.

Her fingers were unsteady as she worked the clumsy buckle of his gun belt and tugged it from beneath his hips. She had never undressed a man before, never even thought of doing so, and her movements were shy and awkward as she fumbled with unfamiliar catches and flaps near equally unfamiliar parts of his body. The belt was unfastened, but the rawhide thong that anchored the holster to his thigh proved to be more difficult. It was wet, and tight and almost impossible to unknot.

The heat between his thighs was an intimate thing, and she tried not to think about it as her fingers probed and pushed at the firm muscle there, trying to loosen the knot. Yet it was impossible to ignore, that sensation of his body beneath her hands, so hard and well formed, so masculine yet so dependent upon her. Her hands grew even clumsier and she felt she should not be touching him there, but even though she knew this there was a certain gratification for the feel of his strength and warmth beneath her touch, and she felt her cheeks heat with the admission.

The thong fell free and she removed the gun belt, stepping back and pushing her hair away from her face with a sigh. That was the hardest part. Matter-of-factly, she leaned forward and began to unbutton his shirt, tugging it off his heavy, uncooperative torso before beginning on the pants.

A month earlier, even a day, she would have never been able to imagine herself doing such a thing. Even now her heart pounded and her mouth felt dry as she loosened the buttons and tugged the garment down over his hips. But he was wet, and he had begun to shiver again, and there was no one to do this for him except her.

Beneath his clothes he wore a tightly fitting undergarment of loosely woven white cotton, and the nature of the material had caused it to dry more quickly, so that, aided by the heat of his body, it was now barely damp. Jessica was glad because she did not know how she could have forced herself to strip him naked, and she was not certain Jake would have thanked her for it even if her ministrations had saved his life. Yet covered as he was the garment left very little to the imagination, and Jessica tried not to concentrate on the definitive lines of his lean forearms and the shading of hair that darkened his chest beneath the material, the way it stretched taut from his ribcage over his flat abdomen to the points of his hipbones, and then gathered loosely over the bulge of his masculinity. . . .

Jessica jerked her eyes away, her pulses pounding with shame and embarrassment, and as she draped the blanket around his lean, hard form she made it a point not to look at him once. But she must have moved him too suddenly or hurt him in some way, because as she tucked the blanket firmly beneath his shoulders he groaned and opened his eyes hazily, then closed them again tightly as he was gripped with a new series of shivers.

The shaking only increased as she tried to soothe him, causing his teeth to chatter and the bed to tremble. He tried to say something, but the words were unintelligible through his tightly clenched teeth. He wrapped his arms around himself, begging for heat, and when he tried to draw his legs up a cry was wrenched from him that tore through Jessica's heart.

Quickly and desperately she scanned the room for some source of heat, and her eyes lit upon the heavy bearskin rug. She was across the room in an instant. She gripped the rug and dragged it by its corners back to him. With much straining and panting, she managed to lift the huge, furry throw onto the bed and across Jake, but it did little good. She watched in helpless torment as he shuddered convulsively.

"Oh, Jake . . ." she whispered. She sat beside him, catching his hands between both of hers, chafing them desperately. "Please, what can I do?"

She leaned forward, laying her cheek against his hot forehead, and another shudder swept through him. "Oh, Jake please."

She knew nothing else to do. She lifted the heavy covers and lay down beside him, wrapping her arms around him and pulling him close, offering him her warmth. And throughout the night she held him.

Chapter X

Jessica slept in hazy snatches lasting no more than a few minutes at a time throughout the night. Jake's chills alternately faded and returned with a vengeance, so that at times it was all she could do to hold him still and prevent him from further damaging his leg. Sometime close to dawn, during one of his quiet spells, she drifted off into mindless exhaustion. She awoke two hours later with a start, realizing that Jake was uncharacteristically still next to her.

Her blood freezing with alarm, she twisted around to look at him. She met a pair of tired, unquestioning green eyes, and her blood began to surge again with relief—and something else.

Her head had been resting on his chest, one arm across his stomach, the other curled around his shoulder. Her leg was thrown over both of his, to keep him warm and still. And both of his arms were around her waist, firmly and heavily, keeping her close. She was aware, as she had never thought before to be aware, of the nakedness of male muscles beneath the thin covering of his undergarment. His shape and warmth and strength no longer seemed strange but wonderfully comforting, peculiarly titillating.

She could feel the springy cushion of hair on his chest beneath her cheek and the firm plane of his abdomen beneath her hand. A muscle in his thigh flexed against hers, and the sensation caused an inexplicable flutter in her stomach, a wash of warmth through her body that had nothing to do with the quantity of covers under which they were lying. There was wonder in the feel of his arms around her, a hesitant pleasure that tingled in her fingertips and weakened the muscles of her legs.

She knew it was inappropriate at the very least, sinful at the most, to be having these feelings, to be so shamelessly aware of his lean, rangy body beneath hers when he was ill and helpless. But looking into his dazed, dusky eyes for a single brief moment that felt like forever, it did not feel sinful. It felt so natural, and so good, and so faintly, inexplicably promising that she almost thought she understood what Jake had meant about the beauty of the things that happened between a man and a woman.

It was that thought, so treacherous and unexpected, that jolted her out of the temporary insanity of sensations and half-formed imaginings. There was a dimming question in Jake's eyes as she struggled to get up, but his arms relaxed enough to allow her to free herself. And then, as she stood above him, confusion pattering in her pulse and alarm tingling her face, he seemed to come back to himself, too. He frowned. "I'm thirsty," he croaked.

Jessica hurried for his canteen.

The fever, low-grade and more annoying than dangerous, clung to him all day like a persistent pest that burrowed itself into the clothing or the skin and refused to be dislodged. He was uncomfortable, tossing and moaning in his sleep, short-tempered and foul-mouthed during the brief moments he was awake. Jessica found some cornmeal and mixed him up a thin gruel heavily sweetened with honey, but he was able to take only a few mouthfuls. She woke him regularly and made him take water; he cursed and glowered at her but always drank thirstily. She bathed his face and hands with cool compresses and did not know what else to do for a fever except to let it burn itself out.

And all day long it nagged at her, that feeling of anxiety and uncertainty that had begun when she had awakened in Jake's arms. She avoided it the way one would avoid biting down on a sore tooth or stretching a pulled muscle, but it was there, aching in the background, waiting for attention.

She was married to Daniel. But Daniel had never made her feel weak and tingling with expectancy just from being near him. He had embraced her, he had touched his cool lips to her cheek, he had smiled into her eyes and made her feel secure and content . . . but he had never created within her the restless sense of excitement and uncertain longing the way Jake did. Were these the stirrings Jake had predicted would come upon her, this need for something indefinable, this quivering sense of something wonderful just beyond her reach?

But she was married to Daniel.

While Jake slept restlessly she washed his clothes in water boiled over the fire and a strong soap she suspected was used for curing hides. She spread them to dry in the sunlight that bathed the porch, and even smoothing out the material that had covered his body sent a curious little thrill of warmth through her that she was afraid to examine too closely.

Late in the afternoon Jake's forehead seemed cooler, and when she checked the crude bandaging on his foot some of the swelling seemed to have gone down, although his skin was now a hideous shade of black-purple. There was, however, no sign of those deadly, spidery red lines creeping toward his heart which would signify blood poisoning. Jessica allowed herself a cautious relief, a surge of hope, and a heartfelt prayer of thanks.

She mixed up a pot of red beans and rice procured from the trapper's larder in hopes that Jake would take some stronger nourishment for supper. He turned his face away weakly from the smell and the sight, but after a time he was persuaded to take some more of the gruel she had made for breakfast. Afterward, he slept deeply and naturally, a sheen of healthy sweat on his face announcing that the fever had finally broken. Jessica arranged the bearskin on the floor near his bed, close to him in case he should need her during the night, and she fell asleep with a smile on her lips.

Jake awoke the next morning with every muscle feeling as though it had been twisted and wrung. His head felt as though it was stuffed with cotton and he was as weak as a kitten, but when he cautiously, very cautiously, moved his leg he received no more than a dull throbbing for his efforts. The fiery agony was gone.

He had felt worse, he was certain. He had received his share of range injuries—snakebites, broken bones, gashes and bruises from the animals he was trying to control—and this wasn't as bad as some of them. But there was nothing he hated worse than being sick and helpless, especially now when he needed all of his wits and strength to take care of Jessica, to somehow get them out of this place.

Jessica. He looked around for her, frowning with the effort of turning his head, and he saw her by the stove, bending over a pot of something that smelled incredibly appetizing. Fuzzily he remembered her finding this place, landing the boat after he had told her not to, dragging him up here . . . how the hell had she managed *that?* She had taken off his wet clothes, too, and cleaned his wound with whiskey that had hurt like hell but had, apparently, kept the infection from spreading. How long had he been out of his head? he wondered. All he could remember was that first night, when he had had the ague and she had wrapped her warmth around him and a series of tousled, confused dreams. . . .

Remembering those dreams and then waking up with her the next morning, looking into her gentle blue eyes, caused something warm and weak to pass through him and his throat went tight. He steeled himself against it, unconsciously tightening his muscles to push himself up in bed. The movement made his leg throb and he swore softly and angrily, but the anger was better and safer than what he had felt a moment before.

Jessica turned, a delighted smile breaking on to her face as she met his scowl. "Good, you're awake. Don't try to sit up by yourself. I'll help you."

He ignored her, grimly pushing himself into a sitting position against the wall as she turned to scoop some of the stew into a bowl. "What is it?" he asked ungraciously as she hurried toward him with the bowl. It smelled wonderful, and he was so hungry he could have eaten his saddle boiled and unsalted.

"Catfish stew. I found some wild tomatoes and onions for flavoring."

She sat beside him on the edge of the bed, and he scowled as she lifted the spoon toward his lips. "I can do it," he told her, reaching for the bowl. Even sitting up for such a short time was making him dizzy, but that was nothing a little hot food wouldn't cure, and he'd be damned if he was going to let anybody spoon feed him while he still had both his hands.

Jessica's gaze was calm and sober, and she let him have the bowl. But she kept a supporting grip on it as he seized the bowl from the bottom, which turned out to be a wise move because his own hands were shaking so badly he would have spilled the hot mixture all over himself if she hadn't been helping. Likewise, he was too hungry to object when she placed a light, steadying hand around his as he tried to bring the spoon to his lips.

It was good. It was so good he couldn't even waste the energy telling her so, but reached greedily for another bite. Her fingers felt strong against his, warm and soft and competent, and she matched the rhythm of her movements to his so well that after awhile he forgot to feel like a baby who was just learning to feed himself and began to enjoy the simple pleasures of her hand around his, sustenance filling his empty belly, strength returning by inches.

When the sharpest edge of his hunger was appeased he paused long enough to ask, "Where did you get the fish?"

She responded matter-of-factly, "I found an old net out on the porch. I seasoned it with some bear grease and the fish swam right in it." It hadn't been that easy, of course. She had spent two bone-aching hours before dawn crouching motionless in the water, waiting for the fish to strike. But Jake needed meat and she didn't know how to shoot a gun, so she hadn't had any choice.

Slow amazement crept over Jake in the brief moment he looked at her, the spoon poised midway to his lips. He knew exactly how hard it was to catch a fish without line, hook or bait. He had been trying to do so since the moment they had begun this hideous journey. But Jessica had done it.

Something in the way he looked at her seemed to make her uneasy, or perhaps it was his hand tightening on hers, but at any rate her hand jarred and the spoon tilted, spilling stew on his neck and chest. "Ouch! Goddamn it woman, what's the matter with you?" He brushed angrily at the scraps of tomato and onion and broth adhering to his skin and then immediately regretted his short temper and snappish tongue. The stew wasn't really hot enough to burn and it had been mostly his fault anyway, but already she had left him, returning in a moment with a damp cloth.

"Damn it, I can do it. I'm not a baby."

He snatched the cloth from her and began to wipe the spill from his skin and his undershirt, but when he glanced at her there was a shuttered, cautious expression on her face that filled him with self-disgust.

She inquired politely, "Do you want any more?"

He did, but it was a form of self-punishment to refuse. "No." He hoped his voice didn't sound as petulant to her as it did to him. He thrust the cloth back into her hand. "I'm finished."

He leaned his head back against the wall and watched her cross the room with a sinking feeling of shame and loss. *You're a prince, Jake,* he thought wearily. *The woman saves your life and you bite her head off for it.* Still, he was filled with faint wonder when he thought of what she had done in the past days. He wouldn't have thought any woman capable of enduring what she had endured since they had begun this journey, but there was apparently nothing she couldn't do once she set her mind to it. A hell of a woman, he thought with a distant, barely recognizable sense of incredulity and admiration. One hell of a woman.

She looked beautiful this morning. She had caught her hair back with a piece of string at the nape of her neck, and its abandoned curls fluffed over her back and shoulders, catching motes of dusty sunlight from the open door and gleaming like polished coal. Her skin was a tawny rose, and even the dark circles of fatigue under her eyes did not mar the graceful, almost regal lines of her bone structure. His clothing, baggy as it was, clung to her shape when she walked, and she had a gentle, subtle way of moving that was a pleasure merely to watch. Jake wondered if his brother knew how lucky he was.

And then something empty and painful knotted in his stomach and he thought, yes, he knew. How could he not know?

Jake released a low breath. He said, "Maria says I'm the devil's very own when I'm sick."

"You're not so bad," she replied as she scrubbed out the bowl.

He was cautiously encouraged. "She used to rap me on the hand with a spoon when I mouthed off at her."

Jessica smiled, but still she did not turn. "I'll remember that."

Jake relaxed a little, feeling comfortable now with letting silence fall between them. He knew he needed to start using the muscles in his leg before they stiffened up on him completely, and he was restless for his strength to return. He also yearned for a bath; he felt pasty with the sweat of fever and suspected he smelled bad. But he knew if he attempted to get up now he would topple to his face and only prolong his recovery.

He ran a tired hand over his bristled cheek. "My face itches," he complained without meaning to complain at all.

She walked over to him, wiping her hands on a towel, looking at him distantly but assessively. "Would you like me to shave you?"

He hesitated. If he tried it he would like as not cut his own throat, but he had never before trusted a woman with a razor in her hand and was loathe to begin now. Yet he had trusted this one with his life, hadn't he?

"If you think you can," he agreed cautiously.

He held himself rigid for the first few strokes, but after awhile the steady, sweeping strokes of the blade against his beard ceased to be terrifying and began to be soothing. She obviously had never done this before; she was unfamiliar enough with the contours of a man's face to have to backtrack several times in her work. But she applied herself to the task with the same intensity with which she did everything else and she didn't nick him once. She wiped the last of the lather from his face and smiled in satisfaction. "You look better."

He ran a grateful hand over his clean jaw and cheek. "Feels better."

There was so much contentment in his eyes for this simple act of grooming that Jessica volunteered impulsively, "If you could take off your undershirt, I'll bathe your arms and—" There she faltered, uncertain what had ever possessed her to suggest such an intimate service, but already he was nodding agreement, unfastening the buttons at his neck.

"That would be good. I feel sticky."

Jessica returned with a basin of vinegar water and a clean towel—she had washed it herself the day before—and sat on the edge of the bed beside him. His chest was lean and strong, just as she had known it would be, and covered with a springy mat of dark hair that rounded faintly as it reached toward his shoulders, narrowed across his abdomen where it crept into the sheet. She had seen him naked that day at Three Hills; she could not imagine why her pulses fluttered so at the sight of his chest. But she had only seen him naked from behind, she remembered, and that only caused the tempo of her heart to increase, sending a rush of color to her cheeks.

But all of this she kept carefully hidden from Jake as she purposely wrang out the cloth and applied it gently to his neck. Jake made a satisfied sound at its soothing, refreshing feel and closed his eyes. Her movements were sure and her face composed as she rubbed the cloth gently across his shoulders and around his neck, then rinsed it in more vinegar solution before applying it to his chest.

The hair on his chest was surprisingly soft and silky, not at all prickly like she had thought it would be. And the muscles beneath were firm, strangely titillating to explore, to caress. Jake's eyes were peacefully closed and his expression was pleasured, but there was pleasure for Jessica, too, in touching him, in discovering the wonders of his strong male body. Something began to blossom in her, a tenderness and a warmth, yet an excitement too, like a question unanswered. And helplessly she knew that Jake had been right. There were things—things she could not even define—that a man could offer her other than companionship and protection. Could she really love Daniel if she felt these things inside when she touched another man?

Perhaps Jake was right. Perhaps it was only gratitude she felt for Daniel. She only hoped gratitude would be enough. It had to be.

Jake opened his eyes as she lifted one arm to wash it, moving from the pit of dark hair down its length to his hands. What strong hands he had. Lean and dark and sprinkled with curling hairs, tapering into slender, calloused fingers that were a pleasure to touch. She remembered that hand curving about her waist while he slept, holding her.

She imagined how it would feel closing about hers in warmth and affection.

Jake was watching her, his expression absent and relaxed. "'A soldier of the Legion lay dying in Algiers,'" he murmured softly, almost to himself. "'There was a lack of woman's nursing, a dearth of woman's tears.'"

She looked at him, curiosity softening the already gentle expression on her face. "Was that a poem?"

He smiled. "Umm-hmm."

She lifted his other arm and began to wash it. Her voice was slightly breathless, but not unpleasantly so. "You know a lot of books, don't you?"

His smile turned the slightest bit rueful. "It gets so lonely on the trail sometimes we read anything we can find, from Shakespeare to the labels on tobacco tins. My mother loved books," he added. "Pa used to tell about the first thing he ever bought for her when they were married, a stack of books from a peddler. I guess he couldn't read too well back then—not many westerners could—but after she died, I remember him sitting in the library for hours, reading and looking at her picture as though by being with her books he could be with her somehow."

Jessica was deeply touched, feeling, through the tenderness of Jake's memory, the power of a man's love for a woman. What would it be like to be loved like that? she wondered.

Then he glanced at her. "Do you read, Jessica?"

"Only the Bible." She concentrated on washing his fingers, a faint flush coming to her cheeks. It seemed much more difficult now that he was talking to her and looking at her.

"We have lots of books at Three Hills." Jake's voice was distantly reminiscent, and he was remembering that day in the library when he had argued with Daniel about Jessica. How could he have been so wrong? And had it been only a matter of weeks since then? It seemed like another lifetime. He turned back to her. "I'll show you when we get home."

When we get home. He had never said that before. Only days before he had been determined she would never call Three Hills home; he had tried to bribe her to keep her away. Now he was going to take her home. The change should have made her happy, but she only felt disturbed, and more confused than ever. *Home . . . to Daniel.*

Skittishly, she moved her thoughts away from Daniel. She invited quickly, "Tell me about Three Hills."

Jake chuckled. "Well, I guess it is something of a story at that. My Pa settled in Texas during the Republic, and the Cherokee made their camp not five miles from where the big house is now. All Pa had was a couple of thousand acres he'd gotten for serving with Houston in the war, and a few hundred head of wild cattle. Then he got into a poker game with some fancy English dude named Hartley—a lot of foreigners wanted to invest in Texas back then—and won well over a hundred and fifty thousand acres." He glanced at her slyly. "Legend has it Pa cheated on that game, but he never would say."

Jessica's eyes were wide. "But didn't Mr. Hartley care?"

"Oh, he cared all right. But back then arguments like that were settled with a gun, and that's the way Pa settled it in the end."

"Your father," ventured Jessica, "sounds like a very—rough man."

Jake nodded. "I guess he was, but it took rough men to settle the frontier. Of course there are probably parts of that story we'll never know. The Hartleys," he added thoughtfully, "still own a section of land adjoining the ranch, but I guess they've forgotten it. They're all back in England now, and don't seem to be holding a grudge."

He shrugged. "Anyway, land wasn't worth much back then and Pa didn't have any idea what he'd done by winning all that land. It wasn't until the Chisolm Trail opened up that you could make any profit in running a big ranch, you know.

"Pa was one of the first to drive cattle north, even before there was an Abilene, and he used to tell us that was my mother's idea, too. And when she made him build that big house the story is that every pioneer who came across to settle would stop by to look at it, because nobody had ever seen anything like it west of the Sabine."

And then, suddenly and without warning, his eyes went opaque, and the pleasant reminiscences faded. "Of course," he said negligently, not looking at her, "most of this happened before I was born, and I only know it secondhand. If you want to hear the real stories, you should ask Daniel."

Daniel. It always got back to Daniel and she could not avoid the subject any longer. Her hands paused in the process of washing his forearm. She made herself look at him and there was distress behind the earnestness in her eyes. She did not know what to say to him, she didn't even know for certain what she wanted to say, but she knew something had to be spoken. "Jake . . . I—I need you to believe that I never meant to harm Daniel, or take advantage of him . . ."

Jake lowered his eyes, and for a moment he looked almost as uncomfortable as she. His voice was very low. "I guess I always knew that."

"It wasn't his money," she insisted, willing him to understand. "I didn't even really think of that. It was just—he was so good to me, and he made me feel good about myself, and . . ." She lowered her own eyes, and her voice dropped a fraction. "I needed someone to take care of me."

Jake looked at her then, long and soberly. "Lady," he said sincerely, and this time the appellation did not seem like a slur. It sounded, in fact, like the most reverent of compliments. "You don't need anyone to take care of you. You take care of yourself better than anybody I've ever known."

Jessica looked at him, filled with a glow of pleasure and pride that came purely from the unvarnished respect she saw in his eyes. A simple thing, but by uttering it he had bestowed upon her one of the highest honors he was capable of giving. And slowly, with a growing satisfaction whose significance was so intense she could barely comprehend it, she realized it was true. *I can*, she thought. *I can take care of myself. Because you taught me . . .*

He smiled. "Daniel said you were a lot like my mother, and I guess he was right at that. She came into the wilderness and built an empire. She fought off cattle rustlers and Indians just like you've fought off alligators and snakes. She even saved my Pa's life . . . just like you saved mine."

Quickly, before the wondrous and tumultuous emotions that were building inside her glowed in her eyes, she turned away and dropped the cloth into the basin, taking up the towel. "There," she said, forcing a negligent smile to her lips as she blotted his skin dry. "Finished."

She had to lean over him to get his shoulder, and to her surprise, he captured a curl of her hair between his fingers. She looked at him, but he was looking at her hair, rubbing its texture between his fingertips with a musing, fascinated expression on his face. "Your hair is so pretty," he said.

Jessica's heart pulsed once in her throat and a rush of what could only be described as delighted wonder rushed through her veins. Jake thought her hair was pretty. No one had ever said that to her before.

Self-consciously her hand went to her hair, and when she straightened up Jake let the strand he had captured drift through his fingers without protest. She turned away to gather up the basin, flustered, and said, "Papa thought my hair was sinful."

When she glanced at him, Jake's eyes were sober. "He was wrong," he said.

For a moment he looked at her and it felt as though the entire world had stopped and sealed them inside a glass bubble. Just the two of them existed, he looking at her and she looking at him, knowing each other, touching each other. But it was just a moment, too brilliant and intense to last more than that. Jessica broke the eye contact first, hurrying outside to pour the water out and hang the cloth to dry.

When she returned, Jake was half-dozing, exhausted by the morning activities. But when she bent over him to draw the cover higher on his chest there was such a soft, hazy expression in her eyes that he had to smile at her. "What're you thinking?" he asked huskily.

She looked embarrassed. She made a great fuss of tucking the blanket around his chest. "Silly things."

"What?" he demanded somewhat foggily.

She shrugged her shoulders and gave him a small rueful smile as she straightened up. "Oh, I was just thinking how long it's been since I've worn a dress." And then her expression grew wistful, and she added, more to herself than to him, "I've never had a store-bought dress. Sometimes I wish . . ." She looked at him, her cheeks brightening even as her expression grew matter-of-fact. "I think you're tired. You should rest."

Jake nodded and closed his eyes wearily. His last thought before drifting off was that when they got back to New Orleans he was going to buy her the prettiest dress in the whole damn town. . . .

"I think my leg will be strong enough to travel tomorrow," Jake said. "We've got to get out of this place."

They were sitting out on the bottom step of the cabin. They had been there four days while Jake determinedly and painfully regained his strength and, with the help of a sturdy walking stick Jessica had cut from a cypress branch, the use of his leg. It still pained him considerably, but the swelling had almost completely gone down and he had been right: there were no broken bones.

The days they had spent there had been among the most blissful of Jessica's life.

They were not completely without incident, of course. Jake became angry with her when she insisted on sleeping on the floor while he took the bed each night, so much so that she finally agreed to trade places just to placate him. He had awakened the next morning with such stiff and aching muscles that she was certain his recovery had been delayed by at least a day, and he did not argue with her about the bed after that. He had gone into a regular temper fit when he saw that she had mangled his boot to such an extent that it had to be tied on with a rope, until Jessica tartly pointed out to him that he would look a fine sight sillier minus a leg than minus a boot. He had hobbled off in dark sullenness, but later that day he brought her a single magnolia blossom plucked from the tree outside, and the simple, wordless gesture filled Jessica with more pleasure than she had ever thought it possible to feel.

She said now, her voice low and lazy with the contentment of a hot, muggy afternoon, "Are you in such a hurry? I've gotten to like it here."

Jake snorted. "You don't ask much, do you?"

She cast him a fleeting, smiling glance. "We've got a roof over our heads, plenty of food, no alligators or snakes . . . It's more than we've ever had before."

Jake looked back toward the swamp uncomfortably. He supposed that to her this bug-infested shack in the middle of nowhere was like a castle, but Jake had been here too long. He wanted to go home.

His gaze turned to brooding as he turned the problem over and over in his mind. He could not calculate exactly how long he had been trying to find a way out of the swamp even before the accident, but he knew it had been too long. There was no guarantee that he would have better luck this time, but the fact that they had finally found signs of human habitation did bode well for the future. If they stayed along this same waterway logic dictated that the area would become more populated until they were out of the swamp altogether. Civilization was near, he could feel it. And home. And Daniel.

The trees grew close to the cabin, with their curtain of Spanish moss and incessant creaking of tree frogs. Jake snatched irritably at a clump of moss that was tickling the back of his neck and said, "If I never see this damn stuff again it'll be too soon."

"I think it's rather pretty." Jessica watched Jake shred the net of grey moss between his strong, graceful hands, absently separating it into strands and bunching it together again with absent, brooding absorption. What beautiful hands he had, she thought. Watching them in motion made her want to lay her own hand atop his, feeling the flex of bone and sinew, the texture of flesh, the sturdy warmth.

Deliberately turning her eyes away from his hands and back toward the sleepy swamp she said, "Aunt Eulalie told me a story about it. Seems there's a legend about an Indian girl who was killed during her wedding ceremony. An enemy tribe attacked and scalped her, then hung her hair on a tree. It blew from tree to tree, turning gray, until every tree was covered with it. And so they say today that the moss will hang forever as a tribute to those who are not fated to live out their love."

Her voice had taken on a rather wistful note at the end, and she glanced at Jake quickly and with an apologetic smile, both for the inadequacy of her storytelling abilities and the silliness of the tale. "Of course, who knows? Aunt Eulalie probably made it up. She made a lot of things up," she added, disturbed by the memory.

But there was a very peculiar look in Jake's eyes, something soft and sad and questioning, and it held Jessica captive for a moment. He moved his gaze away quickly, before she could begin to understand what she saw there.

With an abrupt motion he tossed the moss away, but it caught on an errant air current and floated back toward Jessica, tangling in her hair. She gave an alarmed cry and began to brush at her hair, trying to shake the dry, stringy vegetation free. "Jake, don't do that! That stuff is nasty!"

He laughed. "A minute ago you said it was pretty!"

"It has bugs in it!"

Still laughing, he began to help her pick the moss out of her shiny flyaway curls. He did not know how it happened. He was laughing, and it had been so long since he laughed, and her expression was so comically distressed as their hands ruffled her hair and her lips were so close . . . He never intended it to happen. He had had a thousand opportunities before and had always refused them. He didn't think about it. He didn't plan it. He let his lips touch hers.

It could have ended there. A light, gentle touch, a token of good spirits and affection that meant nothing and could easily have been forgotten. But when he felt her lips part with a startled breath, his own heart slammed to his throat and a thousand sensations prickled his skin and roared in his blood and he couldn't stop. He kissed her again.

The heat and the dizziness that swept through Jessica left her weak. She couldn't think, she didn't try to think. She had never imagined anything could make her feel like this. His lips were soft and questing and rather tentative, but it was as though when he kissed her more than just his lips touched her. It was as though he were infusing something into her, something rushing and powerful and filled with sparks and light. He kissed her and her mind danced away and her breath died in her throat. She was no longer a woman of this time and this place; she was a collection of sensations and wonder caught in a world as unfamiliar as it was beautiful, and all she could do was glory in it, absorb it, let it become a part of her.

Jake could not believe it had happened. He held her face in his hands and looked down into eyes as bright and dazed and shocked as his own must have been. He did not know what to say, what to do. For as much as his mind demanded one thing his body clamored for another. All he knew was the taste of her, the softness and the dearness of her. His heart hammered in his chest, his breath caught in his throat, and every part of him felt more alive, more alert and singing with need than it ever had before. Still, he opened his mouth to say something—her name perhaps. He tried to make his hands release her face. And then he froze.

He had not heard the step behind him, nor the distinctive

clicking of a cartridge. But in that moment he saw Jessica's eyes grow from dazed and soft to wide and alarmed. He felt the tension ripple through her body and his sluggish reflexes registered danger only a moment before he felt something else: the cold barrel of a shotgun pressed firmly into the back of his neck.

Chapter XI

Very carefully and slowly Jake spread his hands palms up, and without turning lifted them to the level of his ears. Jessica looked terrified. Neither one of them breathed.

From behind him a heavily accented Cajun voice said, "I weel t'ink de best for now. A lover's tryst, aha? Running away from de jealous husband, no? And you have stumbled upon de humble home of Jean-Claude Baptiste?"

Jessica got to her feet with stiff and cautious movements, her eyes never leaving the bearded face of the man who held the shotgun to Jake's head. Jake's eyes narrowed, trying to warn her not to move, but she paid no attention. Her relief at actually seeing another human being almost outweighed her fear at his method of greeting.

She said, her voice small and tight, "We meant no harm, Mr. Baptiste. We're lost, and we saw your hut. . . ."

Beneath his coonskin hat and tangled hair and beard the trapper's face was not vicious. It was, in fact, round and florid and rather pleasant. When he looked at Jessica, his expression relaxed into what almost could have been taken for a spark of good humor, and he lowered the gun. "*Oui*, de swamp, she is a treacherous place for those who do not know her."

Jake, still keeping his hands lifted, stood slowly and turned to face the adversary, putting himself between the gun and Jessica. He said, "We didn't mean to trespass. We'll reimburse you for the goods we used."

With a distinctly French sound and a wave of his hand, Jean-Claude dismissed the offer. "Nah, t'aint so often that I see strangers I would begrudge de shelter." He looked at them with avid interest. "What news from de city?"

Jake relaxed, on familiar ground now. Whether in the isolation of the swamp or the lonely trails of the West it was the same: a strange face meant a friendly one until it was proven otherwise, and avidity for news of civilization was the one commodity that never lost its value. He took out his tobacco pouch and papers, offering them first to his host as he began a recitation of the latest elections, prices, squabbles and feuds between Galveston and New Orleans.

Jessica, at first retreating in confusion, soon relaxed in the camaraderie, and at the first break in the conversation put in shyly, "We would be most grateful if you could see your way clear to direct us to the nearest town."

The trapper looked at her thoughtfully, leaning on his shotgun and finishing Jake's cigarette in appreciative leisure. "Ah, pretty mam'selle, this thing you ask, she will not be easy. But..." He cast a shrewd glance at Jake. "For a few coins and a taste or two more of this fine weed, I will take you myself to Cousin Robert's Trading Post. She is not so far away."

The relief that went through Jake all but made him weak, and he could feel it float back to him redoubled from

Jessica. Deliverance, the possibility of civilization, escape at last, an end to this nightmare eclipsed everything else and all Jake could say was, "How soon do you think we could leave?"

Jean-Claude turned his face toward a narrow patch of sky visible through the foliage and squinted at it thoughtfully. "Now," he pronounced at last. "And we shall arrive before darkfall."

Jessica's eyes met Jake's and the dazed joy and incredulous relief she saw there made her want to laugh out loud, to fling her arms around him and hug him hard, and she knew in that moment his instincts were the same. Unconsciously they moved toward each other, but as though a curtain fell between them each remembered what had happened just before Jean-Claude's appearance . . . the embrace that had turned into more, the kiss that was never meant to be. Quickly, uncomfortably, Jake turned to Jean-Claude and began to discuss preparations for the trip; Jessica edged toward the house to gather up their things. Her heart was beating arhythmically and her cheeks burned with an uncomfortable color.

She wondered if things would ever be the same between her and Jake again. She was very much afraid they would not.

When Jake and Jessica crossed the Sabine River and stood at last on Texas soil the elation that filled them was almost a spiritual thing. The nightmare was over, home was before them, they had survived the crucible and reward was in sight. The cloak of oppression they had barely been aware of carrying fell away like dust with the taste of Texas air, the kiss of Texas sun. Home.

The nearest town was less than half a day's ride, and they

made for it instinctively, without discussion, without looking back.

Jake had been stunned to discover that, rather than wandering aimlessly along the waterways that emptied into the Mississippi, they had been progressing more or less steadily west, so that by the time they reached Jean-Claude's hut they were quite near the Texas border; New Orleans was on the opposite side of the swamp. From the trading post Jake had been able to procure a pair of boots, two horses and a saddle for Jessica, though he couldn't say much for any of them. The boots weren't Texas made and the horses sure weren't Texas bred, but he was of no mind to complain. The little horses were surefooted and covered the distance, and Jake was so glad to be back in the saddle again he would have been grateful for a mule.

They reached Double Springs, Texas in early afternoon. It was a quiet little town, nothing much to brag about, with fifty or sixty clapboard houses and half a dozen shops which bordered a central square of hoof-churned mud. The smell of manure and red clay was thick in the air, the road was rutted with wagon tracks and littered with sweepings from the shops, but to Jake and Jessica it was the most beautiful sight they had ever beheld. It was Texas. It was home.

Jake dismounted in front of a dusty building whose sagging sign announced: SALOON—MEALS—ROOMS. Jessica, breathing a sigh of anticipation mingled with relief, slid out of the saddle and tossed her reins over the hitching post next to Jake's. She had surprised Jake by insisting upon riding astride, and though she had never ridden at all before, she had at least managed to stay seated, thanks mostly to the temperament of her gentle mare, and had had little difficulty keeping up with Jake. Her quickly acquired proficiency with a horse did not, however, do anything to condition her muscles to the rigors of riding, and every part of her ached magnificently as she found her feet once again.

Jake grinned at her spontaneously as she stepped up onto the boardwalk beside him. "I don't know about you, but I'll be damned glad not to be sleeping on the ground tonight. What do you say we lay over for a day or two, stock up on supplies and rest before we start out again? I saw a telegraph office on the way in. We can send a wire to Three Hills to tell them when to expect us. Hell, we might even be able to catch a stage for most of the way back."

Jessica's eyes glowed, not only with the prospect of a real bed and good food and even the possibility of never having to get on a horse again, but because, for the first time in days, Jake was smiling at her. The intensity that had absorbed this last part of their journey had precluded all else, so that Jake had barely spoken to her, never smiled at her, rarely taken his eyes off the distant horizon that was his goal. But the urgency had passed, home was in sight, and a celebration was in order. Jessica felt sheer joy bubbling up inside her as she agreed enthusiastically, "It sounds wonderful, Jake. Do you think I could have a bath here?"

He laughed. "Lady, you can have anything you want."

Jessica had never been inside a saloon before, and as she followed Jake through the swinging doors and into the dimly lit interior she felt a bit awed and apprehensive. She was somewhat disappointed to find that it was not filled with horned and tailed creatures after all, and fire and brimstone did not rain from the ceiling the minute she stepped inside. At this time of the day, in fact, it was almost deserted, and very quiet. There was a group of men playing cards in a far corner, and a dusty old man with darting eyes sitting alone and making short work of a plate of stew. Conversation stopped when Jake and Jessica entered, and all eyes turned toward her. That was when Jessica realized what she must look like.

Wearing men's torn and filthy clothes, her hair loose and tangled around her shoulders, scraps of cloth tied around her feet in place of shoes . . . She tried to make herself smaller, shrinking away from the probing, suspicious eyes, yet not wishing to embarrass Jake by staying too close to him. Self-consciously, her hand went to her face, certain it was stained with trail dust, fingering her hair and wishing she had at least tied it back. But Jake didn't seem to notice. He strolled up to the bar and greeted the bartender casually. "Need a couple of clean rooms for the night," he said.

The proprietor was a skinny man with a bristle of tobacco-stained gray beard and narrow, pale, washed-out eyes. His rumpled shirt might once have been white but now blended with the gray of his frayed suspenders. The apron bunched around his waist was dotted with innumerable stains and his fingernails were dirty. He looked at Jessica for a long time, and his lips slowly parted in a nasty, brown-toothed grin.

"Your business, mister, but ain't you wasting your money? We got a fine livery for your squaw, and it won't cost but two bits a night."

There was a burst of laughter from the group at the table and Jessica felt humiliation sweep through her, making her wish that she could fade into the woodwork. She should have waited for Jake outside, she thought desperately. And then, before she knew what was happening, Jake's hand had shot across the bar, grabbing the man's shirt and pulling him off his feet toward him. The laughter abruptly ceased.

Jake's expression was thunderous, his voice deadly quiet as he said, "I've been on the trail for a long time, mister, and shooting snakes has just about got to be a habit with me. So I'd advise you to watch your mouth when you're talking about my sister."

The little man swallowed hard and shifted his eyes around, as though looking for help. He repeated nervously, "Your sister. Right, mister, whatever you say."

Jake slowly lowered the man until his feet touched the floor, and then released his shirtfront with an elaborate display of courtesy, even brushing out the wrinkles. His voice was mild as he said, "Now, why don't you just put two keys in my hand and mind your own goddamn business from now on?"

The bartender reached under the bar, never taking his eyes off Jake, and came up with two keys. "Two dollars a room." His voice was almost, but not quite, surly, and in his eyes was nothing but wariness.

Jake placed five dollars on the bar and took the keys. "I want a tub and hot water sent to the lady's room." There was the slightest deliberate emphasis on the word lady, accompanied by a near smile that could easily have been taken for threatening. "On the double."

The bartender turned to yell for his assistant and when Jake turned to Jessica, his smile was gentle and reassuring. He handed a key to her which had a paper tag on it that had the number six printed on it.

"I'm going to go on down and send that telegram," he said. "Don't let these ass—gentlemen," he corrected himself with a humorous quirk of his lips, "bother you. Just stay in your room until I get back, then we'll go find something to eat."

Because Jake seemed relaxed, so was she. She smiled. "All right," she said softly. The card game had resumed behind them, and no one but Jake watched her as she turned and walked upstairs. The possibility of a bath sounded so wonderful she could almost forget the unpleasantness in the saloon, and something warm and lovely had touched her inside when she heard Jake call her his sister.

The room was small and narrow, a mere partition of a row of rooms on either side of the hallway just like it. It contained a sagging bed with grayish sheets, a washstand with a cracked porcelain bowl and pitcher, and a straight-backed chair. But it was a real roof, a solid wood floor, a real bed with a pillow, and to Jessica it was magnificent. A sigh of sheer luxury escaped her as she sank onto the bed and ran her hand over the lumpy mattress appreciatively.

She thought of Jake's defense of her in the saloon and her eyes softened as a smile crept across her lips. In the past days he had seemed too distant and remote. She had grown anxious, wondering what he was thinking, if he regretted having brought her that far, wondering what they had lost between their last night in the swamp and their first step upon Texas soil and how it had happened . . . Then her smile wavered a bit, because she knew exactly how it had happened.

The memory returned to haunt her, as it had so many times these past days and nights, the memory of Jake's lips on hers, the warmth of his body against hers, the absorbing, tender caress of his calloused hands upon her face. He had kissed her, and even the memory of it could start a repeat of the sensations, the quickened pulses, the tightening warmth in her abdomen, the glorious wonder and helpless confusion because it was like nothing she had ever known before. And even as she treasured the memory, even as her treacherous mind wanted to savor it and explore it and relive it a dozen times and then again, she pushed it aside quickly and in shame, because that was what had changed things between them. Jake had not meant it to happen, certainly it would never happen again, and the sooner it was forgotten the better. Jake had already forgotten it. He had called her his sister.

But her smile was not quite so confident as she assured herself that was exactly what she wanted to be.

Jake was in a bad temper when he left Jessica and the saloon, but by the time he reached the telegraph office his spirits were more composed. After all they had been through, he wasn't going to let a bunch of ignorant backwoods scum upset him. He had survived the most difficult ordeal of his life and come out on top, he was about to enjoy the first real bed and meal he had had in what seemed like months, and the worst was behind him. He had every reason in the world to be feeling good. He was almost home.

The message he sent to Daniel was: "Jessica safe. On our way home. Two days in Double Springs for supplies. Worried about you. Please reply."

The telegraph operator told him the message would be received that afternoon, but Jake knew it might be the next day before he got a reply, depending upon whether or not one of the ranch hands happened to be in town when his telegram arrived. He told the operator he would stop by later in the afternoon, and crossed the street to the barbershop.

After a haircut, shave and bath in the barbershop he was immeasurably restored. He went to check the stage schedule and found a coach leaving the day after next for Fort Worth. Though he personally preferred to ride, he knew the trip was hard on Jessica, and riding those Louisiana nags was almost as bad as not riding at all. He would sell the horses to the livery in Double Springs and wait until he got home to secure a new mount.

He was whistling cheerfully by the time he got to the dry

goods store, where the proprietress was happy to sell him a new pair of pants, a dark blue cotton shirt, and boots that were far better than those from the trading post, and, because he was feeling festive with his new haircut and barbershop sheen, a string tie.

While the clerk was wrapping his purchases Jake strolled over to the female apparel and began to flip through the garments arranged on a wooden rack there. The town was a far cry from New Orleans, and most of the dresses were of sturdy wool or cotton in grays or browns, the kind of thing suitable to a farmer's wife or a shop clerk like the one who was beginning to give him strange looks.

He scowled as he remembered those men in the saloon, and a female customer unable to disguise her curiosity about the rugged cowpoke who was displaying such an interest in women's clothing happened to fall under the full force of it. With a huffy sniff she turned away and began to whisper behind her hand to the salesclerk, both of them nodding and sending suspicious gazes in his direction. Grimly Jake pawed through the ugly dresses until he found what he wanted. It was a simple cotton thing, a bit more expensive than the others, a little wrinkled and dusty from hanging on the rack so long, but it was blue. The color of Jessica's eyes.

The saleswoman, mustering her courage, inquired, "Will there be anything else for you, sir?"

Jake jerked the gown off the hook and strode over to her. "I'll take this," he announced. Then he paused, the frown gathering again as he realized Jessica didn't even have shoes, and he couldn't for the life of him remember what kind of shoes a woman wore with such a dress. And what about the things that went under it, the petticoats and stockings and corsettes and whatever? His annoyance with himself and the attention he was getting from the other customers was mounting, and there was a limit to how big a fool he was willing to make of himself, even for a cause as worthy as Jessica.

He said, "Pick out a pair of pretty shoes to go with it. And all the other frills."

The saleswoman looked at him blankly, and he glared at her. "Everything," he told her, "from the skin up." He could see a dozen speculations rushing through the woman's mind and all of them made him mad. He counted out some bills and dropped them on the counter before she could say anything she would regret. "Bundle them up and send them over to the saloon, room six." He picked up his own package and turned to go.

The woman glanced at the money he had left and quickly collected herself. "But sir," she called after him, "what about sizes? You can't—"

Jake closed the door firmly on her voice and the gawking looks that followed him, stifling a sigh of relief to be back on the street. For a couple just passing through and meaning nobody any harm they were certainly causing a stir in an amazingly short period of time. It was as if these people had never seen strangers before, and in another hour gossip would be all over town about who they were and what they were doing there. Not that it mattered, he assured himself with a shrug. Tomorrow he would bring Jessica back and let her pick out her own clothes if she didn't like what he had bought, and by the next day they would be well on their way toward home.

He struggled to find some sense of satisfaction in that. He had accomplished what he had been sent to do. It was what Daniel wanted, what Jessica wanted. It was for the best, he told himself. Then why didn't the thought of going home make him happy?

He tried to push away the disturbing open-endedness of his own future, but it wasn't easy to do. A worrisome frown marred the contentment that should have been on his features as he walked slowly back toward the saloon.

Jessica had wrapped herself in a sheet and was rinsing out her soiled clothes in the bathwater when there was a knock on the door. She felt born again after bathing and washing her hair, and the only thing that mitigated her joy was the thought of getting back into the filthy clothes. Perhaps once they dried, and if she could get rid of the worst of the stains. . . .

She called out a cautious, "Who is it?" when the knock came again, remembering those awful men downstairs. When a female voice answered she went to the door and opened it a fraction, hiding her sheet-clad body behind the bulk of the door.

The woman looked curious and disapproving, but otherwise harmless. She thrust a bulky package through the door. "A gentleman said I was to deliver this here."

Jessica took the package in confusion and examined it hesitantly, still clutching the sheet high under her arms. "What is it?"

"Just a dress and things. If the size isn't—"

With a little cry of delight, Jessica closed the door in the woman's face, hurrying over to the bed to tear open the package. She couldn't believe what she saw: two petticoats, white cotton stockings, pantalettes, a soft, lace-trimmed chemise, and a pair of high-topped shoes made of soft black leather with mother of pearl buttons. Everything smelled of starch and newness.

And the dress. She snatched it up and held it to her, heedlessly letting the sheet fall away. It was a bright cornflower blue trimmed with ivory cotton lace, and the soft drapery that gathered across the front and into a bustle at back was white printed with tiny blue flowers. It was beautiful, it was feminine, and Jake had sent it to her.

Her cheeks were bright and her eyes were glowing as she brought a fold of the material to her face, luxuriating in the feel of it. "Oh, Jake," she whispered, and she thought happiness would burst her chest. "Thank you. . . ."

An hour later Jake knocked on her door. He had had a walk around town, a shot of whiskey downstairs, and a brief nap in his room. He had changed into his new clothes, polished up his boots, and even worn his tie. It always felt good to get back to civilization after being on the trail, but he could never remember it feeling so good. Maybe it had something to do with all those times he had wondered if he would ever see a real town or eat real food or drink whiskey from a glass again. Maybe it had something to do with the fact that this time Jessica was waiting for him.

She opened the door and the sight of her took his breath away.

It wasn't that he had forgotten she was a woman. It wasn't even that he had grown used to his ugly clothes hiding her feminine features. It was just that he had never imagined before that simply looking at her could make him weak.

The light blue dress dipped low over her bosom, a network of creamy lace shading the contours of her breasts and dripping from the sleeves that stopped just short of her elbows. The frilly drapery of blue print was pulled tight over her abdomen, drawing attention to the smallness of her waist, then gathered into a gentle bustle at the back that reminded him, as it was supposed to, of cradling hips. She had put her hair up, only a feathering of tendrils around her face suggesting the magnificent abandon into which it would fall were the pins released. Her skin was flushed and tawny, and the color of the dress made her eyes as bright as sapphires. She was every inch a lady, she was beautiful, and Jake had not expected to see her like that. Just looking at her started the hungry, aching feeling deep within him which he thought he had left behind in the swamp. He couldn't get enough of looking at her.

Automatically, he took off his hat and smiled at her even though the muscles of his face felt tight. He had to clear his throat. "You look pretty," he said.

Jessica felt a new infusion of excited color to her cheeks, and the way he looked at her made her heart beat faster even as an unexpected wave of shyness swept her. He looked different too. His hair had been neatly clipped, his face was smooth and tanned, he wore a freshly starched shirt, new vest, tie and polished boots . . . even his gun belt had been cleaned. He looked so fresh and strong and so incredibly handsome that Jessica could hardly believe this was the same man with whom she had spent so much time in the swamp. And after a moment, because the strangeness of his nearness was so powerful, she had to lower her eyes.

She murmured, "Thank you for the clothes . . . and everything."

"I'm glad you like them."

It was hard to stop looking at her. He had to force himself to remember why he had come, and it was an effort to make his voice sound normal. "I thought you might like to walk down to the telegraph office with me and see if there's a reply from Three Hills yet. Then we'll get something to eat downstairs before the crowd gets too rowdy.''

Jessica flashed an immediate smile of agreement, not so much because she was anxious to hear from Three Hills, nor because she was hungry, but because she could think of nothing she wanted to do more than to stroll down Main Street in her new gown with Jake at her side.

And she could not remember a prouder moment in her life than when Jake tucked her arm protectively through his and led her down the sidewalk of the ramshackle little town. She had never felt so beautiful before, or cared for, or that she belonged. With Jake by her side she felt there was no place in the world she would not be welcome.

They did not talk much. She could feel the strong beating of his pulse where her fingers touched his wrist and the heat of his arm pressed against her side. When she slowed her steps to peer into a dusty storefront window she caught a glimpse of his lips curving into an indulgent smile, and she was both embarrassed and pleased—embarrassed because she had shared with him her fantasies of walking through a shop and looking at the merchandise, and pleased because the way he smiled told her he did not remember what had happened afterwards.

The telegraph office was busy, and Jessica was glad to remain at the doorway while Jake shoved his way through the crowd. An unsettled feeling came over her on reaching their destination, and she was not looking forward to Daniel's reply as much as she should have been. She wanted to go home—of course she wanted to go home—and she wanted to know that Daniel was well and healthy and waiting for her. Then why did she feel as though with journey's end something very precious would be lost?

''Afternoon, ma'am.''

Jessica turned, startled, toward the sound of the voice, an automatic smile already on her face as she met the man who had greeted her. But her smile wavered and almost faded when she looked into the icy gray eyes above her.

He was a big man, with a long face and hard, strong hands. His skin was pitted with pockmarks, his lips twisted into a grimace of a smile that made Jessica's blood chill. He wore his gun belt low on his hips, below the slight protuberance of his belly, and he leaned with one shoulder against the wall. But despite his bulk and lazy manner he had the aura of a man who could strike quickly and deadly without asking questions or thinking twice. There was a badge on his vest.

Instinctively Jessica shrank back a little. His eyes never moved, and they seemed to be going through her and taking vicious delight in tearing apart everything he saw. She said as pleasantly as she could, "Good afternoon . . . sheriff."

He raised a heavy hand to the brim of his hat. "Sheriff Stratton, ma'am. This here's my town."

Jessica smiled a little weakly, not knowing what to say. He kept looking at her.

"Saw you when you came in this afternoon." His twisted smile arranged itself into something even nastier. He reached out to finger the fall of lace just above her elbow. "Can't say's I object to the change of clothes. You look a bit more like a real woman now."

Jessica tried to move away, but she had no place to go. Her back was already against the wall.

He did not take the hint, but instead let his rough hand drift down to the bare flesh of her forearm. Her skin crawled. "That brother of yours . . ." She couldn't help noticing how he emphasized the word brother just the slightest bit, as though it were a joke she didn't understand.

"He's got quite a temper. We don't want no trouble here in Double Springs."

Jessica's voice was high and not quite steady as she said, "We don't intend to cause any trouble." His finger traveled down the inside of her arm and when she tried to press her arm close to her body, he worked his finger into the crack of her elbow, close to the curve of her breast.

"That's good." He was very close now. His breath smelled rank. "I try to get to know all the strangers that come through here, especially the pretty ones." There was an ugly gleam in his eyes. "Got me a nice little town, runs my way. People learn pretty quick that it pays to be friendly with me."

Jessica's heart was racing and her throat felt thick. Everywhere he touched her she felt contaminated. He put his finger under her chin and made her look at him. There was no mistaking his avaricious look. "Do you know what I mean . . . *ma'am?*"

"What the hell is going on here?" The voice was sharp and furious, and it filled Jessica with relief because it belonged to Jake.

The sheriff straightened up casually and met Jake's eyes with the same low contempt and strength with which he had intimidated Jessica. "Just doing my job, mister," he drawled.

With great effort Jake kept his temper under control. He had seen that animal pawing Jessica and it had been all he could do to keep from stepping in with both fists. Only the gleam of the badge had stopped him. One did not always have to respect the law, but it was a good idea to obey it—or at least give it the benefit of the doubt.

He said icily, "Is it your job to accost ladies on the street?"

The sheriff straightened up, his thumbs hooked innocently into his gun belt but close enough to the Colt at his hip.

Jake tensed his muscles. "It's my job," drawled Stratton, "to check out newcomers."

"Then how about checking her out by keeping your goddamn hands off her?"

Jake's voice was loud, attracting some attention from the telegraph office. Passersby slowed on the opposite side of the street, waiting to see what would happen. Jessica looked at Jake's face, the muscle of his jaw clenching involuntarily, and at the deadly eyes of the man opposite him. "Jake, please."

Stratton said, "I was just telling your pretty *sister* here we don't aim to have no trouble in Double Springs."

"You stay away from her," Jake spat back, "and you won't get any."

A crowd began to gather behind them, murmuring and watching the proceedings with interest.

The sheriff's voice was very low. "You threatening the high law, boy?"

Jake took a step toward him. "You son of a bitch, I don't have to threaten—"

"Jake, please!" Frantically, Jessica laid a hand upon his arm, her eyes pleading as she looked from the hard face of the man before him to the lustful crowd behind them. "It's all right, he didn't mean... couldn't we go now? I—I'm hungry."

Jake took a deep breath, forcing his clenched fists to relax. He knew Stratton; he had met a dozen like him in as many towns up and down the Chisolm Trail. A handful of years ago the man had probably been an outlaw himself, and now kept law and order by gunning down anyone who got in his way. Jake saw his private army, masquerading as deputies or vigilance committee members, materializing from the shadows and moving toward them. No doubt Stratton held the town in the palm of his hand, half through fear, half through blind loyalty, and nobody questioned his methods as long as he got the job done. That was exactly the kind of lawlessness through the law that Daniel wanted to fight in the Senate, for all the good it would do. Men like Stratton would always be there, and they would always get away with their reign of terror. But that wasn't Jake's fight.

He took Jessica's arm, his grip tight on her elbow, but his eyes did not leave Stratton's as he guided her off the sidewalk and around the man, back toward the saloon.

He could feel Jessica's arm trembling beneath his and the rush of shame he felt cooled his temper considerably. He squeezed her forearm bracingly and made himself smile. "Forget him," he said. "We'll be out of this town in a couple of days, and tonight we're going to celebrate. I can just about taste that steak melting in my mouth now."

Jessica smiled, because Jake wanted her to and because when Jake smiled at her something warm spread over her that was impossible to ignore. But she couldn't help remembering the way that hideous man had touched her, and the ugliness in his eyes that had reminded her of her father.

Jessica had never had a meal in a saloon before, and though she tried to relax and enjoy herself she found it hard to do. It wasn't just the noise, the crowd, the activity, or even that awful scene with the sheriff. It was everything. Everything was different now.

Jake sensed it too. The lighthearted relief with which he had ridden into town had dissipated into a dull and ill-defined dread, as though nothing was the way it was supposed to be. For weeks he had seen Jessica as simply Jessica; disheveled, dirty, sometimes desperate, sometimes angry, sometimes exasperating, sometimes amusing . . . but always there, strong and courageous, yet an extension of him. Now he looked across the table and saw a beautiful, well-groomed young woman, and it was like looking at a stranger. Daniel's wife.

Glancing down at the steak and home fries that were set before him, he said, "There wasn't any reply yet."

Jessica looked at him in curiosity, and then realized that he was talking about the telegram. Why should she feel relief to learn there was no reply? Perhaps because, as long as there was no tangible evidence of Three Hills' existence, she could go on remembering it as a hazy daydream. She wouldn't have to think about the time when this journey with Jake would end.

Jake cut into the steak. "That just means they had to take the telegram out to the ranch. It'll be tomorrow before anybody can ride back to town with a reply."

She nodded. She cut her own steak, but found she wasn't very hungry after all. She didn't want to think about Three Hills, about Daniel waiting for her . . . But why not? The only thing that had kept her from going mad these past weeks was the thought of Daniel, of the lovely home and sprawling acres waiting to welcome her. Now it suddenly didn't seem like the only thing worth living for, and the realization distressed her. She couldn't understand it.

Someone started to play a merry little tune on the piano and another group of men wandered in. All of them glanced her way, and Jessica realized that she was the only woman in the place. Her eyes moved uncomfortably around the room, and then she saw a woman coming down the stairs. She did not have to stare to realize that this was one of the notorious saloon girls who made their living in the back rooms of the establishment, and after one quick glance, Jessica jerked her eyes away.

"Her hair," Jessica murmured, without meaning to speak aloud.

Jake looked around until he spotted the object of Jessica's curiosity, and then he chuckled. "God never made hair that color," he agreed easily, and turned back to his meal.

The woman in question wasn't very pretty or very young. Her face was painted with garish red rouge and lip coloring, and the shade clashed with a crop of strawlike orange hair. She was wearing an outrageous black dress that barely covered her knees, and a collection of red petticoats underneath made the skirt stand away from her body in a way that surely wasn't proper even for a saloon girl. But she was the only other woman in the place, and her presence seemed to distract a lot of the attention from Jessica. For that Jessica was grateful. When Jessica looked up again, the woman was looking in her direction, and Jessica smiled at her. The other woman looked startled for a moment, as though she wasn't used to people smiling at her, and then she turned away, leaning up against the piano and starting a conversation with a truculent looking cowboy.

Jessica wondered if Jake spent much time with women like that. She realized it made her sad to think of Jake spending time with any woman.

Which was ridiculous, of course. Jake would marry someday, and he would bring his wife home to Three Hills. She and Jessica would become great friends, and Jake's children would fill the house and take the place of the children Jessica would never have. It would be a good life. They would all be happy together.

But the tension that hovered between them now was a tangible thing, and it was hard for Jessica to imagine the happiness that should be waiting for her at Three Hills.

After a time, trying to force lightness into her tone, she

said, "I guess you're glad not to be eating my cooking anymore."

Jake did not look up. "I never minded." His voice was a little gruff. It flashed before his mind suddenly, the image of Jessica bending over the fire stirring his dinner, flipping her hair out of her way with that graceful little motion of hers, casting him a shy look over her shoulder, and he had difficulty swallowing. A week, he thought. Ten days at the most, and it would be over. She would be home, and safe, and all of this would be like a bad dream. She would be Daniel's.

Jessica let the silence fall. She watched Jake deliberately and methodically cut his steak, and then had to move her eyes away from the flexing of his strong hands. Those hands had pulled her from danger more than once, had held her through the night, gently stroked her hair, cupped her face as the softness of his lips covered hers . . . Deliberately she slammed the door on that treacherous memory, and her stomach began to knot. She found she couldn't eat anymore.

The steak was succulent and moist, but it tasted like sawdust in his mouth. Jake put down his knife and fork and reached for his beer. She looked so lovely and ladylike sitting across from him, her hands folded in her lap, the lace at her bodice casting capricious shadows over the smooth flesh of her collarbone. He just wanted to look at her. He couldn't seem to get enough of looking at her, as though every minute that passed might be their last.

He said after a time, "There's a stage we can get the day after tomorrow. We can be home within a week." His voice sounded strange, a little tight, and the words seemed almost to echo, like something hollow falling into an empty chamber. A week.

Jessica tried to smile, but it fell short. How handsome he

looked, sitting across from her in his dark shirt and tie, his eyes glancing down at his beer, his hair shadowing his forehead, his long fingers moving absently over the glass. He looked sad. She wanted to reach out and touch his hand, to make him smile again, because she knew how he felt. She didn't understand it, but she knew.

"That will be nice," she said, and it sounded unconvincing, inadequate. A week. It *would* be nice. Home. Daniel. And Jake . . . her brother. They were going to be happy. It was going to be good.

Jake did not know how long they sat there, not eating, not saying anything, looking at each other. But he knew it shouldn't be awkward and uncomfortable between them, with nothing to say and too much to feel. Too much wasn't right, didn't make sense.

The place was beginning to get crowded and noisy, and the saloon was no place for a lady after dark. He pushed his chair aside and stood. "I'll walk you upstairs," he said without looking at her. "Then I guess I'll come back down and play some cards."

Jessica nodded, and tried once again to smile as she got up. It would be strange not being with him tonight.

They did not touch or look at each other as they walked upstairs to her room. The noises from the saloon, the piano music, the laughter, the occasional good-spirited rebel yell were only slightly muffled, and Jessica wondered how she would ever sleep. Not that she thought sleep would come easily even without the noise.

Jessica unlocked her door and stepped inside. She turned to say good night to Jake.

"Sleep late in the morning if you want," he said. "I'm going to sell the horses and get some stage tickets, and maybe you'd like to do some shopping for the trip."

Jessica smiled, suddenly overcome by his thoughtfulness. "Thank you, Jake," she said, "for everything." She leaned forward to brush a sisterly kiss across his cheek.

Jake's hands went lightly to her waist, startled. He didn't mean to hold her there, but she did not step away. Their eyes met, hers deep and blue and open and seeming to swallow his; his dark and aching and hungry. It seemed as though they mutually came together, a single breath, a single movement.

There was no conscious decision, no deliberate movement. She was simply in his arms as she was meant to be, his mouth was upon hers, soft and wet and warm, drawing her close, closer . . . There was hunger in their kiss, and joy, and something bursting and building that felt like dying, or being born. His hands were hard on her waist, and then traveling up to her back and her shoulders, tracing her shape, pressing her close. Her hands lifted from his shoulders to his neck, wrapping her arms around him, holding him close, kissing him. There was demand in his kiss, there was dizzied, powerful wonder in hers. Jessica felt herself opening to him, welcoming him. *Jake, oh Jake, it was you all along . . . not my brother, but my love . . .* The truth of it rose up in her throat like a cry and her very blood was singing the refrain and sorrow and need and desperate wonder. *Jake . . . oh, Jake. . . .*

Suddenly he stiffened and tore his mouth away from hers almost savagely. He stood above her, breathing hard, his eyes dark and raw with shock and need, his fingers digging into her ribs painfully as she struggled to let go, struggled to hold on. Her lips felt bruised and every muscle in her body trembled and ached with need, and when she looked at him nothing was hidden in her eyes.

He released her abruptly and his absence was like a blow

to her chest; it left her weak and stunned and too helpless to even speak, to reach for him. He looked at her for a long moment, and the stark agony in his eyes pierced straight through Jessica's soul. Then he turned and strode away.

Chapter XII

Jessica did not know how long she paced the narrow confines of the room, her hands pressed tightly together, biting her lips to keep back the tears of joy or pain or simple confusion. . . .

Jake.

It had been Jake all along, and she had known it, she must have known it. How could she be married to Daniel when she loved Jake? For love was more than just the affection and gratitude she felt for the kind older man; love was powerful and consuming. It opened every part of her and made her belong to him, it was quiet and it was insidious and it was strong and flaming and it had dwelt within her so long that she could not refuse it any longer . . . It was Jake. Only Jake.

And she was married to his brother.

The tinny sounds of piano music floated up to her from the room below, short bursts of laughter, a breaking glass.

Hoofbeats trotted on the hard-packed earth outside her window and in the hallway she heard a woman's giggle, a man's low answering murmur, a door opening and closing.

Her mind raced and her heart ached. She wanted to cry and she wanted to laugh, wanted to reach for Jake and hold him close, to lose herself in the strength of his arms and the sound of his heartbeat. What was she going to do?

At the sound of the knock on her door, her heart stopped, then lurched into a joyous explosion of relief and anticipation. "Jake!" she whispered, and rushed to open it.

At first she was too disappointed and disoriented to do anything but stare. It wasn't Jake who lounged against the door frame. It was Sheriff Stratton.

He stepped inside, closing the door on a sudden burst of song from the saloon. Jessica took an automatic step backwards, too confused even to question his presence. His cold, hating eyes roamed over her once, and a slow grin twisted at his mouth.

"Well, little lady," he said, "I thought it was about time you and I got better acquainted. Your brother," again there was a nasty little curl to the word, "has got hisself into a pretty hot card game, so I don't think we'll be interrupted."

Jessica's heart started to beat loudly and painfully. She managed, "Sheriff . . ." in a kind of question, but she didn't know what she had intended to say.

It didn't matter, for he continued to advance on her, and whenever she took a step back the gleam of lustful satisfaction in his eyes seemed to grow.

"You know," he said, "normally I don't mess with other men's women." Jessica watched in mute horror as his thick, rough fingers went to his gun belt, beginning to unbuckle it. She took another step backwards. "But since you're that cowpoke's 'sister' . . ." His brown-toothed grin widened.

"I didn't figure you'd mind a little entertainment tonight."

The back of her knees pressed into the metal frame of the bed. Jake, she thought, and it rose like a scream in her throat. *Jake*... But she couldn't make a sound.

Stratton released his gun belt and tossed it onto the bed. He took the last step toward her.

Jessica did scream then, but it was choked off almost before it was born by a heavy hand across her mouth. Her breath left her lungs in a gasp as he pushed her down hard on the bed.

Jake held two aces in his hand, and he stared at them without seeing them. The music, the laughter, the blank faces of four strangers who shared the table with him all faded away. Over and over to the sound of his own heartbeat he thought, *How could you have done it? How could you have let it happen? Jesus God, she's Daniel's wife*...

He felt the eyes of the other men on him and he automatically raised the bet a dollar. He had lost the last two hands, but he didn't care. All he could think about was her softness, the taste of her. All he could see was her eyes, filled with longing and welcome, and it invaded his blood, the memory of her, his need for her. Even his skin ached for her. How could he have walked away?

He had promised himself it would never happen again. After that one episode at the trapper's hut, he hadn't let himself get close. He had determined to put it out of his mind, and he thought he had succeeded.

You're not going to do this to Daniel. Or to her, or to yourself. Forget it. She's not yours. She's going home.

His pulse felt like a tight knot in his throat. Every part of him was stiff, aching. He could taste her. All he wanted to do was hold her.

His eyes drifted without volition to the stairs.

Stay away from her. Stay here, play cards, get drunk if you have to, but stay away from her. . . .

He couldn't forget the look in her eyes. She had wanted to call out to him, he knew it. If she had called out, if she had made the slightest sound, he wouldn't have been able to keep on walking.

And if he went up those stairs now, there would be no turning back. He would never let her go.

He set his jaw; his fingers tightened. He turned his eyes away from the stairs and back to the cards.

Jessica's head flailed back and forth as she sobbed, desperately trying to think of some way to escape. His weight was crushing her, his sharp fingers digging into one leg, trying to push her skirts up. His grunts of effort and satisfaction filled her ears and his eyes burned into her.

"That's a girl, fight me," he hissed. "More fun that way." His fingers tore at her petticoat.

She bit down hard on his hand and when he jerked it away she screamed, then screamed again. The music jangled, chairs scraped, people laughed. No one heard her.

She twisted and kicked, she beat him with her fists, but panic drowned her and she knew she had no chance. His breath was hot, his hands bruising on her ribs and legs, and no one could hear her, no one would come.

Her hand flailed backwards, looking for something to hold onto or brace herself against, something to strike out with. Her fingers contacted the smooth leather of the gun belt. With a cry of rage and terror and desperation, she lifted it.

"Whatcha gonna do, cowpoke?"

The man across from him had drawn a deuce. There was

one jack out, two tens, and a queen. Jake was holding a flush, aces high. He looked at the cards for a long time without seeing them. His heart was beating, heavily, steadily, urgently.

Stay. Leave her alone.

Jake calmly folded his cards and got up from the table. Without looking back, he pushed his way across the room and toward the stairs.

Jessica brought the holstered gun down hard on the back of his neck. He swore viciously and grabbed for her arm, but she screamed and twisted, trying to roll away. Then she struck out again with the gun, bucking against him, kicking, striking again . . .

The explosion shook the room. It jerked her arm back with such force that the gun flew from her hand and an agonized bolt of pain shot through her shoulder blade. She thought dimly that she was dying; something had happened and she was dying . . . Suddenly the heavy weight rolled limply off her, the fetid breath was no longer scorching her face, and she was on her feet, gasping and shaking and backing away, staring at the lifeless man on the bed.

Blood had spattered on the wall, on the floor, soaking the white sheets from a gaping hole in the man's back. It was on her hands and face. He didn't move, he didn't breathe. He was dead. *I've killed him,* Jessica thought, but it was a disassociated thing that had no meaning for her. She stared at her hands and the blood and the body on the bed; she heard the uncontrollable series of choked, whimpering sounds that came from her. None of it seemed real, and all she could think was that she had to tell Jake. . . .

Jake burst through the door almost before the echo died.

In one sweeping glance he took it all in. The bloody body on the bed, Jessica in shock beside it, her soft whimpers, and in less than a second he knew it all. The horror, the terror, the decision. Stratton was dead. He had tried to attack Jessica and she had somehow shot him, but he knew these people, he knew this town. The sheriff was dead. Nobody got away with killing the sheriff, especially in a place like this, especially a woman, no matter what the cause . . . He knew they would lock her up. Nobody would listen and she would die if they locked her up again.

A second, no more. In two swift strides he was beside her, grabbing her shoulders, whirling her to face him. "Jessica," he said, "Jessica, listen to me. Can you hear me?"

His face was a dark and intense blur before her. She couldn't stop shaking, she couldn't think. She tried to speak, but only a series of incoherent sounds came through. All she knew was that Jake was there; Jake would hold her and make it right.

Jake shook her until her hair tumbled down and her teeth clacked together sharply and then his face was clear before her, clear and dark and grim. "Listen," he said fiercely. "Go to the livery. Saddle my horse and leave it there. Then get out of town. Do you remember that stand of pecans we passed on the way in? Do you?" He shook her again, until she managed to nod. "Wait for me there. But if I'm not there in an hour, get out. Ride west. Get back to Daniel. Can you do that, Jessica? Do you understand?"

"Yes," she managed. Her breath was hissing in her throat and yet she could hardly breathe; she was shaking all over but she couldn't feel her heart beating. "Yes, I can do that." Because Jake said she must. She would do what Jake told her.

His hands tightened on her shoulders painfully and he propelled her toward the door. "Go out the back stairs," he commanded. "I'll hold them off as long as I can. Hurry."

Jessica ran. She could do it, she could do what Jake told her, she would wait for him . . . She lifted her skirts and sped toward the back stairs. A door opened in the corridor, startled eyes met hers below a mass of frowsy orange hair. "Lord, honey, what's all the commotion—"

But Jessica didn't stop, didn't look back. She ran.

Jake heard the steps on the stairs, the rush down the hall, and he knew it was too late for him to try to follow.

Hurry, Jessica, hurry. . . .

The men filled the doorway, the unarmed saloon keeper and two curious, though somewhat reticent cowpokes. They weren't prepared for violence. The sheriff ran a tight town.

Their eyes bulged when they saw the massacre. "Son of a bitch!"

The saloon keeper rushed toward the body. One of the others drew his sidearm and swung it on Jake. Jake lifted his hands and took a step back, pretending to retreat while edging for the open door as one man went toward the body and the other advanced on him.

"It's the sheriff! God almighty, the son of a bitch shot him in the back!"

"Wasn't even wearing his gun! Shot him in the goddamn back!"

The man holding the revolver on Jake was sweating. He cast a frantic glance toward the other two. "It's him! It's the troublemaker from the telegraph office!"

Jake said quietly, "It's not what you think."

"Get the deputy! God almighty, he's dead! The sheriff is dead!"

"Shoulda seen it coming! Knew he was trouble!"

Jake took another small step, and the other man drew his gun. "Hold it right there, mister!"

Jake knew this was his only chance. He could hold his own with three scared men, but once the trained assassins who called themselves deputies arrived he wouldn't have a chance in hell.

Jessica, hurry, hurry!

The man closest to him jerked his revolver in the direction of Jake's gun belt. "All right, mister, hand it over." He was breathing hard, and the hand that held the weapon on Jake was none too steady. "Real slow like. Butt first."

Jake moved slowly, his eyes never leaving the two men with guns. He took the butt of his revolver gingerly in two fingers, unobtrusively inserting a third into the trigger guard. He slipped it out by inches, and slowly extended it toward his guard, butt first. The man reached out to take it.

Hoofbeats raced past the window. Jake spun the gun around on the trigger guard and fanned it, firing toward the wall behind them. The men hit the floor together, dropping their weapons and covering their heads. Jake kept on firing as he ran out of the room and toward the back stairs.

Jessica hid her horse far back in the grove of trees. Anxiously she paced the periphery, her heart beating off the minutes. It had been more than an hour. She knew it had been. The night was moonless and dark, the grove in which she had hidden far back from the road. No sound carried.

It came back to her, with a wash of weakness and chills, a horror too great to be imagined. The struggle, the explosion, the blood. A man was dead. She had killed him. He had been alive and trying to hurt her and then he was dead. But she hadn't meant it, it was an accident...

Jake. Oh, God please, Jake . . . Why had he stayed? What had he done? He was hurt, or in jail, or—

He had said not to wait. He had said to go to Daniel. How could she leave him? How could she leave him behind?

I'll never see him again, she thought. *He's hurt or dead and I'll never see him again. . . .*

She pressed trembling fingers to her lips, and she tried to pray, but the only thing she could form was Jake's name.

Her horse whinnied softly. She couldn't leave Jake. She had to go back and find him. On trembling legs she turned and started toward her horse. Then she froze.

The silence was thick and black and engulfing. But faintly, ever so faintly from the distant road, she thought she heard the sound of hoofbeats. A single rider, moving fast. It could be a deputy or one of the men from town coming to get her. *Run,* Jake had said. *Go to Daniel.* She couldn't make herself move.

She did not know how long she stood there, muscles paralyzed, breath suspended, bursting with hope and dread and waiting . . . The hoofbeats left the road. A silhouette appeared through the grove of trees, moving closer. She stood still, waiting.

When he dismounted a few yards away she lifted her skirts and ran.

She flung herself into his arms and he held her tightly, crushing her to him, burying his face in her neck. She could say nothing as joy and relief bubbled up inside her, she could only hold him, filling her senses with him. His warmth, his strength, the smell of horse and leather and perspiration, taut muscles straining, heavy breaths rushing, and his heartbeat . . . his heartbeat. Jake, solid and alive and with her.

"I left a false trail," he said. His voice was husky and unsteady, his breath heating her skin where it touched. "They can't send a posse out until morning and by then we'll have a head start."

Jake. Alive, thank God. She wanted to sob aloud with it but all she could do was tighten her arms around him until they ached and lift her face to his and let his mouth cover hers, greedily, hungrily. . . .

It surged around them and through them, desperate release, overpowering need. . . . It was more than relief, more than joy. It was life snatched from the jaws of death, a second chance fiercely seized. It was being born again and not questioning why or how, merely receiving it, cherishing it, holding on and refusing to let go.

Jessica did not know whether it was her weakness or his strength which drew them to the ground. She felt his arms wrapped around her, his mouth tasting her, drawing from her, sending warm swirls of dizzied wonder through her as her lips moved beneath his, lifting to him, holding him, drawing him back to her again and again, unable to get enough of him. The grass was soft and damp beneath her; Jake's heat covered her. Her lips were brushing his face, its texture soft and abrasive, its taste salty and sweet. Her hands stroked his hair, gathering it, holding it, touching it. Her voice was barely a breath as she whispered, "Jake, thank God, I thought . . . thank God—"

His hands drove themselves into her hair. "Jessica, I can't—God, I need . . ."

And then his mouth covered hers, fierce and possessive and hard, and she wrapped her arms around him with a sob that choked in her throat as she pressed herself to him, unable to get close enough or stay long enough. . . .

There was a trembling inside her, a mindlessness, as his

lips moved down to taste her throat, his hand urgently and restlessly tracing the shape of her down to her waist, and then up again. She gasped as his hand closed firmly, warmly, over the swell of her breast, and then he turned his mouth there. His breath heated a flame all the way to the center of her abdomen as it penetrated the material, and then the moisture and warmth of his mouth thrilled her as it opened over her breast, kissing her there. Consciousness receded into sensation, wonderful, sparkling sensation that was a twisting spiral of pleasure and anxiety as it weakened her muscles, rushed through her blood, caused something tight and quavering to knot in her stomach. Her arms tightened around him and she moaned in helplessness and need, for it was Jake, Jake whose intimacy she welcomed, Jake whom she loved.

He tasted the warm flesh of her chest, the softening curve of her breast. His hand moved downward, beneath her hip, and below, and each movement, each soft sound she made sent a new wave of weakness through him and he thought helplessly, *Stop me, Jessica, don't let this happen* . . . But it was too late. It was beyond desperation, beyond need. It was a seizure of something he couldn't control and didn't want to. He only knew that he needed her, that he had almost lost her and he couldn't lose her again. He couldn't let her go.

She felt his hand beneath her skirts, pushing them up to her waist. Cool night air washed over her fevered skin, and Jake's hand was firm against the thin cotton that covered her calf. She was trembling, but not from fear. The dark, starless night was whirling, a flood of sensations bombarded her, and as his hand moved upward that awful aching deep within her intensified and she knew only that she wanted him, wanted him touching her, holding her, staying close to her, as close as he could possibly be.

His fingers brushed against her abdomen, then fumbled with the ties that bound her pantalets at her waist. Everything within her seemed to stop, to focus into clear and sharp relief. The night was still. Jake's breathing was light and unsteady. His fingers were warm as they brushed against her naked skin and a burst of perspiration bathed her body when he touched her. Her heartbeat was wild and erratic, filling her ears, hurting her chest. She felt weak, liquid, waiting. She knew something powerful was about to happen, something that would change her forever, and she was afraid. Then she wasn't afraid because it was Jake, and for him she could give nothing less than all of herself, she wanted nothing more than all of him....

He slipped the undergarment down over her hips, and then off her legs entirely. His torso covered her, his chest hard against her aching breasts, his mouth drinking of hers. There was heat, there was urgency. Somehow his legs had wedged themselves between hers and the rough weave of his pants was a gentle abrasive against the tender flesh of her inner thighs. Time seemed to have speeded up, and then disappeared altogether, so that it had no relation to what was happening to them. There was Jake, and there was Jessica, and there was need that could wait no longer to be assuaged.

Dimly she was aware of his hands pulling at his gun belt, tugging at his clothing. The night was afire with expectancy and the unknown, awash in emotions and sensations and desires never before imagined. And then she felt his thighs naked and strong between hers, flesh against flesh, the embrace of his arms around her, the rush of his breath in her ear, the touch of his lips on her face. And the part of him that was made to fit with her, strong and heated, strange and frightening, pressed against the tender crevice of her most secret flesh.

She knew it would hurt. But the power of giving, the deep and encompassing need for him and what they were about to share had taken her beyond fear, beyond reluctance, far beyond thought. Every pore of her had opened to him, her essence yearned and stretched toward him, and the magnificence of the love that had brought them together filled her, swept her away. There was no past, no future. There was only this helpless moment and what was meant to be.

The power of his thrust rent the night, seared her body and her mind. There was pain, yet there was glory. She clung to him, smothering a cry in his shoulder, and his arms held her tightly, protecting her, cherishing her. She felt the dampness and heat of his cheek against her, the feathering of his hair upon her face, the strong, fast beat of his heart on her breast. He trembled as he held her, strong muscles straining beneath her hands. It was Jake, and this was what she was meant for: to belong to him, to make a part of him a part of her.

The pain faded and he filled her. The power of it was incomprehensible to the mind, this act of nature that bonded souls and bodies, that made them not two but one. This meaning of womanhood, this essence of love. Jake had brought it to her. Jake was the reason she was meant to be, and nothing would ever be the same again. Not ever.

Long afterward Jake held her, fragile and small against him, and all he wanted to do for the rest of his life was hold her. He could feel his heart, slow and steady and powerful, and hers, light and rhythmic. His mind was reeling with sensations and emotions and half-formed thoughts, wonder and weakness and incredible joy, and far deep inside him something was aching and slowly tearing him in two.

All he could think of was Jessica. All he could feel was Jessica, inside his brain, inside the very pores of his skin, deep inside his soul. *Jessica*. He ached for her, he exalted in her, he felt for her all the things it was possible for one human being to feel for another and then even more. There was no way to describe what had just happened between them, touching his soul and leaving him stunned and shaken and helpless. Because it was Jessica.

And there was horror, a dull throb that pushed through the euphoria with slow, swimming motions. *Jessica*. He tried to ignore it, but he couldn't make it go away. Jessica, this dear innocent creature he held in his arms, the woman whose life was so inextricably a part of his, the one woman in the world who had made him whole....

Jessica, his brother's wife.

My God. What have I done? What have I done...

He wanted to hold her, to kiss her, to bury himself inside her again and hide her within him. He wanted to keep her safe, to love her, to make everything good for her and keep her a part of him forever... And he had just done the one thing that could destroy her.

Jessica.

Jake listened to the sound of his heartbeat, watching the still dark world gradually reorient itself. Through the nightmare of the night there had been born a miracle, yet the miracle had given birth to yet another, even worse nightmare, and the cycle of destruction and pain they had set in motion seemed endless. It would haunt them the rest of their lives, and there was no turning back. How had it happened? Dear God, what had they done?

She was so still and soft against him that he thought she

might have fallen asleep. The wave of tenderness that filled him tightened in his throat, burned in his eyes, and it was only with the greatest effort that he kept his arms from pulling her to him again.

Jessica.

How could this have happened? How could he let her go?

"Jessica." His voice was hoarse. He shook her shoulder lightly. Her eyes opened, dazed, and he could not look at her. How could he ever look at her again?

He sat up. His voice was harsh and he hated the sound of it. He hated everything about himself except the part he had given to her. "We have to go. The posse will be here at sunrise. We have to get out of here."

He got up and heartlessly walked away from her. He could hear her soft confused murmur as she rose and rearranged her clothing. He stood still, letting the awful, searing pain grip him. He clenched his fists against it, squeezed his eyes tightly shut.

Without turning, and in barely more than a whisper, he said, "I'm sorry."

Chapter XIII

The night went on forever, measured by the cautious footsteps of the horses as they picked their way through shadowed landscape across unfamiliar trails. Exhaustion and shock eventually took over and Jessica felt as though she were being swallowed by a black abyss of nothingness. Her mind drifted off into a senseless state somewhere between sleep and stupor, and at times she was convinced she had imagined the entire series of events—the struggle, the gun, the blood . . . and Jake.

But she had not imagined what had happened with Jake. Of all else, that much was clear. The unfamiliar soreness of her body shouted it was so, the subtle peace that dwelt deep within her assured her it was real. The world might well end in this black and soundless pit of a Texas night, but one thing would not change, and one truth would never be taken from her. She had loved Jake, and she could face anything for having known that.

The dawn came reluctantly, pushing away the night with scrawny gray fingers, sending motes of murky light through the trees. She did not know how long she had ridden with slack reins, but when Jake pulled up in front of her, her mount halted obediently and dropped its head to drink from the stream. Jake dismounted, and Jessica looked at him foggily, gradually reorienting herself.

Jake had done enough tracking to know how to leave a false trail. Though the course they had taken through the night had appeared to be aimless meanderings it was actually a path carefully and precisely calculated to put as much distance between them and town as possible, while at the same time making certain to mislead their pursuers at all points. They were in the rich rolling redlands of East Texas now, farm country. They had backtracked on their original course several times, and were now almost twenty miles northeast of Double Springs—and that much farther away from Three Hills. But the trail Jake had originally left had led west. He could only hope that by the time the posse realized they had actually gone in the opposite direction it would be too late.

They had crossed this stream more than once, each time emerging on the opposite side from that which a tracker would expect. The place he had chosen to stop was a small clearing in the midst of a thick tangle of hardwoods. The low growth of branches would provide cover from all directions, and a few paces forward a vine covered overhanging rock formed a natural alcove, a shallow cave where they might rest during the heat of the day. Rest was not something they could afford, but the horses couldn't go much further, and common sense told him he couldn't stay alert much longer either. It would be better to rest now than regret it later. He began to unsaddle his horse.

"We'll be safe here for awhile," he said without looking

at Jessica. "Later we'll have to go out and try to find some supplies, but for now the best thing we can do is lay low."

Jessica slid from the saddle stiffly and painfully. Her face was pale and drawn, her eyes dark with fatigue and the remnants of shock. Jake glanced at her, and then quickly away, but not before the twist of pain tightened his chest. It had been his job to protect her, to take care of her, to bring her safely home. But since she had been in his charge he had starved her, led her into the hands of death in a savage swamp, put her through more physical abuse than any woman should ever be required to endure . . . and had turned her into an adulteress. She was being pursued by a gang of lawless vigilantes who would as soon kill her as not, and what could he do to protect her? She was exhausted, she was beaten, she was aching with mental and physical shock. And he couldn't even offer her anything to eat.

Jessica walked over to him. Her voice was small, her face was tight with pleading and confusion. "Jake, we can't do this. We can't keep on running. Why can't we go back, tell them what happened—"

"No." The harshness of his voice made her flinch as he heaved his saddle down and carried it toward the alcove. "You wouldn't even get a trial."

"But it was an accident, it—"

"No, goddamn it!" He dropped the saddle on the ground and turned on her, his face dark, his eyes flashing with hostility and incomprehensible emotions. "The man is *dead,* damn it, a goddamn sheriff shot in the back! It doesn't matter how it happened. Nobody cares! I had to shoot my way out of that room. Do you think they're going to be interested in anything you have to say? We go anywhere near that town and they probably won't even bother with a rope."

Jessica stared at him in slowly dawning horror, recoiling from the truth he implied which simply hadn't occurred to her before. Jake had taken the blame for what she had done. He had used his gun to escape a lynching, and it didn't matter that it was an accident, it didn't matter that she had only been defending herself and Jake had done nothing wrong. He had taken the blame for a murder he had not committed to protect her, and she remembered the torture she had seen in his eyes the night before, the heavy silence that had ridden between them all these hours, and she understood.

She brought trembling fingers to her lips to stifle the agonized cry that wanted to break through, her eyes enormous in her white face. "Oh Jake." It was barely a whisper. "What have I done to you?"

He stiffened himself against the need to sweep her into his arms and comfort her and reassure her and make the horror go away. The anger that she had mistaken in his voice was really desperation, and the last thing he had wanted was to hurt her with it. The last thing he wanted was to hurt her, ever.

"Jessica . . ." His voice softened, and he could not keep the brief wash of aching tenderness from his voice as he took a step toward her. But then he caught himself. He lowered his eyes and moved past her toward her horse. He said wearily, "You haven't done anything to me. All we have to do is get out of this county, stay low until we get back to the ranch. Daniel—" His voice almost choked on the name, and he applied extra effort to tugging at the cinch. "Daniel will fix it."

He could not think about Daniel. He could not make himself imagine facing his brother after what he had done, what he felt. With the last ounce of strength he possessed, he commanded himself to put it out of his mind. One step at a time, one crisis at a moment, for the future was not something he could deal with now. Daniel never had to know. It was an accident, just like—

But there his mind slammed shut. Because it wasn't an accident. It was the only good and perfect thing he had done in his life, and the sorrow and the guilt were tearing him apart inside.

Jessica wrapped her arms around herself to stop the shivers, to hold in the aching. She watched the movements of his shoulders beneath the dark material as he worked the girth, the brush of his hair against the back of his neck, the certainty in his hand as he ran it absently over the mare's flank, calming her. Jessica was filled with love and yearning for him, this man who only hours before had lain with her, a part of her, and had given her the greatest gift it was possible for a woman to know. Intense despair and longing grew and swelled within until she thought no power on earth could ever contain it. She said tightly, "Oh, Jake I never meant for this to happen." She closed her eyes because she could feel the tears burning there, and she held herself more tightly. "Please don't let this happen. I can't let you—suffer because of me." Her voice was torn with pleading, everything within her reaching out to him, but she couldn't make herself move. "Please. Don't you see I love you? I never—"

She saw Jake's shoulders tense, and for a split second he didn't move. Then he applied himself to lifting the saddle. "You can't love me," he said harshly. "You're married to Daniel."

Something within Jessica cried out with that, like a wounded animal helpless against its pain. He carried the saddle over to the alcove, and she took a step to follow him. "I can't help it! You know that it's true. You know—"

He let the saddle fall to the ground beside his, and when he turned to her there was such raw torment in his eyes that she stopped.

"Don't." The single word was torn from him. His hands closed into fists at his sides, and even though his voice softened a fraction the anguish in his eyes went through her like a knife. "What happened last night..." He faltered, groping for words and finding none, hating his own inadequacy, fighting against what he had to say. "It was wrong, it never should have happened. I shouldn't have—" He stopped, and took a deep breath. He saw the hurt and pleading in her eyes and tried vainly to harden himself against it. How could he tell her he was sorry for something that could not be changed? What good would regret do either of them now? What could he say to make her understand what he did not understand himself?

He made his face hard. His fingers dug into his palms. He said flatly, "It was wrong. We have to forget it and get on with our lives."

He turned then and walked a few steps away. Jessica stood where she was, and something strong and calm began to form within her whose source she did not know and did not question. Jake was right. She was married to Daniel. Perhaps what she and Jake had done was a sin, but she could feel no shame for it, and no regret. Before Jake she had never known life, never known the meaning of hope, never known love. If hell were her punishment, it was a small price to pay, for she would never repent for what she knew in her heart was the only right thing that she had ever done.

Her voice was small and strained but clear as she said, "I won't be sorry. I—I know that Daniel is my husband and that—that what we did was wrong, but you can't make me regret it, or be ashamed of loving you."

Jake fastened his hand around a low tree branch, his jaw clenching, his muscles aching. Jessica, don't, he thought. He refused to turn around, refused to meet the hurt in her eyes, the simple honesty in her face. For God's sake, don't. . . .

The tears burned in her throat, ached behind her eyes, but she refused to give in to them. The silence stretched between them like something wounded and alive, suspended between despair and hope, and she wished with all her might that she could do something to make everything right, to erase the pain. What should have been joy was swallowed in sorrow, what should have been a future the two of them could claim was only uncertainty, and all she could speak was the truth, simply and painfully. "Because I do love you, Jake. I have loved you always, and will love you forever. Nothing is going to take that away from me."

He turned slowly. There was an agony of need and reluctance in his eyes, a throb of desperate hope, and Jessica thought her heart would break just looking at him. "God help me," he whispered, brokenly, "I love you too."

He went to her. They wrapped themselves in each other's arms, holding on tight. Her wet breaths were muffled in his shirt, his face was pressed into her neck. There was desperation, and yet there was joy, for even though there was no tomorrow the moment was theirs, and having known so little from life before now, how could they ask for more?

Her heart had begun to beat, strongly, gloriously, with nothing more than being in his arms, and the feel of it surprised her, infused her with warmth. When he lifted his face it was with the same instinct of sureness and welcome that she lifted her lips to his. The kiss they shared was slow and deep and tender, drawing from each other every nuance of need and care. Her blood began to flow again, her lungs to fill with air. Colors played upon the screen of her closed eyes, her skin absorbed the feel of him and it was like being born anew.

His hands moved to her hair, cupping its knotted, tangled curls, caressing them, and then driving his fingers into them as he tilted her head back and claimed her lips again. His mouth opened over hers, moving with a greedy hunger that weakened Jessica's muscles even as his need charged a bolt of heady strength through her. Her fingers closed upon his corded neck, absorbing the damp and heated texture of his skin. And then restlessly, her hands moved down, spanning the breadth of his shoulders, feeling the flex of his muscles, pulling him closer.

He looked down at her, his hands holding her face, his eyes dark with intensity and shadowed with a question, his breath unsteady as he whispered, "Jessica, if we don't stop now. . . ."

Her face was flushed, her eyes bright. Her pulses were light and rapid, her breath a shallow stream through lips that were rouged and parted and still wet with his moisture. The fine trembling inside her was from wonder; the anxious, questing anticipation felt like happiness, begging to be born. And the look in Jake's eyes made her weak, made her brave, and she knew only that she wanted to see that look in his eyes always, for she could never answer his question with anything other than yes.

Searching his face with eyes that were bold yet shy, she whispered, "I don't want to stop."

He looked at her, lashes slowly lowering as he took in every part of her, filling himself with her and the wonder of the promise she offered. Then his lips drifted lightly across her face and he lifted her into his arms.

With utmost care he laid her down inside the alcove, the overhang of entwined branches forming a lacy canopy of green and misty morning sun. She reached for him, a fluttering smile of shy welcome on her lips, and he stretched out beside her, caressing her face with both hands, gently, adoringly. His eyes were emerald, alive with sparks that tightened and darkened with the course of emotions that flowed between them.

He said softly, earnestly, "I only want to love you, Jessica. That's all I ever want."

Her fingers stroked his cheek, rough with the night's growth of beard, and he closed his eyes with the pleasure of the caress.

"That's all I ever ask," she whispered.

They touched each other with fingertips that were discovering beauty for the first time, looked at each other with eyes that spoke of things for which there were no words. Time lost its meaning and urgency drifted away into the gentle morning sun, and there was nothing and no one but the two of them and what they had to offer each other. He began to remove her clothing slowly, and though Jessica was shy at first to be uncovered in the full light of day, that, too, disappeared with the wonder and pleasure she saw in Jake's eyes. With each layer he removed he drank in the sight of her, slowly, almost reverently, not touching her but telling her without words that she was beautiful to him. When he looked at her she felt beautiful. And then, when she was completely naked and unashamed before him, he removed his own clothing.

The sensation of his body, strong and muscled and unclothed against hers as he gathered her into his arms, was dizzying, electrifying. The strangeness of it both frightened and compelled her, yet holding him was a pleasure so great she could not have even imagined it. She let her hands drift over the smooth muscled contours of his shoulders, down his back to his narrow waist, and upwards over his ribs to the arms which encircled her. Touching him, discovering him, filling herself with the presence of him. It was more wonderful than anything she had ever known.

His lips moved lightly over her face, savoring each kiss, prolonging each moment. With both hands he smoothed back her hair, fanning it like a shawl around her head, and then he simply looked at her for a long time. Jessica. His. The infusion of contentment and wonder was intense and powerful, and he wanted her to feel it too. He wanted her to feel everything that he felt for her. He wanted to give her pleasure, and he wanted it so badly that his chest ached and his eyes hurt from the sheer beauty of her.

Last night had been rough and frantic and mindless, less than she deserved and more than either of them had expected. Today there was time. Today there was nothing outside the two of them and he would make the moment last forever; he would draw from it every last drop of pleasure. He wanted to give to her the way he had never given to a woman before.

His gaze was making her blush, and when he ran his hand lightly over the exquisite texture of her skin from hip to waist, she trembled. He brushed her lips lightly with his. "Don't be frightened, Jessica," he whispered. "It won't hurt this time. I promise."

She took a breath that shuddered slightly in her chest, then lifted her hand to his face, smoothing away a lock of hair that shadowed his temple. "I'm not afraid." It was true, for what quivered inside her stomach and speeded her pulses was greater than fear, more powerful than anxiety. It was Jake. Simply Jake.

He kissed her throat and her collarbone, and his hands slipped up to cup her breasts as one strong thigh covered both of hers. She could feel his manhood, hard and heated and swollen, pressing against the soft flesh of her stomach, and the sensation made her gasp. But the gasp turned into an involuntary moan of pleasure as he bent his head and his mouth closed gently over one breast.

Nerve endings flared and dizziness swept through her with his moist warm suckling upon her breast. His hand closed over the other breast, squeezing gently, and then with his thumb and forefinger he drew the nipple to tingling, stiffening life. A strong wire of urgency twisted from her throat to the very center of her womb, and she had to compress her lips tightly to keep from crying out with it. Then both his hands warmed her breasts, kneading them, as his lips trailed a path down her ribcage to the tautening flesh of her belly, where he placed a deep and lingering kiss. Every part of her opened to him, throbbing with a multitude of small and separate pulses; there was an uncomfortable aching between her legs, a confusing demanding urgency that she could not understand and only he could fill.

Her helpless, trembling fingertips followed the path his shoulders took as he moved down her body, pressing a kiss into the hollow of her hipbone, and then upon the sensitive flesh of her inner thigh. She smothered a cry and her fingers tightened on his slippery flesh, then he slid upward again. She caught a glimpse of his face, his eyes bright with pleasure and yearning, before his mouth covered hers. She lifted herself to his kiss with a demand that surprised her, opening her mouth to him, arching her hips against him, her hands moving restlessly over his back. The silky hair on his chest abraded her sensitive breasts, the probing heat of his engorged maleness pressed into her thigh. She felt his heated breath on her face, and when the gentle tasting motion of his lips made a path to her earlobe, new sparks of desire shot through her, causing her to cry out softly.

She felt damp and heated flesh beneath her restless, urgent fingertips, heard the unsteady rush of his breath and her own, a pounding of hearts that seemed to shake the very ground on which they lay. When he slipped his hand down to her closed thighs her muscles clenched instinctively, involuntarily, but then moved apart with his gentle urging. He touched her briefly at the center of her femininity, and her heart lurched into such a frantic explosion that she thought she would surely burst with it. A flood of heat and moisture rushed to the place his hand cupped, and the aching that had begun deep inside her twisted another fraction.

He moved himself above her, parting her thighs further with his strong legs, and his arms slipped beneath her back, embracing her, holding him to her for a long and precious moment. Then he moved his hands to cradle her head. He looked down at her with eyes as bright and deep as the sun-washed leaves above them. He kissed her.

His entry into her body was a slow, sliding intrusion that pressed rather than tore. Unaccustomed flesh stretched to accommodate the strange presence, and Jessica's fingers tightened on his shoulders, expecting the pain. She could feel his muscles quiver as he pushed deeper inside her, and deeper, and soon the discomfort gave way to the sensation of being filled with him, of opening to him. The tightness within her womb seemed to expand and welcome him, to reach for the part of him that invaded her. He was still, holding himself inside her, and she gloried in the sensation.

His fingers, light and unsteady, stroked her hair. "Ah, Jessica," he breathed. "I wish I could make you feel . . . what this feels like to me."

She opened her eyes. His face was damp and flushed, his lips parted, his eyes dark and unfocused and lit with a low and slumberous fire that spoke of adoration and need and exquisite pleasure. She reached a trembling hand to smooth away a strand of hair that was caught in the perspiration on his forehead, and she whispered, "You can. . . ."

A spark quickened in his eyes and he dropped his face to kiss her cheek, lovingly, tenderly. When he started to withdraw from her she gave a little cry of protest and her hands tightened on his shoulders, but then he entered her again, slowly, exquisitely, and this time a little deeper than before. With each of his long, low thrusts she could feel herself molding to him, welcoming him, becoming a part of him. The world began and ended with the rhythm of his movements, withdrawing and filling, embracing and releasing, until it seemed there had never been and never would be anything beyond this moment, this magic they created together.

And then his strokes quickened, became more powerful, and her body instinctively tuned to his, rising to meet him. The fire inside her grew, and she thought she would burst with the need that was swelling and aching and consuming her whole body. She clung to him greedily, helplessly, hearing the sob of her own breath in her ears and feeling only this desperate ache inside her that begged for release and did not know how to obtain it.

And suddenly without warning it came upon her, a ripple of pleasure that began deep inside her and spread in powerfully lapping waves to every part of her body, consuming her, enveloping her, leaving her breathless, helpless. She felt Jake's last powerful thrust, the trembling of release they shared together, the final blending of hearts and minds and souls that carried them beyond themselves to a place where they became one, simply and completely.

Even then they could not part. Jake brought her into the tight protective circle of his arms and legs, his hand entwined with hers, her head on his chest. They trembled in each other's arms, they stroked each other, they had no words to express what they had just shared. They held each other, loved each other, and in the dappled sunlight of the summer morning, they fell asleep.

It was afternoon when Jake awoke. It was with slow amazement that he realized he had actually slept restfully, for the first time since leaving Three Hills almost two months before. And the wonder only increased with the sense of contentment he felt, of rightness deep inside him.

There was no disorientation, no surprise to find himself wakening naked in a sun dappled shelter, and he did not have to question the source of these feelings. He looked down at the woman sleeping curled in his arms and he knew all the reasons why.

She slept with the innocent oblivion of a child, her face resting on his shoulder, her lips slightly parted, her lashes forming delicate shadows on her cheeks. Her hair curled over her shoulder and his arm, and for a moment he was fascinated by the contrast of his large, dark arm and hand encircling her delicate white shoulders, the dusting of jet hair on his forearm mingling with the rich blue-black texture of her curls.

Beautiful, he thought, but the word was a small and impotent description of what he felt. *Jessica, you are beautiful.* Her smooth, feminine body glistened with sparks of dried perspiration in the lacy sunlight, contoured by shadow in soft curves and gentle angles. He wanted to kiss every inch of her, to taste the salt and sweetness of her flesh, to bring her to him again and show her with his body what words failed to prove.

He knew he had no right to feel this good, so content and utterly right about what they had done. The guilt was there, a small dark hovering monster in the corner of his mind, and he knew if he let it it would spring out at him again, ready to do battle. The fear was there, too, a man who was dead and the men who meant to avenge that death. But none of those things could intrude into this time and place. For now, for as long as he could possibly make it, he and Jessica had each other, and that was enough.

She was sleeping so soundly that he could not bring himself to disturb her. Very carefully, he slipped away, moving her head to rest on the cushion of her saddle, and he got up. He covered her lightly with his shirt and slipped on his pants, not bothering with boots as he walked down to the stream.

Leaving his pants on the bank, Jake waded up to his waist in the water, the cool shock of it invigorating his langorous, heated body. He had no soap, that and their other supplies having been left behind with his saddlebags in Double Springs, but the clear water was refreshing as it cascaded over his body, washing away stickiness and lingering fatigue.

He thought no further than the immediate future. He was hungry, and he wanted to find a more permanent camp for them before nightfall. He was not as familiar with this country as he was some of the more western parts of Texas, but he knew it would be hard to track a man through these tangled hills and meandering forests. He had noticed not too far away indications of a farm where they might buy provisions, and once they made a safe hiding place deep in the hills the wisest thing to do would be to stay there, for days or a week, until they were certain the posse had not picked up their trail. Satisfied that none of their immediate problems was insurmountable, Jake stretched out in the stream, letting the water cover his face and head. When he stood up, shaking his hair from his eyes and pushing the cascades of water off his face, Jessica was standing on the bank watching him.

She was wearing his shirt, pulled closed about her but not buttoned, and with her bare slender legs, tangle of hair, sleepy eyes and shy smile she looked like a woodland nymph, a vision forged from the depths of his own imagination. He stood still, breathlessly absorbing the sight of her.

She said, hesitantly, though still smiling, "I couldn't find you. I thought you had left me."

"No." His voice sounded a little hoarse. "I wouldn't leave you. You know that."

He took a step toward her, but even as he did she moved closer to the edge of the stream. She lifted her hands and let the shirt drift down her arms, and before his unbelieving eyes she stepped into the water, beautiful and unclothed and only the slightest bit shy now, moving toward him.

The sense of wonder and delight rose up in him afresh, finding its way to his lips where it formed into a smile of pure pleasure and welcome. "It's cold," he warned, and then laughed as she flinched away from the first slap of spring-fed water against her thighs.

But there was laughter in her eyes too, and the same kind of elemental pleasure that was bubbling within him as she moved forward. "Cold water is good for the constitution," she informed him.

He could see the slight prickling of her flesh as the water moved up over her thighs, covering the dark triangle of curls and then her hips and her small, flat waist, but by the time she reached him, with the water lapping just below the curve of her breasts, he was very warm. He felt drenched by the sun and filled with such deep and contented emotions that he could do nothing but stand there and smile at her.

He moved his hands beneath the water to cradle her hips and she lifted her arms to his shoulders, linking her hands behind his neck. She tilted her face to him, her eyes lightened by the sun to a pure turquoise, her expression tender with just a hint of anxiety. She inquired softly, "Are you sorry?"

"No," he breathed, without thinking about it once, and he drew her to him, warming her chilled flesh with his. "No, Jessica, how can I be sorry?" And it was true, from the very depths of his soul it was true. For the rest of his life, no matter what happened—and he knew it would be bad—he would never regret what they had shared, even if it was no more than this moment.

Jessica inhaled the warm masculine scent of his chest, rubbing her cheek against the silky damp covering of hair. For her, too, consciousness and concern began and ended with the moment. Happiness such as this, which came so rarely in lives such as theirs, was meant to be treasured, savored, stored like jewels against the hard times ahead. She had no regrets. She would never have regrets.

Tightening her arms around him she whispered, "Oh Jake, is it like this for everyone—the way it was for us when we made love?"

She felt the brush of his lips against her hair. And then he took her face lightly in his hand, lifting it to look at him. His eyes were very serious, his voice low as he said, "No. It's never like this. Only . . . for us."

She pressed her face against his chest again, holding him tightly, and he took a long breath, closing his eyes, letting the truth and the power of it go through him as it went through her. Only for them. Rarely, so rarely did two people find that missing part of themselves, that special bond that was meant to be from the beginning of eternity. Most people never even knew it existed, never missed what they had not found. But it had happened for Jake and Jessica. Only for them. When he thought of it he felt reverent and humbled, and then filled with such exquisite, soaring joy that he could hardly comprehend it. They had found each other. How could it be wrong? How could he ever regret what was so pure and right and meant to be?

She moved away from him a fraction and he loosened his embrace, his eyes crinkling with a smile of gentle affection as he looked down at her. She lifted her fingers to touch the small lines that radiated from his eyes, and then with both hands she pushed his wet hair away from his forehead and let her hands trace the shape of his face. How beautiful he had looked as she watched him from the bank, his body strong and perfect as he moved and turned in the water; her only instinct had been to go to him. And now, standing beside him clean and unashamed in the light of the sun, her only instinct was to touch him, to trace his contours and memorize him with her hands as she had already done with her eyes.

His voice held a husky note of teasing as he said, "I watched you bathe once, too. That first morning in the swamp."

She looked startled, and then a little embarrassed. "Why?"

"Because," he said simply, "you are beautiful. And I wanted you, even then."

"I didn't know . . ." She lowered her eyes to his chest, her embarrassed pleasure deepening. "You didn't have to tell me."

He lowered his face to her hair with a breath that was half a laugh and half sigh. His fingers threaded into her hair. How he loved her. He could never tell her how much. "I know," he murmured, and his smile seemed to encompass his whole body. "But you make me want to confess all my sins."

She leaned forward and placed a light kiss on his chest, and he lifted his head, watching the softening wonder in her face as her hands drifted over his breast muscles, tracing the shape of his hard arms and then his neck. The pleasure that filled him with her light, adoring touch made him weak. She looked up at him with innocence and sincerity in her eyes and she said, softly, "You are beautiful, Jake."

"No." His voice was husky, and instinctively his hands came up to cup her breasts, wanting to pleasure her as she pleasured him. "I'm not."

"You are . . ." Her pupils dilated with his touch. Her skin was warm now, and the cool water he scattered over her flesh was a peculiar stimulant, causing her nipples to pucker and tighten with awareness. His thumbs went to those small, hardened peaks, massaging gently, sending ripples of pleasure through her with each motion. She whispered, "To me . . ."

She closed her eyes to the golden sunlight and the wonderful sensation of Jake's hands upon her breasts, her ribs, her back, and then her breasts again, and she let her own hands move over his slippery body, discovering him by touch alone. Sinewy muscles, flat planes, smooth warm flesh. Her hands moved beneath the water, along strong flanks, and then, hesitantly, around his waist and downward, over his buttocks. She looked at him cautiously, but he did not seem to mind. His hands moved, too, beneath the water, to hold her as she held him, and he stepped closer. She felt his tumescent arousal brush against her thigh.

His eyes were alight with the fire she had come to know so well in such a short time, and a thrill went through her with the power they had over one another. He said, "I love it when you touch me, Jessica."

Emboldened, she moved her hands around, her heart thudding with the excitement of discovery and pleasure, and ran her fingers along the strong length of his thighs with their light feathering of hair, and then upward, until her fingers brushed against the swollen evidence of his desire. She felt his breath quicken and his hands closed upon her breasts. "Ah, Jessica," he whispered, and that was all. The intensity of the pleasure in his voice filled her with joy. She closed her hand around him, lightly, hesitantly, her pulses pounding with the strength and hardness of this male flesh. And then, suddenly overcome with shyness and the tremors of resurging need she could not put into words, she wrapped her arms around his waist and pressed herself close to him.

His warm hands covered her back, his heart beat powerfully beneath her ear, and there was nothing between them but spiraling joy, intense pleasure, and desire that swelled and expanded with each breath they took. *I love you, Jessica,* Jake thought, tightening his embrace, and the mere power of the emotion shook him, awed him. His throat was too tight to speak.

I love you, Jessica thought, but the intensity of the emotion was too great to say it out loud.

He bent and lifted her from the water. He lay her down gently upon the grassy bank, and there they made their bed.

Chapter XIV

They purchased provisions from a farm nestled into an isolated hillside, and for over a week they made their camp in a secluded glade deep within the forest. Those were blissful days, complete unto themselves and wrapped in splendor, a small and separate miracle created for them to cherish for as long as it might last. They laughed together, they played together, they made long and exquisite love together beneath the stars or the moon or the gentle beneficence of the midday sun.

They made memories together. Jessica, her hair spangled with wild daisies Jake had picked for her, twirling barefoot in the glade. Jake, awakening drowsy eyed and disgruntled to the tickling sensation of the feather Jessica drew across his face, the annoyance in his eyes slowly lightening into pleasure as she replaced the feather with her lips. Jake's voice, as she lay contentedly in his arms at night, lazily pointing out the constellations to her and recounting the legends that went with each. Jessica's surprised laughter as he awoke her one morning with a cascade of wild blueberries spilling from his cupped hands. Memories, sweet, precious, enduring, each one separately wrapped and treasured, secretly placed in store for the time when memories would be all they had.

They never talked about the future. They each knew it was there, lurking like a hidden foe just beyond the next ridge, and they sought to outwit it in the same manner they had escaped their human pursuers—first by secreting themselves from it, then by pretending it didn't exist. The time they had together, the discoveries they were making with each other, were too precious to allow any intrusion whatsoever, and most especially not reality.

Sometimes Jake fantasized about taking her away with him, riding north to Kansas, and then west, possibly all the way to California. Past the Missouri river no one asked anyone's name, no one cared about the past; nothing mattered except what you could build with your own two hands. He and Jessica could build a whole new life for themselves. . . .

Jessica didn't love Daniel; she loved him, and leaving her with his brother would not be right. Surely there was a way to free her from the marriage, for them to make a life together. He didn't know how, and he was afraid to speak his daydreams aloud, but a little flicker of hope fanned by inventions of the impossible kept his fantasy alive.

When the day came, by unspoken consent, to begin moving again, they rode west, not north. They had used the last of the coffee and flour purchased from the farmer and there was not enough bacon left to make one good meal. They had no choice but to head for a town and supplies.

They were well out of Shelby County, and after almost two weeks with no sign of pursuit, Jake was confident of their safety. But Jessica could not help being nervous as they approached the mid-sized town of Nacogdoches and for a multitude of causes. The first and most obvious was the memory of what had happened the last time they had gone into a town. When she and Jake were alone against the world, they were safe and secure; civilization seemed to preface tragedy. She believed Jake when he said they had outwitted the posse, but she couldn't forget that it existed, and she couldn't help worrying that, once they left their hiding place, the band of officers would be waiting to spring out at them and take them back. But perhaps most prominently she realized that this decision to return to civilization meant an end to their idyll, and soon some decisions would have to be made.

Jessica knew she could not remain married to Daniel, not after Jake, not loving him the way she did. Daniel was a kind and good man and she could hardly bear the thought of hurting him, but she couldn't live a lie. She would have to tell Daniel, and hope he would understand and forgive. But nothing could be solved until they reached Three Hills and talked to Daniel. Together they would work it out. They had to.

Jake was silent and preoccupied for most of the trip, and she knew he was thinking the same thing. Occasionally she glanced at him and caught a dark brooding look in his eyes and she knew he was not worried about the posse or the dangers of returning to civilization—this part of Texas was safe for them, and as long as they kept moving west, away from Double Springs, there would be no trouble. It was what lay at the end of the trail west that worried him. It was facing his brother.

Her tension only increased as they rode through the streets of Nacogdoches, while Jake's only seemed to dissipate. Of course he was glad to see a settlement again; there were dangers in the wild which Jessica, with Jake there to protect her, rarely gave thought to. He would be anxious for news from the outside world and the comforts of a real meal and bed. And in truth, Nacogdoches was nothing like Double Springs. The streets were wide and well-packed, thronged with buggies and wagons and well-dressed men and women on foot. The houses were all neatly painted, framed and boarded; the businesses were thriving. There were two real hotels, a church, and shops and stores of every description. Perhaps it was the teeming activity, the culture shock of all the people and horses and storefronts after living so long with nothing but the ground for her floor and forest animals for company, but Jessica could not feel comfortable.

Jake sensed her nervousness as he helped her to dismount in front of the dry goods store. His smile was easy and reassuring. "We're going to be all right here," he said, and his strong fingers held her waist just a moment longer as he set her feet on the ground, imparting strength with his touch, confidence with his eyes. "Besides," he added, touching her back lightly to lead her onto the sidewalk, "we have to get supplies somewhere. The first thing I want you to find is a decent riding outfit and some boots. That dress is pretty, but it can't be very comfortable for riding."

Jessica smiled a little stiffly and tried to match his carefree mood. The dress to which he referred was far from pretty—washing it in the stream had done little to keep it clean, and it was badly in need of mending in several places. He was right: there were a lot of things they needed.

The little store was crowded with merchandise but not too many customers, a fact for which Jessica was grateful. The storekeeper greeted them from behind the counter, and Jake answered him easily, turning to examine a display of saddle pouches on the wall. Jessica stayed close to him.

"Strangers in town, aren't you?" commented the storekeeper conversationally.

"Just passing through," Jake answered, choosing one of the saddlebags. "We're going to need a little of everything, I'm afraid," he added, bringing his selection over to the counter. "Let's start with some flour, and bacon and coffee; half a pound of salt and three pounds of beans, and my wife needs some comfortable riding clothes."

His wife. The words came so easily that Jake hardly even noticed he said them, but for Jessica it was like a door opening onto something grand and new and right. She *was* his wife in every sense of the word but the legal, yet it felt wonderful to hear such a basic truth spoken out loud. Suddenly Jessica felt good, and relaxed, just as Jake did. They were going to be all right. *His wife*.

The storekeeper, his eyes lighting with pleasure over the prospect of a large order, was more than anxious to help. He eagerly piled their selection of foodstuffs on the counter, displayed for Jake a wide choice of tobaccos, and directed Jessica to the counter that held the clothing. She selected a pair of canvas pants and a shirt and a hat to keep the hot Texas sun off her face, and she was looking at the boots when Jake walked over to her.

"I left some money," he told her, and his hand brushed hers lightly, affectionately. The habit of touching whenever they were in close proximity was a hard one to break, even in public. "Pick out whatever you like and he'll wrap it up for you. I'm going to take the horses over to the livery and see about getting us a room. I'll come back for you. And here. This is for you."

She laughed in surprise and delight as he presented her

with a candy stick, his eyes twinkling. Then he winked at her, stuck another candy stick in his own mouth, and strolled out of the store, his hat tilted back, his hands in his vest pockets, smiling at the thought of how little it took to make Jessica happy.

And happy was exactly how Jessica felt as she took her time over her selections, sucking on the sweet penny candy, relaxing in the strange environment. Tonight she and Jake would share a real bed, like a real husband and wife. Today they would enjoy comforts they had not had in weeks. They could lose themselves in a town like this and no one would question, no one would know. It was going to be all right.

She took her purchases over to the storekeeper, who was pleased to wrap them and pack them into the second set of saddlebags Jake had bought for her. Then her eye was caught by a collection of dried fruit and eagerly she went over to examine it, wondering how much of it they could carry without adding too much weight to the saddlebags.

She was so absorbed in the delight of this new supplement to their diet that she did not even hear Jake return. She was scooping up a sack of dried peaches when he said beside her, lowly, "Let's go, Jessica."

She looked up in surprise. "Jake!" It seemed he had hardly been gone a minute. Then, happily, "Look what I—"

"Don't make a fuss." His voice was quiet, his expression grim. "Just get out of here."

"But—"

"Now!" he hissed, and that was when she noticed the unnatural color of his face, the dark, almost bruised look of his eyes, and alarm shafted through her and began to

hammer in her chest. She dumped the fruit back in the bin and silently followed him outside.

Their horses were waiting where they had left them. Jake said nothing as he arranged the saddlebags and helped her mount, but his eyes followed every movement on the street, examined every face that passed. The tension that radiated from him was palpable, and Jessica dared not question, dared not disturb his concentration. They rode single file at a sedate, almost nonchalant, pace through the town, but Jessica could see Jake's knuckles whiten on the reins as he restrained the urge to whip his horse into fevered flight. She felt panic building inside her and wanted to scream with it, to demand what had happened, what was wrong, but Jake said nothing and she was terrified to break the silence.

When the last of the clapboard houses and neatly plotted gardens gave way to the wide stretch of empty road, Jake lifted the reins and slapped his horse into a gallop, and Jessica did the same, struggling to keep up. Her heart was racing with the pounding of the hooves, her mind whirling with the speed of passing landscape. The wind tore whatever cries she might have made from her throat, and Jake rode as though all the demons of hell were upon him.

The horses were lathered and heaving when at last Jake pulled up under the shade of a gnarled oak. Jessica's muscles were shaking with both the exercise and the fear, the awful, driving unknown fear, and she was gasping for breath.

"Jake, please!" she cried, the words sounding like a sob as she tried to catch her breath. "What is it? What happened?"

Jake was breathing hard, too, and his face was white beneath his tan, shiny with perspiration. He did not look at her, he did not speak as he removed a folded sheet of heavy paper from his pocket and handed it to her.

Jessica opened it with clumsy fingers. It was a poster. Bold black printing sprang out at her.

WANTED
FOR MURDER
JAKE FIELDING
DEAD OR ALIVE

Jessica's heart stopped. The paper drifted from her lifeless fingers and floated to the ground, turning over and over in the breeze until it was caught by a clump of grass on the side of the road. There it stayed, as white and still as a broken tombstone.

Jessica wanted to say no, but the word would not come out; her lips were numb, her breath gone. Only her mind continued to shout denial.

No!

Jake dismounted, relieving his tired horse of his weight, and walked over to the trunk of the tree. He braced his hand against it, staring blankly across the wide stretch of sandy Texas soil dotted with scrub grass and lone pines. He took deep, steady breaths as he let it wash over him. His time with Jessica had been a refuge into daydreams and what might have been; he had been a fool to encourage them. Possibilities and hopes died a quiet, cold death and he was left with nothing but the truth. The truth he should have let himself face a long time ago.

Wanted. As far as the world was concerned, he had shot an unarmed law officer in the back and hanging was too good for him. His description had been circulated up and down the telegraph lines of Texas, the Rangers were at this moment scouring the countryside for him, and he had one chance in a hundred to make it out of the state alive.

Out of the state . . . He had to leave Texas. He would never see home again. Three Hills, with its rolling meadows and deep cool streams, its sprawling trails and valleys, its hard, dusty days and warm, sweet nights . . . Three Hills was all he had, all he had ever wanted. No matter how far he strayed he always knew that home was waiting for him at the end of the trail; spacious rooms and white sheets, good food, quiet times. A way of life as peaceful and as orderly as his mother's flower beds, a little corner of Texas that was life as it was supposed to be. Home. And Daniel.

Daniel.

The thought echoed and twisted through him with a force that momentarily blurred his vision, robbed his breath. Daniel, who always fixed everything, Daniel who had all the answers, Daniel who had depended on him . . . Daniel whom he loved. Jake had shown his love by taking from his brother the only thing he had ever wanted, and Daniel couldn't fix this one. Not ever.

And Jessica.

Her voice was small and shaky behind him. "Jake?"

He turned and saw her white, strained face, but he did not know what to say to her. There was nothing he could say. And he could hardly bear to look at her.

He caught his reins and mounted in a single smooth motion, facing away from her. "Come on," he said simply, nudging his horse into motion. "We've got to get off this road."

Jessica had no choice but to follow as Jake led the way

across the countryside, once again covering his trail as he went.

At sundown they sat beside a small flickering fire, picking at plates of bacon and beans, eating little, saying nothing. Their camp was sheltered from sight by a tall bank, and the leaves of a cottonwood overhead dissipated the smoke from the fire. They were safe here.

Yet it hung over them heavily, surrounded them bleakly: the end of the dream, the beginning of despair. The horror was quiet and thick and enveloping, it invaded every corner of the mind; no words could vanquish it and no matter which way they turned they could not escape it. Reality was upon them, and there was no point in trying to outdistance it any longer.

At last Jake gave up staring at his food and set the plate aside. He sipped his coffee but couldn't taste it. He said quietly, thoughtfully, almost to himself, "I've never shot a man. I've never even thought about doing it." The irony struck him, and he almost smiled, but then he glanced at Jessica and a bleakness crossed his eyes that was awful to behold. He focused upon the black liquid in his cup and he added softly, "But I guess I've done other things that they don't hang people for. Maybe it's right, somehow."

Jessica knew that he was thinking about her and what they had done to Daniel, and a pain twisted inside her chest that she simply couldn't bear. So she ignored it. She got up and took Jake's plate and her own, and walked a few paces away to scrape off the leavings. When she turned her voice was clear and strong, filled with calm decision. "We're going back to Double Springs," she said. "We're going to tell the truth."

"No, damn it!" With an abrupt motion, Jake tossed his

coffee into the flames; it hit the fire with a sizzling hiss. "That's a closed discussion."

"It's the only way! It's—"

"No! A man is dead, Jessica. They'll put you in prison and lock you up for the rest of your life!" He met her eyes with such agony in his that her own heart broke with it. "Do you think I would want to go on living if that happened to you?"

"But I can't let you hang for a crime you didn't commit!" she cried. "How can you ask me to?"

"And how can you ask me to let you go to prison?"

For a moment they looked at each other with helplessness and anguish writhing between them, an endless moment in which they faced the future and reached through despair only to come up empty handed, for there was nothing, absolutely nothing, either of them could do to make things right. Then Jake took a breath and looked away.

"Nobody's going to hang me," he said. "I can take care of myself. All I have to do is get you home safely . . . and then keeping riding west."

She stifled a cry in her throat and moved over to him. "Jake—you can't. You can't leave!" She dropped to her knees beside him and gripped his arm. Her face was stripped and raw, torn with pleading and the pain of a loss too great for her to comprehend. "You can't go on the run like a common outlaw! You can't leave me. Jake, I love you, you can't—"

He said harshly, "You have to forget me." He stared fixedly into the fire, his face tight. "You have to go back to Three Hills and you and Daniel have to make a life for yourselves." Every word was wrenched from him, fought through agony, throbbing with courage born of desperation.

"You have to pretend I was never born, put all of this out of your mind. I'm a wanted man, and you have to forget me."

Her lips parted on a ragged breath, moisture flooded her chest and her throat and her eyes, but what she felt dying and screaming inside her was too intense for tears, too deep and desperate. She brought her forehead slowly to his shoulder. She said thickly, brokenly, "I could never forget you . . . you are my life."

He closed his eyes slowly, tried to steel himself against it, but no power on earth could keep his arms from going around her, from pulling her to him fiercely and possessively. He gulped in air, felt the wetness sting his eyes and seep beneath his closed lashes, and when their mouths met it was with a need so hungry and overwhelming that nothing could ever fill it. Yet they clung to each other, holding off desolation with all the frail strength they had to offer each other. Their lovemaking was frantic, a desperate joining of bodies that was meager protection against the emptiness and separation that waited to claim them. Jessica cried out with the shattering intensity of it; Jake held her to him with an embrace that could crush, but the glory was fleeting, and in the end they could do nothing but part.

Jake pulled the blanket over them and they lay beside each other, their hands entwined but no other parts of their bodies touching, each in their own separate ways trying to come to terms with what they knew must be. The sky was starless, and the emptiness that yawned before them was as black and vast as the night itself.

Swallowing back the tightness in her throat, Jessica said, "I'll go with you."

He spoke to the blank dark canvas overhead. "No. You need Daniel's protection, now more than ever."

She turned to him. "I can take care of myself, you said so."

"You're his wife, Jessica." A multitude of sorrows, past and future, were encompassed in those simple, quietly spoken words. "You belong with him. And I—I can never go back."

For the first time Jake let himself realize the final truth of it. All these weeks Three Hills and Daniel had been a vague and amorphous ideal, a place where he must go, a man who would make everything all right . . . Nothing would ever be right there again. He had betrayed Daniel with more than just his body, by more than just a physical act. He had betrayed him with his heart and soul, the man who had given him everything he had ever known, who represented everything that was good and right and decent about the world; his brother, whom he loved more than any other living being—until he had met Jessica.

For Daniel loved Jessica too. Jake could understand that now. He knew how it was possible for a man to love a woman without ever having her physically. Jake had loved Jessica, secretly and helplessly, before ever having made love to her. He would love her forever, though he might never hold her in his arms again. And he had hurt Daniel in the worst way possible for one man to hurt another. He had not only loved the other man's wife, but he had loved her in a way Daniel was incapable of doing. Daniel would never forgive him for that. Jake would not ask him to.

He could never look Daniel in the eye again knowing what he had taken from him. Deep inside he had always known he could never return to Three Hills while loving his brother's wife. Life as he had known it, as he had always thought it would be, was over. And he said softly, "Maybe it's better this way."

Jessica turned her face back to the sky, the shadowy leaves above blurring until, by clenching her fists and squeezing her eyes shut, she subdued the weakness that would help neither of them now. Grasping at one final straw, she said, "It was an accident. You didn't kill anyone. If we explained that to Daniel he could help you." But she knew, even as she spoke, that it was useless. She knew Jake's thoughts, she knew the truth. It wasn't just the law they were running from now, it was Daniel, the loyalty they each owed him, shattered trust, and the desperate sins they had committed in the name of love.

Jake said slowly and carefully, holding back emotion with every word, "This is the last thing I can do—for either of you. Daniel needs you. I—I promised him. He'll take care of you; you'll be safe. I have to take you home to him." He took a breath and released it softly. "It may not be enough," he finished simply, "but it's all I can do."

With every last ounce of strength she had, Jessica fought back despair. How could she go back to Daniel when the only part of her life that mattered was Jake? How could she live in safety and security with the man whose marriage vows she had betrayed knowing that Jake was living the desperate life of an outlaw? She held herself rigid against the pain, her eyes fixed on the vast darkness above. "Please . . ." she whispered, a plea torn from deep within her soul. "We could go far away where no one knows us. No one would ever find us. And even if—if they did, it wouldn't matter, because we'd be together."

She felt him stiffen; he released her hand and got up to pull on his pants. He made his voice rough, his words harsh. "A man on the run has no room for a woman. I can't take care of you and myself too. A man alone has a chance. You'd do nothing but slow me down."

She knew he meant to hurt her, and she knew why he did it. She bit her lip to stifle the pain and said nothing. Because he was right. There was nothing she could do but let him go. She could not let him endanger himself further for her. Alone he would at least have a chance.

She watched his movements in the dim yellow glow of the fire, a dark and lonely silhouette as he bent before it, pouring out the last of the coffee, banking it with broken branches for the night. *He will go,* she thought. *I will go back to Daniel and he will go . . . somewhere, somewhere safe, somewhere the past will never find him. I'll never see him again. I won't know whether he lives or dies. I'll never see him again.* They had no future together, they never had. From the moment she had begun to love him she had known it was wrong. She could not go with him. She was a married woman, and he was a wanted man. But how could she live without him?

The tears that rose in her throat were thick and helpless. She turned her head toward him. "Oh Jake," she whispered brokenly. "What are we going to do?"

It was a question that had no answer, and each of them knew it. He sat for a long time, his hands clasped between his knees, staring into the fire. He spoke at last, quietly, heavily and without turning around. "I guess . . ." He took a breath, but there was nothing else he could say. "Just the best we can." The fire popped, sparks flared, but the night seemed to swallow up the movement. He focused deliberately on the flames and repeated softly, finally, "Just the best we can."

A light, cool mist was falling as Jake pulled his horse to rest atop a gentle ridge. The landscape below was a patchwork of foggy greens and browns, dotted occasionally with spots of bright color which were the first touches of late autumn in Texas. Neither of them wore coats against the dampness or the chill; Jake's hat was pulled down low on his forehead and dewdrops congealed on his skin. His face was completely unreadable as Jessica drew up beside him.

"This is it," he said.

Thirteen weeks had passed since he had pulled her from Eulalie's house. Not even the changing seasons had marked their time together, and the weeks since Nacogdoches had been a blur of hot days beneath burning amber skies and desperate nights that had no meaning beyond the fact that each one of them might be their last.

Backtracking on their trail, avoiding towns and populated areas, foraging for supplies as best they could, hiding out for long periods of time whenever they found a safe place, they had plotted a slow, convoluted but always steady course west. Three Hills had become a quest, an enigmatic goal with no real substance, an almost quixotic ideal that neither one of them had ever surely believed would be obtained.

Each time they broke camp it was with the very real knowledge that they might not make another one. Every ridge hid a squadron of Texas Rangers with cocked rifles, every stranger they passed on the road was a bounty hunter, every thud of hoofbeats in the silence of the night was a marshal and his deputies. They rode through the days pursued by ghost riders of guilt and justice on thundering steeds; they clung to each other at night with a frantic passion that was only intensified by the knowledge that there might be no tomorrow, and each time they made love it was as if for the last time.

Jessica sat beside him now, the cold drizzle falling off her hat onto her shoulders, and she could not at first believe what he implied. Three Hills. The end of running, the end of hiding, the end of a nightmare that had begun a lifetime ago with a bullet fired from her father's gun.

She looked at Jake, and she could not imagine what he was thinking or feeling as he gazed for the last time over the hills and valleys in which he had grown up, knowing that he would never roam them again. She couldn't believe that, after months of frantic flight and grim despair, suddenly she would look up one morning and they would be home. She had never imagined it like this.

She took a breath and was surprised to find her chest did not want to expand for air. She said, "You'll—have to get a fresh horse and supplies. And we'll talk to Daniel, tell him the truth about Double Springs. There must be something he can do. . . ."

Jake's face was impassive. He said, looking at the horizon, "He's heard about it by now. My even being here is a danger to him." He couldn't go to his brother, but he couldn't leave without knowing Daniel was all right. Maybe he could have one of the men bring him a horse and some money. He couldn't stay.

He lifted the reins and nodded toward the right. "There's a line camp just down there. There will be somebody there who can take you the rest of the way home."

He carefully guided his horse down the slippery incline, and Jessica, numb with the impact of destination at last reached and the implications it contained, followed him wordlessly.

They had arrived at the tail end of the fall roundup, and though the camp was not as busy as it had been, it was by no means deserted. They approached from the back, avoiding the teeming corrals of lowing cattle, the patrolling sentries halfheartedly looking for the last of the strays. They were about a hundred yards from the log building that served as a bunkhouse when a rider moved out from behind a bluff, his rifle raised.

"Freeze in your tracks, mister."

Jake kept up his steady, plodding approach. Jessica, too dazed and exhausted to protest, accompanied him.

The cowhand raised the rifle another fraction, rain glinting off his dark slicker and beading on his unshaven face. His voice meant business. "I said hold it right there, you son of a bitch! We've had enough trouble from you goddamn—" And then he stopped, lowering his rifle, his mouth falling open with an audible snap of the jaw. "Jake! I'll be a son of a—" He swung around in the saddle, bellowing, "Casey! Git up here! It's Jake! By damn, it's Jake—and he's got Miz Fielding with him! Jake!"

He spurred his horse and drew it in sharply beside Jake, his face split with a grin of wonder as he slapped his hand into Jake's and shook it heartily. "I'll be damned and go to hell if you ain't a sight for sore eyes! We'd 'bout give you up fer dead. God *damn* it all, what the hell happened to you?"

And then, suddenly remembering his manners he abruptly withdrew his hand from Jake's and put it to his hat, looking embarrassed as he glanced at Jessica. "Ma'am. That is to say, we're all mighty glad to see you back safe and sound, and welcome home, ma'am." And then, unable to restrain himself any longer, he turned back to Jake. "Where the he—tarnation have you been?"

Jake leaned forward, crossing his arms on the pommel, and allowed himself a slow lazy grin. "Good to see you too, you old horse thief. Though the way you held that gun on me I was beginning to wonder if I'd live to say hello. You been having trouble with rustlers?"

The grin on the other man's face faded into troubled alarm and he said, uncomfortably, "Hell, no, Jake—"

The sound of hoofbeats cut him off as Casey thundered into their midst, reining his horse to a dancing, snorting stop in front of Jake. The two men stared at each other for a long time, Casey's harsh, exerted breath fogging the air, Jake simply waiting. And then Casey lifted his hat, running a wet hand through his thin and graying hair; he breathed, "By God. It *is* you."

His eyes traveled to Jessica and lingered there, cautious and disbelieving as he took in her attire from booted feet to stained and battered Stetson. At length satisfied that it was, indeed, Daniel Fielding's wife, he nodded curtly and said, "Miss Jessica. Glad to see you safe. Welcome back." Then, curtly to the man next to him, "Tom, ride on up to the house. Tell the cap'n they're here. *Move,* boy," he thundered, when Tom hesitated, obviously loathe to miss any of the excitement. "He's waited four damn months, you want to be the one to keep him waitin' longer?"

Tom turned his horse and took off at a gallop, and Jake straightened up. He said anxiously, "How is Daniel? Is he—"

"He's good." Casey squinted in the mist, seeming to focus somewhere just beyond Jessica's left shoulder. " 'Cept near out of his mind worryin' about you two. Miss Jessica, you should come on in out of the rain. Cap'n'll have my hide if I let you catch fever now. We got some stew on the stove, too."

Jessica edged her horse closer to Jake's, for it was beginning to come upon her that this was it. Daniel would be here. Daniel would come, and Jake would go. . . .

Jake reached forward to catch Casey's bridle as he started

to turn. "Casey," he said, "I need a horse. And some money."

Casey looked at him, long and soberly. There was pain in his eyes and reluctance in his voice as he said, "Rangers have been here lookin' for you, boy. I don't know whether you done what they say you done or not, and to tell the God's truth I don't want to know, but if I was you I wouldn't waste no time looking for no horse. They've got this place staked out plain as day, you can bet your last on that."

Jessica heard Jake suck in his breath sharply and felt him stiffen beside her. No, she thought. Not yet, not now. . . .

Casey took out some bills and passed them to Jake. " 'Bout fifty dollars. All I have."

Jake took the bills hesitantly, and looked at them for a moment before tucking them into his pocket. He said, "Thanks." And then he looked at Casey. Only Casey. "Take Mrs. Fielding to Daniel. Tell him—" another shaky breath, and he jerked his horse around sharply. "Tell him I'm sorry." But the words sounded faded and distant, for already he was separating himself from them, moving away.

Casey reached forward and took her bridle, urging her horse toward him. He was saying something to her, but Jessica didn't hear him. None of it seemed real. It couldn't happen just like this. It was like being alive one moment and dead the next, no fanfare, no line of demarkation, no warning. It was simply over. Something deep inside her struggled against it, unwilling to believe it, wanting to cry out against it, but she couldn't make a sound.

Tugging on her bridle once again, Casey said, "Come on now, Miz Fielding, it's time to go home."

And then it was all very, very real: the rain dripping coldly off her hat and down her back; Casey's eyes, stern and determined; the sound of hoofbeats, galloping away from her.

It rose inside her, slowly and surely but with the horrible force of a half-remembered nightmare come true. He was leaving. It was over, just like that. He was gone, and she hadn't even had a chance to say good-bye.

Aching, smothering, writhing, it fought its way out of her chest.

"Jake!"

Nothing but her own echo replied and he kept moving. He did not look back.

July, 1879

Chapter XV

The three drovers were riding east on the Goodnight Trail. They were tired, dusty, and saddle worn; conversation faded from sporadic to nonexistent. They were going home.

Shortly after noon they were joined by a fourth rider. The three nodded silent greeting to the stranger, but did not break their steady, plodding pace. The four rode together in silence.

At sundown they made camp. The newcomer brought cornpone and beef jerky to the usual fare of beans and coffee and they ate as they had ridden, in concentrated silence.

At length one of the men asked, without much interest, "Where're you headed, stranger?"

The newcomer hunched over his coffee, staring into the flames of the campfire. He was heavily bearded, long-haired, and taciturn. Later one of the men would remark that he had a "mean look about him," but his type was not unusual on the trail. He replied, "No place in particular."

The silence was broken by the buzzing of cicada, the chirrup of a tree frog. One of the men got up to make his bedroll.

At length, another spoke up. "We're headin' back from Denver. Drove two thousand head of longhorns. Mean sons a bitches, them longhorns. Ain't no other animal in the world that could make it down this trail."

The first man stretched and scratched his armpit, leaning back against a log. "Makes the Chisolm Trail look like a goddamn Sunday school picnic, and that's the God's truth. But everything's movin' west."

"Goddamn railroads," spoke up another. "Like to know what kind of beef them goddamn Yankees are gettin' once they get 'em off them goddamn cattlecars. Ain't natural if you ask me."

"Nothing left for the wrangler to do but move the herd west," agreed his partner.

"How long since you seen Fort Worth?" The first man addressed the stranger, but no one expected a reply.

"Railroad's damn near ruint it," said another. "God-damn furiners everywhere." To a Texan, everyone who wasn't a Texan was a foreigner.

"Well, hell, I'll be glad to see it, railroad or not. Good Texas whiskey's the only thing that'll get the taste of lime out of my mouth."

"Every cattleman in the state will be headin' in for the auction. Gonna be one hell of a wild time."

The stranger spoke up slowly. "I haven't seen Texas in three years."

"Well hell, friend, you must be 'bout ready to dry up and die."

The newcomer said nothing.

The next morning the three men mounted up to continue their journey home, and a fourth rode with them.

The rolling lawns of Three Hills were alive with color and cheerful activity. Long tables set with spotless cloths and colorful red, white and blue bunting were laden with baskets of fresh bread, pots of chili and spicy barbecue sauce. The hickory-roasted aroma of sizzling pork and beef drifted from the spits out back. Pretty girls with ribbons in their hair strolled arm-in-arm with attentive ranch hands, all done up in their Sunday courting best, and high feminine laughter drifted over the lively sounds of fiddle music as the trio warmed up for the dancing later on. The matrons gathered in groups under the shade trees to gossip and watch the children; the menfolk formed their separate groups to smoke cigars and drink good bourbon and talk about ranching and prices and politics. Cattlemen from all over the state had combined the trip to the Fort Worth auction with a stop first at Three Hills for Senator Fielding's annual barbecue.

Daniel Fielding moved through the groups, greeting each and every guest by name, making them all feel welcome. His appointed term would expire in January and he was standing for election to the same seat. Though it was tacitly understood that the barbecue was as much political as it was social, there wasn't much real need to campaign heavily. Everyone agreed that Daniel Fielding was the best thing that had ever happened to Texas.

"I do declare, Senator, you give the best parties in Texas!"

Daniel's eyes twinkled as he paused beside the group of beaming matrons. "Only because I have the good sense to invite the loveliest ladies in the state," he replied gallantly.

"Oh, pshaw, you turn every head here!" Mrs. Dearing, fat and fifty, beamed at him as she lifted her arms. "Let me see that little one. My word, what a big boy! He's going to grow up to be just as big a heartbreaker as his father."

The women gathered round, cooing like a flock of plump, beneficent doves as Daniel lifted his son from his shoulder and presented him to Mrs. Dearing. "He has a new tooth," Daniel informed her proudly. "And he's just as anxious as can be to show it off, so watch your fingers."

The baby, however, was much more interested in the clump of canary feathers that adorned Mrs. Dearing's bonnet, and a burst of delighted laughter accompanied the determined grasping of his chubby fist.

"I've never seen such a happy baby! Let me see him, Rosalee!"

"I do believe he looks more like you everyday, Senator—although that hair is definitely his mother's! Lord, I never did see the like of curls!"

"Oh, no, Sudie, he's the spitting image of Elizabeth. Just look at those eyes, just as wicked as a laugh and as green as a Texas hill."

Daniel laughed and bent to unwind his son's fist from a lock of Mrs. Dearing's blue-gray hair. "Let's just say he's got his mother's good looks and my obstinance. Come along, Josh, let the nice lady's hat alone and I'll buy you a real canary next time I go to Galveston, how's that? There's a boy."

With only one squeal of protest from Joshua and a chorus of disappointed moans from the ladies, Daniel swung the child back onto his shoulder, where he immediately became enamored of the silver dollars that studded his father's hatband. Daniel obligingly removed his hat and gave it to Joshua to chew on.

"You're spoiling that child, Senator," reprimanded Mrs. Cathcart, though her eyes smiled indulgently. There wasn't a woman present who didn't wish her own husband were a bit more like Daniel Fielding.

"I certainly hope so." Daniel's eyes shone with unmistakable adoration as he glanced up at the toddler on his shoulder. "What else are children for? Besides," he winked conspiratorially at Joshua, "everyone knows that the quickest way to win votes is to kiss babies, right partner?" With that he placed an elaborate kiss on his son's chubby knee, drawing a chorus of laughter from the women. Joshua squealed and bounced up and down happily, crushing his father's hat brim between two enthusiastic fists before stuffing it into his mouth again.

"Honestly, Senator, I don't know why you're wasting your time with a bunch of old crows like us. You leave the baby for us to mind and go on and do your campaigning."

"My dear lady," returned Daniel smoothly, "I certainly will never consider any time spent with this charming group wasted. Your husbands may think they're responsible for the future of Texas, but you lovely creatures are responsible for *them,* just like my wife is for me." He winked and grinned. "You be sure to get your menfolk to vote for me, you hear?"

Fond female eyes watched him move through the crowd, pausing every few steps to show off his thriving young heir, accepting the compliments and adoration with the complete lack of modesty only a proud father could get away with.

"Have you ever seen the like? The man absolutely dotes on that child."

"I dare swear there's never been a man to make such a

fool of himself over a baby. Why, Jessica told me she had to fight tooth and nail to keep him from taking the babe to Austin last session—and the little one not even weaned!"

"She's going to have a handful if she's not careful," Mrs. Dearing warned direly. "That child is growing up spoiled rotten."

"Lord, Rosalee," sniffed Mrs. Lemar. "I never saw a baby less spoiled in my life! Most good-natured boy I ever laid eyes on."

"Besides, she's just as bad as he is. Do you know she kept that babe at breast for months after he was drinking out of a cup—as if she didn't have enough to do without nursing a walking child! I counted the days until I could get my two on good Texas cow milk, let me tell you that, and they didn't suffer a mite for it either. Grew up strong as pines."

"They're both a bit touched when it comes to that child," agreed Mrs. Carson. "But I testify I've never seen a sweeter family in my life."

Mrs. Dearing nodded her head gravely with the rest of them. "I'm the first to admit I never completely agreed with the marriage in the first place, but I can't argue with how it's turned out."

"Jessica Fielding is a lucky woman," pointed out Mrs. Lemar thoughtfully. "To think where she came from, and look at her now."

"Daniel couldn't have made it without her," agreed Mrs. Carson, and then they all turned, smiling, toward the affectionate burst of laughter Daniel and his son had generated from a nearby crowd of young people.

Joshua Coleman Fielding had been born precisely eight and a half months after Jessica was returned to her husband from that dreadful separation that had begun on her wedding day. Everyone congratulated Daniel for his good fortune—to have his adored wife returned safe and sound after such a harrowing experience, his own health completely restored along with an appointment to the vacant Senate seat, and a baby on the way all within a year. There were a lot of male grins and nudges and indulgent, knowing female smiles and joking remarks about not wasting any time. Everyone agreed that Daniel Fielding had endured more than enough tragedy in those months, first with the shooting and his wife's kidnapping and then that unspeakable business with his brother; he was deserving of every happiness and fortune at last seemed to be smiling on him again. No one guessed that those first weeks after Jessica returned to Three Hills were the most tragic of Daniel's life. And no one to this day suspected that the infant son Daniel adored so openly and completely was not his own.

The day Jessica had come back into his life had been like awakening from a nightmare for Daniel. The last he had heard from Jake had been in Double Springs, saying they were on their way home. The next thing he knew the Texas Rangers were swarming all over the ranch claiming Jake had committed a murder in that very town. Daniel never expected to see his brother or his wife alive again.

And then, miraculously, Jessica was home. Alive, unharmed, and returned to him. He had swept her into his arms and the ecstasy that filled him was unlike anything he had ever known. Then he looked into her eyes and he knew his world was about to come to an end.

Hysterical and overwrought, Jessica had poured out the whole story of the accident in Double Springs. Desperately she had begged Daniel to go after Jake, to find him, to stop him, to help him—because Jake was innocent, and because she was in love with him.

Daniel had never known emotions like the ones that battered and clawed their way through him at that moment. The only woman he had ever loved was in love with another man. And that man was his brother.

If Daniel could have found Jake in those first months, he would have killed him. The small edge of resentment, even jealousy, he had harbored for his strong, carefree and favored younger brother on a subliminal level most of his life suddenly sprang forth into a greedy, devouring monster. Jake had everything—power, freedom, determination, virility, charm, choices. Daniel had only Jessica, but Jake had taken her from him too. Forgiveness was impossible, and hatred flowered inside him like a living thing.

And Jessica. The sight of her sickened him, for he could not look at her without seeing her coupled with his brother in the kind of intimacy and surrender Daniel could never know. Jessica, his beautiful, innocent bride, had been despoiled and corrupted by the greedy animal lust of his brother and then returned to him a shattered, discarded woman.

For days he had locked himself in his study, eating little, sleeping not at all, drinking a great deal. Rationality returned slowly and with great reluctance, and he came to see that life went on, and his choices were limited. He had a term in the Senate to fill; people were depending on him. He couldn't let his personal life overrule his debt to his constituents, and he planned to run again once that term was expired. The last thing he could afford was a scandal, and if he threw Jessica out of his house after months of nearly going mad with desperation to have her returned, everyone would know what had happened. And he didn't *want* to throw Jessica out. All he wanted was Jessica, and himself, and Three Hills peaceful and orderly again, life the way it was supposed to be.

He went to Austin; he worked frantically for the people of the state he loved while trying desperately to find some way to forgive the wife who had betrayed him. When he returned, Jessica's belly had begun to round with his brother's seed, and once again Daniel's life was out of his control.

Of course everyone assumed the child was his; of course Daniel let them think so. He and Jessica never even discussed the matter between themselves, and he felt so sorry for her when the stress and fear began to affect her health that he found himself incapable of hurting her further. His own inner torment was mitigated by the support he received from the outside world. To those looking on, Daniel was indeed living the life he had always dreamed of, and he did not find the role that was forced on him of happy husband and proud father to be a difficult one to play. Sometimes, in those dark, confused months before Joshua's birth, he found himself fantasizing that it was more than simply a pretense....

And then, when he held the squalling, red-faced infant in his arms for the first time and looked into the rapt face of his wife, it ceased to be a fantasy. Jessica was his wife. Joshua was his son in every way but the physical, and he loved him with the blind ferocity and desperate, possessive intensity of a grand passion that knows no other outlet. Jake had taken from him one dream, but he had given him another, far greater reality, the one thing Daniel had never thought he would have: a son.

Jessica began to change, too, assuming the responsibilities of the ranch that once had been Jake's and throwing herself into the satisfaction of motherhood as though she had been bred for no other life. The bond of love they shared for their thriving son brought them closer together, and Jessica, too, was his wife in every way but the physical. It was as though those months she had been away had never happened, and there were times Daniel was able to forget he had ever had a brother. When he did remember, it was with only the faintest bitterness and a touch of grief, for to him Jake had been dead for three years.

And there was not a day that passed in which Daniel did not thank the heavens for his good fortune. He was the popular senator, fast growing in power, with the beautiful, smart and exceedingly competent young wife who was the envy of all his contemporaries, and a sturdy young son who held posterity in his hands. The irony was that all of this had been given him by a man he now hated, but that was a truth which occurred to Daniel rarely, and one upon which he never dwelt. He did indeed have the perfect life, and nothing, and no one, would ever threaten that again.

"Hey, Senator, bring that boy on over here!"

Daniel grinned and lifted his hand, making his way slowly over to the holding corral, where five of his neighbors were admiring his new cow pony stock. "Look at that young'un!" exclaimed one. "He'll be sitting the saddle before too much longer."

"I'm having him outfitted with spurs next week." Daniel grinned and set the restless, exploratory Joshua on his feet, where he immediately set off with determined steps for the low boards of the corral. One of the men laughingly scooped him up and turned him in the other direction, where he continued on his curious, chattering journey as though having never been interrupted.

"Haven't seen that pretty young wife of yours today," commented one man.

"She has a few last-minute things to wind up in her office before she leaves for Fort Worth tomorrow," Daniel replied, resting one elbow on the fence and pushing his slightly battered hat back on his head. He kept a wary eye on Joshua, who was managing his long skirts and the stubbly ground with admirable grace and speed, toddling across the lawn in determined and excited pursuit of a butterfly.

"You're not going then?" But there was little surprise in the statement. The ranchers had grown used to Jessica representing Three Hills at cattle auctions, and they had learned to deal with her in the same manner they would with Daniel himself, knowing she had his full support.

"Can't be two places at once," replied Daniel easily. "That's why God blessed me with a wife like Jessica."

"Well, we're gonna miss you, but rest easy we'll keep an eye out on the missus for you."

Daniel laughed. "If you haven't learned by now, the missus can take care of herself."

Some abashed grins went around the group. "Well, hell, Dan, it never hurts for a pretty lady to have a man around to escort her to dinner and such. Wouldn't want her to starve."

"I don't think there's any danger in that," Daniel replied with a twinkle. "Last time she was in Fort Worth she had more escorts than she could seat at one table, if I remember rightly."

"Hot damn, Fielding, if you're not the luckiest man in Texas. How'd you ever find a woman like that anyway?"

Daniel smiled. "No argument there, gentlemen. God knows I couldn't have kept the ranch and the Senate together these past two years without her." Then, "Joshua! Come back here!"

Joshua, advancing intrepidly on the butterfly, ignored the summons.

Daniel, laughing, tipped his hat to them. "Excuse me, gentlemen, I see other duties call. Don't go wandering off now, you still have a speech to sit through before we start dishing up the grub." Then, with another imperious and vain call to his son, Daniel hurried off into a spirited game of tag with the delighted infant.

"Damn fine man," commented one of the men lazily, watching him.

"He's sure got my vote."

Another shook his head in slow amazement, for rarely could the accomplishments of one Fielding be discussed without bringing to mind the travesty of the other. "Who would have thought it about his brother?"

"A thing like that could have ruined another man," agreed his neighbor, leaning on the rail. "But not Dan Fielding."

They ruminated on that for a time. "Heard he killed three men before he got out of Texas."

"I heard he joined up with the James Gang in Utah."

"Horseswaggle," snorted the first man. "The James Gang ain't never been in Utah."

"That Jake always was a wild one," remembered someone else, squinting his eyes against the glare of the sun. "Hot as a firecracker, 'bout as different from Dan as a man could be. Never knew when he was gonna go off. Guess I always did know something like this would happen."

There was a general silence of consent broken only by the snap of matches as a couple of the men decided they had time for one more smoke before the speech began. And then one spoke thoughtfully.

"You know something?" He looked at his contemporaries for a moment, judging their mood. "I never did believe it about old Jake. Not altogether. Sure he had a temper, and there never was a meaner drunk after a drive, but he was a fair man. And a Fielding. Just can't picture him shooting a man in the back."

The silence that fell was thoughtful and disturbed, for the opinion voiced was not a new one. Each of them had secretly puzzled over the same thing more than once over the years.

Finally one spoke up, with a conviction that was undoubtedly more than he felt. "Bullshit, Malone. Daniel is tight with every peace officer from here to El Paso, not to mention the governor himself. Jake Fielding could have amnesty on his brother's word alone if he wanted it. Don't you think Daniel would have cleared him by now if he was innocent?"

The question hung uncomfortably in the air for a moment, slightly perplexing, not easily answered. And then the ranch bell began to clang, gathering constituents to the podium for Daniel's speech, and the uncertainties of justice were easily dismissed for the game of politics. The men stubbed out their cigarettes, pushed back their hats, and strolled over to join the crowd, eager to give a listen to what Daniel Fielding had to say.

The strong commanding tones of her husband's voice drifted in through the open window of Jessica's office, accompanied by an occasional round of enthusiastic applause and cheers. The lace curtain formed a soft blurred screen for the scene outside: Daniel tall and golden on the gaily buntinged platform, commanding the attention and respect of all gathered around him; Joshua supported against Maria's ample bosom at the forefront of the crowd, bringing his tiny hands together with squeals of delight even when applause was not appropriate, generating indulgent chuckles from those around him and reprimands from Maria. Jessica smiled, watching them, and wished impatiently she were outside in the sunshine and festivity, holding her son, cheering her husband.

With a sigh she turned away from the window and back to her desk. "You wanted to see me, Casey?"

The older man looked at her with frowning contempt and raging disapproval that bordered on outright hatred. Though he held his hat in his hand and assumed the closest he could manage to an air of respect, it was plainly evident he would as soon spit on her as speak to her. His resentment ran deeper than merely having to take his orders from a woman, though that would have been enough to cause a man like Casey to despise her. Casey was the only person besides Daniel and herself who knew that Daniel could not possibly be the father of Jessica's baby.

But Jessica had grown accustomed to his attitude over the years, and after all she had lived through it would take more than one man's contempt to unsettle her. The depth of Casey's loyalty to Daniel demanded that he carry out Daniel's wishes, and what Daniel wished was that Jessica be treated with respect. For that reason alone Casey kept his personal feelings to himself.

He said darkly, "Yes ma'am. I want to know what got into your head, talking about bringing them damn foreign cattle to Three Hills. Nobody told me—"

"I wasn't aware, Casey," replied Jessica coolly, "that I had to clear my decisions through you." Then, realizing the quickest way to end this discussion would be by not provoking an argument, she added a bit more patiently, "Brahman cattle are hardly foreign to this country. They've been bred with success in the Carolinas for over thirty years."

"Ugly damn hump-backed critters," growled Casey. "They'll corrupt the whole herd."

Jessica regarded him levelly, resting her fingertips on the desk. "That is precisely the point, I believe. Breeding the longhorns with the brahman will produce a much healthier, heartier stock."

"We've got along just fine without them all these years," returned Casey belligerently, his brows knotting even further in an effort to restrain his anger. "We don't need no woman coming in here and—"

"And how many head have we lost to Texas fever the past five years?" Jessica interrupted shortly. Though her voice was calm and her expression distant and controlled, she could feel her temper begin to fray. The spark of fire in her eyes should have warned Casey. "Have any of you fine cattlemen been able to come up with a solution for *that*? But a mere woman may have, and if I'm the only one who has the guts to try it then I'll be the only one with the guts to succeed. I'm sorry if that upsets you, Casey, but that's the way it is."

Casey glowered at her, seething inside. He had tried, for Daniel's sake, but even before it had become plain what she'd done with that renegade brother, Casey hadn't liked her any better. And then, after she'd proven herself for the whore she was, it was almost too much for a man to ask, just tolerating her. Daniel, however, apparently felt differently. The way he acted, the sun rose and set in this bossy, loudmouthed little tramp who had moved in on Three Hills and claimed it for her own.

The one time Casey had tried to point out the truth to Daniel his old friend had turned on him like a raging bull, threatening not only his job but his life if Casey dared ever make another disparaging remark about Jessica. Daniel's fierce love-me-love-my-dog attitude had left Casey no choice but to swallow the bitter pill with as much good grace as possible, but he had never learned to like it. It was bad enough having her here, flaunting her betrayal in Daniel's face with every move, but in the past years, while Daniel was busy in the Senate, she had virtually taken over the running of the ranch. And she would run it into the ground, Casey was convinced, if he didn't keep an eye on her. For Daniel's sake.

He demanded now, sneering, "And what does the cap'n think of this fine new scheme of yours?"

Jessica replied evenly, "My husband trusts my judgment, as he always does. I haven't made a mistake yet, have I?"

Casey bit back a mumbled retort, at a momentary impasse. Daniel gave the woman entirely too free a hand, that was the problem. But as long as it *was* Daniel approving everything, there wasn't much Casey could do. Still, he asserted stubbornly, "The stockyards ain't no fit place for a woman."

That made Jessica smile, for some odd and wistfully bitter reason, and she couldn't help thinking about the places she had been and the things she had done in her life which weren't "fit for a woman." The brief retreat into the past was both painful and frightening, however, and she quickly pulled herself from it, squaring her shoulders and meeting Casey's gaze firmly. "The matter isn't open for discussion, Casey. If you don't want to go with me I can easily find another one of the men—"

"No," Casey interrupted, glaring. Someone had to keep an eye on the woman, and it was a job he trusted only to himself. "I'll go."

"Good." Jessica kept her voice distant and pleasant. "Then there's nothing left for you to do but go on out and join the party, and be ready to leave first thing in the morning. I'll be out directly."

When he was gone Jessica allowed herself a weary sigh of relief and sank down into her chair, suddenly in no mood to join the festivities herself. She had hoped these encounters with Casey would grow easier with the passage of time; in fact they had only grown worse. Maybe it was Casey, maybe it was the trip tomorrow that she really didn't want to make, maybe it was just the heat. But she was suddenly very tired.

Three years before a terrified, battered and confused young girl had run to Daniel Fielding and thrown herself on his mercy. Three years before—to the day—Jessica Duncan had become Mrs. Daniel Fielding and had set in motion events that would change the lives of everyone involved in more ways than they could have ever dreamed possible. It seemed like a lifetime ago.

The woman who presided now over the office that controlled the affairs of Three Hills Ranch bore no resemblance at all to the helpless young girl who had so gladly and trustingly put her life in Daniel Fielding's hands. Barely twenty-two years old, Jessica Fielding was the wife of one of the wealthiest and most influential men in Texas. Daily she made decisions that affected the lives of hundreds. She was respected by men and envied by women; she spoke and people listened; she ordered and they obeyed. She was lovely and well groomed, refined and gently mannered, and, whether gracing her husband's arm at a lavish political dinner or issuing quiet, clipped commands to the ranch hands, she was a figure who radiated authority, whose presence was not ignored. She was strong and wise and capable. And at this moment, she felt far older than she had ever expected to be.

The moment she had seen her husband of only a few hours crumple beneath the force of her father's rifle she had thought that was the worst thing that could ever happen to her. Those awful days of madness and captivity in Eulalie's house had proven to her that she was wrong. Faced with death in the swamp, dragging a weak and injured Jake to safety while alligators raced toward the scent of blood had not even been the worst. Standing in a tiny room above a saloon with blood on her hands and a dead man on her bed she had thought surely that was the end, that was the worst that could ever happen to any woman. Looking into Jake's eyes and knowing that he had condemned himself to the life of a fugitive to save her, listening to the sound of his horse's hoofbeats disappearing . . . Then it was over. That was the greatest agony she could ever know. But it had only begun.

The worst was looking into her husband's eyes and seeing the cold fury of hate form there when she begged him to save his brother's life. Feeling his arms shove her roughly away from him, the agony of betrayal that tore at his face, knowing that with her love she had sealed not only Jake's fate, but that of this kind and generous man who had given her his name and his love and whom she had repaid with treachery.

That was when she knew she could endure no more. Those were the dark sleepless nights of endless emptiness, the days haunted by the specters of the two men whose lives she had destroyed. The will to survive that had brought her through deepest desolation to the greatest joy and then back again began to wither, and die. Wherever she reached she grasped only emptiness, and there was nothing left to live for.

But even then a new life was taking hold inside her, growing, demanding the right to live. Joshua. Jake had ridden out of her life and, as far as she knew, to his death, but he had left a part of him inside her that grew and thrived each day. They had come together in love and created a miracle, and as long as she had Joshua, Jake would be with her forever.

Joshua. Truly a miracle child, not only for Jessica but for Daniel as well. Jake had given them a gift of love that brought new life to everyone it touched and how this had come to be no longer seemed to matter. For Joshua Daniel began to smile at Jessica again, and to put the past behind him. For Joshua Jessica began to forgive herself and build again. For Joshua's sake they became a family.

But Jessica did not forget, even if Daniel had managed to. Every time she looked into her son's dancing green eyes she saw Jake, and sometimes the pain that gripped her heart was so severe she had to turn away, unable to bear the beauty of her child or the memories he kept alive. Every day Jake haunted her. As servants brought in stacks of wood against the winter cold she thought of Jake, stretching his hands over a small campfire or trapped in some snowy mountain pass. When she sat down to an elegant candlelit table with jewels at her throat and witty guests on either side Jake was with her, hungry and waiting. She scanned each newspaper with suspended breath, dreading the news of his capture, yet when none came aware of a poignant stab of disappointment mixed with relief, for it he were captured at least she would know he was alive.

Sometimes at night she dreamed of Jake, dying alone and helpless, calling her name. She would bolt upright in bed, her heart thundering in her ears, her breath sobbing in her chest, the sound of his voice rushing through the room like an echo. Then she would go to the nursery and scoop up her sleeping son, running her hand over his silky black curls, pressing a kiss to his flushed cheek, holding him against her breast so tightly that he whimpered. Jake. He might be lost to her forever, but she had his son. . . .

Jessica roused herself from her reverie and got up from the desk, turning toward the window once more as she fortified herself to go out and greet her guests. It was the time of year, she knew, and the memories it brought. Generally she enjoyed her duties at Three Hills and threw herself into the responsibilities demanded of her with a frenzied energy that filled her days and blotted out her nights in exhaustion. But she dreaded the trip to Fort Worth, and if there had been any way Daniel could spare the time himself, she would have begged off. She was so very tired.

Joshua, in the middle of Daniel's speech, had become so vociferous in his demand for attention that Daniel had relented and brought him up on the platform with him, joking about the young Fielding showing the makings of a politician already. Jessica could not help smiling at the picture he made, supporting a now-contented Joshua with one arm while gesticulating adamantly about the future of Texas with the other.

And that, she realized with a slow and unexpected swell of contented pride, was the meaning of it all. Jake's son would roam the meadows and brooks of Three Hills as Jake had done, under the beneficent umbrella of Daniel's love and protection. Jessica would apply all her considerable strength and acumen to making the ranch a better and more prosperous place for his son to inherit, Daniel would work to make Texas a freer and stronger state in which he could grow up. Joshua did not belong to their past and could not be tainted by it; he was their future. And though there might be nothing Jessica could do for Jake now, she was doing the best she could for his son.

Jessica moved outside, through the throngs of applauding guests who cheered the conclusion of her husband's speech. She stepped up onto the platform and, laughing, took the eager, squirming child from Daniel's arms, then lifted her cheek for a kiss. They stood there for a moment, the three of them silhouetted against a brilliant blue sky, Daniel's arm around Jessica as he gazed down into her laughing face fondly, Jessica's arms around Joshua. They were the perfect family, and for that moment—just that moment—neither the past nor the future shadowed their happiness.

Chapter XVI

They made a peculiar pair, the smartly dressed, confidently striding young woman and the shuffling, disgruntled ranch foreman as they moved through the streets of the sprawling, bustling cattletown of Fort Worth. But the city was a conglomerate of all types of people: the wealthy rancher with his richly stitched boots and gold watch fobs, the wrangler just in from the drive eager to stir up a little dust and have some fun, the Eastern reporter or merchant with his celluloid collar and striped suit, the occasional Indian or Mexican wrapped in a serape.

The bawdy houses were doing a booming business and the saloons stayed open twenty-four hours a day. The periodic report of gunfire as an enthusiastic cowpoke expended some energy by firing his weapon into the air was no cause for notice, nor was the delighted squeal of a saloon girl as some ardent gentleman swung her over his shoulder and carried her through the dust and traffic of the crowded street to his own room.

Jessica stepped matter-of-factly over a drunk sprawled in the doorway, quelled the leering grin of a young drover with a single cold look, and quickly pulled her gray linen skirts out of the range of a tobacco-spitting mule driver who was trying to persuade his team in the most colorful language imaginable not to detour by way of the sidewalk. Another time she might have found all the excitement and gaiety of the booming town invigorating after long peaceful months at Three Hills, but today all she could feel was impatience. Casey's growling disapproval was not improving her temperament any.

"Ugliest critters I ever did see," he grumbled for what must have been the tenth time in as many minutes. "Crime against nature, that's what they are. You bring them things back to Three Hills and we'll be the laughingstock of the county."

"It's over," Jessica returned shortly, gathering up her brief train in one hand to step off the sidewalk and over a mud puddle. "I've bought them, they belong to us, and that is that. The men will start driving them home tomorrow, and you can feel free to go with them. I've still got some business to take care of at the bank that will keep me here a few days longer."

"No ma'am," Casey returned stubbornly. "The cap'n said I was to stay with you, and stay with you is exactly what I'm gonna do."

"I assure you, I can manage just fine without you."

Casey glared at her. By rights he should leave her to fend for herself. He didn't know how any of them would ever recover from the humiliation dealt the ranch by the sight of a woman, coolly mingling with the herders and ranchers and auctioneers amidst the teeming stench and confusion of the stockyards, calmly examining those filthy deformed beasts as though she knew exactly what she was doing, then lifting her voice to be heard high and clear above those of men as she actually bid on them. And the worst was she didn't even realize what a spectacle she had made of herself. She wasn't aware, even now, of the way eyes were following her, carefully masking disapproval and distaste. A woman rancher! Who had ever heard of such a thing? She was making a fool of Daniel right before his very eyes and he was allowing it—even encouraging it! And that, of course, was the crux of the matter. Every instinct within Casey told him to ride off and leave her—and those unnatural beasts she called cattle—to fend for themselves, but Daniel had entrusted him with a charge. He had to obey.

Scowling fiercely, he said, "I'll stay."

"Fine." Jessica nodded curtly. "Then you can do me a favor. Take a message to the Curtises and thank them for their invitation, but tell them I won't be able to accept after all. I have some paperwork to do before I go to the bank, and I'll dine in my room tonight."

So now he was an errand boy. Casey's lips tightened but he said nothing as he touched his fingers to his hat and swung in the opposite direction to do as she bid.

Jessica released a breath as he departed and relaxed her furious, determined stride to a more leisurely pace. Actually, she had nothing to do that night, but she did not think she could take one more unnecessary moment of Fort Worth's frenzied gaiety, not to mention Casey's suffocating presence. An evening of hotel food was a small price to pay for a little peace and quiet.

She missed her baby terribly, and up until the very last minute she wasn't certain she could leave him. The raucous shouts and whinny of horses and the thunder of the train engine were no substitute for high childish laughter, his sweet voice calling the delighted litany of "Mama! Mama!"

or even the crash of glassware and the inevitable temper fit when Maria scolded him. She missed his bouncing dark curls as he ran across the room, the devilish gleam of mischief in emerald green eyes when he was especially pleased with himself, the sweet smell of his skin and the strong grip of his chubby little arms around her neck when he thought she was displeased with him. She didn't know how she could possibly stay away from him for nearly a week. And it almost made her smile to realize that she needed her young son far more than he, in all likelihood, needed her.

Next time, she determined, Joshua would be old enough to come with her—if indeed there would ever be a next time. So far she had not found a single thing about Fort Worth that would encourage her to come again.

The railroad had brought prosperity, and with it expansion. There were signs of building and renovation everywhere. Scaffolding and workmen littered the streets as new storefronts were raised, and canvas tents dotted every alleyway to accommodate the crews brought in by new builders and merchants. The hotels and rooming houses were full to overflowing with people come to stay and people just passing through, for even as the railroad had made travel from the East easier, it kept pushing inexorably west, taking with it as many people as it brought in. Once Texas had been the center of the world to the frontiersman, now it was just a crossroads, and that in itself was rather sad. The land was growing fast, and everything was changing.

It was with a stifled sigh of relief that Jessica left the hubbub of the street for the relative quiet of her hotel room. The hotel Daniel had chosen for her was the most respectable in the city, away from the noise and spillover of the saloons and pleasure houses, and it was furnished quite comfortably, if not elegantly, with a chenille covered bed, a writing desk and standing chifforobe for her clothes, as well as a stuffed easy chair and footstool in the corner. She had been lucky to get a northern exposure, and with the lazy shadows from a spreading oak darkening the room it was quite a bit cooler inside than it had been on the streets.

Shrugging out of the crisp linen jacket, Jessica went over to the mirror to unfasten her hat. Her reflection in the shadowy room looked a little overheated and slightly mussed, curls escaping damply around her face, the feathers on her hat drooping tiredly. Jessica shrugged and pulled off the hat, glad that the day was, for the most part, over. She tossed her hat and jacket onto the dresser, and that was when she heard a movement behind her.

Jessica whirled, her hand flying to her throat, a strangulated gasp tearing at her lips. She couldn't scream, she couldn't move. She could only stand there, her heart pounding wildly, her eyes wide with fear and alarm.

The man who rose slowly from the shadows of the corner chair was tall and darkly bearded, lean and taut, every inch of him radiating coiled alertness and danger. His dark hair straggled over his collar and met the faded bandanna he wore around his neck, and his clothes were dusty and travel worn. His face was dark and shadowed and as hard as granite, the face of a man who rode with danger as his daily companion and had learned to outwit it at whatever cost. And his eyes . . . his eyes were as green as a Texas hillside . . . they had once danced with merriment and sparked with temper, had softened with gentleness and flamed with need . . . they now were hard and unreadable and as old as time.

"Hello, Jessica," he said quietly.

She did not know how much time passed that she stood

there, paralyzed in every muscle, every thought, every emotion. And then suddenly her heart leapt into an explosion that was like the shattering of the bars of a cage after an eternity of imprisonment, something beaten and cowed by despair suddenly infused with strength and racing toward life, toward freedom. She whispered, "Jake!" And her eyes grew wide with it, her blood suddenly surged with it . . . *Jake.* Alive.

The incredible, rushing joy swept her, taking away her breath, her speech, her capacity for anything except the need to touch him, to fill her sight and senses with him.

She took one small instinctive step toward him, her hand outstretched, her heart in the fierce incredulous glow in her eyes . . . And then she stopped. Jake. Jake who had saved her life more than once, who had held her in his arms and made her know the reason she lived, Jake who was a part of her, whom she loved with the sweet desperate intensity that would span all time. Jake, with the bearded face and hard eyes, a man who had seen too much and known too much and done too much to ever be the same again. Jake, whose taut, wiry body reflected experience hard earned, a fight for survival in which determination was his only ally. Jake, whom she didn't know anymore. . . .

They were about five steps apart, and she didn't seem to be able to move any further. She stared at him, and he looked at her, and it was as though the very air between them was charged and strained, keeping them apart, pulling them together. Her trembling fingers went to her lips as though to stifle a cry, and she could feel the short pants of her breath against her fingertips. Her heart kept pounding, pounding. She couldn't get enough of looking at him, of filling her eyes with him, of simply knowing he was there, and alive. The emotions that warred within her were intense and paralyzing. Jake. But not Jake. Here, but not hers.

She let her hand flutter away from her face. She couldn't stop her eyes from searching his face, wonderingly, despairingly, questioningly, hungrily. She whispered, "What—what are you doing here?"

Jake could feel it too, the intensity, the shock, the desperate awareness that was so thick it froze his muscles. Jessica. So beautiful. And so different. Jessica of the wild dark hair and huge blue eyes, in stained and baggy clothing and dirt-streaked face. He had carried that picture of her in his head so long it had become almost like a talisman. Jessica, innocence and determination, unquestioning trust and blazing courage . . . Jessica, the girl he loved.

There stood before him a woman he barely recognized, tailored, refined, controlled. Her hair was twisted severely atop her head, only a few of the familiar curls escaping about her face. Her starched white blouse with its high leg-o-mutton sleeves and tight cuffs was the height of fashion, her slim gray skirt and smart walking boots elegant and rich. Her figure was fuller and softer. Her eyes were older. There was a thinness about her face and a set to her mouth that he did not remember; it spoke of pain. *Has life been good to you, Jessica?* he thought. *Tell me it has and it will all be worth it.*

He should never have tried to see her. He should not have come.

He said, never removing his eyes from her, "I got to feeling homesick. I thought I could see Daniel . . . just once."

She couldn't answer. She could only look at him.

His throat ached, looking at her. "You look good," he

said hoarsely. So much time, he thought in dim and distant wonder. A lifetime. . . .

"So do you." It was barely a whisper. To her, he looked beautiful. He was life, he was hope, he was an answer to her only prayer for years. He was Jake. And he was there.

His heart was pounding, slowly, steadily. It felt as though it had just begun beating again for the first time in years. Jessica. He hadn't meant to see her. He truly hadn't. He had resigned himself long ago to the fact that he would never see her again. And even after he had seen her arrive with Casey and without Daniel he had sworn to himself he wouldn't go to her, that he would stay away from her . . .

He saw it rise up in her eyes, the pain and the need and the hunger, and her words, whispered and shaky, held a bubbling cauldron of emotions too intense to define. "Oh Jake, where have you been?" Almost she moved toward him. Tightly, she held herself in check. Only her eyes reached out to him. "What have you been doing?"

He looked at her for a long time. His face was schooled in blankness. He replied simply, "The best I can."

She felt a quiet rending deep inside her. It was the sound of a heart slowly breaking in two.

A heartbeat passed, then another. Jake wanted to touch her. Just to reach out his hand and make sure she was real. He wanted it so badly that his eyes ached and lungs constricted and he couldn't make his hand move.

He said, "I hear Daniel's doing well." His voice sounded strained and odd, and it hardly seemed to belong to him.

"Yes." Hardly a breath. She hadn't moved, not once, from her poised position when she had turned to see him standing there. But her eyes were alive. "We—think he's going to be re-elected."

"Good." The words drifted between them like chaff on a summer breeze. "It's what he always wanted."

"He's . . . very happy." She was hardly aware of what she was saying. *He can't stay. He has to go. This can't happen.*

"Good." That was what he had wanted to know. It was the only reason he had come. He had to leave. He couldn't stay.

He made himself concentrate. "How's the ranch?"

"Good." Her mouth was dry. Her heart was pounding so forcefully against her breast that the material of her blouse fluttered with the movement. And in Jake's eyes, deep within them and visible only to her, was a fire, low and intense. The same fire that was burning within her. "I just bought some new stock. Brahman."

Faintly, so very faintly that she might have imagined it, she thought his lips curved into a smile. "I heard." And his need for her pulsed inside him, suddenly and powerfully. The sensation was so intense, so swift and consuming, that it blinded him, and it took all the strength at his command to steel himself against it. She was not his. He had to leave.

But he couldn't make himself move toward the door. His throat felt raw, as did every nerve ending in his body as he said, "I just needed to know—" There he almost faltered. He couldn't stop looking at her. Aching for her. Filling his mind with her for all the days and weeks and years that lay ahead. "That you were all right."

Don't go. Jake . . . Don't go . . .

She whispered, "Yes."

"I'm glad." It was husky, barely above a whisper. He couldn't stay. And he couldn't even make his eyes move away.

She made herself say it. She had to say it. The words tore

her apart inside and came out shaky. "It's dangerous for you to be here."

He took a breath. It hurt his chest. "Yes. I have to go."

There. It was said. He turned toward the door.

Let him go . . . Jessica clenched her fists.

Jake put his hand on the handle. *Don't let me leave . . .*

"Jake."

She was across the room before she realized she had moved. Her hand was on his arm, her eyes caught in the turmoil and raw flame of his. His skin flared to life beneath her touch, her pores flooded with the presence of him. Their mouths met.

It was meant to be a brief kiss, a single, final good-bye. A last touch, a last taste, a brief glimpse of what might have been. It was hungry, it was primal, it was all-consuming. Her arms went around his neck and he crushed her to him so tightly that it hurt. His mouth devoured hers and her body strained into his. Muscles ached, senses whirled, passion flared and desperation consumed. And when they parted, breathless and unsteady, each took a part of the other that could not be returned. They looked at each other, and nothing but the truth, naked and wanting and unashamed, was written in their eyes.

Jessica took a step away from him. Slowly, her hands went to the buttons of her blouse.

A collage of sensations flooded Jake as he went to her. The soft feather bed, the smell of starch and sunshine and clean muslin. Her skin, dewy and quivering beneath his unsteady fingertips, her dark hair spread like the rippling sheen of a waterfall against the pillow. Her face . . . ah, her face, tight with wanting, aflame with need. He wanted to kiss her face, and her face alone, over and over again, but lost in the vortex of demands, all he could do was fasten his lips to hers and drink from her. The softness of her against the hard length of his body, her curves, full and lush and womanly beneath his hands. She tasted as sweet as tears, drugging heat, velvet softness. And she touched him . . . she touched him.

Jessica ran her hands over his back in long sweeping motions, gathering him to her, exploring, touching, reassuring herself he was truly there. He was sinew and bone, tough and rangy, slick with perspiration and heat. Her fingers dragged across the stern cords of his neck and tangled in his long hair, traced the shape of lean, taut buttocks and tightened there, hungry and unashamed. Her breath came in ragged gasps between the fever of his kisses and the moisture from his mouth mixed with hers as she demanded more. His skin felt so good against hers, so sweet and solid and good, muscles straining and crushing, so strong, so alive. His hard thigh pressed into her hip, his fingers closed on her flesh, his mouth drew from hers. Jake. Jake who was dead but now alive, Jake who had come back to her, Jake, real and solid and strong . . . She was drunk with him, blinded by him. Her heart roared and her breath faded and every part of her body was invaded by him, yearning for him. Jake. Only Jake. . . .

He wanted to touch her, to caress her and kiss every inch of her, to drown in the sensation of her and make it last forever. But the thunder of his heart shook his whole body and the fire that consumed him went beyond the throbbing, straining swell of his loins. For years, for an eternity of days and nights he had carried the ache inside him, pushing it back, trying to forget it, trying to conquer it, yet it burned now stronger than ever, and what had been restrained so long could not be held in check another moment. Oh, he wanted to taste her, to savor her, to let himself believe it was real and to cherish the moment, but her slender calf was winding itself around his, her hips were straining toward him and his skin was bursting, his reason lost. His hand closed around her thigh and her legs parted for him. He felt himself slide against the moist heated center of her and nothing mattered except the stiff, driving need in his loins. He plunged inside her.

Her flesh was tight around him and he knew he hurt her; he heard her startled cry but he was lost in the fierce consuming need, he could not stop, he could not pull back. He clutched her to him, drove deep inside her, and then she was arching against him, her legs winding around his and her cries were of pleasure and yearning and desperate, desperate need. He felt the bite of her nails on his back, the press of her mouth against his shoulder, her softness enveloping him, closing around him, drawing him back again and again. His breath was a harsh scraping in his chest, his heart a dim and distant thunder, his head exploding with mindless, blinding need. She sobbed his name as with one last strong plunge the peak burst upon him helplessly, overwhelmingly. Buried inside her, clinging to her, suspended with her, the essence of him spilled forth and was absorbed by her, became a part of her, and what he had given to her was his very soul; what he had taken from her was her own.

Weakly they clung together, their bodies still fused, shattered breaths and heartbeats struggling to find a mutual rhythm. Neither could let go of the other. Neither could bear to believe that this, like so much else in their lives, must soon be no more than a memory.

Jake's hand was unsteady as he lifted it at last to stroke her wet, flushed face. Jessica gave a whimper of protest as she felt his fullness slide from her, his weight leave her, but almost immediately she was with him again, pressed against his chest, wrapped inside his arms and legs. His heart pulsed through her body, his breath fanned against her hair. She loved him. Oh, how she loved him. The past years without him had been nothing but a barren dream landscape, an imitation of life through which she only drifted. Her body was battered and exhausted, but alive for the first time in three years. Her mind, her heart, her senses were full of him.

She tilted her head to look at him, feeling the swell of renewed wonder, the gift of the impossible come true. Lightly she ran her fingertips over the thick silkiness of his beard, tracing the familiar shape of his face underneath. Jake. So different, yet still Jake. And still hers. She let her fingers drift over the network of lines that radiated from his closed eyes; they were deeper than she remembered, engraved by sun and wind and hard times into his burnished skin, but she thought now some of the wary tension had relaxed from his face. The set of his mouth and the line of his brow did not seem so severe. Her palm brushed lightly over his lips; they parted to caress her skin.

"I love you," she whispered. "Every day and every night for the past three years I have loved you."

His eyes opened, deep and bright, alive with a hundred thoughts and emotions too intense for words, and yet he struggled to express them. "You've haunted me," he said huskily. His eyes went over and over her face, absorbing it, adoring it, assuring himself she was real. "I tried to get away from you, but like a ghost you rode beside me. . . ."

Her voice was tremulous. "How could I have ever thought I could live without you—"

And in a rush, "Jessica, thank God I've found you—"

On a single breath their arms tightened around each other in a fierce embrace, his face buried in her hair, hers pressed into his shoulder. Their eyes squeezed tightly closed, their arms strained until the muscles began to weaken, and as tightly as they held each other it wasn't enough. It would never be enough.

He whispered, "I can't bear to leave you again."

"I can't bear to let you go."

But then slowly it began to creep through them, the truth there was no way to avoid, and it left in its wake a desolation they could not hold at bay no matter how hard they tried. Gradually Jake's arms loosened and he sat up. Jessica had no choice but to let him go.

He sat on the edge of the bed for a moment, his back to her, and Jessica wound her fist tightly into the tangled sheets to keep from reaching up and pulling him back to her. Don't, was the only thought her heart could pulse. Don't go . . . Not yet, not now.

But when he stood it was only to reach for his clothes. He pulled on his pants but did not button them. He walked over to where he had left his shirt, and he fumbled in his vest pocket for tobacco and papers. With his back still to her, he asked quietly, "Does Daniel know?"

Know? With the brilliance of a summer lightning storm it burst upon her: Joshua, with his tousled black curls and laughing green eyes . . . Joshua, the gift of life which had come from Jake, who did not know he had a son.

In a rush of wonder and joy she took a breath to tell him, she even reached out her hand to share the precious moment with him, and then she stopped. A dozen new and conflicting visions flashed through her head. Joshua, riding proudly on his father's shoulder, squealing with delight as he ran into Daniel's arms. Daniel's eyes hardening with hate when he heard Jake's name. Jake, lean and tough and hard, a man whose love for her had caused him to suffer things she could not even imagine and who had changed in ways yet unknown to her. Jake, whose life was at risk even being in Fort Worth. What would he do when she told him? What would he think?

He will go to Three Hills, she knew. *He will try to see his son, and if the Rangers don't kill him Daniel will.*

And a distant yet firm voice of reason warned her to be careful, to think clearly, for more lives than one depended upon this truth. She heard herself answering simply, "Yes."

Jake took a deep breath. With hands that were almost steady he managed to roll and pack the cigarette; he struck a match. How strange it was. When last he had seen her the guilt of adultery, the travesty committed against the brother he loved had consumed him. It had been the single most important driving force behind his torment. Now he had only renewed the dishonor, yet he was hard put to even feel shame. He had not escaped the guilt, nor forgotten it, but how pale it seemed in light of all he had suffered for love of his brother and his brother's wife in these past years.

And now, for the very first time, he let himself wonder if they had made the right decision in those frantic last weeks together three years before. The doubt, so new and unexpected, shook him profoundly. All this time he had told himself he had had no choice: law and honor had insisted that he return Jessica to her rightful husband and leave Texas on his own. But could anything be right which had caused this much pain? Not only to Jake, but to Jessica, and to Daniel, who had had to live with his wife's infidelity and his brother's betrayal.

No. Squaring his shoulders, unconsciously tightening the muscles of his neck, he assured himself it could not be so. *No, it was right. It was right, it was best, it was the only thing we could have done. Jessica, tell me it was right. . . .*

But Jessica, her voice tight and high with distress and determination, only said, "You can't go on living like this."

Jake inhaled the harsh blue smoke. He stared out the window at the bustling street below, dozens upon dozens of people laughing, talking, moving to and fro . . . any one of whom might shoot him in the back for the reward the moment he stepped out of this room. A familiar sight, a familiar knowledge. And he answered, with no emotion at all in his voice, "I have no choice."

Choices. Choices he did not even know about yet. Joshua, who would never know his real father. Jake, who would never know he had a son. There was no choice for them as long as Jake was a fugitive, running from a crime he didn't commit and a brother he loved. But if he were free . . . Dear God, if he were free. Would the choices be any easier to make? How could she live with herself knowing he would never have the chance to find out?

She sat up in bed, winding the sheet tightly about her, rigid with desperation and hope. "Jake, we've got to tell the truth. It's been three years, tempers have cooled. There's a new sheriff in Double Springs now, and even the laws have changed. If—if I went back, there might be someone who remembers, someone who saw something, who knows the truth." Her voice almost choked in her throat and her eyes were torn with pleading. "Jake, we've at least got to try."

He turned slowly. His face was blank, but his voice was rough with the plain truth. "And if we fail?" he demanded calmly. "You'll end up in jail and I'll be hung."

And neither one of them would see their son again. How could she choose between the man she loved and the child who was his only legacy? Was it worth the risk?

Her face was pale and taut and her fists gripped the sheet

tightly at her breast. Her voice cracked as she said painfully, "Nothing has changed, has it?"

With all his soul he wanted to sweep her to him and tell her everything was going to be all right. To erase that awful bleakness from her face and with his two strong arms reshape the world for her, to *make* everything all right. But he had learned long ago the futility of racing from the truth. All he could say was "No." It tore his heart out to say it.

She looked at him for a long time. His bare chest, his knotted shoulders, the swath of dark hair that thickened on his spare abdomen where his unbuttoned pants parted. The emptiness in his eyes, the sadness on his face. Everything had changed. And nothing.

Her eyes were full and dark and brilliant with unshed tears. Her lips trembled as she slowly lifted her arms to him. "Make love to me," she whispered.

He came to her. Once again they clung to each other, once again they tried to convince themselves that this brief moment would last forever. They tried to push away the past and ignore the future and simply lose themselves in each other. It wasn't enough, but that, for the moment, was the best they could do.

Chapter XVII

Jake awoke the next morning with a feeling deep down inside that was so strange he barely recognized it. In the first few drowsy, sun-softened moments he could almost imagine he was back in his own room at Three Hills, the feather mattress and real sheets beneath his body, the jingle of bridles from the stable and the disgruntled early morning curses coming from the bunkhouse; the smell of coffee and sausage drifting up from Rio's kitchen. But if he was at Three Hills he would have been up hours before, and the soft, sleeping woman curved next to him would be only a figment of his imagination. And realizing that this was not imagination, the feeling of lazy contentment and security within him only deepened. He might not be at Three Hills, but he was home.

Jessica was lying on her side with her back to him, her knees slightly drawn up, one arm cradling the pillow against her cheek. His arm was around her waist and throughout the night their hands had remained entwined, his body cradling hers. Waking up to find her there was not waking up at all; it was merely the continuation of a recurring dream.

A smile of which he wasn't even aware caressed his lips as he brought his face forward slightly to brush against the rich curls that spilled down her back. Gently he disengaged his hand from hers and let it roam, very lightly, over her silky skin. He did not want to wake her. He simply wanted to touch her.

Three years before she had been young and underfed; her body had been as hard and lean as his. Now she was soft and full and womanly, and he reveled in the changes. Her small belly was no longer taut and concave, but a gentle hill of feminine flesh. Her breasts were ripe and heavy; the nipples were more prominent and instantly aroused by his touch. She gave a soft and sleepy moan of pleasure when she felt his caress, and his own breath quickened with her awareness. He bent to kiss the delicate curve of her spine, and she caught his fingers, bringing them to her lips.

He felt her gentle smile; he traced the shape of that smile and then the silky underside of her lips, the tip of her tongue. When his fingers returned to her breasts, they were slick with her moisture. He took intense pleasure from the pleasure he was giving her as he gently traced the shape of those tautening peaks, caressing, massaging, adoring.

With his other hand he stroked her back, the silky tangle of curls, the gentle dip of her waist. Her hips were fuller now, her thighs rounder. Every inch of her delighted him, warmth and softness and femininity. He pressed himself close, inhaling the wonder of her. She smelled of sweetness and sunshine and him.

She turned in his arms and her eyes met his with drowsy unabashed welcome. She slipped one arm beneath his as her leg covered both of his; her other hand played with his hair.

They looked at each other lazily, contentedly, absorbing the peace of being in each other's arms.

He let his hand drift down her back again, exploring the texture of her hair, the softness of her buttocks, the curve of her thigh. He kissed her forehead and the corners of her eyes. He fastened his hand around her knee and gently moved her leg to rest higher on his hip. He pulled her close.

She touched his face, her fingers curious and exploratory against the strangeness of his beard. That made him smile and she traced the shape of his lips as he had done with hers. He kissed her fingertips, gently drawing each one by turn into his mouth and her face softened with the sensation. *So many pleasures, Jessica,* he thought. *So many pleasures we could know.*

He slipped his hand between their bodies and positioned himself against her. Her eyes widened as he slowly entered her, and watching her was exquisite. He urged her leg up to his waist and then pressed his fingers against her hips, guiding her. Her eyes drifted closed.

"Look at me, Jessica," he murmured. "Let me see your eyes."

Her eyes fluttered open, and it was the most beautiful sight Jake had ever seen. Deep with passion and hazed with pleasure, questioning and delighting, her eyes were full of him. He brought his hand up to lightly caress her face, and the wonder that grew within him expanded to every pore of his body. It felt like a smile of sheer joy. Jessica. So beautiful. And his.

Her hands moved, stroking his neck, his back, his arms. Their bodies moved in long, slow, delighted rhythms of love. Sunlight dappled the bed and scattered across their entwined bodies in lazy, whispered caresses. They watched each other, they gave of themselves and learned of each other through their joined eyes. The tension built but it was not an urgent thing, and when release came it was in endless suspended ripples of drifting pleasure, lapping waves of delight that captured them as one, so that what was felt by one was redoubled in the other, sensations enhanced to exquisite beauty because they were so completely shared.

They rested together but did not part. They caressed each other and held one another and murmured endearments until Jake began to harden inside her again. The sensation of himself growing within her, of her soft, welcoming flesh expanding to accommodate him, was unlike anything Jake had ever known, and the deepening wonder in Jessica's eyes only intensified his own. *It should always be like this,* Jake thought as he began to move inside her. *Just the two of us, always. . . .*

They lay together quietly as the sun grew higher in the sky, slanting rays gradually changing angles across their bodies. They didn't talk at first, for there was no need for words. It was, for a time, as though they had been together always, and together they savored the illusion.

It was a mistake, Jake knew clearly. *It was a mistake to leave her. It seemed right then, it seemed like the only right thing, but it was wrong . . .*

But how could it have been a mistake? He looked at her, he felt her beneath his hands. She was the vision of a pampered, well-cared for woman. She had not suffered from his absence in any physical way; she had only benefitted from it. If she had gone away with him she would not have been the woman he held in his arms now. Could she have survived what he had been through in those years? How could he have asked her to?

And then he remembered Jessica in the swamp, and on that endless, hazardous road back to Three Hills. He remembered her as he had seen her the day before, striding through the streets of Fort Worth with Casey in tow and a town filled with ranchers and cowhands bending to her will, and a sweep of fierce possessive pride filled him. Yes, she would have survived. Jessica could survive anything.

But that did not mean he had the right to ask her.

Smiling a little with the memory, he said, "I saw you yesterday at the auction."

Jessica looked up at him, her heart giving a queer little tug at the thought of Jake in the crowd, watching her, so near and yet unknown to her. And then she wondered if he had been pleased with what he had seen. Did he realize that, in so many ways, she had stepped into his shoes at Three Hills? That she now gave the orders he once had given, made the decisions that were his to make, commanded the respect and obedience of the ranch hands which once had been due only him? Would he understand if he knew?

But the curve of his smile was encouraging, and she ventured softly, "Were you surprised?"

He chuckled, and the sound was strange, for she had not heard it in so long. But it was indescribably wonderful. "Hell no. I don't know how I could have been. If there was ever a woman who could stand up and make men take notice, it's you."

Her relief, her pride and her gratitude, was consuming. Jake was not disappointed in her. He was pleased with what she had become. Daniel allowed her the freedom to be and do her best; he had opened doors for her that were closed to most women. She had always respected him for that and been grateful. But even in Daniel she had sensed a hint of reticence, of censure, that he was afraid to voice. Jake, however, expected nothing less of her. Jake was proud of her.

But she had to know more. She needed the reassurance that he did not resent, even on the smallest level, her actions on his behalf. "Jake," she questioned, watching his face, "would you have done it—bought the brahman, I mean? The other ranchers are saying I'm crazy, and even . . ." But she didn't want to bring Daniel's name into the conversation. She finished lamely, "Even those who don't are just indulging me, I think. But I want it to be the right thing for Three Hills." *For more reasons,* she thought, *than I can tell you right now.*

He was thoughtful, his mind riding back over the trails he had covered the past years, recalling as if from a dream the many times he had imagined himself still a part of Three Hills, making decisions instead of following orders. How good it felt now to allow that imagination a small place in reality, to pretend that it mattered.

"They're moving west, you know," he said after a moment. "That's where the market is. The longhorns are the only breed with the stamina to make it, but once they get to the Rockies they break down with the cold and disease. Everybody's complaining about needing a stronger breed, or a different breed. Yeah," he decided, looking at her. "I think I would have tried it. If anybody's going to find an answer it ought to be Three Hills."

She embraced him swiftly, pressing her face into his chest. He could not know how much his approval meant to her, how it freed her in ways even her own strong will or Daniel's indulgence could not do. She had tried so hard to do the best for Three Hills, to do it as Jake would have done it, for the sake of his memory and the future of his son. To have his spoken approval was a blessing she had never dreamed would be hers; it was more than she ever would have asked for. It made everything worthwhile.

And yet what could it mean if Jake could never return to claim what she had built for him?

Jake sensed her slight withdrawal, the shadowing of her mood, and he guessed her thoughts. Since the moment he had set foot in Texas it had been with him, the memory of home, the loss of what he could never have again. And now he was suddenly hungry for details, to draw and capture from her every moment of her life in the three years he had been away. So much time had passed, he had missed so many things.

She had taken over for him. Daniel could not have done it. Daniel's ambitions had always lain in different directions; he had never had the passion for ranching that Jake did. But Jessica had stepped in. She had seen the need and filled it as she always had. He wanted to know what she had done, how she had done it; he wanted to know about the ranch hands and the stock and the market and the drovers, and just as he opened his mouth to begin the questions he stopped.

Because he really did not want to know. Hearing about what was gone would only hurt him, and he had spent too much energy in the past years refusing to look back to begin that pointless course now. Because memories, as he had already learned, were debilitating, torturous demons whose presence he could not afford. Instead he let his mind drift forward, and he said almost absently, "Good cattle country in Colorado. Rough land, but damn beautiful. There are places where a man could lose his soul just looking at the sky."

Jessica caught her breath in still expectancy, because this was the first time he had given any hint as to where he had been, what he had been doing. And she wanted to know, she desperately needed to place him against a background for those years that had been missing in her life. But she lay silently against him and would not push.

His fingers toyed with her hair. "I never thought I'd feel that way about any place but Texas. But there's a place near the Divide . . . the Indians call it Gold River. I don't know why, there's never been any gold there as far as any white man knows. I wish you could see it Jessica."

He felt everything within him still with the echo of what he had said, and the sudden import of what it implied. It wasn't too late. He had left her once and it had been wrong, but now—

No. Leaving her had not been wrong, it had been the only honest thing to do and it still was. She was wealthy, secure, respectably married. She had Three Hills and Daniel took care of her. She took care of Daniel. It was good.

It was insanity. He would never ask her to leave all of that, not for what he could offer. Out of Texas he was safe from the Rangers, but there were bounty hunters everywhere and he had had his brush with more than one over the years . . . Yet the bounty hunters were looking for the desperado he had allowed himself to become. If he were a respectable citizen, if he claimed a piece of land and settled down, with a woman. . . .

Crazy. He silently cursed himself and tried to put it from his mind. Once before he had allowed himself daydreams, imagined everything would work out and he would find a way for them, and the next thing he knew he was staring at his name on a wanted poster. He wouldn't be so foolish again. He had never expected to see her again and these past few hours had been a luxury he did not deserve. It was best to be grateful and let it go.

How could he let her go?

She was happy with Daniel. Daniel took care of her, and

even that was more than he deserved. He should be grateful. And Daniel needed her. How could he harm his brother further?

His heart was pounding slowly and steadily. When he took her chin in his fingers and lifted her face his hand was slightly unsteady. He couldn't ask her. He had no right.

Her eyes were so blue, so open, so utterly his. *Leave it alone, Jake.*

He said hoarsely, "Jessica, come with me." And then on a rush he couldn't seem to stop he added, "I'm not saying it would be easy. I can't offer you much, if anything . . . But there's land for the taking across the mountains, and nobody cares who you are or what you've done. It would be rough, I won't lie to you about that, but we've been through worse, Jessica, and it would be a chance . . . For God's sake, Jessica, it might be the only chance we've got."

She stared at him, the impact of his hurried, intense words rushing through her like a physical force. Her mind reeled and whirled and her first, joyous and determined instinct was yes! It was what they should have done long ago, what she had begged him to do. It wasn't too late, there was a chance . . .

And then, tumbling and chasing themselves, a dozen conflicting thoughts and needs and emotions filled her mind. There wasn't just herself to consider, there was Joshua, the baby Jake didn't even know existed. And Daniel. Daniel might let her go but he would never relinquish Joshua. He would follow them to the ends of the earth, they would never be safe from him. And even if she somehow managed to escape, there was so much . . . How secure they all were, living in their comfortable little world at Three Hills. Joshua, the son of a senator, pampered, adored, provided with the best of everything. He would have the best education, a rich inheritance, a powerful, adoring father, or he would be the son of a fugitive, living in poverty, never knowing security or permanence or the truth about his parents' past. . . .

Shameful, hateful thoughts, but as hard as she tried to ignore them she couldn't push them away. *Oh Jake, I only want to do the right thing. For you, and for your baby.* And how could she answer him?

Jake saw the light fade from her eyes, the reluctance creep into her face, and with her hesitance he felt something go through him that was like a slick knife between his ribs. His hand fell away from her face and pain filled him. He had been a fool to even think it.

Quick pleading leapt into her eyes, and she said, "Jake—"

A stern knock on the door froze them both.

"Mrs. Fielding? It's Jenkins from the desk. Are you there?"

Jessica threw a quick alarmed glance at Jake. His face was tight and his hand had instinctively gone over the side of the bed toward his holster on the floor.

"Mrs. Fielding, I'm sorry to bother you, but there's a man downstairs from the bank. He says you were supposed to meet him."

The bank! She had forgotten. She looked again at Jake and saw in his eyes what he wanted her to do. She tried to make her voice as normal as possible through the pounding in her throat and she called out, "Yes. I—I overslept. Please tell him I'll be there shortly."

"Yes ma'am."

The footsteps retreated and she felt Jake cautiously relax. Quickly she returned to him, a torment of indecision on her face. "Jake, I—"

"You'd better go." His voice was calm, almost matter-of-fact. But his face wore a strangely shuttered expression, his eyes were as blank as they had been when she had first seen him the day before. "Best not to arouse any suspicion, just do what you're supposed to be doing here." He tossed the covers aside and began to dress.

He was right of course. Anything out of the ordinary would be reported to Daniel, for half of Fort Worth was filled with gentleman ranchers who felt it their bound duty to keep a protective eye out on the pretty young Mrs. Fielding. Any variation from her normal activities would arouse a bevy of solicitous concern, something neither she nor Jake could afford. But she couldn't leave Jake like this, with so much yet unsaid between them, a life-changing question hanging unanswered in the air. . . .

"Jake, we have to talk." She wound the sheet around her and got up on her knees, reluctant to leave the bed as though that simple movement would put an end to anything that might have been between them. "Jake, you can't go yet. I have to keep my appointment or they'll be suspicious, but we have to talk. Wait for me. Will you promise you'll wait for me?"

Jake hesitated in the process of stuffing his shirt into his pants. His back was to her, but the pleading in her voice etched a poignant picture of her face on his mind. He closed his eyes but the picture did not go away. A few more hours. A day, or two, that's all he would have. What would be the harm in waiting for her? He wasn't ready to walk away, not just yet. Not like this.

He said at length, "I don't guess I've got anything pressing me to be anyplace else."

With a huge sigh of relief Jessica got out of bed, and hurrying behind the screen, began to dress. There was too much, far too much hammering for her attention and she couldn't think clearly. She had to tell him. But how could she? How could she, in these frantic moments as she rushed to keep an appointment and tried to school herself to act natural among the impatient bankers and Daniel's close friends, turn to Jake and say, "By the way, there's something you need to know. . . ."

Oh, no, she had to be careful about the way in which she told him. She had to have a plan in mind, an answer to his question, some way to insure his reaction. He was still the man she loved, but he had changed so much. How could she know how he would react to the news that he had a son? And how could she tell him in the same breath that he would never see that child?

Jake was completely dressed when she came out, idly standing at the window and staring down at the street below. For just a moment alarm gripped her, but she pushed it away. He wouldn't risk trying to leave her room in broad daylight. He would wait for her. Of course he would.

"I'll—I'll be as quick as I can," she said. When he did not turn, she prompted, trying to keep the urgency out of her voice, "Jake? You will be here, won't you?"

He turned. His smile was rather distant. "I'll be here."

She left hurriedly, not wanting to, not having any choice. And she couldn't get the awful nagging suspicion that he might not be there when she got back out of her mind.

Jake watched her leave the building and walk down the street toward the bank. A woman of style, a woman of quality. Heads turned when she passed, gentlemen tipped their hats and greeted her by name. Suddenly he remembered the girl whose only wish had been to be able to walk through a real store and look at the merchandise, to smell the perfumes. He had always said she deserved more. Now she had it.

For the love of God, who was he fooling?

Jessica had built a life without him. Daniel had forgiven her, he had taken her in as his own. That was a gift not to be taken lightly. She had everything she had ever wanted, everything he had wanted for her. Why should she give it up now? What had ever possessed him to ask her?

He couldn't wait around for her to come back and make excuses why she couldn't go with him. He didn't want to see the reluctant and apologetic look on her face, he didn't want to hear the words. He had been crazy to come and crazier still to have stayed. The least he could do was spare them both the agony of good-bye.

On that decision he turned toward the door. Another soft knock froze him where he stood, his hand going to his revolver, silent curses exploding in his brain. And then a voice.

"Jake? It's Casey. Let me in."

He released a slow breath. Jessica must have seen Casey downstairs. He would have preferred no one else know he was here, but it was done now. And, damn, it would be good to see a face from home just once before he left.

He opened the door cautiously and Casey slipped inside. The two men looked at each other for a long time. Casey had changed hardly at all; Jake was almost beyond recognition. The two men acknowledged this while saying nothing.

Jake, slowly filling with the pleasure of familiarity, was the first to speak. "It's good to see you, Casey."

Casey looked at him soberly. "Wish I could say the same, Jake."

Casey had been in a fury of turmoil ever since he had seen Jake slip into Jessica's room the day before. By some chance Casey had arrived back at the hotel before Jessica. When he saw Jake he had started toward the room, planning to get rid of Jake and avert disaster. But then Jessica had returned. Casey had been able to do nothing but slip back into his room and let fate have its way.

He had waited for Jake to leave, marking the time by the depths of the tragedy that was building. When Jake did not leave within fifteen minutes, all hope passed that this would be a casual meeting and leave nothing changed. After an hour Casey knew the two of them were coupling in their animal passion and the vision made him sick. When Jessica didn't leave her room for dinner he knew plans were being made. And when Jake still hadn't left her room that morning there was no hope for it: the cheating bitch had told him everything, and even now they were planning to steal that boy from Daniel and run off together.

And that, Casey knew, would destroy the man to whom he owed his life.

He had confronted Jake not knowing what he was going to do, but knowing he had to do something. He was all that stood between Daniel Fielding and the loss of everything he valued, and the very least Casey could do was try to make Jake see reason. Seeing Jake so battered and weary, Casey even thought that he might have a chance at success.

Casey took off his hat and leaned one hip against the dresser in an easy stance. "You look like hell," he told Jake frankly.

Ruefully Jake ran his hand over his beard. "I guess I do at that." It was beginning to occur to him to wonder what Casey thought of finding him in Jessica's room, but he didn't wonder very hard and the answer did not concern him overmuch. It only went to show how little conscience he had left, not to feel even the slightest embarrassment at being more or less caught with his brother's wife.

So he met Casey's speculative gaze without shame or

regret and asked the only thing he was interested in knowing. "How's everything at home?"

Casey seemed to think about it for a long time before answering, and there was a firm and sober look in his eyes that reminded Jake of the man's past military career. "Good," he said at last, and the word was like a quiet challenge. "Damn good."

Jake waited for the rest, and Casey did not disappoint him.

"Listen, Jake, I only come up here because you and me go back a ways and I figure you got a right to know. I don't hold nothing against you personally, understand, though I can't say's I approve of some of the things you've done." There was a flicker of something ugly in Casey's eyes then, and Jake knew he was not referring to what had happened in Double Springs. He knew it by the way the other man's eyes shifted to the rumpled bed behind him.

Jake kept his gaze and his tone even. "Go on."

Casey returned his eyes to him. "I don't know what she's told you, and I sure don't know what the two of you are planning, but I think you owe it to yourself—and your brother—to do some hard thinking before you go off and cause any more heartbreak. They're happy, Jake."

With a sharp indrawn breath that sounded like a hiss, Jake swung away, dragging his hand through his hair. He should have known it was coming. But that didn't mean he had to listen to it.

But Casey persisted relentlessly. "To look at 'em you'd think they was just any other married couple. I know you can't change the past, but I wouldn't rightly reckon she's thought about you once since you been gone, and the way she carries on with the cap'n I'd *sure* give it some thought before I gambled away my future on a woman like that."

Jake said tautly, without turning, "Casey—"

"And as much as it pains me to admit it, the cap'n needs that woman." Casey knew when to press his advantage. He could tell he was getting through to Jake, for despite all he had done, Jake had always had a soft spot for his brother. "Why else would he have kept her? Now you think about that Jake, and you count your blessings. He took her back with no questions asked, and that baby . . . Why, he loves that boy like it was his own. Things are good now, Jake—"

Jake froze. He heard nothing after the word baby. He turned, very slowly. *"What?"*

Casey stared at him. Jake's eyes were very dark and his lips seemed to have lost color. He was looking at Casey as though he had never seen him before and Casey furiously wracked his brain to try to remember what he had said to put that look on Jake's face.

"What baby?" Jake demanded.

Jesus Christ. Casey couldn't answer. He could barely even think. He could only stare at Jake and see his shock and the anger rising. *Jesus Christ*. She hadn't told him. The cheating, lying little bitch hadn't told him, and if Casey hadn't interfered no one might ever have been the wiser. Jake might have left as he had come. . . .

He thought quickly. Casey had never been inspired in his life, but he knew the future depended upon his being so now. And, gratefully, he was. He said, "I thought you knew. It was in all the papers." He forced an uneasy laugh. "But then I guess you ain't been reading too many newspapers have you?"

Jake stood poised, his eyes never leaving Casey's face. Casey licked his lips nervously. "Well, you know Daniel, so it shouldn't come as no surprise. Took in an orphan kid a while of years back, made it like his own . . ."

His eyes like steel, Jake drew his revolver and pointed it straight at Casey's chest. "The truth," he demanded quietly.

Casey began to sweat. He hadn't seen it coming. And he'd never seen eyes like that on anybody. He straightened up slowly, and the movement of the revolver followed him. He licked his lips again. "Hell, Jake, what're you so all fired—"

Jake cocked the hammer. His face was so taut his cheekbones stood out prominently above his black beard. "I'll blow a hole in you, you son of a bitch. *What baby?*"

Casey had no doubt in the world that Jake would do it. He had killed once, hadn't he? At least once. And Casey had never seen a more murderous look on any man's face than the one he met across the barrel of the Peacemaker that was leveled at his chest.

"All right, goddamnit!" He was sweating in earnest now, and he threw his hands up in a gesture that was half surrender, half outright terror. "What do you want from me?" The words were spat with as much contempt for himself as for the woman to which he referred. "The whore came home already breeding, and you and me both know it wasn't your brother that got her that way!"

The two men faced each other for what seemed like an eternity. Not a flicker of emotion crossed Jake's face. The hand that held the revolver didn't waver. And Casey became convinced that Jake was going to shoot him after all, just for the hell of it.

Then Jake slowly released the hammer. He said softly, "Get out of here."

Casey wasted no time doing so.

With the reflexes of a man who had received a mortal blow but stubbornly refused to die, Jake lowered his pistol and returned it to the holster. He stood staring at the place

Casey had been, his expression unchanging, his eyes registering nothing. He stayed that way for a very long time.

Jessica's heart was in her throat as she rushed into the room scarcely an hour later. She had pushed along the business with the bankers as fast as she had dared, neglecting too many of the social amenities, causing the two pillars of Fort Worth's economy to cast her curious, surprised looks toward the end of the session. And all the while her mind was racing, leaping back to Jake, shadowed by the dread premonition that something was wrong, that when she returned her room would be empty . . . Oh, why? Why had she had to leave like that? Why had he chosen that very moment, with so little warning, to ask her the most important question of her life? And what answer, even now, could she give him? Assuming she ever saw him again.

Her eyes swept the room as she flung open the door, and the relief that flooded her as she saw Jake lounging on the bed left her weak. His ankles were crossed, his arms linked behind his head, his eyes fixed upon the door and registering no reaction at all to her flurried entrance. That should have bothered Jessica, as should the still, closed expression on his face. Had she been less worried, less overwhelmed with relief, she would have noticed that his relaxed posture was underscored by thrumming tension; that he looked less like a man awaiting his lover's return than a dangerous animal coiled to spring.

But Jessica, joy glowing in her eyes and coloring her cheeks, noticed nothing except that he was there. She went quickly to him, sitting on the edge of the bed beside him. "Oh, Jake I was so worried that you wouldn't wait, that you would decide—I hurried—"

His hand moved with the swiftness of a striking snake,

closing about her wrist with a steely grip that made her gasp aloud. His eyes were fire and ice. He said lowly, "Why didn't you tell me?"

She stared at him. His hand was hurting her and what she saw on his face plunged her into a turmoil of confusion and fearful hurt. All she could manage to say was, "Jake, what—"

His fingers tightened, wrenching a smothered cry from her. "Why didn't you tell me about our baby?"

The question, spiteful and harsh, reverberated in the room, pummeled Jessica's head. Disbelief, dread, shame, sorrow and fear warred for precedence among the emotions that were assaulting her. And the churning anger and contempt in Jake's eyes, the pain beneath that . . . But her voice seemed to have left her, her strength was ebbing as the certainty of this horror grew, and her voice was barely a whisper. "How did you find out?"

His eyes narrowed a fraction, yet his voice was smooth even as his fingers tightened, almost unconsciously and most painfully, on her wrist. Her fingers began to throb. "Well, it certainly wasn't from the proud mama, now was it?" Then shortly, "Casey. Am I the only man in Texas who *doesn't* know?"

"Jake," she pleaded, "I was going to tell you—"

He swung to his feet and released her with an abruptness that sent her sprawling on the bed, cradling her throbbing arm against her chest and biting back a cry of pain. He whirled on her, his eyes flaming, his face wild with rage. "Were you? Or were you hoping I'd meet some Ranger on the street before you got around to it? That would have saved you a hell of a lot of trouble, wouldn't it?"

"Jake, please!" she cried, almost sobbing, but he was

out of control. She had never seen him like this and he terrified her even as she was torn apart inside with his pain.

"By God, you've got it all, haven't you?" he flung at her. "Fine house, devoted husband, and bastard child you can fob off as his! You've got it all worked out! And to think I thought you would give it all up to come with me!" He gave a harsh, ugly bark of laughter. "By God, that's rich!"

"Jake stop it!" she screamed. "What was I supposed to do? You left me! You—"

"And you damn sure took advantage of it, didn't you? I always knew you could take care of yourself!" And even as he spoke he knew she was right. He even knew that it wasn't her he was angry with but life, fate, the brutal circumstances that had branded him an outlaw and given his brother everything that was his—*everything*.

Jessica pressed her hands to her face, breathing hard, protecting herself from the hatred in his eyes and the fury in his voice, struggling for strength, for some way to reach him. But Jake couldn't seem to stop himself; he wanted to strike out, to hurt something, to destroy something, and it didn't matter if what he destroyed at that moment was himself or the woman he loved. He took a short, tense stride toward her, bunching his fists to keep himself from dragging her to her feet.

He bit out, "It's been good for you hasn't it, Jessica? Damn good! You've built yourself a little fairy-tale world and fit right into it, and you call that living. Well, let me tell you something about living, lady—it's hard and it's ugly and it's damn sure not fair! Maybe it's time you and Daniel found that out for yourselves!"

Jessica lifted a pale and torn face to him. Her eyes were

dark with agony, an agony almost as intense as his own. "Jake, you've got it all wrong. Please. . . ."

And for just that moment he stopped. It washed over him, suddenly, forcefully, and perhaps for the first time. His baby. His *son*, born of this woman and the love they had shared. A love that had changed his life, that had cost him his brother, his home, his freedom, everything he had ever known. But his son. He had a son that would be forever his, that no one could take from him . . .

He looked at her long and steadily, and his eyes, the torment in his face, stripped from Jessica anything else she might have said. When he spoke his voice was quiet, deadly final. "I've given up my life for you, Jessica, but I won't give up my child. You can't keep him from me."

He turned and strode away, and the door slammed loudly behind him.

Jessica could do nothing but sit there, her fingers pressed to her lips, and let the tears stream down her face. She couldn't call out, she couldn't make herself move. He had taken everything from her when he walked out the door.

Listening to Jake's horse's hoofbeats fading in the distance all those years ago . . . looking into her husband's eyes and seeing his hatred there . . . She had survived that. She had thought that was the worst that could ever happen to her. But until this very minute she had never had any idea what the worst could really be.

And it had only begun.

Chapter XVIII

Daniel's eyes were volcanic. "How the hell," he demanded lowly, "could you have let this happen?"

Casey stood before him, his eyes focusing bleakly on the hat he held in his hand. There was nothing Daniel could say to him that he had not already said to himself, no filthy name he could call him Casey had not already called himself. All he had wanted to do was protect Daniel. Instead he had set wheels of destruction in motion that could not be turned back. If shooting himself would have done any good, he would have cheerfully done so.

Daniel leaned back in his chair, one hand curling into a fist atop his desk. His eyes moved unseeingly to the wall of books behind Casey and his mind drifted back to that last angry encounter with Jake, in this very room. Jake, with his volatile temper and his stubborn determination. He should have known, even then. Daniel should have known that whatever happiness he might ever reach for would always be blighted as long as Jake was in the picture.

Jake. A chill gripped him as the truth of it washed over him again. Jake was back in Texas, had been with Jessica, was even now on his way to Three Hills to destroy everything Daniel had built for himself. Over the years he had pushed Jake's existence so far back into a corner of his mind that his brother hardly even seemed real, much less threatening. But it was like a recurring nightmare, something that just wouldn't stay dead, and now Jake was close and he knew everything. There was no way to ignore him any longer. Daniel had done everything in his power to see that Jake never entered their lives again, but he had failed. Now he was going to have to face the consequences.

Daniel got up and walked to the window. He pushed aside the curtain and looked out over the peaceful lawn, still and green and lush in the July sun. Jake was not going to do this, he thought fiercely. Daniel had worked too hard, wanted too badly, and he was not going to let Jake take them away from him.

Jessica was his. Jake might have put his physical brand on her, but she belonged to Daniel; she always had. He had taken care of her, he had lived with her, he had loved her first. Joshua was his, too. Jake was young, he was strong, he was determined. He could build a life for himself if he was wily enough; he could start again. But Jessica and Joshua were all Daniel had. He would not give them up to his brother. He couldn't.

He spoke quietly but firmly. "I want armed guards to patrol the perimeters twenty-four hours a day. Tell them that my brother is on his way back here and he means to harm my wife and son. Their orders are . . ." He took a brief breath and still did not turn. No regret backed the words, just determination. "To stop him."

Casey's face hardened with satisfaction and he gave a curt nod before turning to leave. He would make it up to Daniel, he vowed silently, and he would begin by changing the order to shoot to kill.

They had left on the one o'clock train, less than an hour behind Jake. Jessica knew that on horseback and by the cautious, circuitous route Jake would be forced to take he could not possibly reach Three Hills before they did—and she knew just as certainly that Three Hills was exactly where he was headed. Still, she had clenched her fists and stared white-faced out the window the entire way, urging the train on, willing it to gain speed.

She had not even paused to inform the household of their return, but raced blindly up the stairs, snatching her dozing son out of a startled Maria's arms and holding him tightly, smothering sobs of relief and fear in his sleepy warm skin. She did not know what Jake was going to do, and she did not know whether she feared more for the man she loved or the child he could take from her. But Jake, so violent and volatile, used to taking whatever he wanted and deprived now of everything, raging with hurt... She didn't know what he was going to do, and that was what terrified her the most.

Jessica knew that while she shut herself in the nursery, playing with her delighted son, Casey was downstairs telling Daniel everything. And for one last time she let it sweep over her: the desolation, the sorrow, the guilt of the pain she had inflicted on the man who had committed no crime except to love her. By the time she gathered her courage to go to him, she knew there was nothing left to say, nothing left to do, nothing left, in fact, for them at all.

Daniel heard her enter the library and turned slowly. He expected the sight of her to invoke hatred, the rage of betrayal renewed. What he felt, in fact, was exactly the opposite.

She was holding Joshua, her hand cradling his head, his fists tugging at her curls. Mother and son, so much alike, so beautiful. Her face was white and distressed yet painfully brave, and Daniel was suddenly gripped by a possessive love so intense it left him shaken. They were *his*. He had paid the price for them in forgiveness and devotion and love. He had battled himself and society and Jessica's betrayal for their sakes, and he had won. No one would take that victory from him now. No one would destroy what they had built.

Jessica looked at him, and the depth of pain in her eyes gripped his heart. She said brokenly, "Daniel—I'm so sorry—"

He stepped over to her and put his arm gently around her shoulders. He knew in that moment that he would move heaven and hell to keep her and the family they had made. There was a stiffness, almost a grimness behind his smile, and his voice was rough as he said, "Don't worry, Jessica. You're home now. Nothing is going to hurt us."

The days that followed were a string of endless hours brittle with tension. Manpower was doubled at the line camps, and armed men patrolled the borders at regular intervals, although had Daniel thought to question or had Casey not been too stubborn to listen, any one of the men could have pointed out that such measures were futile. Jake had roamed the hills and valleys of the ranch since he had been old enough to walk. He was as at home in the woods and meadows, the caves and copses as any forest creature, and he knew ways in and out of Three Hills that none of the men ordered to stop him could even begin to guess at.

Denying Jake Fielding access to what he was determined to have was an exercise in futility, and the men began to place secret bets on how soon Jake would outwit them all.

As the days passed and nothing happened Jessica tried to convince herself that Jake had regained his senses, that he would not endanger himself or his child by returning to the ranch. During the day life almost regained its sense of normalcy, despite the fact that Daniel seemed unwilling to let Joshua out of his sight even for a minute, and long and worried looks from her husband seemed to follow Jessica everywhere she went. She played with Joshua, she attended to household business, she and Daniel had conversations about the ranch just as they had done before, and it became increasingly easy to pretend everything was all right. But at night she could not close her eyes without seeing Jake's agonized and enraged face. And she had nightmares.

She awoke from one such dream in the dead of the night to the sound of her own gasp being torn from her throat. Her body was damp with perspiration and her thundering heart shook her entire body. She could remember nothing of the dream except that Jake needed her and she had been unable to reach him, and Joshua. . . .

Joshua.

Not bothering to put on her robe, she swung out of bed and raced down the hall. She flung open the nursery door and halted there, her heart pounding and her breasts heaving, arrested by what she saw.

A brilliant moon flooded through the open window and painted Jake's silhouette silver. He was standing beside the empty cradle, a still sleeping Joshua in his arms. His head was bent low over the child, one hand cupped against his head of silky curls while Joshua, his thumb stuck contentedly in his mouth, slept on his father's shoulder.

For the longest time they remained like that, father and son, mother poised just on the outskirts, her hand extended as though to protect them, or gather them close. Then Jake said quietly, "He didn't even cry when I picked him up." His voice was thick and a little uneven, deeply infused with a note of wonder.

He turned, and in the moonlight his face was wet with tears. Jessica thought her heart was incapable of breaking again, but she looked into Jake's face and everything within her was torn in two.

He asked softly, "What's his name?"

"Joshua," she whispered, and she was never certain afterward how she even formed the words. "For your father."

She thought he nodded. He lowered his head again, brushing his bearded cheek against the baby's hair, and she saw his hands tighten, just once. She reached for him with her mind, her heart, her soul; she ached to enfold him. She couldn't make her arms move.

He moved toward her. Gently he transferred the sleeping child to her arms. "He's a fine boy," he said huskily, and his hand lingered to caress Joshua's hair. Then, in a broken whisper, he said, "Take care of him for me, will you?"

He turned away from her, toward the window. A moment later he was gone.

Jessica tightened her arms around her baby. Squeezing her eyes shut, she whispered, "Oh Jake, what have I done to you? *What have I done?*"

Jake had climbed the spreading oak that spanned the north side of the house so many times in his reckless youth that doing so now was instinctual, requiring little concentration. Blindly he reached for familiar handholds, his mind numb and his eyes blurred. Dimly he knew that this action, so familiar from his childhood, was now being performed for the last time, and perhaps on an even deeper level he knew that these last moments marked an end to more than just his past. But it hardly even mattered, for he had just left the best part of himself behind in that room, the only part of himself that he cared about. Even as he dropped lightly to the ground, he knew that it was over. And he was almost glad.

He felt the steel revolver press into his ribs with no surprise. He didn't even try to turn around.

"You did it Jake," Daniel said quietly. "I'll give you that. I don't know how you got past the guards the first time, but you're sure as hell not going to do it again. Let me have your gun."

Daniel was surprised at the level tone of his voice, the steadiness of his nerves. For all the hatred and rage he had felt for Jake over the years, he had often wondered how he would react if, or when, he came face-to-face with his brother again. He had expected blinding, incapacitating fury, had feared remorse. He felt nothing now but calm and certain determination. He could do what he had to do to protect his family.

Jake could have fought, and the chances were that he would have won. He could have run, for he didn't think Daniel would shoot him in the back. Both alternatives briefly occurred to him, but were rejected with a sense of weary relief. And in a strange way he was glad to have it end here, at his brother's hands, where it should have ended years before. He unfastened his gun belt slowly and handed it to Daniel without turning around.

Daniel took the belt, and his revolver against Jake's ribs

did not waver. It was very peculiar how little he felt. He did what he had to do.

"All right," he said quietly, "we're not going to raise a stir. Just walk slowly around back. We're going to the old barn."

The old barn was one of the first outbuildings that had been constructed at Three Hills. It was built sturdily of logs, with a firm iron bolt on the door. The needs of the ranch had long since outgrown it, and now it was used only for storage of old tack and outdated equipment. Jake and Daniel had played there many times as boys.

Their way was guided by moonlight, their steps certain. They were halfway across the yard when Jake spoke. He had to know. "If I ran now—would you shoot me?"

Daniel hesitated, but only fractionally. His voice was steady. "I think I would," he said quietly. "So please don't."

Jake said nothing.

The door screeched as Daniel pulled it open, and then with a sharp nudge of the revolver, urged Jake inside. The moonlight from the open door was enough to show him what he needed, and he went to get a coil of rope hanging from the wall. "Put your hands behind your back," he ordered shortly.

Jake complied.

Daniel wound the rope tightly around Jake's wrists, jerking it into a knot with a ruthlessness that made Jake wince as the rough hemp bit into his skin. When it was done Daniel commanded, "Sit down."

Jake sank somewhat stiffly to the hay-strewn dirt floor, and Daniel went to work binding his ankles together. For the first time in three years Jake looked at his brother, and even shadowed and dim as his vision was, the sight made the pain in his chest tighten and twist. How much older he looked. How grim. In swift succession memories flashed before his eyes: Daniel, his face alight as he told Jake of his impending marriage; the glowing bridegroom on a torchlit lawn as he placed Jessica's hand in Jake's so confidently, *You are the two people I love most in the world.* And Daniel as Jake had last seen him, lying weak and white and begging Jake to return his bride to him. God, how had it happened? Jake thought weakly. How had it ever come to this?

"Daniel, I'm sorry." Jake's voice sounded distant, bleak, and painfully inadequate. "I never meant for this to happen."

Daniel looked at him, and for the first time, with the shock of recognition, he felt the stab of pain. Jake. *Damn it Jake. I loved him, trusted him. He had been my brother.* Determinedly, almost viciously, he pushed the emotion aside.

His voice was harsh, his words angry and defensive. "Do you think I enjoy this?" He drew another loop of rope around Jake's ankles and pulled it tight. "I can't let you back into their lives. They're mine, they're all I've got—" Something strange caught in his throat; he cleared it with a short breath. He concentrated on knotting the rope. "I can't," he said simply as he stood up.

Daniel looked at Jake for a moment, and there seemed to be a hint of sorrow in his face. There was nothing but resignation in Jake's expression.

"What are you going to do with me?" Jake asked at last.

For a moment Daniel seemed not to hear him. And when his eyes focused again there was nothing there, not regret, not satisfaction, not even anger. "First thing in the morning I'll ride for the marshal," he answered matter-of-factly. "You've left me no choice, Jake."

Jake nodded, and in simple acceptance of his fate, turned his head to rest against the wall.

Daniel stood for a moment longer, then turned and left him, bolting the door firmly.

When Daniel reentered the house his heart started to pound, and it felt as though it would burst right out of his chest. Only when he stood above his sleeping son's cradle did it begin to calm. He reached out a hand that was not quite steady and touched the baby's head, taking strength from the small form that was all he knew in the world worth living for.

"It couldn't be any other way, Josh," he said huskily, forcing determination into his voice. "It couldn't be."

He walked past his wife's closed door and into his own bedroom, all the while reciting the litany. *It couldn't be any other way.* But the reassurance seemed hollow, and it was almost dawn before he slept.

Bright morning sunlight fell across Jake's face, causing him to wince and smother a moan as he turned his head. He tried to move his arms and the pain that shot through his shoulders was blinding. A voice roared above him, "Where is she, damn you!"

Jake blinked at the hazy silhouette of his brother shadowing the doorway, trying to focus on what he had said. He struggled to sit up but his muscles were like rawhide and his mouth felt as though it were stuffed with straw. "What?" he mumbled foggily, rising to a sitting position.

The blow sent him reeling back against the earth floor. It snapped in his neck and blurred his eyes, and when his head cleared Daniel's face was throbbing above him, red and distorted, fists clenching convulsively at his sides. "*Where is she?*"

"What the hell are you talking about?" Jake shouted back, struggling briefly against the rope that bound his hands. He felt a trickle of blood run from his cut lip into his beard, and his whole mouth tasted coppery. He struggled again, furious at his inability to defend himself. "What's the matter with you?"

"You know damn well what I'm talking about!" Daniel took a step forward as though to haul Jake to his feet or fasten his hands about his throat, but stopped himself short. "Where is my wife? Where was she planning to meet you?"

Jake stopped his futile struggles just then, anger and confusion halting in its spiral and disappearing with a burst. He stared at Daniel. "Jessica's gone?"

Daniel's mouth curved into a sneer; his fists clenched tighter. His head throbbed with the memory. All night he had struggled with his conscience over how to tell Jessica about Jake, or whether to tell her at all; he had even delayed coming out to check on Jake that morning in the vague hope that he might have escaped. He had appeared at the breakfast table only to find the place across from him deserted, and to be told by Maria that Miss Jessica had left at sunrise with no word of when she would return. She had acted very strangely, reported Maria worriedly, and held on to that baby as though she might never see him again. Was everything all right, did Daniel think?

"She didn't know," Daniel said, breathing hard. "She didn't know that you were tied up out here. She went to keep whatever tryst you made last night, and you're going to tell me where it is or by God I'll kill you right now and won't regret a minute of it. *Tell me*."

Jake's mind whirled, retreated, but couldn't escape. Jessica. He knew exactly where Jessica had gone.

He looked at Daniel, dread and disbelief warring on his face. "She had an idea," he said slowly, "that if she could go back to Double Springs . . . somehow she could prove what really happened, and clear my name." Then he added anxiously, "You've got to stop her, Daniel. You don't know what she might do or say. You've got to go after her!"

Daniel stared at him, and there wasn't an instant's doubt that Jake was telling the truth. His face was tight and torn with alarm, his eyes in turmoil. Jake said urgently, "Go, for God's sake! They'll put her in jail!"

Daniel thought quickly, and the scenario grew in horror. He had worked too long and hard to prevent exactly this kind of thing to let it all fall apart now. He was so close—so close to having Jake out of their lives forever. At best he would be several hours behind her, but there was still time, with luck, to avert disaster . . . He said roughly, "Nobody's going to put her in jail." And he turned.

"Daniel."

Nothing but the quick command in Jake's voice made Daniel turn back.

Jake said quietly but inarguably, "I'm going with you."

The two men looked at one another for a long time, each set of eyes filled with emotions that only the other could fathom. Daniel took out his knife and bent to cut Jake's bonds.

The journey that had taken an eternity on horseback three years before now took a little over six hours by train. The landscape Jessica once had seen only for its hiding places and watering holes now seemed appallingly civilized, small towns and mail depots every few miles, farms and houses dotting the countryside. With the arrival of the railroad everything had changed.

Double Springs was nothing like she remembered it. There was the train depot and new storefronts, two new boarding houses that advertised hot meals, and a real hotel with two stories. The streets were lined with boardwalks and filled with wagons and carts.

She did not know what she was going to do, did not know what would happen to her. She had only known, as she looked into Jake's eyes the night before, that she had no choice. She had taken everything from him. The least she could do was give him back his freedom. It was a truth too long hidden, an action long overdue. But having resolved herself to the only possible course, she had known she could not delay another moment.

In the back of her mind there had always been the certainty that the truth was not a secret shared by only her and Jake. Someone, somewhere in the town must have heard or seen something that could corroborate her story, and that was her first hope. The scandal would be terrible for Daniel, and for that she felt regret. But if the truth were finally brought to light there was the possibility that she would be cleared of an accidental shooting and Jake, most certainly, would be totally exonerated.

During the trip she had wracked her brain replaying the nightmare that had occurred behind that closed door three years before, and hope began to wane, then finally die. No one had seen anything. How could they have? Her word alone would have to stand, and though it might not be enough to save herself, it would certainly save Jake. It had to.

She would tell the truth. It would be up to a judge and jury to believe her. And if they did not . . . If they did not she would go to prison. She would never see her baby again, but, surprisingly, she felt no fear. What she was doing was nothing more nor less than she should have done at the beginning. She could not give Jake back the three years he had lost from his life, she could not give him his home, his brother, his child. But she could give him this. At least this.

She pushed open the door of the saloon, and the sense of déjà vu that swept her was so potent it was almost breathtaking. The same sawdust littered floor, the same scarred bar, the same suspicious, grizzled barkeeper. A group of men were playing cards at a corner table, striking the perfect tableau of an early afternoon three years before. Conversation ceased, all eyes turned to her . . . only the last time the eyes had been filled with leering derision for the bedraggled, filthy girl in men's clothing. Now they fastened on the smartly dressed young lady with wariness and curiosity. That almost made Jessica smile.

She did not know what she had expected to find there. Perhaps nothing, perhaps everything, perhaps only some little thing that would jog her memory. The memories were there, all right, but none of them were helpful. Perhaps coming here was nothing more than a tribute, a final good-bye to the past, a fitting end. And then she saw her.

Leaning against the bar, wearing a short gold dress that was stained and mended in places where it wasn't supposed to show, was a woman with bright orange hair. Like a series of tintype photographs, images flashed before Jessica's eyes. A woman coming down the stairs in a black and red dress. Jessica's eyes meeting hers in a tentative smile. A door opening, frowsy orange hair, alarmed eyes. *"Lord, honey, what's all the commotion?"*

Jessica's heart was pounding and her palms were wet beneath her white gloves as she slowly crossed the room. The woman's eyes narrowed with suspicion and she straightened up at little as Jessica approached. Jessica was certain she would not be able to make her voice work. *Oh please, God. . . .*

"Excuse me, ma'am," she said, "could I have a word with you, please?"

Daniel used his influence to obtain a private car for the trip to Double Springs. They were on their way by noon.

Jake sat by the window, Daniel blocked the aisle. Casey was in the seat behind them, alert and taciturn, and Jake knew that, out of the view of other passengers, a revolver was pointed at his back. He tried to dredge up amusement for the thought of Casey riding shotgun on him, or sorrow for the fact that Daniel thought it was necessary, but he couldn't manage either.

The hours chugged by in snips of passing landscape, and Jake kept his face turned toward the window, watching. It seemed to him that the years of his life were flashing by with the same steady speed, and he was dimly fascinated by the show. He hadn't lived long, but he had lived fully. More, when it came right down to it, than he had ever wanted to. And now he was only tired.

At last he said, not turning away from the window, "It was a good thing you did, taking care of them." His voice was heavy, but not sorrowful. Simply truthful. "I didn't thank you for it."

Daniel said sharply, "It's not yours to thank me for anything. Jessica's my wife and Joshua's my son. They were mine to take care of."

Jake was silent for a long time. When he turned to Daniel his expression was quiet, but in his eyes there was a peculiar struggle, pride wrestling with the question he was uncertain how to ask. "The boy . . . You won't tell him, will you?"

Daniel was startled, just for a moment disconcerted. Then he said gruffly, "Of course not."

Jake seemed to relax. He faced the seat straight ahead. "I mean . . . not even that he had an uncle. I think it would be better, especially while he's young. Later, maybe you can make up some story."

Daniel realized abruptly that Jake was talking about his own death. He opened his mouth to say something, but then swallowed hard and said nothing. Jake turned back to the window, and after awhile Daniel looked away.

The woman's name was Lottie. She agreed to sit with Jessica at one of the sticky tables near the door. She looked at Jessica with a cautious indifference that was not completely borne out by a spark of curiosity in her eyes. "Sure I remember you." She shrugged, and then a quick and almost embarrassed softness flitted over her harsh features. "Remember you sittin' right here that night—smiled at me like you didn't have a brain in your head. Thought at the time that wrangler you were with shoulda known better than to bring you into a place like this."

Jessica tried to keep her breathing even. Her fists were clenched under the table. "But later," she said, calmly. "Do you remember what happened later?"

"You mean the shooting?" The woman's eyes grew opaque. "Yeah, I remember. I was coming upstairs about the time Stratton was knocking on your door. Remember thinking it must've been yours because what else would he be doing there?"

Jessica didn't dare to even blink.

Lottie's face was perfectly composed as she continued

mildly, "Son of a bitch deserved to be shot, if you ask me. You ain't the first woman he'd tried that on. You're the first one that got lucky, is all."

Hope was suspended inside Jessica like a balloon ready to burst. "Then you know . . ." Her voice was shaky. "You know what he tried to do to me?"

Again Lottie shrugged. "Heard you screaming. Figured the rest. Had a customer, you know, and there wasn't nothing much I could do about it, not that I make it a policy to get involved in other folks' troubles, but you'd looked kinda sweet and I felt sorry for you. Heard the gun go off, but by the time I got to the door your young man—Fielding, they say it was—was bounding up them stairs . . . By the time I got some clothes on and got back to the door you was running toward the back like some wildcat. So I figured it was over."

She said it so matter-of-factly, not knowing her simple, concise memory could save the lives of two people . . . Jessica's heart was racing. She hardly even heard her own voice as she said, "You heard the shot *before* Jake came up the stairs. You know he didn't fire it."

The other woman looked at Jessica as though she were slightly dim-witted. "'Course I know it. Don't take no genius to figure out if the man wasn't even in the room when the gun went off he didn't shoot anybody."

Over. It was over. There was someone who could corroborate her story, who had heard everything, had seen Jake and could prove his innocence. Lottie could tell a jury that not only did Jake not fire the gun, but that she had heard Jessica fighting off an attacker. They both would be free. It was over.

Swiftly, Jessica clutched the other woman's hand. Lottie looked startled, but did not try to draw away. "Please,"

Jessica said. Her pulses were fluttering like a thousand mad butterflies. "Please, will you come with me to the sheriff and tell him what you just told me?"

Lottie looked at her, but her eyes were touched with pity and her smile was a little sad. "Honey, it won't make no difference. I told 'em two years ago that boy didn't shoot nobody. And it's not that I wanted to see you in any trouble, honey, but it just didn't seem right to lie about it . . . hell, it wasn't no skin of my teeth one way or another, right? I could only tell what I saw." But she shrugged and withdrew her hand. "Didn't make no difference. This town is sewed up tight where Jake Fielding's concerned. Somebody wants to see that poor kid hang, and they want to see it bad." Her eyes were stern, her voice certain. "You're wasting your time, honey. There ain't nothing you or me can do to change anything now, and I learned a long time ago that the best thing you can do sometimes is to pretend you don't know so much. That way you stay out of trouble. If I was you, I'd just go on home and forget all about it. Not too much else you can do."

The train wouldn't move fast enough for Daniel. It didn't help to tell himself that this train would pass through Double Springs a mere three hours after Jessica's and that there was nothing, absolutely nothing, that could happen to her, nothing she could do until he got there. Over and over he asked himself why. Why, after all this time, did this have to happen? Why, after all he had done for her, did she have to turn against him again? *It was over, damn it, Jessica, over. You could have left well enough alone.*

She would try to confess to the long-ago crime, he knew. He also knew she wouldn't succeed. There might be a scandal, but he could hush it up. He had covered up worse.

No, it wasn't what she had done that worried him so, it was *why.* Was she so unhappy with him that she would go to jail rather than stay with him? Didn't she care at all that she might never see her son again? What could she have been thinking of when she rushed off on this noble impulse? Jake could take care of himself, they both knew that, and her heroics were doing nothing but complicating the situation.

Jake. That was another thing he tried not to think about. A dozen times he had reminded himself of all the demanding reasons he had been forced to bring Jake along. He had had no choice. He was certain he could handle things in Double Springs, but if not, if something went wrong, it wouldn't hurt to have Jake as bargaining power. And it was time to end it, they both knew that. How could he ever sleep again knowing that Jake might at any moment come bursting back into his life, ready to destroy everything he had worked so hard to protect? How could he raise a family, build a career, salvage anything at all for himself out of life with his brother lurking in the background threatening it all? He had had no choice, damn it. Jake and Jessica had left him no choice.

Jake sat stalwart and silent beside him, looking out the window. Looking at it all for the last time. In the past two hours he had said nothing. But what was there to say?

Daniel closed his eyes slowly and stiffened himself against insiduous emotions. *Oh, Jake, for God's sake why?* Why did he have to come back, why did he have to let Daniel catch him? Why didn't he escape when he had the chance? He had hated his brother for so many years and for so many reasons, but he had never expected it to end like this between them. Not like this.

He couldn't bear the silence any longer. He glanced at Jake, whose profile was stern and strong. Still Jake, always able to face anything with equanimity. And maybe that was the basic difference between the two brothers. Jake could accept losing. Daniel could not.

The insensibility of it, the waste and the wantonness of it all rose up in Daniel like bitter gorge, and the anger he felt was not for himself or his brother, but for the twisted fate that had brought them here. And even as he realized this he tried to redirect his anger toward Jake. Bitterness roughened his voice when he demanded, "What the hell ever possessed you to do such a thing?" Jake turned, nothing but curiosity in his eyes. "That's the one thing I never understood. You were always such a selfish son of a bitch, but you stood right there and took the blame for a crime you didn't even commit. Why?"

Jake smiled faintly and shrugged as though it were of no consequence. "It wasn't so hard to do at the time." And then a vaguely troubled shadow crossed his eyes and he added more thoughtfully, "Her father used to lock her up in that wagon, did you know that? And that place—her aunt's house—there were bars on the windows. They wouldn't even let her have any clothes, or a candle. Hell, Dan, she's been a prisoner all her life in one way or another. I couldn't let them lock her up again," he said simply. His eyes met Daniel's with nothing more than a quiet statement of the obvious. "I just couldn't."

Daniel looked at his brother, and it was as though he had never seen him before. It was as though, at that moment, he had never seen a lot of things before, and something went through him that was deep and uncomfortable and far too disturbing to face. He wanted to say something, felt he should say something in denial or defense, and he even drew a breath to do so. But then the first warning whistle sounded, announcing their approach to Double Springs, and the moment was gone.

Daniel turned and stared straight ahead. But his eyes were troubled, and as hard as he tried he couldn't seem to push back that peculiar, unsettled feeling that threatened to make him look at things he simply didn't want to see.

Chapter XIX

"You knew," Jessica accused in a hushed, disbelieving voice. "You've known all along. You had a witness willing to testify to Jake Fielding's innocence and you've done *nothing!*"

It had been late afternoon when Sheriff Luther McCall rode in, dusty and ill-tempered from a futile afternoon of chasing down a mountain lion that had attacked two men and innumerable livestock during the past month. He had gotten off a couple of shots at the animal, too, but in the end it eluded him and he had been forced to return to town much sooner than he planned. Jessica Fielding was waiting for him in his office.

Her husband's telegram had preceded her by four hours.

McCall took off his gun belt and laid it on his desk, shaking the dust out of his hat before sitting down. Calmly he took out a box of ammunition and began to reload his weapons, to all appearances intent upon ignoring Jessica.

In the past hours Jessica had begun to put together a horrifying picture of what was happening in Double Springs, a picture with too many pieces missing, but she couldn't make herself believe it. She couldn't be so close only to have victory elude her now.

She placed her hands on the desk, leaning forward to get the sheriff's attention. "That woman in the saloon," she insisted, "Lottie, she heard everything. She saw Jake come up the stairs *after* the gun went off. She's willing to swear to it now, if only you would—"

"It don't matter how many witnesses you got ready to swear, Miz Fielding," McCall interrupted calmly, not looking up from his work. "What is, is what is. No point in trying to change it now."

Luther McCall had learned practicality the hard way. When he had first taken office he had had as much respect for the truth as the next man, and in his own way he still did. But it hadn't taken long to see how little one man could do to change the way things were, and he had enough troubles without stirring up things that had happened long before he came to this town.

He was acutely aware, as all lawmen were, that job openings in this business only came about one way, the same way he had gotten the job. He intended to postpone creating a vacancy in Double Springs for as long as possible, and he had learned the easiest way to do that was to mind his own business. He kept the peace; he put his life on the line for a dollar a day and so far he had been lucky. He had few complaints.

He had read Senator Fielding's telegram and had made certain that he was not in his office when the two o'clock train pulled in. He had hoped that by now Fielding would have come to collect his wife and he wouldn't have to deal with any of it. Let the good senator handle his own domestic problems. He had handled everything else.

"But he's innocent!" Jessica cried. "I shot Sheriff Stratton in self-defense! You know that! Lottie said you know that!"

McCall only replied, "It's out of my hands."

"What do you mean?" Jessica couldn't believe it. They were so close, so very close, but everything was whirling out of control. Nothing was making sense. "We could end it all here, don't you understand that? Why won't you listen to me?"

McCall rotated the cylinder of his revolver, snapped it in place, and laid the gun on the desk again. When he looked at her it was with reluctance, and a touch of pity, but a great deal of resignation. It was obvious the poor woman didn't understand. In his opinion, she had a right to.

He said, "It's your husband you need to talk to, Miz Fielding, not me or Lottie. Seems to me you and him is working at cross-purposes. He's got it all taken care of."

Something cold and insidious began to creep through Jessica's veins. She stared at him. She didn't want to know, she was certain she didn't want to know, but she heard her own voice cautiously demanding, "Daniel? What—what has my husband got to do with any of this?"

The sheriff met her eyes evenly and without much concern. "He's a rich man, a powerful man. My guess is he's paid a lot of people a lot of money to make sure the truth never comes out."

Jessica's head reeled. She couldn't absorb what she had heard, much less believe it. It made no sense. Why would Daniel do such a thing? Daniel, so good, so scrupulously honest . . . How could it be true?

She said a little hoarsely, "Are you saying that my husband . . . *paid* to have Jake charged with this crime?"

McCall shrugged. "Or to keep you from being connected

with it. All I know is you can confess as many times as you want, you can drag up Moses himself to testify for you, and it won't make a blessed bit of difference. I don't reckon there's a lawman in the state that would arrest you."

No. It was impossible, she thought. This nightmare would end, it couldn't go on forever. Daniel would not be a party to this. Daniel knew Jake was innocent. He wouldn't have his own brother hung, not after she had told him, after she had pleaded with him . . . Her eyes were wild and dark but her voice was firm as she said, "You're lying."

McCall opened his drawer and took out a yellow scrap of paper. He handed it to her. "See for yourself."

He got up and walked to the coffeepot on the stove.

Jessica wanted to crumple the incriminating sheet and toss it into the flames. She wanted to scream denials and beat her fists against the strong back of the man who walked away from her until he recanted his perfidy. She wanted to turn and run from the office. But her eyes were drawn to the writing on the paper.

My wife arriving 2:00 P.M. Remember our bargain.
Will follow on 5:00 train with prisoner.
D. Fielding

Jessica stared at it for a long time.

Sheriff McCall turned, a tin cup of coffee in his hand. "Can I pour you a cup while we wait?" he offered politely.

Jessica let the paper drift from her numb fingers. The whistle sounded, announcing the arrival of the five o'clock train.

They were the only ones to get off at Double Springs. Casey grasped Jake roughly by one arm; Daniel took the other. He walked between them without objection, a bit bemused by the sight of the place that had meant so much to him and about which he remembered so little. How strange. He had vaguely expected something larger than life, brilliant in detail, invoking a flood of memories and dread. All he saw was another dirty little town indistinguishable from dozens like it scattered across east Texas. He idly wondered whether the Pearly Gates would be as disappointing.

They were across the street from the sheriff's office when the reality of it struck him, and his muscles clenched instinctively. Daniel drew his gun. "Don't try it Jake," he advised quietly.

Jake looked at him, and the brief surge of fight-or-flight energy drained away, leaving him only empty and sad. This was it. This was really it.

"There's no need for that, Daniel," he said wearily, but Daniel's eyes were cold and he did not lower the gun. Casey's grip on Jake's arm tightened, urging him forward, but Jake held firm. He didn't remove his eyes from his brother's. "I'll go," he said. "But under my own power. A little dignity isn't too much to ask, is it?"

Daniel hesitated, and desperation mingled with the impatience in Jake's tone. "For God's sake, man," he said, "put that fool thing away! Jessica might be in there. Do you want her to see you like this?"

The debate was clear in Daniel's eyes, but at last some better judgment ruled. He reholstered the revolver and nodded curtly to Casey to release Jake's arm. "All right," he said. His eyes were narrowed against the setting sun. "Casey, you wait here, but keep watch. He's slippery and has a lot to lose. We wouldn't want anything to happen," his eyes fastened on Jake's in a challenge, or a warning, "just because he gave his word not to try to escape."

Casey nodded, however reluctantly, and stepped back. His fingers curled tensely, almost eagerly, above his holster. He wouldn't disappoint Daniel. Not again.

Jessica saw them through the window. She saw Daniel pull his gun and point it at Jake with a dim and spiraling horror that was too great to be believed. Daniel wouldn't do this, she thought, Daniel wouldn't turn his own brother in, not now, not when they were so close. *No.*

She saw the men on the street; she saw the sheriff walking toward the door with his back to her. She saw his loaded revolver lying on the desk.

She began to inch silently toward the desk.

Outside the door Daniel paused and looked at Jake. He didn't want to do this, he thought angrily, but Jake had left him no choice. There was no other way.

He might have voiced his thoughts; looking into his brother's eyes he might have said something, or done something . . . But just then Sheriff McCall opened the door.

"Right this way, gentlemen," he said. "I've been expecting you." He glanced at Daniel. "Your wife is here, Senator."

They stepped inside.

Jessica withdrew the revolver from the folds of her skirts. Leveling it with both hands, she pointed it directly at the sheriff.

"It won't be hard," she said. She was breathing irregularly, but her voice was much stronger than she expected it to be, and the determination in her eyes was real. Desperation was her courage, for her choices were ended. "I've seen a man die before, I can do it again. I've lived through worse. A lot worse."

For a moment the three men were a frozen composite of shock and disbelief. They saw the gun; they saw her eyes.

They saw a woman who would do what she had to do to save the man she loved.

And the voices burst on her at once. Daniel's, horrified, "Jessica, for God's sake—"

The sheriff's, quiet and wary, "Now Miz Fielding you be careful with that thing—"

"Move back, both of you!" Her voice was loud, but the gun didn't waver. Neither did her determination. "Step away from him."

"Jessica, please—"

"No, Daniel." But she did not look at him. She kept her eyes trained on her target. "Jake has paid with three years of his life for something he didn't do; it's my turn now. I don't want to shoot this man, but if I do you won't be able to fix it this time, and Jake will still be free." Slowly, using both thumbs, she pulled back the hammer. "Now move away from him, both of you. Jake, ride out of here."

Slowly, very cautiously, McCall and Daniel moved away. But Jake moved forward.

Jessica's hands tightened on the revolver. "Jake, *go!*"

"No, Jessica," he said quietly. His face was very sad. "It's over. I'm tired of running."

She cast a desperate glance toward him, holding the gun steady. "Jake, please."

Jake kept moving toward her. "I can't let you do this, Jessica. Joshua needs you. This is not the way."

He was standing in front of her now, his eyes tired, his face filled with sorrow. He reached up and closed his hand around hers, gently lowering the hammer of the revolver back into place. Her hands began to tremble beneath his; she felt the sobs rising, shaking her whole body. He took the gun from her and handed it behind him to the sheriff. Jessica flung herself into his arms.

She held him fiercely and his arms went around her tightly as the sobs broke through. Once she had promised him she would never let him see her cry and through everything she had kept that promise . . . but now it was too late. It was over, there was nothing she could do except let the sobs of terror and despair break through.

Jake closed his eyes, lowering his face to her hair, blinking back the tears that burned his eyes and clogged his throat. He held her to him, his heart filling with her and breaking for her and knowing that this time it would be for the last time. *Oh, Jessica, don't . . . don't . . .* But he couldn't let her go, and she couldn't move away from him. They clung to each other as though to their last breath of life.

Daniel watched them, and the shock on his face began to turn to pain, and the pain into something else . . . something he did not want to recognize but could no longer ignore. She would have done it, he realized. She would have killed for him. She would have given up her baby, her home, her life for him.

And Jake. What had it been like in that moment when he had made the decision to protect her, to take responsibility for a crime he didn't commit so that she might go free? Had there been any hesitation, any doubt? Any moment when he questioned why or wished there was an easier way? Looking at them now, Daniel did not think so, and it was something he could not even imagine. Both of them were still willing to give up their lives for the other, even if it meant never seeing each other again.

Jessica. He had loved her, Daniel thought bleakly, in his own way. But it hadn't been the right way. It never could be the right way.

Jake felt a heavy hand fall on his shoulder. He tightened his hands briefly on Jessica's waist, imparting strength, forcing determination. "Jessica," he whispered into her hair. "Stop it. Please. It's time."

Jessica caught her breath and choked back a sob. She tightened her fists on Jake's back but she couldn't step away, she couldn't let him go, not yet. *Please, God, let me be strong just one more time . . .*

It was Jake who stepped away, clasping her arms firmly, moving her back. Jessica compressed her lips tightly together as she lifted her tear-ravaged face to him. She tried to be strong. She didn't want him to remember her like this.

McCall said gruffly, "Come on, Fielding."

Jake turned.

"I don't think that will be necessary, Sheriff."

Daniel spoke quietly, and three pairs of eyes swung to him. But he fixed his gaze only on Sheriff McCall. "I think once we have a talk with Judge Baily the charges can be dropped against my brother. Obviously, my wife is guilty of nothing more than self-defense." He took a breath, and it was a little unsteady. "The judge is a—close friend. I'm sure we can have this matter cleared up before dinner time."

McCall released Jake's arm, his relief obvious. "I think you've made the right decision, Senator," he said.

Daniel looked at Jessica. "I hope so."

Daniel walked over to her. He lifted his hand and with a gentle touch gathered a tear from her shocked, reddened face. His smile was stiff with pain, but there was relief in his eyes, a quiet and simple satisfaction that could only come from looking at a ledger that had finally been balanced.

"I've made mistakes, Jessica," he said softly, "I've committed crimes just as great as yours or Jake's, but all in the name of love." His eyes dropped briefly, and he added, "Now maybe there's a chance—if not for atonement, then at least to learn from the past. I don't have to make those mistakes again. And I won't be the cause of any more suffering.

"I thought I could protect you with my love," he said, raising his eyes to her again. "But what I was really doing was keeping you prisoner. Because you were never mine, were you? Any more than Joshua was."

She bit her lip, hardly trusting her voice to speak. She searched his eyes, not daring to believe what he had said, what he had done, but knowing, somehow, it was true. He had freed Jake, and now he was freeing her. "Daniel, I—"

But his finger drifted to her lips, pressing gently there, and the spark of pain in his eyes silenced her. He turned to Jake.

The two men looked at each other. There was so much between them, things that could never be said, things that could never be recalled. Nothing could be changed now, it was too late for both of them. But Jake had to try. The need to try was burning inside him. "Daniel," he said hoarsely. His face was raw with pain and need and gratitude and regret. "I never—"

But the swift agony that crossed Daniel's eyes revealed he had reached his limit. He said harshly, "Not now. It's over." He turned. "We'd better get to the judge's office before he leaves."

They stepped out into the amber sunlight, Jessica first, then Daniel and Jake. The sheriff stood in the doorway. Jessica stepped off the sidewalk and onto the street, but Jake held back. He touched Daniel's arm.

"Dan," he said softly, and Daniel looked at him. Jake did not know what else to say. "Thank you."

Daniel knew he should answer. He wanted to answer. But what could he say to Jake that would bring back those lost years? For Daniel's sake, Jake had lost a lifetime . . . Joshua's lifetime. Nothing could ever bring that back. Daniel struggled with himself, trying to find forgiveness—for himself, for his brother, for the woman they both loved. He wanted to say something to make it all right, but knew there was nothing. Still, he had to try. Then his eyes sharpened.

Casey stepped out from the shadows of the building across the street, sliding his gun from his holster. Casey, whose last instructions had been to shoot Jake if he tried to escape. Casey, whose blind loyalty to Daniel was unfaltering. Casey who could not know . . .

The instant seemed to be frozen and the future hung in the balance. No one else saw Casey. It was in Daniel's hands.

Casey lifted the gun and leveled it at Jake. When he drew back the hammer, Daniel almost thought he could hear the sharp click of the mechanism in the still, hot air.

It could have been over then. In that moment, everything could have changed.

And all Daniel could think was, *Jake. . . . my brother . . .*

Years of hatred, anger and betrayal dissolved into a single vision of clarity as time resumed its pace. Alarm tore across Daniel's face and he flung up his hand.

"Casey, no!"

Everything happened at once. Daniel lurched forward and pushed Jake out of the way just as the explosion tore the air. Jessica screamed; Daniel staggered backward to the ground. Casey, his face torn with shock as he saw the bullet meant for Jake rip through the man he had been trying to protect, lurched forward, crying out hoarsely. Instinctively the sheriff raised his gun and another shot rang out. Casey fell forward in the street, his revolver flying from his hand.

And then it was all in slow motion. Jake heard the deep distant thrumming of his heart, an eerie background chorus for the weighted, underwater movements he made to reach his brother's side. He heard Jessica's smothered, whimpering cries, saw a blur and scurry of movement as people rushed from stores and saloons, heard voices, smelled the acrid mixture of smoke and dust. And in a series of stilted flashbacks superimposed upon the scene was a madman on a horse, a young girl screaming, a bridegroom falling to the ground. Jake, cradling his brother in his arms, pressing his hands into the wound, screaming for help and praying Daniel wouldn't die. . . .

And now a different place, a different time. Jessica knelt beside him in the bloodstained dirt, drawing Daniel's head into her lap, gasping with broken sobs. Jake gripped his brother's arms and whispered breathlessly, "It's all right. Hold on—the doctor's coming."

But it wasn't all right. Daniel knew it. The bullet that had ripped through his back left a gaping, flowing hole in his chest; blood trickled from his mouth. He looked at Jessica and tried to smile. When his eyes returned to Jake they were foggy.

"It's all right," he whispered. Again he tried to smile. "This—is the way it should have ended—before."

Jake drew in his breath, gripping Daniel's shoulders tightly. Jessica's trembling hand stroked Daniel's forehead and Jake bent low. "Daniel, I'm sorry." His voice was choked, barely intelligible. He held him tightly. He couldn't let him slip away. "For everything. No matter what—you're my brother, and I've always loved you."

Daniel's breath was harsh, but his face was peaceful. He answered simply, "I know."

A pain gripped him and Daniel fought against it. His face twisted with it, then relaxed. His brow knotted with effort, his eyes narrowed with concentration, as he lifted his hand. He touched Jake's face, weakly. "Promise me. . . ."

"Anything."

"Take care . . . of our son." Daniel's hand fell away; his eyes drifted closed. He was still.

Jake squeezed his eyes shut, lowering his face to Daniel's shoulder. He held him tightly. And after a long time someone pulled Jessica to her feet; he could hear her crying. Then a gentle hand touched his shoulder and he had to let go.

Jake drew Jessica into his arms and stroked her hair. He looked at his brother, and then, for the first time, he did not see what was lost. He saw what was left behind for him to cherish and protect. And love.

"I promise," he said softly.

He turned Jessica in his arms and, leaning on each other, they walked away.

Epilogue

1880

The sun was just setting against the Rockies when the man rode up, his son sitting proudly on the saddle before him. The woman came to the door of the small ranch house, her face breaking into a laugh of pleasure at the picture the two of them made.

Three Hills, and the past it represented, had been sold at auction to the highest bidder. With the proceeds and some breeding stock, Jake and Joshua and Jessica had pushed westward, out of the shadows and into the future they would build for themselves. They now owned fifteen hundred head of sturdy longhorn-brahman stock, a rough log cabin they had built themselves from the hardwood timber that grew in such abundance in the foothills, and free grazing range that stretched as far as one would care to wander. It was not yet a dynasty, but it was a beginning.

Joshua slid impatiently from the saddle, immediately fell on all fours, and scrambled quickly to his feet, having no time to waste on his mother's cry of concern or inconsequentials like scraped hands and knees. "Mama, Mama, look what I found!"

He raced onto the porch, panting with exertion, his face glowing with excitement. In his grubby hands he held a shiny rock. "Papa says it's just fool's gold, but I don't care, I'm gonna keep it!"

Jessica bent with appropriate sounds of respect to examine his find, but already Joshua was racing away, eager to store this treasure among the others, a dried rattlesnake skin, an Indian arrowhead, a rusty wagon hitch, a railroad spike. Laughing, Jessica called over her shoulder, "Wash up for supper!"

Jake dismounted and tossed the reins over the hitching post, smiling as he walked toward her. Every time she saw him Jessica was filled with renewed wonder and joy, for every time was like the first time. The sun glinted off his tousled hair as he whipped off his hat, illuminating his smooth brown skin and the crinkled smile lines that radiated from his eyes. He was so tall and strong, his gait easy and confident as he came to her, and every day he grew more beautiful to her.

He stepped up on the porch and bent to kiss his radiant young wife, his hand resting with possessive affection on her belly, which was already rounded and full with their second child. Jessica turned in his arms, and the kiss that was meant to be a brief greeting deepened easily into something more, lasting longer than either had intended.

The moment might have lasted forever had not Joshua, clamoring for his supper and tugging on his mother's skirts, interrupted them. With a teasing scold, Jake bent down to scoop up his son, tucking him against his hip. Husband and wife draped their arms around each other's waists, and smiling into one another's eyes, they turned to go into the house.